DANGEROUS TALENTS

FRANKIE ROBERTSON

Castle Rock Publishing
Tucson, Arizona

DANGEROUS TALENTS

"A great tale of adventure and romance, beautifully imagined and deeply engaging from beginning to end!"
~**Diana Gabaldon**, bestselling author of *Outlander*

"Grabs you from the start with excellent pacing, fascinating characters and culture, and a satisfying romance. I want more!"
~**Jennifer Roberson**, bestselling author of the Sword Dancer series, The Chronicles of the Cheysuli, and *Lady of the Glen*

"Romance, peril, and magic: what more could anyone ask?"
~**Dennis L. McKiernan**, author of the Mithgar series, and the Faery series

DANGEROUS TALENTS

Copyright © 2012 Frances R. Gross

Cover art and formatting by Jaycee DeLorenzo
of Sweet 'N Spicy Designs

Published by Castle Rock Publishing.
http://www.CastleRockPublishing.com

For Les Reese, a talented writer, gone too soon.

acknowledgments

This book is better due to the generous advice of the Working Title critique group: Dave Felts, Larry Hammer, Jill Knowles, Earl W. Parrish, Roxy Rogers, and Janni Lee Simner, and has benefitted from the attention of the Tanque Wordies critique group: Dennis L. McKiernan, Diane Turner, and John Vornholt. A special thank you to Martha Lee McKiernan for plying us with delicious desserts.

My editor Rochelle French at Edits That Rock helped put the final polish on *DANGEROUS TALENTS*, and Jaycee DeLorenzo of Sweet 'N Spicy Designs demonstrated cheerful patience and professionalism as she designed the second, third, and fourth versions of the cover.

The Saguaro Romance Writers chapter of the Romance Writers of America is an amazing group of people. They've been extraordinarily supportive, and have given me a safe environment to learn and grow as a writer.

Most especially, I want to thank my husband Brian, for his unending encouragement and support.

chapter one

"YOU CAN PAY ME the rest now."

Cele Montrose pointedly looked around. There was nothing but steep rock, scraggly brush, prickly pear, and saguaro cactus in sight. Then she cast a sharp look at her guide, Berto. He'd stopped beside two ancient stone cairns that rose shoulder high on either side of the pitiful excuse for a trail. "I don't see any petroglyphs."

Berto's dark brown eyes wouldn't meet hers. "They are close. Just a little way farther on. You get there easy."

"So take me there."

"No. No. This is as far as I go."

"You promised to take me to the glyphs. That's our deal." Cele had met Berto at Udall Park before dawn so he could take her to see the Fifth World petroglyphs. Most experts doubted they existed, but a few sources claimed they were unlike any others. Cele couldn't resist and had sent out feelers for more information. Berto had responded to her queries.

"This is a sacred place," he said. "I cannot go. I wait

for you."

"Sacred?" *Crap*. She wanted very much to photograph those petroglyphs, but she *didn't* want to get in trouble with the Tribal government. "But we're not on the rez."

Berto met her eyes. "No. They do not come here. Not for many years."

"Then what's the problem?"

Her guide's gaze slid away from hers again, and she started to wonder if she'd made a mistake coming here alone with him. She'd checked Berto out. He'd worked for a couple of her archeologist friends, all of whom had spoken well of him, so this morning she'd followed his battered pickup north and east of Tucson, down a little-used dirt road and past a sagging, metal gate. From there the old track rose steeply into the foothills, twisting and turning into the Catalina Mountains. It was much too rough for her vehicle, so she'd parked her Civic and climbed into Berto's ancient Ford.

Eventually, the road grew too rutted even for the truck, and they'd started to hike through the scrub. Berto had said it would only be a short walk, but if she'd known they'd be bushwhacking, she'd have worn jeans instead of hiking shorts, no matter how hot it was. He'd followed a trail that looked like little more than an animal track until they'd reached this place marked with drystacked rocks fitted neatly together to form two five sided towers that rose shoulder high. There he'd stopped and shifted nervously from one foot to the other.

"Berto, what's the problem?" she repeated. *Are there smugglers in the area?*

His eyes darted all around before they returned to hers. "The spirits walk here."

Cele relaxed. He wasn't worried about somebody shooting him. "The spirits?"

"*Sí.* This is the place where the Old Ones disappeared. Sometimes the spirits who took them come looking for more."

Cele grinned. "That's a cool story. I'd like to hear the rest of it. You can tell me while you take me to the petroglyphs."

"No. I will not go beyond *la señal de madrina.*"

The sign of the godmother? Was he using this nonsense to jack up the price? "No glyphs, no more money."

"Pay me what you agreed!" Berto took a step forward, and Cele retreated beyond the towers, lifting her hands, ready to use her self-defense skills if necessary. The guide, however, didn't follow.

She'd paid him half, and she already had a spot picked out on her wall for these photos. Her mother had taken an impressive collection of photos of Southwest Indian artifacts and petroglyphs, and Cele wasn't going to let superstition prevent her from adding to her mother's legacy. "Look, if your story is a good one, I can sweeten our deal. How does another forty sound?"

"No!" Berto's posture grew even more rigid, but he didn't come any closer.

Cele frowned, confused by his flat refusal. "There's no way I'm going to pay you before I see the glyphs." *And I'm sure as hell not going to pay him before I'm back in his truck.*

"This was a mistake. I should not have brought you here. Forget the money. We go now." Berto wiped his sweaty palms on his jeans.

Shit! He was really scared, not just greedy. Cele stepped forward, one hand outstretched. "Wait a minute! I'll tell you what. How far is it? I'll go, take my pictures, and then you can take me back to town. Then I'll pay you the rest. Okay?"

Berto hesitated, and then nodded. "Okay. I wait. One hour."

"Two."

The guide shook his head. "They are close, the glyphs. An hour. No more."

Resigned, Cele sighed. Now that she knew how to get here, she could come back and stay longer on her own. "Okay. One hour."

Berto gave her directions, and she left him pacing on the other side of the stone markers.

Less than twenty minutes later, Cele was peering over the edge of a narrow defile. Distinctive, light gray petroglyphs decorated virtually every surface of the dark gray rock face, like some prehistoric message board. Her mother would have loved photographing this site.

I have to get closer. She was going to get the first pictures of the Fifth World petroglyphs. She'd share them with the archeologists at the university, but just as Tenen and Tufts had kept the location of Kartchner Caverns secret for twenty years, she wouldn't tell where she'd found these glyphs. From Berto's behavior, she didn't think he would either. Which was a good thing. She didn't want these beauties defaced by souvenir hunters.

She looked for a way down. *It's only about twenty feet.* Even better, it looked like weathered handholds were cut into the descent.

Cele carefully lowered herself over the edge and climbed down. When she reached the bottom and stepped away from the wall, she heard a low humming. She nervously looked around for a swarm of bees, but as her gaze swept the walls, she forgot her fear. The glyphs were so clear, more distinct than any she'd seen before, as though they'd been carved only yesterday.

Is this a scam? Had Berto carved these glyphs himself?

She moved closer to examine a spiral carving. Even though they were distinct and clear, the indentations of the pattern were weathered, just like the surface of the rock. She'd bet that these petroglyphs were just as old as Berto claimed.

Amazing. She stepped back to take in the panorama.

Decorated by long dead hands, the rock face was alive with images in motion. Stick figure gods danced with a huge boar over the walls, and the spiral of the universe swirled before her gaze. A man and a woman slithered up a rainbow spanning the handholds she'd descended.

Not trusting her eyes, Cele blinked and looked again. The images were quiet.

Of course they're quiet. They're stone. She dug her camera out of her fanny pack.

The humming grew louder. It had a rhythm now, like a drumbeat. *Where's it coming from?* She scanned the area, but saw only a raven sitting on the crest of the wall. *Where did he come from?* She hadn't seen him fly in.

The raven regarded her with a sharp eye, then cawed. She raised her camera to take his picture, but an odd urgency suddenly gripped her. She had to get out of there. *Climb out! Now!* The thought felt like a command. Cele glanced at her watch. She still had forty minutes left before she had to get back to Berto, but she couldn't shake the feeling that time was running out. She had to leave. Cele slung the strap of her camera over her head.

Grabbing the handholds, she pulled herself up. The throbbing hum quickened, and her fingertips tingled in time with it. She climbed faster, in time with the beat.

Her arms ached with the effort, but she didn't care. She was almost there, almost to the top. Just a few more feet, and she'd be safe. Then abruptly, she was jerked away from the stone.

Cele clutched and scrabbled at the rock. She tried to

cling to the cliff, but the ledge slipped from her out-stretched fingers. Her stomach lurched as she fell, suddenly weightless.

The granite walls disappeared. A rainbow arc rolled out beneath her. Surrounded by shimmering color, she slid down the bow into the dark.

She fell in silence; even her scream made no sound.

Small rocks and sand bit sharply into Cele's cheek. She opened her eyes on the desert ravine, viewed from the odd angle of being face down in the dirt.

What happened?

She pushed up to her hands and knees, and then sat and checked herself over. *No blood, no broken bones, no dizziness. So far, so good.* She licked her dry lips and took a long drag from her water bottle. Light glared over the edge of the ridge, making her squint.

How long was I out? It must have been hours. The sun had traveled far to the west, casting most of the narrow cut in shadow. Berto would be long gone and Elaine would be frantic. Her roommate might even have called Search and Rescue.

Cele winced. *I hope not. I'd never live it down: a rescue operator being rescued.*

She dug out her cell phone. No signal. *Of course. I'm in a narrow canyon. Duh.* She'd have to hustle to keep things from getting out of hand.

Cele picked up her hat, stood, then stared. *What the...?*

No prickly pear cactus with their flat pads sporting inch long spines studded the hills. And interspersed with the prickly pear there should have been tall saguaros stretching their arms for the sky. But there wasn't a cactus in sight. A chill crept over her, despite the heat.

Cele turned, examining the rock walls rising on three sides of her. Etchings covered the shadowed rock faces all around her, from the ground up to the top. *At least* that's *the same.*

Then she realized it wasn't.

The cliffs were darker and the images were different. No figures crawled up either side of the cleft. There were no handholds, either.

Instead of cactus, thorny bushes grew six feet tall and just as wide, dense with small leaves and long thorns. The other plants were different, too. A chill that had nothing to do with the temperature shivered down her spine. *This isn't right.* She drew in a steadying breath, but the spicy, intertwining scents were unfamiliar. This was all wrong.

Cele groped for an explanation. She'd taken a tumble. Had she hit her head? Wandered off in a fog of confusion? But that wouldn't explain the change in vegetation. And her memory was clear right up to the moment when she'd fallen.

I didn't fall! She hadn't lost her balance, or slipped. Someone had yanked her off the rock face–but there'd been no one around. *And that rainbow.* She looked up at the clear blue sky. *There's no way I could have seen a rainbow.*

Nothing made sense. Her pulse pounded.

Another raven–or was it the same one?–landed on the lip of the defile, sunlight flashing off his blue-black wings.

"I have to get out of here," she told the bird. "I'll figure it out when I get home." She started to climb.

The raven watched as Cele tested each toehold carefully before trusting it not to crumble beneath her. Her arms quivered. Her muscles burned. The bird stepped aside as she pulled herself up to sit on the edge, but it didn't go far. Her shoulders burned from exertion and she glared at the corvid. "Don't look so smug. You have wings." Then she looked behind her.

The path was gone.

The ground was unbroken desert—in both directions. The trail should be there. It had to be.

But it wasn't.

Cele scrambled to her feet. The mountains rising behind her were wrong, too. Her heart lurched, skipping a beat. She turned and turned again, looking for some familiar thing, but there was nothing.

"*No!*" Her scream echoed off the cliffs.

Everything was different. Everything. It couldn't be. But it was.

Her breath came in short gasps as her heart tried to pound its way out of her chest. *This can't be happening! The world doesn't change in the blink of an eye!*

She scrambled up the hill. Maybe at the top she'd see something she recognized. Loose rock rolled from under her feet as she bent forward, half climbing, half crawling on all fours. At the top, she stared desperately across the valley. No glint of sun on windows, no buildings stood tall, no cars moving on long roads that ran straight for miles. No roads. Nothing.

Icy fear raced down Cele's back and she covered her face. *This isn't happening. It's not real. I must have hit my head. I'm hallucinating.* But her head didn't hurt. She wasn't dizzy. She dropped her hands and stared again.

Where she'd hoped to see a sprawling city of a million people, she saw only desert scrub. No city glittered in the valley; it wasn't even the same valley.

Where the hell am I?

Her legs wobbled and she sat down hard on a nearby rock. Her mouth ached, parched from fear and exertion. She gulped several swallows from her squeeze bottle.

The container was light when she slipped it back into its holster. Then she froze. Her other bottle was already empty. She hadn't planned on a long hike. She had almost no water left. Fear choked her as she remembered briefings at work about dehydration and desperate victims dying in the desert.

She was in deep, deep trouble.

Cele sucked in a shuddering breath, then another, trying to steady her frantic pulse. She was an emergency services dispatcher. She'd responded to difficult situations before. She knew how to function under stress. *I need to stay calm and think.* But her mind kept racing like a hamster on a wheel.

Everything she knew told her to stay put so Search and Rescue could find her quickly. But Search and Rescue would never find her here. She was nowhere near where she'd told Elaine she'd be. She checked her phone again. Still no signal. And the little GPS icon was missing.

What am I going to do?

Water. She had to find water.

The raven cawed and flew east, along the base of the hills.

Birds need open water too. Maybe if she followed it, she'd find a stream flowing out to the valley. It wasn't likely, but it was the only chance she had. She started walking.

Cele kept on searching even after the sun set. The raven was long gone. A full moon rose before her in the cloudless sky, huge and yellow as it topped the mountains, casting long shadows toward her. She kept walking, hoping to find a stream, unwilling to stop, unwilling to accept that she was lost in an alien landscape.

The moon was high when she stumbled and fell, too exhausted to rise. She allowed herself two tiny sips of water from the bottle, swishing the liquid around her mouth before swallowing. The tepid water didn't come anywhere near close to satisfying her thirst, but she had to make her water last.

Her stomach cramped with hunger and she tried to ignore its empty complaint. *I'll just close my eyes for a second. Then I'll go on.*

Cele startled awake, heart thumping, hands clutching the earth. She wasn't falling. *It was just a nightmare. Just a replay.* Except her hair had been black in the dream, instead of blond. She laughed sourly. *Why should I expect my dreams to make more sense than reality?*

Insects churred in the dark, and something rustled in the bushes to her right. She'd been too tired to worry about scorpions, snakes, or mountain lions before. Now she looked around nervously. Moonlight silvered the desert, cutting sharp shadows on the sand. She struggled to her feet, shivering. As hot as it was during the day, the desert temperature had dropped during the night without the concrete and asphalt of the city to hold the heat. She rubbed her arms and stared with amazement at the sky.

She'd never seen so many stars. Even with a full moon, the panoply of light was breathtaking. And strange. Where was the Big Dipper? Where was Scorpio? She searched the heavens until the stars seemed to spin.

I'm not in Kansas anymore. Or Tucson. Her stomach tightened painfully at yet more proof she was far from home.

If only I hadn't insisted on seeing those petroglyphs. But second-guessing the past wouldn't help now. She pulled out her phone. She wasn't surprised to find no signal. Resigned, she gathered her things. Something was missing. She looked around. Her camera! It must have come free of its strap when she'd fallen.

The loss felt like a blow. It wasn't the most up-to-date model, but it was the last camera her mother had bought before she'd gotten sick. She'd been so proud of it. Cele blinked back tears. Her mother was gone. Her camera was gone. She was lost. But she was still her mother's daughter and she wasn't going to just lie down and die. Cele put on her hat and resumed her search for water.

She tried to be methodical. She walked back up into each cleft, between hills where the plants grew thicker, hoping to scent moisture or hear the distinctive burble of running water. Thorny branches clawed her legs and arms as she edged past shadowed thickets. Each time she worked her way into a new defile, a peculiar certainty warned her she was wasting her time and energy. Water wasn't there. But she had no foundation for that surety, so she continued to search in the logical places.

When the first graying of the eastern sky announced the coming dawn, she drank a small swig of water, cool and chilled by the desert night. Cele had never tasted anything so sweet. There was only a tiny bit left. Should she drink it now or save it? Did it matter? She stared at the squeeze bottle, her mouth aching. Then she up-ended the container and swallowed the precious liquid. That was it, the last of it. If she didn't find water soon, she wouldn't have the strength to keep looking. She would die, desperate and delirious. Ruthlessly, Cele pushed away the ugly thoughts.

The sun and the heat rose higher as Cele's spirits and strength dropped lower. Her mouth itched and tickled and ached for moisture. She tucked a pebble in her cheek to suck on. It helped a little, but not enough. She finally took shelter beneath the low hanging branches of a scrubby tree between two hills. She was so tired. Her eyelids drooped and she didn't try to resist.

The sun was again sinking when Cele awoke. Her head ached and her scratches stung. She didn't want to move, but she made herself crawl out from under the tree. Once again, she checked her cell. Not only was there no signal, the battery icon was empty.

Damn it! She flung the phone against a nearby boulder. It shattered. Her head swam with the sudden effort and she steadied herself against a rock. She had to get out from between the hills to where the air was moving.

The sun glowed bloody behind her on the western horizon as she rounded yet another hill, looking for dense vegetation that might be a promise of open water. The growth here appeared a little greener than in the open desert, so once again she hiked into the cleft between the hills.

Once again, that feeling, that damn *knowing*, told her she'd be disappointed. *There's no water here.* Cele shook her head and was struck with a wave of dizziness. She was becoming delirious, imagining things. She had to examine every possibility. What if she died because an irrational hunch had kept her from checking the right spot?

The heat weighed upon her like a lead apron in a dentist's chair. Cele slumped on a shaded rock to rest, trying to dredge up enough hope to go on. Two rocks over, a lizard postured as if doing his push-ups.

She'd stopped trying to figure out what had happened to her. She didn't care anymore. Water was the one thing, the only thing that mattered. That feeling, that stupid *knowing*, still nagged at her. There was water somewhere not too far ahead. She had maybe another hour of light left, and she wasn't going to waste it feeling sorry for herself.

She stood, and what she saw brought her up short. Heart hammering, Cele blinked and rubbed her gritty eyes, wondering if she'd begun to hallucinate. About fifty yards away, two oddly dressed men rounded the edge of the hill.

chapter two

cele's heart jumped as a jolt of adrenaline hit her. Search and Rescue had found her! She took a step and waved her hat. "Hey!" she tried to shout, but it came out as a croak.

The men saw her and stopped abruptly, eyes wide. One of them turned and whistled two sharp, high notes, followed by a third, lower tone.

Quickly, seven more men rounded the hill. The tall, powerfully built hikers wore long-sleeved, rough-spun shirts and scuffed leather pants tucked into high boots. Broad-brimmed hats shaded their bearded faces, and they carried leather packs and blanket rolls on their backs. They were armed with spears, knives, swords, and bows.

This isn't Search and Rescue.

They weren't here to save her. They looked dangerous.

She didn't care. They had water. Without it, she was dead. She waved and stumbled toward them. "I need help," she croaked. "I need water."

One of the men spoke softly and gestured; immediately, all but two of the band fanned out, moving quickly into the hills. When she stopped in front of the remaining men, one of them grabbed her arm and pulled her under an overhanging rock, knocking her hat to the ground.

"Hey! What—?"

A calloused hand clamped over her mouth and a rough whisper sounded close to her ear. "Be silent woman, or I will ensure it."

Her self-defense training almost kicked in, but the flood of adrenaline had cleared her mind. Even if she overcame this man, there were eight others, and without water she couldn't escape them for long. She stood, tense and quiet, watching the other man.

He crouched by a tumble of rocks, scanning the hills with sharp gray eyes. His beard, which had been neatly trimmed not too long ago, was a reddish brown, bleached gold on the surface by the sun. Most important, he had two bota bags hanging from his shoulders.

Her tongue rasped like sandpaper. Water was so close, and she couldn't get to it. She tried to turn her head, to free her mouth so she could ask again, but her captor held her too tightly. His grip on her mouth pressed grit into her flesh. Time and more time passed, while nothing moved.

Suddenly, the gray-eyed man directed a gesture to someone she couldn't see. Over the next few minutes, his squad quietly returned from the hills. The leader's gaze remained fixed on her while his men made their reports. There was no sign of outcasts, they told him. They'd found where she'd rested, nothing else.

Cele paid scant attention to their conversation, riveted instead on the leather waterbags slung from their shoulders. The leader made a sign and her captor took his hand from her mouth, but kept a tight arm around her waist.

Her knees wobbled. She'd have fallen if he'd let her go. "Can I–" Her voice cracked from disuse and thirst, and she coughed. It felt like her throat was shredding. Her captor's grip shifted from restraint to support as she doubled over and clung to his arm, racked by the effort to clear the dust. With a snatch of breath, she croaked a single word. "Water?"

Dahleven bit out an order. "Give her water, Falsom." *What in the Nine Worlds is a woman doing here in the drylands alone?* This was a complication he did *not* need. Their mission was difficult and dangerous enough without this, too.

With one hand, Falsom unslung and unstopped his waterskin, then steadied it as the pale-haired woman upended it with shaking hands. Dahleven considered her through narrowed eyes. She was indecently dressed. Even the Daughters of Freya had more modesty. Her arms and long legs were bare and scratched, yet her hands were as smooth as any lady's and diamonds glittered in her ears. His eyes lingered on her high cheekbones and green eyes, then wandered down to the light golden skin revealed by the open top buttons of her shirt. Her bedraggled state suggested she'd been in the unforgiving drylands for some time. Why she was merely pink and not blistered he could not understand, unless that was her Talent. But it was a minor puzzle, compared to her mere presence.

The woman tried to drink again, but Dahleven stepped closer and pushed the waterskin away from her lips. Too much water too soon, and she'd be sick. "Who are you? How did you come to be here?"

Her voice was barely a rasp. "My name is Celia Montrose. I'm lost. Can you get me back to town?"

A town! In the drylands? In the mountains? Does she mean Kotaki in the Tewakwe Confederation? But Kotaki was five days north, over the pass. And this lady was no dusky-skinned Tewa. "What town do you speak of?"

"Tucson, of course."

"And where is this *Toosahn*?"

She stared at him as if he was demented, then tried to drink again.

It went against his grain to deny her, but he had to have answers and thirst was a powerful motivator. His men's lives could depend on what she had to say. He held the waterskin away from her parched lips with a firm grasp on her wrist. "No. First you answer my questions."

Her eyes sparked. "Look—" The woman broke off, coughing.

He relented, allowing her another sip of water.

When she caught her breath, her voice was clear and impatient. "If I knew where Tucson was, I wouldn't be lost, would I? I wouldn't be dying of thirst and exposure, and I certainly wouldn't be playing Twenty Questions with *you* in the middle of the desert."

Her arrogance surprised him, but he wouldn't be put off. "How did you come to be here, lost," he raked his eyes over her bare legs, "and exposed?"

He noted the fear that began to replace her anger. Guilt mingled with satisfaction. He wasn't in the habit of terrorizing women, but fear sometimes revealed truth.

"I was hiking and I fell. I must have hit my head. When I woke up, I couldn't find the trail."

"What trail were you following? Where were you going?"

"It wasn't a marked trail, exactly. I was taking pictures. If I still had my camera, I'd show you."

Though she spoke in a strange rhythm, he could understand her well enough. But some of her words made no sense. *Camera. Toosahn.* Dahleven suppressed a shiver of dread. *She may be Fey-marked. That would explain much.* Those the Elves touched were never the same afterward. In any case, it would take time to get the truth from her if she were not too mad to know it, and he didn't have time to interrogate her here. It would soon be dark and they still had a distance to go. This puzzle would have to wait.

Dahleven turned to his squad, issuing orders. "We move. We camp at the spring tonight. Sorn, watch the woman."

Cele clenched her teeth. *Who the hell does this guy think he is?* He ordered her around as though he had the right to. And the way he looked at her, as if she were in her underwear, scared her.

The man who gripped her took the waterskin from her hands before she could take another drink and handed her off to another man, the one called Sorn. Her new keeper's grip was just as firm as he wrapped his long fingers around her right biceps, but somehow his touch seemed less threatening. He scooped her hat off the ground and handed it to her. Cele looked up at him. She got a quick impression of height and dark hair before he urged her forward and she was forced to pay attention to her feet or fall on her face.

"Wait!" The leader's voice stopped Sorn, who pulled Cele up so short she almost fell.

"Give me that." The leader pointed to her belt pack.

"What? Why?" Cele asked. It was sheer stubbornness. She was in enough trouble. What difference did it make if he wanted her pack?

In answer, he reached for the strap hooked around her waist.

"Hey!" Cele batted at his hands but had enough sense not to try any of the more effective self-defense moves she knew. Sorn still had a firm grip on her arm.

The leader ignored her, pulling at the waist strap of the pack. He examined the plastic clasp in an oddly diffident way, touching her no more than necessary, then said again, "Give this to me."

"No." She must have lost her mind. She would never have held out on a mugger like this. But the word was said, and she wouldn't back down for no good reason.

The leader drew his knife. The double-edged blade must have been a foot long. *That's a good reason.* Cele sucked in a noisy breath and drew back from the threat as she groped for the catch. "Okay, okay! It's yours." Her hands fumbled, then the plastic clasp released. She thrust it out to him at arm's length. "Here, take it if you want it that bad!"

He looked at her oddly, then sheathed his knife with one hand while taking the pack with the other. Then he walked off into the dusk.

The others had already left in twos and threes and Cele quickly lost track of them in the fading light. They continued in the direction Cele had been headed: east, along the base of the hills. Sorn set a brisk pace and it was all she could do to stay on her feet. When she stumbled, he stopped and gave her more to drink, then a moment later urged her forward again. But his grip on her arm shifted, and she felt he wasn't so much restraining her as holding her up.

She began to steal glances at her escort when she could take her eyes off her feet. Cele couldn't make out details, but she sensed his vigilance in the way he held his head. His alertness wasn't centered on her, but on the country around them. She thought of trying to escape, then dismissed the idea. She was too weak. He'd catch her in a second.

If he wasn't wary of her, maybe she could get some information from him, find out how much trouble she was in. Was she being "rescued" by drug runners? There was a lot of drug traffic this close to Mexican border. Or maybe they were *coyotes*, people who smuggled illegals across the border. They'd have no qualms about leaving her here to die—if they left her alive at all.

A slow death in the desert might be better than some of the other things they could do.

Cele stole another look at her captor. The leader might be ready to knife her for her belt pack, but this guy seemed a little safer. "You're called Sorn?" she asked in a raw whisper.

His attention snapped to her, then returned to their surroundings. His look didn't have any of the speculation men's eyes so often held. "Yes." Sorn's voice was so low Cele doubted it could be heard two paces away.

"I'm Celia Montrose."

"Yes, my lady, I heard."

My lady? Maybe these guys are historical re-creationists. But they act more like hysterical survivalists. Don't upset him. Start with a nice basic question. "Where are you taking me?"

"To a spring a little way from here. We'll camp there tonight."

"And then?"

"And then Dahleven will decide."

"Dahleven?"

"Lord Dahleven. The one who spoke to you before."

Lord *Dahleven. The one who trades water for information.* What would he do with her? Memories of

20

the day's heat shriveling her flesh and the shivering cold of the previous night flashed through Cele's mind, accompanied by thoughts of *coyotes* abandoning people to die a slow and horrible death. "Will—will he leave me in the desert?"

Sorn frowned as though he didn't like what he was thinking. "No. That he will not do."

"What are you guys doing out here?"

Sorn refused to answer any more questions, and in only a few minutes more they were at the camp. Cele *knew* water was here, and very close, even before she heard the faint splashing and smelled the distinct odor of wet dust. *Well, of course, Montrose. They told you there's a spring.* But it was more than that. She *felt* it.

Six men sat scattered around, eating and talking. Conversation halted as she and Sorn came into camp. Every eye turned to her. Cele caught herself edging closer to Sorn, but then she made herself straighten and stare right back at the men. She wasn't going to let them intimidate her. Most of the men turned back to their dinners, but one rose and came toward her. His face was pleasant and his sandy hair fell forward into his face. His beard, like most of the others, had been closely trimmed some days ago. Before he could speak to her, Dahleven barked his name.

"Fender!"

The young man's head whipped around. "My lord?" He glanced back at her long enough to give her a lopsided grin and a wink before he changed course for Dahleven.

She couldn't hear what was said, but Dahleven's expression was stern. His words had only part of the effect he probably wanted, though. The younger man didn't approach her again, but after he gathered his sword and bow, he caught her eye with a tilt of his head, then gave her half a smile and a little shrug as he headed out of camp. Fender's good humor would have been reassuring if *Lord* Dahleven hadn't ordered him away from her.

Cele looked around as she passed among the men. Each man's gear was neatly organized in the same way. Blanket, waterskins, pack, weapons. Very precise. Very military. She remembered the way they'd silently obeyed the hand signals Dahleven had given them. *Who the hell are these guys*? Maybe they were survivalists after all. But she hadn't heard anything lately about a group like this operating near Tucson.

Tucson. That brought her up short. She wasn't near Tucson anymore. She wasn't near *anywhere* anymore. No anywhere she knew of. Something strange had happened to her when she'd fallen past the petroglyphs. So strange, she probably shouldn't be thinking of her danger in terms of survivalist fruitcakes or *coyotes*. So strange that she had no way to guess what these guys might do next. All she could do now was keep her eyes open and hope for the best.

The moon crested the eastern mountains, bathing the landscape in its reflected light, throwing sharp-edged shadows from every rock and bush. Dahleven sat on a low rock shelf, talking in quiet tones with another man. Once again, Cele was impressed by the power leashed in his tall frame. The ripple of muscle beneath his leather leggings and the unconscious grace of his gesture as he pointed over the hill made it clear he was at ease in his body. There were probably very few who could best him.

Dahleven had taken off his hat, and when he glanced up Cele could see his brows were drawn together in a frown. The bright silvery light from the nearly full moon washed the color from his shoulder-length hair, and his dark, shadowed eyes sent a jolt of apprehension through her as they paused on her own. Then, as quickly as he'd looked up, he returned to his conversation.

Unreasonably, she felt irritated by his casual dismissal of her. She should be glad he wasn't turning those dark gray eyes on her, though he'd probably be questioning her again soon enough. What answers could she offer? None that would satisfy him, she was sure.

Sorn laid out his gear in the same orderly way as the rest of his companions as Cele sank onto the sand in an exhausted heap. He spared her a half-smile and handed her his waterskin. "You can rest and eat now."

Cele eagerly took the skin. The water caressed her throat, soothing the parched tissues. She took off her hat and poured some water over her face, delighting in the wetness dancing over her hot skin. Then she drank again. It tasted flat, like leather, but nothing had ever tasted so good.

She hadn't slaked her thirst when Sorn pulled the skin from her lips. "Not too much. You'll sicken yourself."

She knew he was right, but it was hard not to lunge after the bota as he tugged it away.

Cele's hunger flared as she watched Sorn cut a strip from a thin slab of dried meat. Her mouth tingled and watered and her stomach rumbled loudly. But before she could reach for the jerky he held out to her, Dahleven came over, her pack dangling from his fingers by the woven nylon strap. Behind him, two men gathered their weapons and disappeared into the night.

Without preamble, he asked, "What are you doing here, my lady, alone in the drylands, without escort?"

"My lady" again. How courtly. If only his tone didn't make his words sound like a threat. Cele felt herself at a disadvantage, sitting on the ground while he glowered over her, so she struggled awkwardly to her feet. She was even more tired than she'd thought. Dahleven reached out and grasped her hand, helping her to stand.

She lifted her brows in surprise. *Chivalry isn't dead, even among kidnappers.* "Thanks."

He dropped her hand, looking annoyed. "Answer my question."

She tried to make her voice strong and calm. "As I told you before, I was hiking." She wasn't going to tell him about the petroglyphs. "I fell and couldn't find the trail again." *Heck, I couldn't even find Tucson again.* "If you hadn't come along when you did, I don't know what I would have done. I was out of water. You probably saved my life. Thank you." *A little flattery never hurts, and it's no more than the truth. Never mind being dragged through the desert after being half strangled and threatened with a knife.*

"Forgive me for being so unclear in my query. *Why* are you in the drylands? And how did you come to be here *alone*? And dressed so...unusually?" His gaze lingered on her scratched and scabbed legs.

Cele didn't like the way his gaze made her feel like she was standing there in her underwear, and she wished again that she'd worn jeans instead of shorts. "I *told* you. I was hiking!"

Dahleven snarled at her with a curl in his perfectly formed lips. "You've told me nothing!"

"Look, one minute I was climbing, and the next I was falling into the Twilight Zone. I don't *know* what I'm doing here. This isn't where I'm supposed to be! Just show me the way back to Tucson and I'll get out of your hair!"

Cele had started out calm, but by the time she finished, she was screeching at him. She never lost control this way. She was practiced at staying calm under stressful circumstances. She hated him for causing it, and hated herself for giving into it.

Cele braced herself for a blast of returning anger. She didn't give a fat rat's ass whether he was happy or not. She'd had enough of his bullying.

But Dahleven didn't snap her in two. He didn't even shout. He just looked at her hiking boots, then at the pack in his hand, rubbing his thumb over the nylon strap. He pursed his lips and nodded slowly as though he understood something. Then he stunned her by returning the pack. "I'm glad I didn't have to cut this from you. I would be sorry to have destroyed its usefulness. This buckle is most remarkable. Of what material is it made?"

Cele was only dimly aware of the men around her relaxing again. She was too busy trying to cope with Dahleven's sudden change of direction, her mind fogged by hunger and thirst and fatigue. He hadn't been threatening to stab her earlier? He'd only meant to cut the strap? *Maybe he's not a potential murderer, but he's still an arrogant, lecherous, overbearing bastard.* She stared into the shadows that hid his eyes and wondered what was behind his change of attitude. "Plastic, of course." Her voice was still sharp with irritation.

Dahleven gave her answer a blank look, then pulled her map, folded inside a plastic bag, from inside his vest. "This is a fine map. Remarkably detailed. Where is it of?"

She'd forgotten the map. Cele reached out and Dahleven handed it to her. "This will prove it! It's a map of the foothills north of Tucson." She pulled the plastic zipper apart and unfolded the map.

"Ah." Dahleven retrieved the bag and examined it more closely. He pressed the edges together, then pulled them apart again as she had. "Wonderful." Then he returned the full force of his attention to Cele.

Hasn't he ever seen a sandwich bag before? The intensity of his gaze drew her back to the map.

The light from the nearly full moon revealed the markings clearly enough. Cele followed the curved line of a road with her finger. "This is about where I fell, I think. And over here is—" Cele stopped, confused. She recognized various trail icons, and the topographical lines that indicated changes in elevation, but the words were incomprehensible. She knew the little marks said "Tucson" and "Coronado National Forest," but she couldn't read them. She blinked hard, then brought the paper closer to her face. The letters were clear. Lack of light or blurred vision wasn't the problem. The words simply made no sense.

"My lady?" Sorn asked.

"I can't read it." Cele said softly. "I should be able to read this," she said louder. She couldn't have a brain injury bad enough to keep her from reading without having other serious problems. "What's going on here?" Panic edged her voice and she looked wildly from Dahleven to Sorn and back again. "What's happening to me?" The world had twisted strangely about her yesterday, changing its shape, and now she was changing, too.

Dahleven kept his eyes on her while he spoke in an even tone to Sorn. "You were about to offer Lady Celia something to eat, were you not?" Then he knelt, picked up a rock, and scratched something in the sand.

It was the words, "Are you hungry?"

She could read it!

Cele's laugh had a ragged edge, but some of the tightness in her chest relaxed. "Yes! Yes, I am." Her panic receded, but her confusion remained. Why couldn't she read her map when she could read what Dahleven had written?

Dahleven redirected her thoughts. "I regret we can offer only a cold supper. A fire could be too easily seen at a distance." He offered her his hand and led her to the low rock he'd sat on earlier, then seated himself on another a little distance from her.

He watched her while she ate. She half expected him to keep badgering her with questions she'd already answered, but he didn't say anything; he just watched her. His steady gaze made her nervous. She tried to ignore him, but he made that impossible by apologizing for retaining her Swiss Army knife.

"You are clearly no enemy known to us, but even a small blade can draw blood," he said, as though the knife were more a danger than she was.

She found his courtesy as puzzling as his arrogance was annoying, but she said nothing and kept chewing the spicy dried meat Sorn offered. It was salty and delicious. Unfortunately, Dahleven stopped her from eating anywhere near enough.

The day's heat fled and the night turned chilly. With the edge taken off her hunger and no longer warmed by her anger, Cele began to shiver.

Dahleven offered her a warm hand to help her rise. "You'll sleep with me and Sorn tonight. We—"

Alarm and anger flared through her. Cele snatched her hand back. "Not in this lifetime!"

She should have seen this coming. His motives were clear now. He hadn't been protecting her from that younger man's attentions, he'd been saving her for himself. That's why he'd softened his approach—to make her more compliant. And if she didn't cooperate? Cele's fears crystallized with sharp cutting edges. She might have been mistaken before about his intentions with the knife, but it was clear Dahleven wasn't the kind who accepted no for an answer. Still, "no" was all he was going to get.

chapter three

DAHLEVEN BLINKED with surprise at the woman in front of him. The moonlight had turned Lady Celia's fair hair to silver, but her face was tight again with stubborn anger.

"I'm not sleeping with you, any of you, now or ever!"

The camp fell silent.

"You will–"

She cut him off again. "You think you can pass me around? Buy me with a little food and water?" Rage vibrated in the air around her. "I'll fight if I have to. I won't be your toy, and I won't let you rape me."

Dahleven gaped. How could she think such a thing? He'd offered no insult.

"Rape! My lady, no!" Sorn burst out. Lady Celia turned to him with a quickness born of fury, making Dahleven glad she was unarmed. Sorn rushed on before she could speak. "The night is cold, and we travel lightly. We all share our blankets to keep warm, and we have none to spare for you to use alone."

Lady Celia searched Sorn's face. Her expression slowly softened as the truth of his words penetrated. How did Sorn inspire such trust in women? It was almost as if he had a second Talent. Dahleven watched the anger run out of her like water from a broken jar, leaving her soft and small and vulnerable. His men relaxed as the tension dissipated.

Lady Celia dropped her gaze and ran a hand through her hair. Then she brought her gaze back up to his and straightened her shoulders. "I'm sorry. I misunderstood."

Dahleven acknowledged the apology with a nod and kicked himself for being a fool. The woman had endured two days alone in the desert and a rough rescue by a troop of strange men. He shouldn't be surprised by the conclusion she'd jumped to. A woman with any breeding and modesty at all would balk at sleeping between two dirt-encrusted men. He made a second mental correction. Had he thought her soft and vulnerable? The woman had the pride and honor of a Jarl, apologizing directly, without excuse. Her character was as worthy of admiration as her fine body.

At the thought of her body, Dahleven's gaze traveled down her exposed legs, and up past shapely hips to her breasts. They would fill a man's hand perfectly, with a bit left over for kissing.

Dahleven cleared his throat and looked away, embarrassed to find his thoughts running uncomfortably close to Lady Celia's fears. Then he looked back at her scratched and bruised legs. They needed attention. A *Healer's* attention. "Ghav! Come attend to the lady's injuries."

"I'm fine. I'm just tired."

Is the woman always contrary? "I'm sure you are, but I'd like our Healer to attend you, as you're my responsibility, now."

Her brows rose, sparks flashing in her eyes again. *Now what?*

"*Your* responsibility?"

Her mouth opened to continue, but Sorn put his hand lightly on her arm. "Ghav is a skilled Healer, and he can take the ache and sting from your bruises. You'll feel better for letting him tend to you."

Lady Celia looked at Sorn. She pressed her lips tightly shut, glared briefly at Dahleven, then nodded to Sorn. "All right."

Ghav had come up quietly during the last skirmish. He gestured with a small flourish at the rock Lady Celia had just been sitting on. "My lady?"

Dahleven watched as Lady Celia seated herself. A strange combination of expressions flashed across her face in response to Ghav's gesture. Suspicion, and...surprise? Unease? Was she not accustomed to courtesy? Perhaps he should revise his opinion of her social standing. Yet her bearing declared her to be at least a high-standing freeman, and perhaps the daughter of a lord. The woman was a puzzle, and one he'd have to solve. Such puzzles could be dangerous.

Dahleven shook his head, then pulled Sorn aside so they could talk privately. Sorn's eyes always saw clearly, especially where women were involved. "What is your estimate of her? Is she what she claims to be?"

Sorn rubbed his bearded chin between thumb and forefinger before he spoke. "She feels fair to me."

If it had been anyone but Sorn, Dahleven might have questioned whether the lady's looks had turned his head, but his friend saw deeper than that. His intuition read women almost as well as Ragni's Talent of Empathy.

"Granted, she's no Tewa, but we saw Outcast Nuvinlanders mingling with the Renegade Tewakwe in that camp two days ago. She could be one of them, play-acting to save her skin."

Sorn snorted. "You don't believe that any more than I do. No Nuvinland woman, Outcast or not, would go about dressed—or undressed—as she is."

An image of Lady Celia's bare legs, scratched and bruised, surfaced and lingered for a moment in Dahleven's mind. He glanced over to where Ghav tended the lady. Were he a healer, he could be the one smoothing salve on those long legs. But that was not his Talent. Dahleven forced his thoughts back to the subject at hand. "True. And no Nuvinlander or Tewakwe ever had gear such as she carries. Did you see that buckle? And the map!"

"And the Lady was truly distressed when she couldn't read it," Sorn added.

"But she read what I wrote in the sand."

"Could she be Fey-marked?" Sorn asked softly.

An involuntary shiver made Dahleven twitch. "Perhaps. But she doesn't quite have the feel of it. I once met a man who'd been taken by the Fey. He saw things that weren't there."

"Then perhaps it is as she says. She is not of Alfheim."

They were silent again, mulling over the implications.

If she wasn't of Alfheim, then she must be from Midgard. *That realm must have changed greatly since Freyr led our ancestors from it.*

Somehow, Lady Celia had traveled the Bifrost, just as their Vinland ancestors had some eight hundred years ago. But why was she here alone? Surely only a god could open the way for her. "Why would Freyr bring a solitary, half dressed woman to Alfheim?"

Sorn shrugged. "Who knows why the gods act as they do? Perhaps a Tewakwe Shaman invoked *their* gods and brought her across."

"But why, then, is she wandering alone in the drylands rather than safe in the Confederation? And why *this* woman, who is clearly not of their people?

"Could someone with a Great Talent have pulled her unwilling over the rainbow bridge?" Sorn's voice dropped, as if he didn't want to speak the thought aloud

The hair on the back of Dahleven's neck rose. Was it possible? Would Baldur and Freyr allow it? No one had used a Great Talent in Nuvinland for a hundred and fifty years. But who then had brought her here? And how?

Which brought him back to Lady Celia and the puzzle she presented.

"She may well be an innocent," Dahleven said, "but we know nothing about her. I put her in your charge, Sorn. Watch her, and help her keep pace tomorrow." They'd have to move fast to get their news about the Outcast and Renegade alliance back to Nuvinland in time for the Althing.

Ghav knelt at Cele's feet, moistening a fairly clean cloth. He looked more like a bear than a Healer. Curly hair covered the backs of his huge hands and sunburned arms and the hair on his head was prematurely gray. Most of his beard remained dark, but two stripes starting from the corners of his mouth were nearly white. Bushy eyebrows sprang from his forehead and were much darker than his hair, still showing most of their original brown.

Cele tensed in anticipation as Ghav prepared to clean her scratches.

He looked up at her. "I'll not hurt you, my lady."

Cele tried to relax. His touch was surprisingly gentle for a man with such large hands, and when he cleaned her scrapes it didn't hurt at all. He worked slowly, holding the cloth against a particularly stiff scab, letting the warmth of his hands sooth the soreness, though she no longer had any pain that needed easing. When the scrapes and bruises on her arms and legs were all clean, he unstoppered a jar containing a light brown ointment and daubed it on the scratches.

Cele had started to relax under Ghav's gentle, painless ministrations, but she came alert and pulled away a little at the first application of Ghav's concoction. "What is that?"

"It's nothing to fear, my lady. This will prevent the wounds from going bad."

"What's it made of?"

"Are you a Healer, my lady? Do you know herbs?"

Cele shook her head.

"I won't recite them, then. Various herbs have the properties of preventing putrefaction in a wound. This is a decoction of such herbs, mixed in an oil base to preserve it. May I continue?"

Cele nodded, feeling ashamed. She'd assumed these people were ignorant and primitive because they carried swords and leather waterskins. Ghav's explanation reminded her she shouldn't measure things here by old familiar yardsticks.

The brown ointment was cool but warmed as Ghav rubbed it in. It absorbed quickly, leaving only a slight sheen from the oil base. "This will also keep the scabs from cracking and splitting," the Healer said as he finished. He rose, just as Sorn returned. "Lady Celia is well, and her wounds aren't deep. She needs rest more than anything else, now."

"That, and more water," Cele interjected.

"I'll make sure you get both," Sorn said, offering her a hand to rise.

He'd refilled his waterskins while she'd been with Ghav. He handed one to her. "So, my lady, you would fight us all?" Sorn gave her a teasing grin. "I will sleep sounder tonight, knowing I have a warrior of such prowess at my back."

Cele tensed. Was he mocking her? But there was no malice in Sorn's twinkling eyes. Her anger evaporated and she chuckled in spite of herself.

Sorn took a good bit of time smoothing the ground and whisking away pebbles. The men not on watch grinned at his meticulous preparations as they doubled up to share their blankets. His efforts flung a bit of grit too far and struck one man on the back of the neck. The man startled and growled, "It's not a bridal bower, Sorn. Leave off."

Cele was practically asleep on her feet when Sorn finally spread the blanket, sat down at the edge, and pulled off his boots. He pulled a second blanket over himself and flipped the corner up so she could crawl in next to him. Suddenly, Cele was wide awake again. Sorn had been nothing but kind. He'd made no sexual overtures, given her no lustful looks, but she still felt awkward about lying next to him.

Cele sat down on the far edge of the blanket and began unlacing her hiking boots. She didn't hurry. Maybe he'd doze off as quickly as the other men had. Cele heard him shift behind her and when she turned to look, she saw with relief he'd turned his back to her. She took her time unlacing her other boot. Sorn hadn't moved. He was probably asleep already. Carefully, Cele lay down as far away from him as she could and gingerly pulled the blanket over herself. Soon the men's soft snores were complementing the desert's own night-song. Sorn remained still. She relaxed and her pulse began to return to normal.

"You must leave room for Lord Dahleven, my lady," Sorn said softly. "It will be cold when his watch ends and he'll want his share of the blankets."

Cele tensed again, but she knew he was right. Slowly, she inched toward him. She lay curled on her side facing away from Sorn's back, but she stopped short of actually touching him.

Sorn made a noise but didn't say anything.

Despite her nerves, it felt wonderful to lie down. Sorn had done a good job of smoothing the ground. His warmth crept between the blankets and gradually enveloped her, soothing her tired muscles. She was much more comfortable than she'd been the night before, but sleep wouldn't come.

She wasn't surprised. It had taken her a long time to be comfortable with Jeff, her ex. She had even less reason to relax now. And though they hadn't hurt her, and had even been gruffly kind, she didn't know these men.

All around her, the desert night noises chirped and rustled, accompanied by the soft snores of the men. The stars turned silently overhead. Sorn breathed evenly. Eventually, the last two days of fear and worry, sun and exhaustion, took their toll.

Cele jerked awake, heart pounding. For a panicked moment she didn't know where she was. She lay curled around a warm body and someone had just moved close behind her. Cele's pulse pounded in alarm.

Memory returned as Dahleven fitted himself to her contours, trapping her front and back. He brought the desert chill under the blanket with him. Instinctively, Cele pulled away, closer to Sorn's warmth, but Dahleven had the same idea, snugging close to the heat of her body until they lay like three spoons in a drawer. She didn't want to stay sandwiched like this between the two men, but she couldn't escape without causing a ruckus. Cele waited, tense and listening. The nearby desert was quiet but for the sounds of the sleeping men. Dahleven's body quickly warmed. He kept his hands to himself. Her heart slowed as her surge of adrenaline faded, and pressed between two heat pumps, her muscles eased of their own accord.

Dahleven's breathing changed, deepened. *He must be asleep.* Gradually, with no threat to keep her alert, Cele's eyes closed. She was so exhausted that she barely surfaced when he flung a muscular arm across both her and Sorn. Half dozing, Cele felt only the soothing warmth of his broad chest behind her and his thighs, hard with muscle, tucked under her own. Without further worry or thought, her fatigue overcame her.

The eastern sky had begun to hint at the coming day when Dahleven awoke. It was time to be up and away, but he didn't move.

In their sleep, the three of them had shifted position. Dahleven lay on his back with his arm around Lady Celia and with her head pillowed on his shoulder. Her arm rested on his chest and her body was softly molded against his side. She'd flung one leg across his thighs. The Lady had been in the desert for two days, and smelled like it. But underneath the sharp tang of her sweat, the fragrance of flowers lingered in her hair. Dahleven drew in a deep breath, savoring the hint of delicate perfume.

Lady Celia shifted slightly, and Dahleven became acutely aware of her curves pressed against his chest, hip, and thigh. His morning wood twitched. He liked the way she felt, nestled along his side. A bird trilled, announcing the coming day, but Lady Celia's even breath told him she still slept. He imagined rolling her beneath him and kissing her awake. Filling his hands with her nicely rounded breasts. Pleasuring them both until they fell sated onto the pillows of his bed.

Dahleven pushed the heated images away. They weren't in his bed, nor in private. Neither had the lady consented.

They ought to be on their way. The pale gray light was growing, and his men made the best time during the cool of the morning. But a few minutes more wouldn't hurt.

Sorn raised his head to look at Dahleven with a grin and a glance at the woman between them. Dahleven's sworn brother knew him too well. *He's happy now. He's caught me indulging myself.* It didn't happen often enough by Sorn's standards. He wouldn't rib him in front of the others, but by Odin's Eye, when they got home, Sorn would ride him hard.

Dahleven answered with a shrug of his eyebrows. Sorn's grin widened before he began moving carefully away, silently as usual. Then, with exaggerated care, he tucked the top blanket around Lady Celia before pulling on his boots.

Cele awakened to a quick draft of chill air. She hadn't heard Sorn leave, but his departure left a void of warmth at her back. Muzzy with sleep, she smiled at his trying not to wake her, then snuggled closer to the remaining source of warmth.

Dahleven.

She froze and came fully awake. *Oh, hell.* How could she have gotten into such an awkward position? It was one thing to sleep close for warmth, another to wind up entwined like lovers. It amazed her she'd slept at all, let alone slept pillowed on Dahleven's shoulder. Maybe she could ease away before anyone, especially Dahleven, noticed. After her accusations last night, the last thing she needed was to send mixed signals.

Unfortunately, the camp was already beginning to

stir. Cele heard the men around her grunt and mutter as they pulled on their boots, got to their feet, and went beyond the perimeter of the camp. Sorn hadn't let her drink much at any one time last night, but he'd encouraged her to drink often. Cele became painfully aware of her bladder.

She also became aware the rhythm of Dahleven's breathing was not that of a sleeping man. She sat up abruptly to find him returning her gaze, clear-eyed and alert.

How long had he been lying there awake while she cozied up to him like some stray cat?

Dahleven sat up and reached for his boots. He didn't look at her as he said, "Good morning, Lady Celia. We'll move soon. Sorn will escort you away from camp so you may...accommodate your needs." Then he stood and walked away without another glance.

Amusement warred with annoyance and quickly won. *He probably doesn't know any words that are suitable for a "lady" to hear in this situation. I wonder if polite people ever refer to such vulgar things as bodily functions here? Probably not.*

Her amusement faded as Sorn returned to lead her beyond the camp. As he took her outside the main area of activity, Cele's discomfort with the situation increased. This was one of the reasons she took short day hikes: taking care of business in the wide-open spaces had never appealed to her. Before they'd gone far, Sorn stopped. Cele continued on a few steps then turned back to him. He handed her a wooden trowel and turned his back.

"What's this for?" Cele asked.

"For digging a cat-hole."

Sorn sounded like she had asked if water was wet.

"Here?" Over Sorn's shoulder, Cele could clearly see the camp and the men in it. Very little obscured the view, only one scraggly desert bush that was more stem than leaf. Cele marched around Sorn to face him. "I don't think so! There's no cover here. I'm not going to drop my drawers here in full view of God and everybody!"

Sorn refused to look at her, but he spoke firmly. "Here. Now. To go further from camp would both endanger you and waste time."

"Endanger me? What are you talking about?"

"We're on the edge of enemy territory. We are not here by invitation."

"What are you talking about? What enemies?"

"Our trade caravans and borders have been raided and attacked. Those responsible are not far from here. It's not safe for you to wander off, searching for the perfect bush to hide behind. No eye will violate your privacy. Lord Dahleven has said it."

And what Dahleven says is law, judging by Sorn's refusal to look at me.

"Please, hurry. We have far to go and must make haste."

Cele's bladder seconded the need for haste. She looked at the digging tool in her hand, and then over her shoulder at the camp. The men there were all busy—with their backs turned to her. Cele looked again at the tool, at Sorn with his carefully averted gaze, then went back around behind him.

Sorn's explanation didn't make sense. She's seen no one but Dahleven and his men in the last two days. Just going out of sight for a few minutes wouldn't put her at any risk. Cele thought for a moment about just walking on and finding her own spot, but Sorn was obviously under orders. He'd try to stop her. She'd have to let him or break his arm. Not a good choice. He'd been nice to her, and this wasn't worth fighting over.

Cele scratched a little trench in the sand. She didn't

look around to see if anyone was looking when she dropped her shorts. If she saw no one, she could pretend no one saw her. Besides, Lord Dahleven had Spoken.

Breakfast was the same as it had been the morning before and the morning before that and every morning since they'd left Nuvinland. By the Talents, Dahleven hated journey bread. It kept a man on his feet, packed small and carried light, but it tasted like how the inside of a boot smelled.

Kepliner and Knut were standing watch while the rest of the men ate, sitting together in a loosely formed circle. Usually they gathered in small twos and threes, quickly ate their morning meal and readied themselves to move out, but this morning they all wanted to take the measure of Lady Celia.

Dahleven watched Lady Celia's face as she bit into the ration Sorn gave her. The corners of her mouth drew downward and her lips puckered, but she only paused for a moment before she continued chewing. Then she actually smiled at Sorn and took another bite. Well, she *had* been in the drylands for two days. *By the Hidden, I hope I'm never so hungry as to be grateful for journey bread.*

"Lady Celia, I have some dried fruit here." Halsten pulled his pack into his lap and began to rummage. "That bread Sorn's foisting on you is foul stuff. You'll like this much better. It's chewy, but still sweet." Halsten handed her a packet wrapped in waxed cloth.

Lady Celia turned the power of her smile full upon him as she accepted his gift. "Maybe just one piece. I don't want to take all you have left," she said, unfolding the cloth.

"No, no. You keep it. It's good energy on the trail."

"Thank you," she said, lightly touching the back of his hand. "That's very generous."

"Would you like my nuts?" Lindimer asked, reaching behind for his pack.

Falsom snickered and Sorn cuffed him.

Ghav and Fender started reaching for their packs as well. *What's the matter with all of them?* They'd only been away from home and women for two weeks. Maybe that was Lady Celia's Talent: turning men into fools. In its place, that could be a pleasant game to play, but he had a mission to complete and men to lead safely home. It was time to put a stop to this.

Dahleven stood up. All eyes turned to him, including Lady Celia's big green ones, framed with long lashes. She'd washed her face and neck, combed her hair, and braided it neatly. Curling wisps escaped the butter-yellow braids that reached just to her shoulders. She looked more like the lady he'd first thought her.

"We'll move soon. Be ready."

The men immediately began to disperse, gathering their equipment. *Good. She hasn't robbed them of all sense.*

"I'm ready now. I can finish this on the trail if you want to get going." Lady Celia gestured with the fruit in her hand and stood. "I won't hold you up."

A night's rest has improved her temper, at least. Dahleven inclined his head.

"Where are we going, anyway?" she asked.

"Quartzholm," Sorn answered.

The information only made her frown. "Will someone there be able to help me go home?"

Maybe Father Wirmund would have some good news for her, though Dahleven didn't have much hope of it. "Perhaps." He changed the subject. "Have you filled your water containers?"

"First thing." She paused, and blushed. "Well, second, anyway."

"Good." He started to turn but was stopped by the touch of her fingers resting lightly on his arm.

"I, uh, want to thank you." Lady Celia spoke in a low voice only he and Sorn could hear. She blushed again and stammered on. "Actual privacy would have been better, of course, but lacking that, well, I appreciate your, uh...Oh hell! Thanks for telling your men to give me some space this morning."

Give her space? She used words strangely at times, but her meaning in this case was clear. "No thanks are necessary." He turned again to go. *Does she believe we would do otherwise? Probably. Last night she thought I'd proposed to rape her.*

"Just the same, I don't see why I couldn't have gone around a hill or something."

Does she argue about everything? Reluctantly, Dahleven turned back to her. She looked like a lady, but no lady he knew would discuss this. Then again, no lady he knew would have survived two days in the drylands so well. "I'm sure Sorn explained to you."

"Yes, but—"

He refused to talk about the subject anymore. "This conversation is pointless. Get ready to move. We cannot slow our pace to accommodate you. You must keep up."

Lady Celia's green eyes widened. Then they narrowed as though she'd reached a decision.

Dahleven turned away before she could vent her annoyance. *She's probably decided I'm an ass.* That shouldn't bother him, but it did.

Something about the woman threw him off balance. It wasn't just that she'd popped into Alfheim as his ancestors had. She distracted him from his duty. He must get his men and the information for which they'd risked their lives safely home. Instead of thinking of that, he'd lingered this morning, enjoying the feel of her against him, and now he was rattled by her thanks for an ordinary courtesy. What was the matter with him? He was as taken with her as his men, admiring her stubborn courage and her long, lovely legs. He couldn't afford that kind of distraction. None of them could. Not in hostile territory. He didn't expect trouble from the Tewakwe, but the Outcasts and Renegades were still a threat. A very serious threat to a party as small as theirs.

He signaled their departure to the others and tried not to think about how Lady Celia's green eyes slanted over her high cheekbones. Instead, he forced himself to focus on Pathfinding the quickest way home to Nuvinland.

The general direction was clear, even without the use of his Talent. But he could find the quickest or easiest route without the use of a map simply by concentrating on where he wanted to go. He needn't have been there before, which made his Talent especially valuable for reconnaissance.

Now that they were climbing into the hills, they walked single file, traveling in two groups of four while he took the lead. Sorn walked behind Lady Celia where he could keep an eye on her; Fendrikanin was in front to help her over the rough spots. Falsom ranged above them on the ridges, using his Talent of Heimdal's Sight to scout their surroundings. The other team followed several minutes behind to lessen the risk of drawing the attention that a combined group might attract.

Dahleven looked back at Lady Celia as she walked between Sorn and Fendrikanin. She looked down, concentrating on her footing. Then she glanced up and met his gaze. She frowned and her eyes narrowed again. Pointedly, she looked away from him.

He continued to watch her over the course of the morning. Though he set a brisk pace, she didn't lag.

He regretted his brusqueness. It wasn't his habit to be rude to women. She probably wasn't responsible for the inconvenience she presented. She probably shouldn't be blamed for the effect she had on the men, either. Nevertheless, her presence was a distraction. A woman, especially a beautiful woman, didn't belong on a drylands mission. He and his men needed to stay focused and move quickly.

Good advice. Now, all he had to do was follow it.

chapter four

what a jerk!

Cele refused to meet Dahleven's eyes when he looked back at her, checking on her again. Well, she'd said she could keep up, and by God she would. Her legs ached and she felt a blister rising on her left heel, but she kept to the brisk pace he set.

They traveled single file. Fendrikanin walked ahead of her, Sorn behind. Most of the sparse vegetation was comprised of thorn bushes, with the occasional Spanish Dagger-like plant thrown in. The group's path twisted through the spiny growth. A careless hiker could easily find her leg impaled if she didn't watch her step.

Dahleven led the way with an unconscious grace. She'd seen that same smooth gait in some of the firemen she'd met and in her self-defense instructor. They walked with confidence, trusting their bodies to do whatever was needed. Dahleven moved the same way. He never hesitated or looked at a map, just forged ahead, never pausing, never slacking his pace. Just looking over his shoulder now and then to see if she was falling behind. *Jerk.*

They walked in relative silence, the crunching of their footsteps on the sand the only noise. They didn't talk, and Cele didn't miss the conversation. She needed all her breath to keep up.

The sun moved higher in the sky. Cele felt like they'd been walking for hours, but the eastern range looked no closer than it had when they'd set out this morning. In fact, as the sun rose, the mountains seemed to recede. She pulled one of her water bottles from its holder and took a long draw, then put it back without taking a second drink. No one had warned her to conserve. Sorn could see every time she drank and said nothing to caution her, so water must not be a problem. Just the same, maybe she'd hold off a little. After enduring nearly two days of thirst, feeling the weight of the remaining water on her hips gave her comfort.

As she thought about water, Cele experienced the peculiar certainty again. Yes, there was water ahead, and Dahleven's course led them toward it. She gave herself a mental shake. There was no way she could know that. *Don't flake out.* She was in enough trouble without imagining things.

The morning wore on and her blisters grew more painful. Cele started to think about raising the white flag and asking to rest, but she hated the thought of giving Dahleven the satisfaction. He hadn't said it in so many words, but he clearly expected a *lady* to slow them down. She wouldn't care so much if he hadn't been such an ass about accepting her gratitude. Thanking him had been embarrassing enough without being called pointless. Cele gritted her teeth. She hated being dismissed.

Dahleven raised his left arm over his head, then signaled in that direction. Cele noticed Falsom's attention immediately rivet on him.

"What's happening?" Cele asked.

Dahleven veered toward a spur of rock thrust outward from the hills.

"He's calling a break," Fendrikanin answered, following Dahleven around a tumble of boulders that had long ago broken from the cliff. Sharp spikes of the Spanish dagger-like plant grew in every crack and joint between the stones.

On the far side, Dahleven waited by a cleft at the base of a sheer rock face that rose thirty feet before breaking back to the ridge above. The two sides of a long crack had shifted, creating a cave that ran deep into cool darkness. As soon as she came close, Cele knew: *There's water here.*

Sorn stepped into the shade near the entrance and peered into the cave. "Nice and cool. This will be a good resting place."

Dahleven snorted a laugh. "I'm glad you approve."

Cele tried not to show her surprise at his unstuffy response. Instead, she sat and began removing her hiking boots and socks. The air on her hot, tired feet felt wonderful, and she wiggled and stretched her toes.

The other men came around the spur of tumbled rock. Ghav came and knelt before her, shaking his head at her new collection of scrapes and bruises. "Those blisters must have pained you. You should have said something." He rummaged through his pack. "I have a salve that will help."

"Thanks. They feel better already." She was surprised to realize her statement was true. Just as it had last night, Ghav's mere presence made her aches and twinges fade away.

"Of course they do." The Healer found what he was looking for. "Now, let's tend to your hurts."

Fendrikanin stooped twenty feet to Cele's left, kneeling by a cleft eroded into the hillside. When he straightened, his hands and beard were wet. "The water's sweet, and there's plenty of it."

Dahleven joined Fender, kneeling by the spring, and placing something Cele couldn't see into the water. "Accept our gift in return for your bounty," he murmured. He paused a moment, then rose and returned to the cave opening.

What was that all about?

"Drink as much as you want, and refill your bags." Dahleven directed his comment to the group in general and gestured toward the small rill. He turned to Fendrikanin. "Will we have water tonight?"

The other man closed his eyes for a moment, then shook his head. "It's hard to tell this close to the spring, but I think we'll have a dry camp tonight.

Dahleven nodded and leaned against the rock face to Cele's right, arms crossed, watching her.

Trying to ignore his scrutiny, Cele watched Ghav clean her blisters, but the leader soon made that impossible by coming close and crouching nearby.

He picked up one of her boots and examined it closely. "These are very finely made."

Cele looked at him cautiously. "Scrimping on footwear is a false economy, in my opinion."

"Very wise." Dahleven continued to examine the boot. "Of what materials are these?" His gaze lifted to hers and stayed there, intent and waiting.

His scrutiny was unsettling. The stormy grey of his eyes swirled around his pupils and Cele felt she was being swallowed by his steady, unwavering gaze.

"Lady Celia?"

She missed a beat while trying to remember his question. "Uh, leather, nylon, and the usual assortment of man-made products, I guess." Then the oddness of his question struck her. *He was impressed with my belt pack, and the sandwich bag, too.*

Cele looked closely at him. She'd noted the presence of leather boots and waterskins, spears and swords. Now the absence of plastics and synthetics struck her forcefully. It was the final blow, and it hit her harder than the changed landscape and vegetation, or even the missing city. She was lost. Profoundly lost. Completely severed from everything she knew and loved.

Cele felt her eyes filling, and looked away so Dahleven wouldn't see. She'd been around enough macho types to know he already resented having to haul a woman along with him. His attitude would only get worse if he caught her weeping.

Ghav startled her by smearing his brown ointment on her scraped knee and she jumped, shaking loose a tear. Ghav said, "My apologies. I didn't mean to startle you." Then he looked up at her face and paled. "Are you in pain?" he asked urgently. His concern seemed out of proportion to her injury.

"Not at all."

Ghav still frowned doubtfully, and Cele tried to reassure him with a shaky smile. "I wish the doctors back home had your touch."

Ghav looked relieved. He pointed at her face. "The tears alarmed me."

Cele quickly wiped the dampness away, wishing Ghav hadn't called attention to it. "It's nothing. Don't worry about it." But the tears kept slipping down her cheeks.

Ghav drew a rolled bandage from his pack, but Cele stopped him.

"I've got just the thing for this." Cele pulled out her first aid kit, complete with the pack of adhesive bandages. "Here's one just the right size," she said, applying it.

Ghav was delighted and inspected it closely. "How wonderful! It sticks to the uninjured skin on either side. Do you have larger bandages like this?"

"No, but I have gauze and tape." Grateful for the distraction, Cele showed him the contents of her first aid kit, including the empty tube of antibacterial ointment. "I finished this off before you found me. It does what your brown stuff does: prevents infection."

"You might not have needed so much bandaging if you'd been dressed properly," Dahleven commented. "Do your people not have clothing to equal your footwear? I don't understand how you kept the sun from burning you, but you obviously haven't been as successful avoiding thorn-bushes and rocks. Heavier clothing, *any* clothing, would have given you greater protection."

There was that look again. It made her feel indecent. She'd dressed appropriately for a short hike, but Dahleven's intense gaze made her feel like she was half naked.

Ghav intervened. He waggled his bushy gray eyebrows at Dahleven, then turned to Cele. "You must tell me more of the healing arts of your home. The differences must be as great as in your customs and dress."

"Indeed." Dahleven got to his feet and began climbing to where Falsom kept watch near the top of the ridge.

Sorn poked his head out of the cave. "Ghav will keep you talking about healing and herbs all day if you don't stop him. Come in out of the heat."

Ghav laughed. "He's right. Go. Rest. We'll talk later."

Cele put on her socks, then gathered up her belt-pack and boots and followed Sorn inside.

"How's your knee?" Sorn asked, sitting down cross-legged on Cele's left.

"It looked worse than it was. Ghav fixed me up so it doesn't hurt at all."

"He has a Talent for that."

"I guess so." Ghav had a talent for healing. Sorn had

a talent for kindness and Dahleven had a talent for pissing her off.

Cele changed the subject. "I don't know anything about anything or anybody here. Tell me about yourselves."

A twinkle appeared in Sorn's eye. "I've been in Lord Dahleven's company now for six years. I like roast duckling, sleeping late on holidays, and my favorite color is blue."

Cele snorted, and dug Halsted's dried fruit from her pack. "What about your family? Do you have brothers and sisters?"

"None living. My only brother died before I was born. The fever took my mother and sisters five years ago, so it's just me and my father now. What about you? Do you come from a large family?"

"No," Cele said around a mouthful. She didn't want to talk about herself. She was more interested in what Sorn's life was like. "What's your father like?"

"He's a jeweler. His Talent is Enhancing Beauty, so everyone wants one of his pieces. When I was younger, I wanted to be just like him."

"You wanted to be a jeweler?" Cele couldn't keep the disbelief out of her voice. Sorn seemed so comfortable in his skin, she couldn't imagine him doing anything else. Certainly not making jewelry.

Sorn chuckled. "No. I wanted his Talent. When he was young all the women wanted to be seen with him."

"Because he made them jewelry?"

Sorn gave her an odd look. "Because his Talent made them beautiful. Before he learned to harness it, his Talent ran loose. Anyone within its aura appeared more beautiful. When I was young, I thought being surrounded by beautiful women sounded pretty good."

That sounded new-agey. "I doubt you had much trouble gaining the attention of the ladies, even without your father's talent thingy."

"You have the truth of it, Lady Celia! Our Sorn here is a smooth hand with the ladies. He's not lonely much of the time, are you Sorn?" Fendrikanin grinned and winked at Cele.

"Shut it, Fender," Sorn growled.

"That's right. Our Sorn here seldom lacks feminine companionship. Or should I say, *sisterly* companionship?" Fendrikanin leaned forward to push his jibe home with a direct look.

Sorn rolled his eyes. "Yes, Fender, back home I'm surrounded by women. Thronged. Hounded."

"I'm a little confused," Cele said tentatively. "I thought you were an only child?"

"He is, but half the ladies of Quartzholm would adopt him if they could." Fendrikanin's eyes glinted with his joke.

"We won't discuss *your* reputation with the fairer sex, as there is a lady present." Sorn looked away from Fendrikanin with exaggerated disdain, but there was a sparkle of humor in his eyes. "Actually, he's right." Sorn's mouth twisted in a rueful grin. "The ladies at home do love me—as a brother. Whenever you see me engaged in conversation with a woman, it's a safe bet she's asking advice on how to deal with her beau."

Cele didn't say anything, chagrined to recognize a similar feeling within herself. Of course women talked to Sorn, he was easy to talk to. Sorn was comfortable. He was...safe. "I see your problem."

"Now it's my turn to ask a question."

Cele grinned. "You can ask."

"A true lady. She promises nothing." Fendrikanin sketched a bow.

Cele laughed and inclined her head.

Dahleven appeared in the cave entrance. He gestured and Knut left the cave. Cele wondered if he would quash the conversation like the sudden appearance of a study hall monitor.

Fendrikanin seemed undeterred. "We were just sharing confidences. Care to play?"

"It sounds like a dangerous game. Whose turn is it?" Dahleven asked, sitting against the opposite wall. He bent his legs to avoid blocking the entrance and propped his elbows on his knees.

Cele glanced at him with surprise at his unstuffy reply and saw a smile lurking around his lips.

"Lady Celia's, but she has reserved a lady's prerogative." Fendrikanin grinned at her.

Cele knew she was supposed to ask, and knew she shouldn't, but did anyway. "To which of my prerogatives do you refer?" she asked with mock dignity.

Unrepressed, Fender replied, "Why, to change the rules at any time, my lady."

Cele had to laugh, and so did everyone else, including Dahleven. "And don't you forget it." She wagged her finger at Fender.

"You've heard about me," Sorn said. "Now tell us about your family, Lady Celia."

"I'd rather hear more about this Talent thing you mentioned."

Sorn's eyebrows rose, and Fendrikanin darted a look at Dahleven.

What did I say?

"Do you not have Talent among your people, Lady Celia?" Dahleven's face and voice were very casual. Too casual.

Cele answered carefully. "We have people back home who are talented in art and music. Or we might say someone has a talent for fixing things, but that sounds different from what you're talking about."

Sorn's brows were drawn together. "We have those among us who are skilled in the Arts as well, but Talent is a separate thing."

"Separate how? Are you talking about some kind of magic?"

Sorn glanced at Dahleven, who gave a slight nod. "Our Talents are neither trickery nor ritual magic," Sorn said. "They're part of us, but separate from gifts of skill. A man might have a Talent for shaping wood, but no skill for woodcarving. So he might become a cooper or a wainwright. My father could have applied his Talent by working with paint, or cut stone, or fabric and laces, but his skill and his heart lie in working with metal and fine stones. His Talent enhances the natural beauty of his creations, and the beauty of those who wear them."

Cele wasn't sure what to think. Were these guys serious? It sounded like they were talking about psychic stuff, and they obviously took it very seriously.

"A few poor fools have Talents of little use. I know one fellow whose Talent is imitating sounds and voices. Entertaining, but not of much value," Fendrikanin added.

Cele thought of the highly paid performers back home who'd built their fortunes on mimicry, but said nothing. *Home.* She'd been there only three days ago. Now it seemed very far away.

"*Do* you have Talent among your people, perhaps called by another name?" Dahleven asked softly. From Lady Celia's questions, he feared he knew the answer already.

Falsom came in off watch and picked his way past the others. A little of the midday heat drifted in with him. It would be a while yet before the day cooled enough for them to move on. Dahleven wished they could have kept moving, but none of them, bred in the mountains, tolerated the lowland heat very well, so they rested each midday while in the drylands.

Lady Celia waited for Falsom to pass before she answered. "I don't think so. Not the way you talk about it."

Fendrikanin studied the ground. Dahleven felt awkward, but he forced himself to meet Lady Celia's eyes. What did you say to someone who was Talentless? Sorn reached out and squeezed Lady Celia's hand. To his surprise, Dahleven wished he were the one comforting her.

Lady Celia gave Sorn a quizzical look. "What's wrong? You all look as though someone died."

Dahleven exchanged an embarrassed glance with the other two men.

Sorn broke the awkward silence. "We're just sorry that you're...Talentless."

"You're new to Alfheim. Your Talent could still Emerge," Fender suggested.

Dahleven knew that was unlikely, but he didn't gainsay Fender. Talent Emerged during puberty, not in well-grown adults. "It's rare among us that a child fails to develop Talent," Dahleven added gently. It generally meant pitying glances and ostracism.

Understanding broke over Lady Celia's features. She removed her hand from Sorn's grasp. "You mean it's like a deformity to be without Talent, don't you? From your point of view, I'm not quite whole."

All conversation had ceased. Falsom froze, still standing. No one spoke.

"Well, I've never had a talent, and until I got here I never knew anyone who did, so I don't miss it. In fact, people who claim to have unusual abilities like that are considered a little flaky where I come from, so it's not a problem for me. And, no offense, but while your Talents are handy, they hardly seem essential."

Dahleven said nothing. No one else did either; there was nothing to say. Many people coped with their shortcomings by viewing them as unimportant. No good would come of persuading the Lady otherwise.

"You said some among your people have unusual abilities?" Sorn asked.

"So some of your people do have Talent?" Fendrikan-in joined in.

"A few people claim they can move small objects without touching them, or see things that are far away with their minds, but they can't always get it to work when they want it to. Most people are pretty skeptical about that sort of thing."

"It sounds like Talent is rare among your people," Dahleven said.

"Maybe. But if it doesn't work consistently, what good is it?"

"Our Talents are consistent." Dahleven spoke softly but firmly. He wanted Lady Celia to be clear on this point. He didn't want her thinking of them with the same distrust she obviously had for the Talented among her own people. Maybe they deserved that doubt. He and his men did not.

Lady Celia was thoughtful for a moment. "Do you all have only one?"

Dahleven nodded. "One is enough."

"What are they? If you don't mind me asking."

"Pathfinding," Dahleven said.

From Sorn: "I'm a Cat Foot."

She nodded, understanding his unusually silent movement now.

"Water Finding," Fendrikanin said softly.

"Heimdal's Sight." Falsom finally sat down.

Lady Celia looked confused. "What's that?"

"Like Heimdal, I can see things at great distance."

"Oh. And Ghav's Talent has something to do with healing, doesn't it?" Lady Celia looked around for the healer. "Pain. You stop pain, don't you? That's why you were upset when you thought I was hurting. You were afraid your Talent wasn't working."

Talentless or not, Dahleven admired her quick understanding.

"You've so recently arrived," Ghav said. "It's possible my Talent might have had no effect on you, but the lack of your response still would have distressed me."

Lady Celia nodded. "Yes, of course."

They fell silent again. *Ghav was right to silence me out there*, Dahleven thought. He'd been thinking ill of her for looking like a lady and dressing like a—what? A sex thrall? The lady Celia, however, kept the pace like a soldier, without complaint, and faced the truth without flinching from it. She might be Talentless, but his criticism was out of place, even if her lack of clothing was a hazard to her well-being and a distraction to his concentration.

Sorn again broke the tension. "Now that you know about our Talents, tell us about yourself."

Not for the first time, Dahleven thanked the weavings of the Fates for Sorn's presence, as his friend redirected the conversation with instinctive empathy.

A wicked twinkle glinted in Lady Celia's eye. "I've been an emergency response operator for three years and a supervisor for two. I like pizza, hiking at dawn, and my favorite color is green."

There was a perfect pause, then Fendrikanin hooted his laughter.

Sorn touched his forehead in mock salute. Then he asked, "What's 'pizza?'"

Lady Celia's eyes widened and she put a hand on Sorn's. "You've never had pizza? No, I guess you wouldn't." She smiled. "It's wonderful! You put meat and onions and cheese and mushrooms and spicy tomato sauce on thin bread and bake it. I'll make you some, sometime."

Dahleven wished she'd offered to cook for him, then crushed the thought. "Tell us of your home and family. Your life there must be very different."

Lady Celia looked at him as though she were surprised he could be civil. Well, he supposed he'd earned that.

"It *is* different. I live in a valley full of people—about a million of them. We have cars and planes and television. Of course we also have car accidents, gunshot wounds, and heart attacks." Her mouth twisted into a sour moue on the last few words.

Dahleven didn't recognize all of her words, but he understood what she left unsaid. She missed her home, but she hadn't been happy.

"And your family?" Sorn prompted.

"There isn't much to tell." Lady Celia's eyes dimmed a little as she looked off to the side. "My mother died two years ago after a long illness. My cousins live on the other side of the country, so I hardly know them. The family pretty much shunned my mother after she met my dad. She didn't have much use for them either. I share a house with my best friend, Elaine." Lady Celia's eyes came alive again. "Poor Elaine! She'll be out of her mind with worry."

"And your father?" Fendrikanin asked.

"My father was never part of the picture. He took off before I was born. Mom raised me on her own."

"He deserted a woman bearing his child?" Kep burst out.

Dahleven felt the same, but he kept his flare of outrage and disgust under control, wishing young Kep had more restraint.

The lady shrugged. "It happens. I never suffered for it. Mom saw to that."

"Your mother sounds like a remarkable woman. I wish I could have had the honor of knowing her." Sorn said.

Lady Celia smiled at him.

Score another one for Sorn.

Lord Dahleven set an easier pace for the afternoon's leg, and Cele found herself wondering about the world she'd fallen into and worrying about the one she'd left behind.

She didn't like being regarded as defective.

Apparently, everyone here had something called a Talent. What it was—psychic ability or whatever—she didn't know, but not having one marked her a cripple. *Talent-challenged.* Well, she was fine without one. They'd just have to get over it.

Elaine would have called Search and Rescue nearly two days ago. Cele hated to think of them climbing the hills, searching for her to no good purpose. How long would they look before they called off the search? How many days would she be featured on the evening news, with the anchor solemnly intoning, "...and still no sign of the missing woman"?

In a month, I'll be a face on a milk carton.

Would she still be here in a month? A year? Would she ever get home? And if she did, how would she explain where she'd been? What explanation could she offer that didn't sound crazy? *No one believed Dorothy, either.*

Maybe it would be like in the fairy tales. She'd get home and find that no time had passed at all. Or maybe she'd be a real, live Rip Van Winkle, and twenty years would have flown by in a night.

Dahleven looked back at Sorn and gestured for him to come forward. Sorn jogged past her to join him. The gray-eyed leader had surprised her. He'd been brusque to the point of rudeness this morning, and he'd made her feel like she was walking around half clothed. But then in the cave he'd been civil, nice even.

Sorn was another matter entirely. His kindness kept this wacked-out weirdness from getting to her. She wished she could introduce him to Elaine. Her roomie would love him. A flare of embarrassment made Cele roll her eyes. She sounded like a sister, trying to fix up her brother with her best friend. From the sound of things, Sorn didn't need another sister.

Cele looked ahead to where he walked with Dahleven. Sorn had a runner's build: lean and wiry. His dark brown hair just touched his shoulders. *He'd be perfect for Elaine.* Dahleven's muscular frame was more to her own taste. His broad shoulders tapered down in a classic "V" to a narrow waist. Dahleven might be confusing and annoying, but he did have a really nice ass.

"Do you believe her tale?" Dahleven asked without preamble, when Sorn joined him. "Is she truly ignorant of Talent and all the rest?"

Though Sorn was younger by two years, Dahleven had always trusted his opinion. Even when they were boys, Sorn saw through the mess that obscured most complex questions. And, his romantic life notwithstanding, Sorn understood women. Something Dahleven, as most men, didn't even try to lay claim to.

"Yes, I believe her. And so do you. That's what scares you. Lady Celia's presence is an omen of change."

"Indeed." Dahleven gave Sorn a tight, lopsided smile. "How did she get here? Who brought her?"

Sorn shook his head, his own worry showing in the tightness around his eyes. "Whether it was the gods or a

Great Talent, the Lady is here unwilling. She deserves some consideration for that, no matter which way that wind blows."

Dahleven looked over at Sorn. His friend raised his eyebrows in gentle challenge, as if to say, *You know I'm right.*

Dahleven inclined his head, silently acknowledging the criticism. Then he grinned. "That's why I put you in charge of her, Sorn. I don't have time to coddle a lady right now, but I know she'll be safe in your care."

Sorn rolled his eyes and shook his head. "It's easy duty. She's pleasant and funny and proud and honest. You'd know that for yourself if you did more than growl at her."

"I've noticed." He wasn't blind and deaf. He'd noticed, all right. He'd noticed that Lady Celia's green eyes flashed like razor-edged emeralds at him, but softened like a meadow on a spring day when she looked at Sorn. He'd noticed she had a distracting shapeliness and an honest character to be admired. He'd noticed it would be too easy to spend time thinking about touching her instead of getting his men home safely.

Dahleven jerked his head. "You'd best get back to her."

Cele trudged onward as the sun dropped lower in the sky. At least her feet didn't hurt much anymore, since Ghav had slathered her blisters with his ointment. The terrain opened up a bit and then the footing became soft, as Dahleven led them through a dry wash. Steep banks rose to either side, though a tumble of large boulders had broken from the right, narrowing their path for a short way. Sorn turned and waited for her. Fendrikanin passed him. She was nearly even with Sorn when his head jerked up and his attention focused on the hills to Cele's left.

Then all hell broke loose.

chapter five

AN ARROW WHIZZED by Cele's left cheek just as Falsom's shout, "Tewas!" cut off abruptly.

The next instant Sorn pushed her between two boulders and a thorn bush. "Stay there!"

The rock scraped Cele's shoulder and knees. Screams and shouts of battle surrounded her, piercing like the thorns clawing at her back. An arrow skittered off the rock above her head and rebounded into the tangled branches of the thornbush.

She had only a narrow view of the fight—mostly of Sorn's back as he lunged and danced away from his opponent's attack. Dahleven's voice rose above the chaos. "Back against the banks! Into the rocks!"

Ululating cries rose from several places on the wash's banks above them. Hair rose on Cele's arms and the back of her neck and her hands felt clammy. No battle cry in the movies compared to hearing one first hand.

Cele craned her neck, trying to see what was happening. The thornbush at her back stuck sharply into her shoulder and scraped her cheek. She flinched back, ducking her head again. Over the pounding of her heart, she heard metal ring in a quick slide across stone, and a sharp *Crack!* of splitting wood. Grunts of painful effort joined thudding footfalls, adding to the din as the second group of Dahleven's men joined the fray.

The gut-wrenching cries of pain made her skin feel too tight. She'd heard terrible things over the phone lines as an emergency response operator. She'd listened to people in pain and danger, even people dying, but nothing compared to this. Men screamed and fought only two feet from where she stood, wedged between two rocks.

With a shout of effort, Sorn pushed his opponent back to the left and out of her field of view. Then, from the right, a brown-skinned warrior with a bladed club rushed at him. Sorn couldn't see his danger.

"No!" Cele' reacted without thought, surging from between the rocks. The warrior was side-on to her, his club raised and ready to come down on Sorn's head, when her snap-kick connected with his knee.

The enemy warrior shrieked and collapsed on the sand. Sorn turned at her shout, but he didn't thank her for saving his life. His eyes widened and he pushed her back toward the rocks as he faced another foe coming close behind the first. The new opponent didn't have time to check his momentum in the soft sand. He seemed to fold almost gracefully over Sorn's blade. Sorn shifted his weight, trying to turn back to the bloody enemy he'd left behind him. But the deep sand betrayed Sorn, shifting beneath his feet. The warrior's bladed club caught him full in the belly.

"No!" Cele swept up Sorn's fallen sword with both hands and lunged at Sorn's attacker. The blade was horrendously heavy, but her horror and anger gave her strength. He looked surprised when the steel sliced the side of his neck, but he dodged backward, knocking the sword out of her hands with his club.

She was going to die.

Then Fender was there and his blade was between the warrior's ribs.

The fight ended abruptly. One moment the clangor of battle surrounded her, a moment later all she heard was the pounding of her heart in her ears. She fell to her knees beside Sorn.

An instant of silence was broken by Dahleven's voice. "Halsten, find out what happened to Falsom. Knut, up on the banks. Keep your eyes sharp. Fender, see to Lady Celia."

Despite the warning, Cele jumped when a hand touched her arm and pulled her to her feet. Fendrikanin grasped her tightly by the shoulders, turned her this way and that, looking her over.

"She's unharmed," he said over his shoulder.

Cele pulled away from his grasp, intent on getting to Sorn's crumpled form, and Fender let her go. She took a step, then her vision narrowed. Black dots danced in her eyes. The young warrior caught her as she started to topple. He pulled her aside to sit on an outcropping.

Too much adrenaline, a fuzzy part of her mind observed. She put her head between her knees and closed her eyes. That made it worse, giving her the sensation that the rock was turning beneath her. Cele opened her eyes again and stared at the sand between her feet, the sounds of death echoing in her mind.

Her head cleared enough to let her sit up, but her stomach churned. Cele clamped her jaw tightly, taking shallow breaths, refusing to throw up. She hated feeling weak.

Cele's awareness of her surroundings returned slowly at first as she noticed the small, immediate things. The rock she sat on was warm. There was a fine grit in the hollow where her hand rested. The edge of the rock was sharp.

Abruptly, the rest of the world snapped into focus

with awful clarity. Lindimer was binding Kepliner's arm. Knut stood above the wash, tense and alert. Five men with dusky skin and black hair lay dead, face down in the sand.

The dead men were dressed in leather leggings and sleeveless shirts, details she hadn't noticed during the frenzy of danger. Their limbs sprawled at odd angles. Blood soaked the sand beneath the nearer one. The one Sorn had saved her from. Cele looked away.

"Better now?" Fender asked, his voice sounding oddly thick.

She nodded, unable to speak. Only a few steps away, Dahleven knelt by Sorn while Ghav examined his wound.

Sorn! Cele stood and found her legs surprisingly steady. Moving to Dahleven's side, she asked, "Can I help?"

"Good, you've got your wits back." Dahleven rose. His voice was rough and he had a bloody scrape on his neck and a pinched look in his eyes. "Yes, you can help." He cleared his throat. "Ask Ghav what to do. We must move, and quickly, and it will be hard on Sorn. Ghav may have his hands full with all of us tonight; the Renegades sometimes foul their claws."

"And so saying, you should be cleaning that hide of yours," Ghav said. "Come here, Lady Celia, and I'll teach you the ways of tending a belly wound."

Dahleven took a step back, making room for Cele. He looked at Sorn a moment longer with a tight expression, then straightened and walked away.

Sorn's clothing was ripped and drenched with blood, more blood than she'd ever seen before. This was her fault. If she hadn't shouted, Sorn wouldn't have been distracted. He wouldn't have been vulnerable. *He wouldn't have seen that third warrior, either.* One of them would have killed him. Or her. But guilt and doubt still choked her.

"Lady Celia?" Ghav's voice jerked her attention back to the bloody scene before her.

Self-recrimination wouldn't help Sorn. Cele forced her thoughts into professional mode, wrapping herself in calm detachment. Her medical knowledge consisted of first aid training and what she'd learned from flipping through the medical flowcharts while on the phone with panicked callers. Nevertheless, she knew that the smell rising from Sorn's wound meant his bowel had been perforated, and that was bad news. Very bad news. *He needs surgery and antibiotics.* She wanted a cell phone and a Medevac helicopter.

"Lady Celia." Sorn's voice was tight with pain.

"I'm here." She knelt and took his hand, her professional detachment cracking. His touch released too many feelings.

"You are...uninjured?" Sorn's breath came out unevenly.

"I'm fine." Cele tried to keep her voice steady. "You saved my life." Her feelings jumbled together. In only a short time, she'd started to rely on his kindness and humor. What would she do without him? No one had ever risked his life for her before. How dare he put that burden on her?

She looked at Ghav. She couldn't keep all of the accusation out of her voice. "He's in so much pain! Can't you do something?"

The expression on Ghav's weathered and lined face flickered at Cele's tone, but he answered with a calm voice. "I'm blocking as much of his pain as I can, my lady. Beyond that, I can only use my knowledge and skill to help him."

Cele dropped her eyes and pressed her lips together. Ghav was doing his best, but that wasn't the answer she wanted.

"Sorn, I must hurt you more if I'm to help you at all." Ghav bent over Sorn so he could look directly into his eyes. "Chew these leaves. They will dull the pain somewhat." The Healer pulled three leaves from a small clay pot filled with oil and stuffed them into Sorn's cheek. "Chew," he commanded and waited to see his patient's jaw begin to move before he continued by unrolling a leather pouch filled with obsidian knives, metal tongs and tweezers, what looked like finishing nails and twine, needles and thread.

Ghav untied Sorn's breeches and began to pull them away from the bloody gashes in his lower abdomen, then paused. "My lady, this will be an ugly business. I must clear his wound of clothing and I cannot pause for a lady's delicate sensibilities."

What's he more concerned about, my reaction to the wound or Sorn's privates? All she said was, "Get on with it." Cele glanced at Sorn's face. His breathing slowed a bit and his eyelids drooped over glazed eyes.

Ghav folded the front flap of Sorn's pants down all the way, not quite revealing his genitals. Four gashes bled profusely, but only one appeared deep. That wound was enough to threaten Sorn's life. Ghav pulled the obsidian knife from its sheath and started to set the tip to Sorn's belly.

Cele's hand shot out, grasping Ghav's wrist. "What are you doing? Aren't you going to sterilize that?"

Ghav stared at her, startled.

Right, Montrose. The wound is already filthy and I'm worried about a few more germs?

Cele released his wrist. "Sorry. It's just that where I come from, we believe that clean wounds heal better."

Ghav's voice was a bit testy. "Here, also. May I continue?"

Cele nodded, then as Ghav was about to cut she asked, "Have you ever treated something like this before?"

"Twice."

Successfully? She wanted to ask, but said nothing.

Ghav must have guessed her thoughts. "This is a serious wound, my lady, and the treatment for it is limited. A great deal will depend on Sorn." Ghav lengthened the deep gash, cutting gradually down through the layers of tissue, careful not to further cut the bowel that lay beneath. He nodded toward his bota. "Get that and pour it in the wound."

Cele picked up the skin and hesitated. She'd been drinking it with no ill effects, but the idea of pouring untreated, unsterile water into Sorn's shredded belly went against the grain. "We really should boil this first."

Ghav looked at her impatiently. "My lady, pour it now, or I will summon someone who will. I must cleanse the waste from his belly before I bandage the wound, and I must do it now before he loses more blood."

Cele poured half the bota into Sorn's wound.

"Now come over here help me turn him to his side."

The two of them turned Sorn and Ghav pulled the edges of his wound apart. Sorn moaned. Bloody, vile smelling liquid poured out.

None of her experience had prepared her for this. Cele's stomach clenched. *No. I won't be sick. I won't. Not now.* She didn't want to be here, seeing this, doing this to a man who'd been so kind to her, who'd made her laugh. But she couldn't leave him, either. Cele swallowed tightly and her stomach pulled back from her throat a bit.

They did it twice more, using two of Ghav's three botas, before Ghav felt he could sew Sorn's bowel. He selected a curved needle and a length of thread from his pouch. Cele pushed questions of sterile, dissolving sutures out of her mind. Ghav had to use what was available. He took small, delicate stitches, putting Sorn's insides back together. She was amazed at how deftly Ghav worked with his huge hands.

When he finished stitching Sorn's interior, Ghav rinsed the wound yet again. The liquid sank into the sand. It still carried blood and stank of fecal matter, but less than before.

"That was the last of my water," he said. Ghav sat back on his heels and wiped a forearm across his brow, pushing his graying hair off his sweaty face. "I should do this again, but we won't reach the spring till tomorrow morning, at best."

Cele reached behind her for one of the squeeze bottles in her belt pack. "Use mine," she said, pulling open the top. Unbidden, the memory of desperate thirst rose in her mind. The dry, furry tongue, the near delirium, the aching need. Her mouth itched; she felt parched already.

She pushed the unwelcome images away. They'd reach a spring tomorrow. Short rations weren't the same as no water at all.

Ghav gave her half a frown, but he took the container. When the wound was as clean as he could make it, he packed a poultice of herbs over the wound and wrapped a bandage tightly around Sorn's middle.

"Aren't you going to sew him up?"

Ghav shook his head. "The wound needs to drain."

Dahleven rinsed the wound on his neck. The water ran clear; the bleeding had stopped. *Damn.* Dahleven scrubbed at the wound till it bled again, then bent and emptied the skin over it. *That'll have to be good enough.*

Knut called out, "My Lord!" The lookout nodded to

where Halsten helped a slumping Falsom navigate the scree leading down to the wash bed.

Fender scrambled up and pulled Falsom's other arm across his shoulders.

Falsom had barely settled to the ground, propped against a rock, before he started apologizing. "I don't know what happened. I didn't see them. I didn't see a thing." Falsom's head wobbled wildly and Dahleven eased it back to rest against the rock. Falsom winced. "Agh, my head!" He put both hands up, awkwardly groping as though he couldn't quite find it.

"Don't punish yourself, Falsom. They must have Talents that blinded you to their presence." The trader caravans that had been attacked reported certain Talents being suppressed and the victims suffered blinding headaches. One man had died from the effect.

Falsom had been lucky.

But he wouldn't stay lucky if they remained here much longer. None of them would. Most likely they had encountered the Renegades by chance. Their enemies had probably seized an opportunity to attack what seemed to be a small group, until the other half of Dahleven's company, the second group of four, arrived. The Renegades hadn't liked the odds then, and had taken to the hills. *Cowards.*

Dahleven ran a hand down the back of his neck, wincing as much at his thoughts as the pain when he scraped his wound. *We can thank that "cowardice" for saving our necks.* He had two men down, and two more with wounds that might be fouled. Water was a good day's march away unless they went back, closer to the Renegade encampment. That was too dangerous. The Tewas could return at any time with reinforcements. They had to move. Now.

Dahleven stood. "Halsten, Fender, make two litters with spears and blankets—"

"No! I can walk on my own." Falsom started to rise, but Dahleven pushed him down easily. "Well, maybe with a little help, but I can walk."

Dahleven hated to lose an additional two spears to the making of a second litter, not to mention the men needed to carry it. He looked closely at Falsom. The man's eyes already focused more steadily and his head didn't wobble as much. He might make it with help. "All right, you can walk." Dahleven turned to Kepliner, whose bandaged arm rested in a sling. "Kep, stay with him. Fender, Halsten, we'll still need a litter for Sorn."

Dahleven walked over to where Ghav and Lady Celia bandaged Sorn. His sworn brother's face was white under his tan, contrasting sharply with his dark hair, and his face twisted with pain. Ghav wore his usual placid expression, but Dahleven had known the older man all his life, and they'd seen battle together before. The narrowing of the Healer's eyes reflected his worry.

Nearly as white as Sorn, Lady Celia didn't hesitate to follow the directions that Ghav gave her. When they finished, she stood quickly and turned toward him, but she was too close and tried to take a step back. The deep sand hampered her and she wavered. Dahleven reached out to steady her. Lady Celia's face paled even further under her sun-pinked skin and her uncertain balance worsened. She was going to faint at his feet. He reacted instinctively, putting his arm around her to steady her against his body.

She was nearly as grimy as the rest of the company, but when her head fell against his chest under his chin, he smelled flowers again, as he had the night before. The scent of her hair and the feel of her body against his produced a familiar and unwelcome response. A post-battle cock-stand wasn't unusual. *But this is neither the time, nor the place, nor the person.*

Dahleven dragged his mind away from the inclinations of his body, but he kept his arm around Lady Celia. "Ghav, we can't stay here."

He didn't ask if Sorn could be moved. He'd seen enough wounds. Sorn obviously needed quiet and rest. He shouldn't be jostled over the mountains. Dahleven wished he could let Sorn heal before forcing a march. If they could stay put just a day or two, that would give his friend a better chance to recover. But he didn't have that choice. None of them did.

Lady Celia stiffened and tried to push away. Dahleven let her, but kept one hand on her arm to steady her. Color had returned to her face and her eyes sparked with anger. *She's feeling better.*

"You're going to move him? You can't! He's all torn up inside. He needs rest!" Lady Celia jerked her arm out of his grasp and stood stiff and rigid with anger. She seemed oblivious to the tears tracking through the dust on her face.

Dahleven resisted the impulse to reach out and wipe the moisture away. He couldn't afford tender feelings toward this woman. He didn't know who she was or why she was here. Just because she'd come from Midgard didn't mean she was benign. He believed her explanations, as Sorn believed her, but wiser men than they had been led astray by a pretty face. He had a responsibility to get his men and his information back to Quartzholm. He couldn't afford to trust her, to give her a weapon by explaining that he would give almost anything to restore Sorn.

"We haven't got time for this." Dahleven looked past her to Ghav. "We'll move as soon as the litter is ready." Then he turned away from the emotion on Lady Celia's face.

A moment later she grabbed his sleeve as she jumped in front of him. "Don't you walk away from me! This is important! Sorn is seriously injured. Moving him now could kill him. Don't you care about that? You have a responsibility to him!"

Anger flashed hot and cold. Cold won. Dahleven grasped her wrist and pulled her hand from his shirt. He didn't release her, but held firm and leaned close. His voice was tight and low with controlled rage. "Do not attempt to teach me my responsibilities, my lady. I know them better than you. Right now they include not allowing a larger party of Renegades to return and finish what these have begun." Dahleven gestured broadly at the five bodies that lay across the wash from them.

Two of the dead lay belly up. Blood from a mortal wound stained the chest of one and the rictus of death had begun to distort his face; another no longer had much of a face at all. A surge of satisfaction washed through Dahleven as Lady Celia glanced at the dead Tewakwe and she paled, but she didn't wobble or faint. The anger in her eyes receded, but didn't disappear entirely.

Dahleven released her wrist. Her hand fisted tightly, as though she'd like to hit him, but she stood quite still, glaring at him.

Fendrikanin coughed then said, "The litter is ready."

Lady Celia looked at Fender and the tension broke.

Dahleven nodded. "Good. Let's move."

Cele was grateful that Dahleven set a slower pace than he had in the morning, but it was still difficult for the men carrying the litter. No one complained; they all wanted to be further away from Renegade territory.

Movement took its toll on Sorn. Ghav stayed close, walking by the side of the litter when the way through the hills allowed it. He couldn't shield Sorn from his pain entirely. The men carrying the litter did their best, but they climbed uneven ground and they couldn't keep from bouncing him. Ghav dosed him with more of the herbs from his store, but a groan occasionally escaped Sorn's lips when the going was particularly difficult.

After one such jostle, Cele jogged forward till she came even with Dahleven. "Is this the easiest path...you can find?" she panted, out of breath. "This is too hard on Sorn. Couldn't we move faster...and easier on the flat?"

Dahleven glanced at her and shook his head. "Easier, but not faster—or safer. This way leads more or less directly to the pass we're headed for. Going back down to the valley and then climbing back up would cost us time and still cause Sorn to suffer. And the Renegades watch the trade trail in the valley."

Cele pressed her lips together. It wasn't what she wanted to hear, but it made sense. And at least he had explained instead of just dismissing her.

She waited for the litter to catch up with her, then resumed walking beside it. She noticed Dahleven looking back at her, one eyebrow cocked. She didn't think much about it; her attention was all for Sorn.

The vegetation changed as they climbed further from the desert floor. The passable ground widened and scrubby trees replaced the thornbushes, but the footing was still uneven. Cele walked to one side of the litter when she could, and Sorn held her hand. He kept his eyes closed, but she could tell from the pressure of his fingers when each new jostle increased his pain.

They traveled hand in hand until the party paused again for the men to change who carried the litter. The rotation started to repeat, and Cele offered to take a turn. She wanted to *do* something, and it was the only thing she could think of.

Dahleven took her hands in his and turned her palms upward. His hands were warm and firm and callused.

Cele's office worker's hands were soft and pink and scratched from her few days in the desert. He shook his head. "No. Ghav has enough to do without you tearing your hands to rags." Then he turned away to speak to Lindimer.

Cele's anger flared at Dahleven's dismissal. That he was right only made it worse.

The afternoon wore on. The leather straps of Sorn's bota bags chafed Cele's shoulders but she refused to complain, not when the rest of Sorn's pack had been redistributed among the others. Everyone was carrying a heavier load than usual. Dahleven led them upward along the ridges, as straight east as the terrain allowed. It was a little cooler here than lower in the foothills, but the air was just as dry and Cele's mouth cried out for moisture. She refused to give in to her thirst and didn't allow herself relief until she saw the others drinking. They were all on short rations. At a normal pace they would have reached water by midmorning the next day, but they were moving slower now, and they'd used a lot of their water cleaning wounds.

They walked until the fading sun robbed them of enough light to travel safely, then they made another cold camp. They stopped at a wide spot in the lee of a cliff that rose thirty feet.

Ghav was by Sorn's side as soon as his bearers put him down, close below the ridge face. As the Healer pulled back the blanket that covered Sorn, it was immediately apparent that infection had set in. Sorn's abdomen was swollen and darkly discolored. Red streaks swept outward from his wounds and the bandages were putrid with drainage. Cele choked back a cry and her stomach roiled at the vile smell.

Fendrikanin volunteered his water to cleanse the wounds, but Ghav refused it. He merely expressed foul fluid from the wounds and covered them again. Sorn groaned and clenched his hands in the dirt as Ghav worked.

Cele wanted to scream, but instead she knelt and clasped his hands in her own. His grasp hurt, but Cele welcomed the pain. If he hadn't been protecting her, this might not have happened. This was worse than watching her mother die. Much worse. It hadn't been easy to see her mother in pain, but at least Cele hadn't felt responsible for the cancer.

Sorn's clasp eased as Ghav applied fresh bandages. Then the healer left to tend Kepliner's arm.

Ghav was halfway across the camp before Cele realized what was about to happen. "I'll be right back," she assured Sorn, then she jumped and ran to catch up with the Healer. "You should wash your hands before touching Kep's arm," she said in a low voice.

Ghav's eyes narrowed. "Cleanliness is important, but you seem overly concerned about it, my lady. That's fine for a lady's chamber, but it's a luxury we can't afford in the field, especially when we're already short of water."

Cele put her hand on his arm. "Please, believe me. I know what I'm talking about. Back home we know a lot about this. You carry Sorn's infection, his...fever, on your hands. You could take it to Kep's arm if you don't wash first," she pleaded softly.

Ghav took an impatient breath, then let it out slowly as his expression became thoughtful. "All right. I'll sacrifice some water to rinse my hands. We haven't any soap with us. And when we're safe in Quartzholm you will explain to me more fully what you think you know about healing."

Cele poured water while Ghav scrubbed his hands

together in the flow, shaking his head all the while. Then she returned to Sorn.

He slept. *Thank goodness.* Though his eyes had remained closed most of the day, she knew the pain had kept him awake. He was as exhausted as if he'd climbed every step himself.

The evening chill followed quickly on the heels of twilight, and Sorn shivered. Cele looked around. Dahleven was nowhere to be seen, but his gear was close by. Cele appropriated Dahleven's blanket and doubled it over the one already covering Sorn.

His shivering didn't ease. Cele lifted the edge of the blankets covering him and crawled in close beside him. He was feverish and stank of sweat and shit and pus. Pillowing her head on one bent arm, she draped the other across Sorn's chest and inched closer, breathing through her mouth to avoid the smell. In a few minutes, Sorn's shivering eased.

"Thank you, my lady," Sorn whispered.

Cele startled. "I thought you were asleep."

"No. Ghav's herbs have worn off a bit. I'm awake for now."

"Are you in pain? Should I get Ghav?"

"No, my lady. The pain is tolerable now that I'm still." Sorn turned his head so he could look at Cele. Their faces were quite close and Sorn spoke softly. "Let's just talk for a bit."

"Okay." Cele fell awkwardly silent. She and her mother had talked easily before her death two years ago, until the pain meds had put her into a coma. *Pain meds!* "I'm an idiot! I have some Tylenol in my kit. It'll help with the pain." She started to get up but Sorn stopped her.

"Save it. I may need it more later."

Cele lay back down. The Tylenol probably wouldn't help that much, and she didn't want to think about how much worse his pain could get. Her eyes looked everywhere but at his face.

"Don't worry yourself about me, my lady. I'll recover. I promised my father I'd be back for Fanlon's Feast, and I never break an oath. It's quite a celebration. I'd hoped to partner a dance with you, but I think that must wait."

Sorn's confidence eased Cele's concern only a little. Attitude counted for a lot in recovery, but the red streaks near his wounds alarmed her. They probably meant septicemia. That could be why Ghav hadn't bothered to clean the wound again. If Sorn's blood was infected, there'd be no point in putting him through the torture of it. But she certainly wasn't going to tell that to Sorn. As for conversation, Sorn had provided an opening, and Cele seized it. "Tell me about your father. Do you look like him?"

"No, I take after my mother. Father is shorter and stocky, like Halsten. His fingers are thick as sausages, but he can do the most delicate work with them." Sorn fell silent for a moment, then went on. "He likes to laugh a lot. He was always teasing Mother, and she always rose to the jibe. I think sometimes she did it to humor him. I don't know if he ever guessed." Sorn's eyes were a little unfocused, as if he pictured a private scene in his mind, and a thoughtful smile curved the corners of his mouth.

"My mother didn't laugh much," Cele said, "but she was always in a good humor. Nothing ever seemed to upset her." She felt herself blushing as Sorn looked at her. "Certainly *she* wouldn't have nearly fainted *twice* in one afternoon."

Sorn shook his head. "She might have fainted three times if she'd seen what you have today."

Cele's voice was critical. "It's not what I expect of myself."

"Have you much experience with combat then, on

which to base such expectations?"

Sorn's question zinged home and Cele grimaced. She thumped him gently on the shoulder and was rewarded with a brief grin. "You're more like your father than you think."

They fell silent again, and Cele groped for something to say. "Is there anybody special waiting for you at home?" Then she remembered Fendrikanin's teasing and wanted to kick herself.

It didn't seem to bother Sorn. "Oh, I'll have nursing aplenty when I return—of the sisterly sort. I'll not lack for scolding either, for not dodging fast enough." Sorn looked in Cele's eyes. "This wasn't your fault, my lady. Things happen in battle. Don't blame yourself."

"But if I hadn't distracted you—"

"If you hadn't acted, one or both of those Renegades would have crushed my head from behind. If you hadn't acted again, the other would have finished what the first began." He pulled a cuff bracelet from beneath his sleeve, then pushed it onto Cele's left forearm. "You saved my life twice over, and I thank you for it."

The waning moon had just peeked over the ridge, and Cele could see a gold cat embossed into the silver cuff.

"I can't accept this. It's too valuable."

"More valuable than my life?"

"Of course not!"

"Then accept this, and my thanks."

Cele shut her mouth on her protest, unconvinced, but somehow feeling a little better.

Sorn changed the subject. "You know about me. What about you, my lady? You've been gone from your home for days now. You don't wear the arm-bands of a married woman. Is there a man tearing his clothing in grief at your absence?"

Cele's mind flashed to Jeff. Six months gone now, but

his abrupt departure still left a bitter taste in her mouth. "No. There's no one like that waiting for me."

Her face must have shown more than she intended, because Sorn gently asked, "There's an unhappy tale there, I can see. Will you share it with me? Some have found me a good listener."

She'd told only Elaine the details of how Jeff had left, and only because she'd needed a place to stay in a hurry. It had hurt too much at first, and later she'd been too embarrassed. But Sorn lay there waiting, breathing a little fast, but with such calm acceptance and concern that Cele found herself telling him the story.

"Well, it's nothing very unusual. There used to be someone, but he left." Sorn was silent, and Cele found herself elaborating. "Jeff and I lived together for a year. We were engaged—"

"Engaged?"

"To be married."

"Ah, betrothed."

She liked the old-fashioned word. "Yes, betrothed. Then I came home one day and found a note that said he'd taken a job across the country, it had been fun, and to have a great life. And oh, by the way, the new tenants would be moving in at the end of the week so I had to get my stuff out of the house right away."

The appalled expression on Sorn's face was gratifying and encouraged Cele to continue.

"I was in shock for two days, and when I finally had the wits to ask, none of his friends would tell me where he'd gone. By then, I was out of time. The house was in Jeff's name and he'd rented it out from under me. So I moved in with my friend Elaine.

"I was such a dope! In hindsight there were signs that he was flaking out on me, but I loved him. I thought we'd work it out. I trusted him. I built up this fantasy that he was different. I told myself that he wasn't like my father, that he would always be there. He said he would, anyway. I guess I had to learn the hard way that words aren't worth very much. At least he didn't leave me pregnant."

She'd only planned to tell Sorn the basic facts, but his attention had drawn the words out of her. And now that they were out, she felt lighter than she had for months.

"The cursed Oathbreaker!"

The force of Sorn's outrage startled Cele.

"Lady Celia, among us a man who breaks an oath of that sort would pay a heavy fine and bring dishonor upon his family. The cur doesn't deserve your regard."

"I sort of figured that out, just a little too late."

"Men of that stripe are wise in the ways of deception. You shouldn't punish yourself for loving him. "

"But I should have seen him for what he was!"

Sorn squeezed her hand lying on his chest. "The heart is a wayward thing and goes where it will. You loved him and forgave him his flaws. Better a loving heart than a suspicious one."

A hard knot that Cele hadn't realized she carried began to dissolve. "Thank you."

After a moment, he said, "I would ask a favor of you, my lady."

Cele brightened, anxious to do something in return for his kindness. "Ask."

"Do not judge us all by what that Oathbreaker did. No man in this company would act as he did, nor anyone I know."

Caution and doubt made Cele pause. *Men always stand up for each other.* But the earnest look in his eyes made Cele retract the thought. Sorn was serious, and this was a different world. "Okay. I'll make you a deal. I don't know if I can trust words and promises just yet, but I'll judge you by your own actions, not Jeff's." *Or my father's.*

Sorn gave her a half smile and Cele became aware of how rapidly he was breathing. She touched his face and was dismayed at how hot his skin was. No wonder she wasn't feeling the chill, curled against him. He radiated heat like a furnace. Cele started to pull away, but Sorn held her arm. "I'll be right back," she said, easing from beneath the blanket. "I'm going to get that Tylenol."

But Ghav was already there. Cele watched, her arms crossed tightly, as he gave Sorn two different kinds of herbs to chew. Within a few minutes, Sorn breathed more easily and his eyelids drooped. The Tylenol wouldn't have worked half as well.

Cele relaxed. Sorn's bracelet almost fell off and she pushed it up past her elbow, where it fit better.

Ghav stood and turned to Cele. "You must eat, and see to your own needs." When Cele started to protest, he held up his hand. "Don't be selfish. You need to stay strong. I can't spare time caring for a woman faint with hunger. Go."

Dahleven returned from setting the order of watch and stretched out next to his friend. Many times they'd shared blankets, hunting together as boys. Sorn had been the better hunter, moving so quietly up on their prey he could hardly miss, he came so close. But Dahleven had been the one to lead them to their quarry in the first place. They'd made a good team, and better friends.

The camp was subdued. Sorn's injury affected everyone. One by one, each man stopped a moment beside Sorn and bluffly exchanged a few words, offering nuts or fruit, though Ghav wouldn't allow anything but a few sips of water.

They'd been lucky in more than one respect: the Renegades hadn't fouled their claws, so Kep and Dahleven's wounds hadn't begun to fester. Falsom would recover. He'd fallen into a heavy sleep as soon as they stopped to camp, barely staying conscious long enough for Halsten to roll him in a blanket, but otherwise he seemed to be whole.

Sorn slept restlessly, despite the herbs Ghav dosed him with, and Dahleven was barely able to doze at his side. So, when Lady Celia finished eating and returned to Sorn, Dahleven waved her off toward Fendrikanin. *No sense in her going without sleep as well.* She took a breath as if to protest, but then clamped her mouth tightly shut and turned away. Dahleven sighed. He'd offended her again. Well, he couldn't help that. She needed her rest whether she knew it or not.

Sorn stirred again and woke. He gave Dahleven a weak smile. "Like old times, eh?"

Dahleven grunted. "Too much so. You always were one to lie abed. We'll never catch any game with you flat on your back all day."

Sorn's smile widened. "You should try it. The ladies like a man who knows his way around in bed."

"So this is just a ploy to gain the lady's sympathy? I can think of better ways to attract women."

Sorn shifted position and gasped. Dahleven's gut twisted in sympathy, but he maintained a mocking expression.

"Use them then," Sorn said. "I can't wait to see. You won't catch one with that grim face, though. Women like a man who laughs now and then."

"I laugh."

"Not enough."

Dahleven's pretended humor failed him. "I can't find much to laugh about just now."

"Ah, my friend. Our fate is in the hands of the Norns,

and they weave as they will. My death blow came defending a lady. It's a good death. But your fate is much different, I suspect. Though tied to the same lady."

Dahleven let Sorn's reference to his death pass without comment. He was right; it would be an honorable death. The skalds would sing songs of his deeds. "The lady is a puzzle."

"She's more than a problem to be solved. She's a woman—as you already know." Sorn grinned.

Dahleven groaned. "I know it too well."

"Your fates are woven together. Enjoy it."

"The Gods respect and reward a man with courage enough to grasp his fate—and change it," Dahleven countered.

"Some fates shouldn't be changed. A man needs more than respect to make a life. He needs joy. Take it where you find it." It was an old debate between them, and held the comfort of a ritual. Sorn's eyes drooped and his smile softened. His voice was muzzy with coming sleep. "Don't turn your back on joy, my brother."

Sorn's fevered voice awakened Cele. His querulous moans had already roused Dahleven and Ghav. Cele slipped from beneath the blanket she shared with Fendrikanin and went closer. She stopped a few steps off to Dahleven's side, where he knelt, facing Ghav across Sorn's supine form. Dahleven hadn't wanted her near Sorn before, and she didn't want to be sent away again.

A slight breeze bit cold and sharp, raising gooseflesh on her arms and legs. Cele hugged her arms tightly, trying not to shiver, and looked down at Sorn. Fever flushed his face, and his breath came rapid and shallow.

"Is there nothing that can ease him?" Dahleven asked.

The healer looked across at him. Dahleven's usually calm face was carved by fatigue and worry. His eyes pleaded with Ghav.

Cele knew how he felt. She'd asked the same questions herself, but seeing the naked emotion on Dahleven's face twisted something inside her. An irrational, half-formed hope tried to flicker to life. She wanted Sorn's recovery too much to accept anything less, and Dahleven wanted it too. He led these men. They respected him. They obeyed him. Somehow Ghav would do what Lord Dahleven demanded. He would save Sorn. Cele saw the same expectation on Dahleven's face, etched by silvery light and shadow. She wanted it for herself, for Sorn, and when she saw the anguish in his eyes, she wanted it for Dahleven, too.

Ghav's low voice rumbled almost below the threshold of hearing, as if he were as reluctant to speak the words as they were to hear them. "There is only one thing that will ease him now, and it will come soon enough."

Hope shriveled in Cele's heart as Ghav's words repeated in her mind. She looked at Dahleven. His expression barely changed, but the subtle tightening of his face, the slight sag of his shoulders betrayed his pain. Her vision blurred as her eyes filled, and hot tears spilled down her cheeks. She turned her face away.

There was nothing more anyone could do. Ghav had done his best. Sorn would die, and no one could do anything about it. No one *here*. At a hospital, with modern antibiotics and sterile surgical techniques, they could probably save him. But she might as well wish them both on the moon.

She hated feeling helpless. She'd felt like this when her mother lay dying those last two weeks in the hospital. She'd hated it then, and she hated it now. What was

she doing here, anyway? Why did she have to start caring about Sorn just to watch him die?

Cele's shoulders slumped and she hugged herself
tighter.

There was one small thing she could do, if Dahleven
would allow it. Cele went to Ghav's side and knelt.
"You're both tired. Let me stay with him."

They hesitated. *At least they're not saying no right
away.* Cele looked to Dahleven for a decision. She saw
the doubt flicker across his face. He probably didn't
want to leave his friend in the care of a stranger. Cele
saw the negative forming in his face when Sorn decided
for him. He reached out and grasped Cele's hand with
hot fingers.

Ghav nodded and rose, saying, "He will thirst. Only
let him sip. Call me if his pain increases." Then he went
to slip under a blanket beside Kepliner.

Dahleven looked at the face of his friend as though
he were reading the future there. He grasped Sorn's other hand. "Until later, my friend." Then he rose and went
to speak with the sentries.

Cele looked at Sorn's hand clasping her own, grateful
beyond words for his vote of confidence. Her eyes
threatened to fill with tears again, but she blinked and
swallowed them, unshed. Then she snuggled close under
the blanket with him, propping her head on one hand.
When she looked at his face she saw him regarding her
with aware, fever-bright eyes. She wanted to thank him
again for all the small kindnesses he'd shown her, for his
forgiveness, but all the words that she thought of
seemed inadequate, so she remained silent. But she
thought the half smile he gave her said he understood.

"Dawn will be a long time coming," he said. "Sing to
me."

Sing? She'd never sung without music to guide her
and drown her mistakes. Her experience consisted of

singing along with the radio, and in church as a child. "I'm not very musical."

"I'm not very critical."

Cele's mind went blank. The only songs that came to mind were hymns and Christmas carols. She sang "Amazing Grace" and "Away in a Manger." She was trying to remember the words to "Oh Come All Ye Faithful," when Sorn interrupted her.

"Do you know any happy songs?"

"Happy songs?" she asked stupidly.

"Those who crafted the songs you sing...seem not to have been very cheerful." His voice came in painful gasps. "Could you sing a song with a smile in it?"

Cele became very aware of the limits of her musical knowledge as she tried to think of an upbeat tune. All she could think of was "Sleigh Ride" which had always set her toes tapping. It seemed terribly inappropriate, but Sorn liked it, so when she finished she started over again, singing softly, "...Our cheeks are nice and rosy, and comfy cozy are we..." By the end of the last chorus Sorn had fallen into a fitful doze.

She watched his labored breathing. It was no worse than when Ghav left, but it was so ragged that she wondered if she should call the healer anyway. Suddenly, Dahleven appeared out of the darkness. He lay down on Sorn's other side. Cele expected him to dismiss her, but he only said, "Two will keep him warmer than one."

They stared at each other across Sorn, the knowledge that he was dying hanging in the air between them. Then Cele looked away, at her hand held in Sorn's. When she glanced back at Dahleven, she saw he'd been staring at their clasped hands too.

"I heard you singing." Dahleven's voice was rough.

Cele grimaced. "I'm sorry. He asked. I didn't mean to disturb the rest of you."

"No. It was...very nice. You...have a good voice."

Cele suspected that wasn't what he'd meant to say, but she let it drop.

Time passed. Cele tried to avoid Dahleven's gaze, but no matter how their eyes danced away from each other, they kept meeting. Cele lowered her head, pillowing it on her bent arm to avoid staring at Dahleven, but after a bit she felt herself drifting off and propped her head on her hand again. She forced her drooping eyelids wider and tried to focus on Sorn's breathing. She thought that maybe it came a little easier. After a few minutes she found herself drifting again. She blinked furiously, trying to clear the gritty feeling from her eyes.

"I'll watch. We need not both lose sleep."

She searched Dahleven's face, then flicked her eyes away again, feeling guilty for nearly falling asleep. "I said I would stay with him."

"You have, and you've brought him comfort. But he sleeps now. You may as well lay your head and rest a bit, too. I'll wake you if there's need."

Dahleven watched Lady Celia's face relax in sleep. He was grateful for her tenderness toward his sworn brother. He looked again at her hand clasped in Sorn's. Sorn had very nearly sworn him to care for her earlier, as a man would ask his brother to protect his lady. Dahleven remembered the words of Lady Celia's song, "We're snuggled up together, like birds of a feather…" It was a song of courting. Sorn had at last found a woman who saw him as more than a friend. Could such feelings grow in less than a day? Dahleven's gaze traveled to where Sorn still clasped her hand, and then to the cuff he'd given Sorn that now wrapped Celia's arm above her elbow. It wasn't a betrothal band, but it was all Sorn had to give in this place, and rested in that spot. Apparently, Sorn had made his choice, and the lady had accepted.

Sorn's breathing came fast and ragged and smelled terrible, though it was hard to separate from the stink of his wound. It was worse than Ingirid had smelled after he and Sorn had thrown his older sister into the sulfur springs. The memory triggered an involuntary smile. He and Sorn had been partners in mischief since they'd gotten lost in the tunnels below Quartzholm together, long before his Talent Emerged. They'd sworn brotherhood in his tenth summer, their difference in rank of no consequence to them.

Dahleven's heart felt like a stone ground to dust by Sorn's suffering. In all the adventures and dangers they'd faced together, he'd never imagined that Sorn could die.

Cele startled awake as Dahleven pulled her hand free from Sorn's stiff fingers. Dahleven's shadow loomed over her as he knelt beside her, the first faint graying of dawn behind him. Sorn's chest lay still, no longer struggling with painful breaths. *He's gone.* She made a short, sad little moan as Dahleven pulled her first to sit, and then to stand.

She'd known these men for just over a day, but she felt smaller, bereft by Sorn's death. Cele looked up, into Dahleven's eyes. The pain there mirrored her own. He put his arm around her shoulders and she felt as though he'd given her permission to share his grief, a permission she hadn't realized she needed until he touched her and led her a little way apart from the camp.

His kindness broke her tenuous self-control. Her eyes stung and filled; tears tracked her cheeks. Dahleven hesitated a moment, then pulled her closer. Cele's arms slipped behind his shoulders. She gasped in damp, sobbing breaths, feeling as though something in her chest might explode and suffocate her. Fear and loss crashed in on her. She was so far from home. Her mother was dead, Jeff was gone, Elaine was beyond reach, and now Sorn was dead, too. He'd offered her friendship. His easy, instinctive gift for putting her at ease had made this strange world easier to bear. Conflict twisted and knotted her heart. She wanted Sorn to still be alive, but she was relieved his suffering had ended.

Cele pressed her face against Dahleven's chest and shivered in his arms.

Fender brought a blanket and draped it around her. Dahleven continued to hold her, rubbing slow circles on her back. The pressure in her eased, and she drew a deep, shuddering breath. She could hardly think. She sniffed wetly, then pulled away enough to free one hand to wipe tears from her face. She was embarrassed at losing it, but surprised and grateful for Dahleven's kindness.

Dahleven pushed her far enough away to look at her. He gave her a bleak half-smile, and with both hands on her shoulders, he pushed her gently down to sit on a rock. He pressed some dried fruit into her hand and put a waterskin by her. "Try to eat something. We must attend to Sorn." Then he walked away.

Cele felt calmer after her tears, though an ache still filled her chest. Part of her mind was appalled at breaking down, but she was too numb to worry about it. She couldn't eat, but Cele sipped the water while the sky slowly brightened and the men built a cairn over Sorn's body. The stones made an empty clack as they set each one in place. The lonely sound went on and on. Cele tried to shut it out, but it penetrated, echoing in her head. Then they finished and there was silence. The sun gleamed obliquely over the mountains, filtering through the scrub trees on the ridge above. With the last rock laid over Sorn's body, the men gathered close and began to sing.

Sunbeams shafted through the trees in a shallow angle as their voices rose and fell, blending in a powerful rhythm that Cele felt in her heart. The beauty of their deep male voices carried her with them and closed her throat again with tears of longing. They sang of the brotherhood of men striving for a common goal, the exultation of vanquishing a foe, the need to protect hearth and family, the desire for a woman, the love of children. Cele felt it all. It felt *right*; it felt whole, and she wanted to be part of it, to belong to it.

Then they fell silent.

For a moment it seemed as though the whole world stopped. Then the gathered men moved apart and began breaking camp. Their actions were quiet and purposeful, but the sudden movement in the new silence jarred after the ceremony.

Cele felt as though she'd stepped outside of time and the activity of the men around her had nothing to do with her. Sooner than she expected, Dahleven pulled her to her feet. The company moved on, leaving Sorn behind, under his blanket of stones.

chapter six

THE ROUTE DAHLEVEN chose grew steeper, but his Talent assured him that he led his men rightly. It pulled at him, strong, while he concentrated on his goal, more like a niggling, half felt itch when he thought about other things. To be sure, there were many right paths, but he concentrated on finding the quickest. If Sorn had still lived, he would be seeking a different, easier route; men couldn't carry a litter when they climbed as much as they hiked. Now, with no litter, they could travel a more direct, more difficult path, and make up the time they'd lost.

They needed the speed. The Althing would open in three days' time, at Fanlon's Feast. The Jarls would be discussing the danger to Nuvinland's borders, and how best to meet it. He and his men must get home with the information they'd gathered if Nuvinland was to avoid war with the Tewakwe. There was no glory to be won in fighting the wrong opponent. But he would gladly have sacrificed the time to have Sorn still with them.

Dahleven reproached himself for the selfish thought. Sorn's death wound, honorably gained in battle, entitled him to feast in Valhalla. Even walking the misty ways of

Niflheim until the return of Baldur would be a better fate than the agony of a belly wound. He wouldn't call Sorn back to that.

Dahleven's heart clenched in a tangle of pride and anger and guilt. Sorn had stood his ground before the onslaught of the Tewa's bladed club, defending Lady Celia. He'd fought valiantly, vanquishing his attacker, refusing to succumb to his wounds until the threat to her had passed. If not for her, Sorn could have given way, defended himself with greater flexibility. He might still be alive if Dahleven hadn't put the lady in his charge.

Dahleven wouldn't risk more of his men to protect her. He'd watch the lady himself rather than assign her to another. Fendrikanin or Ghav would make more sense as a chaperon, but he wanted—no, needed—to keep a close eye on Sorn's betrothed himself.

Dahleven turned and reached down to help Lady Celia scramble up the steep slope. Her firm grasp closed on his wrist as he held hers. Her face contorted with effort and she grunted softly as she pulled herself up the rock. Dahleven put his other hand under her arm to help and she nodded her thanks. There were smears under her eyes where she'd wiped away tears when she thought he wasn't looking.

The image of her hand clasped in Sorn's rose in his mind. It seemed unlikely that deep affection could grow in so short a time, but her broken-hearted sobbing had confirmed it. *In less than a day, Sorn won her heart and then broke it by dying. The skalds will tell the tale.* The thought was spiked with frustration and anger at himself. *I won't be jealous of him. Not over her.*

As soon as she was steady, he released Lady Celia and resumed the climb. He relished the punishing physical demands of the mountainside. It held back the stabbing sense of loss.

And what of the lady? Her grief for Sorn seemed genuine and deep, but what was her part in all of this? It was too much of a coincidence that she appeared in Renegade territory just as Nuvinland was facing the possibility of war, instigated by an unknown enemy. Was she truly an innocent? How far should he trust her? Could he trust her at all?

Sorn did.

Sorn. His loss cut sharp and deep. Pride in Sorn's honorable death carried him only so far. After that, the pain took over, slicing like shards of obsidian.

Cele grunted as she pulled herself up the steep slope. She was grateful for the hard pace and difficult terrain. It kept her from wondering why Dahleven's face clouded when he looked at her, and it kept her from thinking about Sorn. She had to concentrate on every step to keep from falling on her face or tumbling back down the craggy hillside. *When, exactly, do foothills become mountains*? She'd bet they'd made the transition.

The trees grew taller and closer together as they climbed, and the low brush grew thicker. Dahleven was often by her side, giving her a hand up over the awkward spots or holding branches aside so she could pass more easily. Why did he stay so close when he frowned every time he looked at her? Did he blame her for Sorn's death? *He'll have to get in line.*

Cele felt the bracelet Sorn had given her hug her bicep. No matter what he'd said, Sorn had died because of her, because he'd been protecting her. He might have died anyway if she hadn't been there, but he also might have been only wounded, like Kep. He might not have been hurt at all. Instead, he was dead.

The day wore on and the air grew cooler as they climbed, but it was bone dry and the company was short of water. Cele tried to keep her mouth shut and breathe through her nose, but the hard climbing forced her to gasp, parching her tongue till it felt like paper. She tried to imagine eating an orange to trick her mouth into moisture, but she was too tired and too dehydrated. They wouldn't reach the spring until the evening. They'd lost time yesterday, slowed by carrying Sorn's litter, and more that morning by burying him.

Cele's head throbbed. Her world narrowed to nothing more than thirst, moving forward, and the raw ache of Sorn's death.

At last, Dahleven called a rest. They paused in a narrow defile, perched in a stair-step fashion on the slope. Falsom had recovered and sat at the top of the "stair," watching their back-trail. They traveled all together now since the rocky ground wouldn't raise a dust cloud that would reveal their location.

Cele sat on a narrow shelf beside Dahleven and shook her head when he offered a strip of jerky. She didn't have much of an appetite, and she didn't think she could chew the desiccated meat. She closed her eyes, exhausted in body and heart. She could rest her body, at least. A moment later, she felt dried fruit pressed into her hand. She opened her eyes.

"You must eat." Dahleven looked at her with a surprising mix of pity and concern. His deep voice was soft but firm.

Cele started to refuse, but she knew he was right and took a small nibble. The deep red flesh of the fruit still had a sharp tang; her mouth tickled and started to water. Maybe she could eat after all.

She looked out at the landscape spread below. It had a rugged, unforgiving beauty similar to the mountains back home.

Home. It almost seemed unreal to her now. So much had happened in so short a time. It filled her mind, crowding out the details of her former life. Supermarkets and rush hour and performance reviews seemed vague and unreal compared to hiking till her bones ached and holding a dying man in her arms.

Too soon, Dahleven called for them to resume their trek. At least the air had lost its oppressive, strength-sapping heat. Cele sensed urgency in Dahleven, but he never failed to pause and offer help over the rough spots.

She hardly knew what to make of him, now. He was still stern and brusque with his frowns and his orders to eat, but underlying that she glimpsed something else. *Losing one of his men can't have been easy for him.*

Cele drank the last of her water at the mid-afternoon break. It was only a swallow, and she was too thirsty to hold it in her mouth first. She swallowed convulsively, and the liquid ran down her throat and was gone. She up-ended her squeeze bottle again in a forlorn hope for a few more drops.

"Here." Dahleven stood before her, holding out one of his botas.

Automatically, Cele took it. It was about a quarter full. His other bags hung light and flaccid from his shoulders. This was his last water.

Cele's throat ached for a drink, but she thrust it back at him. "Thanks. I'll be fine."

Dahleven shook his head and pushed the bag back at her. "We share on the trail. Drink what you need."

She wanted it too much to argue. Pulling the stopper, Cele tipped the bag to her lips. The water tasted stale and flat and delicious. She closed her eyes and savored it, rolling it around her tongue before letting it slide soothingly down her throat.

Somehow, she made herself stop at only two swallows. When she extended the bag again to Dahleven, he gave her a small smile as he took it, then drained the last of the precious liquid. A moment later, he gave the signal and they were climbing again.

Dusk came early, the sun's low slant cut off by the folds of the mountain's ridges. The short rations had sharpened Cele's strange certainty that water was ahead. She knew where the spring was before Fender told Dahleven, before they heard the first musical cascade of the rill. It pulled at her, like a thousand painless hooks in her skin. Despite her fatigue, her pace increased, matching Dahleven's. On the other side of a rare flat space a broken rock face rose. There, tumbling over the rocks was one of the sweetest sights she'd ever seen. Crystalline liquid eddied in several small pools before it ran off the stone and disappeared into the soil at the base of a huge tree with quivering leaves.

Cele started forward, but Dahleven put out his left arm, blocking her while he scanned the area and the heights above. Fender went forward while Dahleven signaled to the others. Two men disappeared down their back-trail, while three others climbed to vantage points above the stream. Fender knelt by one of the small pools and brought the crystal liquid to his lips in his cupped hands. A moment later, he turned and smiled, moisture dripping off his sandy beard.

"It's safe." Dahleven stepped aside and drew Cele from behind him. "Stay here." He went forward and knelt next to Fendrikanin at the stream. Taking something from the pouch at his belt, he cast it into the stream, murmuring the same words as he had at the last spring. "Accept our gifts in return for your bounty."

Who is he talking to? she wondered, but when he returned to her, her mind jumped back to what he'd said before. "What did you mean, 'It's safe?' The water?"

He shook his head. "Partly. Our enemies could have fouled the stream. But my main concern was ambush. Thirsty men are often careless."

A shiver ran up and down Cele's back. She never wanted to hear the sounds or see the results of battle again.

Ghav gathered skins from the other men and helped Fender fill them. She noticed that neither Fender nor Dahleven drank.

Dahleven held out his bota bags to her. "They'll finish more quickly if you help them, Lady Celia. The sooner the skins are filled, the sooner we can all drink."

"Of course." Cele took his waterskins and her own to the stream. Light danced on the clear shallow flow and struck sparks from some of the stones in the streambed. They looked out of place. She started to reach for one but Ghav stopped her.

"Leave it be, Lady. 'Tis a gift for the sprite."

Is he kidding? "The sprite?"

"She who lives in the stream, of course. Fill your bags so we can all slake our thirst."

Ghav's words about a sprite made no sense, but she understood about thirst. As she plunged the neck of a bota into the cold current, Cele's dry mouth pinched and watered. She marveled at the men's self-discipline. No one drank until all could drink. The liquid comfort was so close, only an arm's length away, burbling and laughing over the rocks, teasing her fingertips with its cool moisture. Her parched tissues ached with anticipation, and quick on the heels of her thirst came a sharp stab of hunger. She filled another bag and tried to ignore her body's demands. Ghav and Fender weren't slaking their thirst, and neither would she, not until the rest could drink, too. She didn't want to seem weak or sacrifice whatever respect they might have for her. She wasn't sure why it mattered, but it did. If they could do it, so could she. And once her mind was made up, waiting to slake her thirst became easier.

Dahleven was almost satisfied with their camp. They'd climbed higher, above the stream, so their sentries could see anyone who approached from that direction. It wasn't the most defensible position, but it was the best they could do.

He hadn't been so cautious two nights ago, when they'd found Lady Celia, nor at the midday break yesterday. Had that contributed to the attack? He didn't think so. It was more likely ill luck, a chance encounter. A bad chance. Tewakwe seldom traveled this side of the Thorvald mountains, but who knew what the Renegades and Outcasts did?

Dahleven pulled himself back from his musings to hear the last of Fendrikanin's tale of how Sorn won an oar-stepping contest at the last Festival. It was traditional for a dead man's companions to toast him for three nights and tell of his deeds. They hadn't any mead or ale to honor Sorn properly, but his stories would be told, and by the third night they'd be home. Then the beer and wine would flow, and the golden tongues of the skalds could give Sorn the honor he deserved.

Ghav cleared his throat and the men's attention turned to him. "Let me tell you, Sorn was quieter than a mouse, and I have the tale to prove it.

"A year ago this month, during the Feast of Fanlon, our Sorn was strolling home in the dark hour before dawn, when he came upon one of his sweet friends weeping. Now Sorn was weary from drink and dancing, but he had the tenderest heart any sister could wish for, so he could hardly pass by without stopping. 'My dear,' says he, 'Why are you weeping?'

"And the young maid answers, 'I've been with Rolf, and he's asked me to marry him.'

"'And that gives you cause to weep?'

"'No, of course not!' she says, blushing as maidens do. 'But I've stayed out past the time when my father expected me home. His anger is a fearful thing. If he learns that Rolf kept me out so late he'll beat me and lock me in the house for a year.'

"Sorn had witnessed the man's anger himself, so he knew the lady spoke the truth. 'The lights are out,' he suggests to the girl, 'Slip in through the kitchen door.'

"'I daren't,' she says. 'Father is such a light sleeper. He wakes at a mouse's sneeze.' And at that, the young maid begins to weep again.

"Sorn thinks for a moment, then tells the girl to dry her eyes. 'I'll help you,' says he."

Someone groaned, anticipating the trouble Sorn's kindness would earn him.

Ghav continued. "As soon as she dries her eyes, Sorn scoops her up into his arms. The girl squeaks, and Sorn says, 'Be as quiet as the dew, and I'll get you inside.' And Sorn carries her into the house and up the stair, making less sound than an owl's wing.

"He sets the lady down at her bedroom door, nods a silent farewell, and makes his way back down the hall. But then, just as he's passing by the old man's door, a mouse runs out of its hole, its little nails skritch, skritch, skritching on the floor. Sorn stands still and silent, and for a moment he thinks himself safe. But then the mouse comes closer, its little feet loud in the quiet night. Inside the room, Sorn hears the girl's father cough and stir.

"Sorn knew what he had to do. Quick as lightning, before it could take another step, Sorn scoops up the mouse, runs down the hall, and out the kitchen door as quiet as a butterfly." Ghav paused, as if savoring the anticipation of his audience.

"I know this is true, because I came along just as Sorn emerged onto the street. There he was, stepping out of a dark house, breathing hard and red in the face. 'What mischief have you been up to this Feastnight?' ask I, knowing the sort of fun young men are like to have.

"'Why, none at all,' says he.

"'And I suppose that's a mouse in your pocket?'"

"'Yes, indeed, and here it is!' and he dangles the furry mite by its tail in front of my nose."

The men groaned softly, grinning. Dahleven just shook his head. It was an outrageous mangling of what really happened, but true to Sorn's spirit. He flashed Ghav a smile before he stood. The rest took his signal, and they quickly dispersed to their blankets.

Dahleven hesitated, then offered Lady Celia a hand to rise. He liked the way she wrapped her long fingers around his wrist in a practical grasp. She got to her feet slowly, despite his help. *She'll be stiff in the morning.* He gestured to Ghav, and the older man escorted her beyond the edge of camp. Dahleven wasn't ready to perform that intimate courtesy.

Something had changed between them today. She no longer prickled every time he offered her help. She was still proud, but it was an honorable pride, and she hadn't quenched her thirst until the last waterskin had been handed out.

He stood for a moment, staring at his blanket. *It might be better if we were still biting at each other.* He remembered how it felt, with her soft curves pressed against him. *Was it only yesterday morning?* Then he remembered her fingers clasped with Sorn's and her desolate sobs, and shook himself. The woman was grieving for his sworn brother.

Ghav returned with Lady Celia, his blanket tucked

under his arm. "I thought you might want to share my blanket with me."

Dahleven looked at his old friend with relief. Though Ghav couldn't ease the pain of Sorn's loss, with him as chaperon, sleep might come easier. "An excellent idea," Dahleven said.

Ghav spread his blanket and lay down by the edge. Lady Celia took the middle, pulling in tight to take up as little space as possible, trying to avoid touching, and being touched. Dahleven shook his blanket, letting it float down neatly upon the three of them. As he lay down with his back to her, he tried to ignore the faint fragrance of flowers.

Cele was running. In the distance, her mother and Sorn were playing cards, perched on the rainbow colored rails of the train track. Sorn bid two hearts. Cele shouted, but no sound came out. Coming down the hill, a train raced toward them, picking up speed. She'd never get to them in time! She ran and ran, heart pounding, legs pumping, but the distance never got shorter. There was nothing she could do. If only they would look up, get out of the way, but they didn't. Her mother slapped her cards down triumphantly. A royal flush, all hearts. Cele screamed at her mother to move, but again she made no sound. The ground shook. The train bore down on them, its huge old-fashioned engine belching thick black smoke. Suddenly, Dahleven ran by. He'd get there in time, but he could only save one. She kept running. Then she tripped and went sprawling. Dahleven stopped, turning his back on Sorn and her mother to help her up.

Cele jerked awake, gasping, clammy with leftover fear. No! Her heart pounded. Her mother was dead. Sorn was dead. If she'd been faster, if she hadn't fallen...No, she hadn't fallen. She'd shouted. And Sorn had died.

Cele covered her face with one arm, but the nightmare's images remained sharp and accusing. She groaned. *It was just a dream. Just a dream.* She sucked in a deep breath. *But Sorn is still dead.* And it was all her fault.

Dahleven touched her shoulder. "Are you all right?"

Cele lowered her arm, feeling embarrassed. Dawn had barely begun to pale the eastern sky, but Dahleven and Ghav had already risen, leaving her alone in the blankets. At least she wasn't waking up wrapped around Dahleven like a clinging vine. "I'm fine." She started to get up, but as soon as she moved, the muscles of her thighs and calves screamed. She winced and gasped as pain lanced through her legs.

Dahleven crouched by her feet. He gave her a wry smile and spoke softly. "We're all feeling yesterday's climb, Lady Celia, but not as terribly as you, it seems." His breath fogged in the cold mountain air and his deep voice rumbled like a big cat's purr, soothing away her nightmare. Hesitantly, he asked, "If you will permit me, I can rub away some of the stiffness."

Cele suddenly felt warm. Anticipation danced around the idea of him touching her on purpose, and she didn't like that feeling. *Don't be ridiculous*, she told herself. She wasn't attracted to him. She didn't even like him. Well, maybe a little. He'd been kind to her after Sorn died, after all. But not in that way. She just needed a bit of help to get moving. She nodded. But Dahleven didn't put his hands on her directly. He began massaging through the blanket.

Involuntarily, Cele tensed and drew in a sharp breathy gasp. She needn't have worried about any erotic undertones. The pain was terrible as his hands forced blood into her sore muscles.

Dahleven's hands stilled but remained on her thigh. Now that he wasn't rubbing, his large hands felt warm and comforting. He looked at her, his face drawn in concern. "My apologies. Your muscles are badly knotted." He lifted her leg, moving it through its range of motion.

Cele winced as her muscles protested, but didn't stop him. It had to be done if she was going to do more than hobble today. She looked into his gray eyes and saw compassion swirling in storm-cloud depths—something she wouldn't have given him credit for two days ago.

"You must have been suffering yesterday. You should have said something."

"I didn't want to slow us down. We needed to make up time." Cele repeated what he'd said, but without reproach.

Dahleven nodded, as if acknowledging more than they had spoken aloud.

Abruptly, he pulled his hands away. Their absence left her feeling chilled. "I'm an idiot. Ghav should be doing this and taking your pain, rather than causing you more." Dahleven looked past her. "Ghav, come here, would you? Lady Celia has need of your Talent."

The older man came over, his brow furrowed with concern.

"Yesterday's climb has knotted her legs." Dahleven rocked back on his heels and stood, making room for the Healer.

Ghav's face relaxed. "I can help with that." He pulled the blanket aside, then poured some amber liquid from a flask into his palm. The oil bore a soft fragrance reminiscent of cinnamon. Ghav warmed the oil first in his hands, then smoothed it onto Cele's calves and thighs.

Cele tensed, anticipating the pain she'd felt before, but it didn't come. The soreness in her legs had begun to fade with Ghav's arrival. Now, as he touched her, it disappeared entirely, in spite of his kneading massage. Cele relaxed and leaned back on her braced elbows, watching him curiously. The effect of his Talent hadn't been so obvious before, when he doctored her scrapes. They hadn't hurt as much. Sorn had explained about Talents, but now she realized she really hadn't understood. Ghav's ability was almost...magical.

No. There has to be another explanation. The oil might carry a drug that was being absorbed through the skin. *But the pain faded before he even touched me.* The power of suggestion? But she didn't believe it was that, either.

In this place, a man could take away another's pain. Or move silently. Or find a path just by thinking about it.

It didn't fit into her understanding of how the world worked. But this was a different world. And whether it made sense or not, she had felt it, heard it, and seen it.

What a blessing Ghav's Talent would be for a paramedic. An E.M.T. would love to ease a person's pain just by showing up. But it would be a curse as well as a blessing. Pain carried a message about what was wrong; a message Ghav couldn't hear when he got too close to his patients. *Everything has a price.*

Then she noticed Dahleven was still standing there, frowning, as he watched Ghav's hands on her muscles. He seemed lost in thought. *Is he worried I'll slow them down today?*

The sky was lighter now, and the men not on watch started crawling out of their blankets.

"Hey! Lindimer! Why didn't you wake me for my watch?" Halsten called as he threw aside his blankets.

Dahleven stiffened, all attention. Ghav stopped rubbing Cele's legs.

Halsten and Fendrikanin came to Dahleven, sleep banished from their faces.

"My Lord! Lindy and Knut didn't call us for sentry duty." The urgency in Fender's voice made it clear that he wasn't just remarking on getting a few extra hours of sleep.

"Find them." Dahleven ordered.

Falsom and Kep went one way, Halsten and Fender another, moving quietly, though not as quietly as Sorn would have.

Dahleven pulled his sword, and Ghav wiped his hands, grabbed his bow, and knocked an arrow.

"What is it? What's happened?" Cele asked.

Dahleven raised a hand, commanding silence as he scanned their surroundings. Cele pulled on her boots to be ready, though she wasn't sure for what.

A minute passed. Two. Three.

The crunching of brush announced Fender and Halsten's return a moment before they appeared, bearing Lindimer between them. They laid him on the ground gently, as if he slept, but one glance told Cele that Lindy would never wake again. His eyes were frozen wide in surprise, his mouth open in a silent shout. His throat had been slashed. Dried blood covered him like a grisly bib.

Cele swallowed convulsively and shut her eyes, but the image continued to swim in her mind. She didn't want this. She didn't want to be here, to look death in the face again so soon. She gazed up at Dahleven. He stood tall against the dawning sky, looking down at his murdered man. A muscle in his jaw bunched.

Halsten stood and reported. "We found him where he stood sentry. There's no sign of a fight. What could have happened?"

Fendrikanin still knelt at Lindimer's feet. "His Talent was Heimdal's Ear, and the moon was still bright last night. He'd have heard anyone before they got that close, even a Cat Foot, and seen them, too."

Falsom and Kep came back into the camp. Kepliner's forward momentum faltered half a step when he saw Lindimer.

"We saw no sign. No footprints other than our own, no sign of Tewa or Outcast," Falsom said.

"And no trace of Knut," Kep added.

"Why would they carry him off?" Halsten asked. "They left Lindy where he lay."

For a minute no one answered, leaving the question hanging in the air. Then Fender spoke. "No one carried him off. He left. After he killed Lindimer."

Dahleven nodded, slowly. "Yes. So I think, also."

The faces of the gathered men were stone, but flames of anger and horror flickered behind their eyes.

Dahleven broke the silence. "We must hurry. He's had half the night to find his *friends*," he spat the word, "and lead them back to us. Let us hope he's had some trouble locating them." He looked at each man as he spoke. "Falsom, Kep, stand sentry. Lady Celia and I will fill the waterskins. Fender, Halsten, Ghav, you must build a cairn for Lindy in too short a time."

Dahleven turned immediately to gathering the waterskins. Cele got to her feet and followed, grateful for a reason to leave the vicinity of Lindimer's bloody body.

First Sorn, and now Lindy. Brave men, both. Dahleven swallowed the sour taste that rose in his throat. All of them bore the same risks, but that didn't make the loss of a man easier to bear. *And Knut, that whoreson!*

Dahleven hoped a priest would have a chance to strip that dog's get of his Talent before Dahleven killed him. *May he freeze in Niflheim.* The Council would declare Knut Outcast, and every man's hand would turn against him to slay him on sight, without hesitation. But as far as Dahleven was concerned, Knut's life was forfeit now.

Dahleven forced himself to bank his anger. He needed a clear mind to safeguard Lady Celia and get his remaining men home. As the two of them climbed down to the rocky rill, Dahleven was grateful the lady didn't pester him with questions. Then he looked into her pale face, and guilt pinched him. She'd been through horror after horror, yet here she was helping rather than becoming hysterical. *There is much to admire about her. Sorn was a lucky man, though for too short a time.*

"Stay close," he said. "I won't let any harm come to you."

She nodded. "I know."

Those two words shouldn't warm him as much as they did.

Ghav and the others had built an adequate cairn over Lindimer by the time he and Lady Celia returned. Not as good as Lindy deserved, but it would keep the scavengers from his bones. He asked Lady Celia to roll up the blankets, then went to join the others. It pained him to do so, but prudence required that he leave Falsom and Kepliner on sentry, so only four of them sang Lindimer's death song. Lindy should have had more to sing his passage out of Alfheim.

As Dahleven lifted his voice to blend with the others, he noted that Lady Celia stilled her movements and listened. Then he left his concerns about Great Talents, Tewakwe, Renegades, and Outcasts behind. His heart rode on the song, feeling the universal concerns of men, those things that defined them and bound them together: the fierce love for a newborn child; the pleasure of sliding into the soft warmth of a woman; the brotherhood of shared danger; and the joyous triumph of a foe vanquished.

When their song ended, Dahleven gave the order to move on, with a heart feeling both empty and full.

Thanks to Ghav's Talent, Cele's muscles no longer screamed with pain. She managed to keep up even though the climb was just as arduous as the previous day's. She was glad to put distance between them and their last camp, though there was no way to leave the sadness behind. The image of Lindy's stiff, staring face and his grisly bib of blood rose in her mind. She was glad Dahleven pushed them hard. Their pace kept her from thinking too much about what would happen if their enemies caught their small group. Dahleven gave her every possible assistance, but he didn't slow for her.

The men around her were hyperalert. Their tension showed in their posture and actions: the way one or another of them would halt the group with a sudden word or gesture and everyone would listen, scanning the mountainside for movement. Their wariness was contagious, and Cele found herself jumping at every bird's trill and broken twig.

They made the pass by late morning. Patches of snow still lay on the northern face of the slope, even in midsummer. When they reached the crest, Dahleven paused and drew Cele up to stand beside him. "This is Nuvinland."

A high valley opened below them. Though trees obscured some of the view, Cele could see thick pine forests draping the mountains on either side. Lush green grasses grew in the wide meadows that broke up the forest, with flocks of tiny white and black flecks ranging over them. *Sheep*, she supposed. Other open areas looked more like tilled land and terraced fields. In the distance, on the right side of the valley, the sun winked off a pink granite wall that thrust out through the forest. It had an apron of bare ground and a cluster of buildings for a skirt, miniaturized by the distance. Far below, a river sparkled silently, too distant for the sound of its rushing waters to reach her ears.

Cele's throat tightened. *This is what Sorn longed to return to.* "It's beautiful."

Dahleven was silent for a moment, then nodded. "It is." Then he gave the signal to continue on. The slope heading down into the valley was much shallower, making for an easier descent than the climb had been. They'd only descended a hundred feet or so when Falsom shouted from the crest above them.

"Renegades!"

A second later, arrows began thunking dully into the ground around them.

"Downslope!" Dahleven shouted. He grabbed Cele just above Sorn's bracelet and pulled her along as he began to run, his feet slipping in the drifts of needles.

Cele heard a cry, and took her eyes off her feet long enough to glance behind. Halsten had fallen, an arrow in his back. Ghav turned too, just as more than a dozen black-haired, dusky-skinned men came careening down the slope at them. Ghav hesitated, then resumed his barely controlled retreat.

The group separated as they fled before the larger force. Falsom, Kep, Ghav, and Fender veered off to the left as the ground dropped down; Dahleven and Cele found firmer footing on a rocky outcropping to the right. Dahleven slowed enough to glance over his shoulder, and Cele followed his gaze. The pursuit had split, too, and five men followed them.

Dahleven raced down the mountainside, half running, half sliding, sometimes jumping, and Cele went with him, pack banging against her back, arm still locked in his firm grasp. They rounded a wall of rock, and suddenly the ground dropped away in front of them. Dahleven hauled back on Cele's arm so abruptly she almost fell on her butt, scant inches from the edge.

"Odin's Balls!" Dahleven released her and turned to face the enemy that had yet to appear around the upthrust. He started to pull his sword.

To Cele's surprise, he slammed it home again, and ran to the rock wall behind them. "Get out of your pack!" he said, shrugging quickly out of his own.

What? Cele didn't understand, but she didn't hesitate. She imitated Dahleven and shucked her own pack, hanging onto the straps.

He grabbed her free hand, and pulled her into a scrawny thicket growing against the rock-face. *He's crazy! We can't hide here.* The bush wasn't nearly thick enough to conceal them. But Dahleven kept pulling, and Cele followed, until suddenly she slipped into a fissure in the rock. It was tight, and she could hear him grunt and jerk, then he was free and dragging her through. Her breasts brushed the walls as she sidled in. The pack in her hand stuck and Cele jerked harder on the straps to yank it free.

The interior opened a little wider but they still had to walk sideways to get through. They turned a corner and suddenly they were in a more open space. A faint trickle of light came from the narrow entrance, along with the distant shouts of their enemies as they discovered their quarry missing.

Dahleven put his finger to her lips. They stood very still as the men outside argued about where they might have gone. Cele tried not to breathe too loudly. Eventually, the voices moved away.

Then Dahleven towed her farther into the cave, and the dark swallowed them.

chapter seven

CELE BLINKED, vainly trying to see in the dark with eyes adjusted to the bright midday sun. The only sounds were the rasp of her and Dahleven's hard breathing. He pulled her onward, deeper into the stillness of the cave. She gripped his hand tightly, taking reassurance from its warmth and strength.

A moment later, she lost even that small comfort when Dahleven released her. She heard him shrugging his pack on, so she did the same. Then his searching hand pulled hers to the back of his belt.

"Hold on," he commanded tersely.

Cele felt his body shift as Dahleven drew his sword and heard the slithering whisper as the steel pulled free of its leather sheath. His posture shifted as he raised his left arm over his head. Did he intend to fight their enemies in the dark? But he didn't turn to face the entrance, but instead continued on, deeper into the mountain, moving at a slow, deliberate pace.

Cele reached out with her free hand, finding only

emptiness. What waited for them in the blackness? The only cave she'd been in was Kartchner Caverns, a well-lit tourist attraction. Were there bats in here? Wild animals? They didn't have Kep with them to scare cave dwellers away. Fear rippled down her spine. She wished she had a flashlight, but she hadn't needed one for a morning hike.

A sharp *ting* bounced off the rock and Cele jumped. Dahleven must be using his sword to defend himself against stubbed toes rather than Renegades or creatures of the dark.

The sound of their footsteps, the echo of their ragged breathing, gave her the sense that the ceiling and walls were several feet away. As long as she didn't run into any stalactites, she'd be okay. With much taller Dahleven in the lead, she stopped worrying about bumping her head and concentrated instead on her footing, though the ground was surprisingly even beneath her feet. The air smelled stale but free of the dank odor of moisture.

The echoes of their footsteps changed, and Dahleven pulled her to the right. Cele's hand abruptly encountered stone. They were turning a corner.

"There's a drop here. Less than a foot." After straining her ears for clues, Dahleven's voice startled her.

He took her hand from his belt and put it on his shoulder. She felt him step down. He stopped, waiting for her to follow. She found the edge and eased herself down several inches. Again he stepped down and waited. Cele felt her way forward, then carefully lowered herself. They continued down five of the regularly spaced steps.

Stairs? She thought. *In a cave? Not ADA compliant.* Cele swallowed the edge of a hysterical giggle. They weren't tourists, and this wasn't Kartchner Caverns. Then Dahleven turned another corner and stopped. The space they were in felt like a small alcove, and she was suddenly standing very close to him. He pulled her hand from his shoulder, and Cele's heart jolted with panic as she lost contact. But he only took a short step away to sheath his sword.

"Can you find your way back?" She hadn't planned to ask it, but it popped out of her mouth anyway.

"Certainly." Dahleven sounded surprised.

Duh. His Talent is Pathfinding. "Sorry. I forgot—"

"Quiet."

Cele listened.

Nothing.

The dark hung closely, like the deep folds of a heavy velvet curtain, damping even the soft susurration of their breath. No other noise disturbed the endless silence. *What are we listening for?* She felt as if the world had stopped. Cele concentrated on the reassuring pressure of Dahleven's shoulder against hers.

When Dahleven spoke, Cele jumped. He put a reassuring hand on her arm. "It's all right. They don't follow."

"That's great! Then we can wait a while and go find the others." Cele winced at the nervous sound of her voice, but she was glad they'd soon be above ground.

"No. The Renegades may not follow, but they may well be waiting for us. And the others will be far away, if they still live."

Cele heard the slight dip in Dahleven's voice when he said *if they live*, and realized how worried he must be for his men. Sorn was dead, as was Lindimer and probably Halsten. They could all be dead, and she didn't even know who was trying to kill them, or why. So much had happened, she hadn't even thought about asking questions until now. "Who are these Renegades? Sorn said something about caravans being raided, but we don't have anything they'd want. Why did they attack us?"

"The Renegades are Tewakwe who have been exiled from their Confederation." Dahleven shifted and Cele felt him lower himself to the ground. "There's room enough to sit."

Cele joined him. The floor felt thick with powdery dust and was surprisingly smooth. Obviously manmade. She propped against the wall next to him, shoulder to shoulder. She'd tried to avoid touching him any more than necessary when they shared a blanket. Now she needed the contact. "Why did they attack us?" she asked again.

"I think they're working with our own Outcasts to start a war between Nuvinland and the Tewakwe Confederation. If they're successful, the chaos of war would make it easy for them to pick the bones of both peoples. The first attack upon us I think was pure bad luck. This one, today, was the fruit of betrayal." Dahleven's voice was bitter. "Thanks to Knut, they know we discovered their camp and guess their plans. They want to stop us from returning to Quartzholm with that information. If we don't make it, the Council of Jarls will bring a vote of war before the Althing."

"But if they're waiting out there for us, how are we going to get to this Quartzholm?"

"We'll continue on through the mountain."

"*Through* the mountain?" Her voice was a little shrill.

"These mountains are cross-cut with hidden tunnels. By using them, we'll avoid the Renegades."

Cele took a deep breath of cool, stale air and blew it out slowly, but couldn't get all the fear out of her voice. "In the dark? Won't that slow us down a lot?"

"No, not in the dark. At least, not the whole way. This tunnel isn't much used, but when we reach the Knot we'll find torches. We'll be able to move quickly then.

And the tunnels are a shorter path than traveling over-land."

"Too bad no one left any torches where we came in." Cele's voice was still edgy.

"That's something I'll see changed when I return." Dahleven found her hand and pressed it between his own. "I'll not lead you astray. This I promise."

Promises. In her experience, the promises men made weren't worth much, but she'd made one to Sorn, and she'd keep it. She wouldn't judge Dahleven by her father or Jeff. He hadn't broken a promise to her yet. He hadn't made any, either, until now.

"Okay. Let's go then." Lady Celia leaned forward to rise.

Dahleven heard the determination and controlled tension in her voice and nodded to himself. She was anxious, but calm. She'd be all right. He'd known sea-soned warriors who panicked in the tunnels, even bright with lighted torches. And very few were comfortable in the absolute dark. He didn't like it much himself, but he had played throughout the tunnels as a boy, and his Talent gave him the advantage of knowing he could never be lost.

Dahleven gently tugged her back to rest against the wall. "In a bit. First, we'll rest and eat."

She sagged against his shoulder. "Okay."

Lady Celia slipped the waterskins off her shoulders and shrugged out of her pack. He heard the *snick!* of her belt-pack's unusual buckle. She drank from the strange bottles she carried and fumbled a bit with the ties of Lindimer's pack. Before long she worked them loose and soon he heard and smelled her nibbling on dried fruit and jerky. He liked the way she focused on the task at hand. Yes, she definitely would be all right. *She'll be a good companion in the dark.*

A second interpretation of his thoughts followed hard on the first. He traveled down that warm path, indulging in the pleasant images that brought to mind. Her shoulders would be warm and softly curved, her skin soft under his hands. Her feisty attitude promised passion and he could almost feel the velvet weight of her breasts—

The need to shift to readjust the fit of his pants brought him back to the moment with an embarrassed grimace. At least the lady couldn't see his discomfort. He tried to redirect his thoughts.

He remembered her as he had last seen her, dirty and disheveled, legs scratched and scabbed, braided hair loose and awry from the headlong rush downslope, eyes wide in alarm. The image failed to soften his interest. *My taste in women has taken quite a turn.* He scratched an itch and recalled his own unwashed state with a wry grimace. *I'm not much of a prize either, at the moment.*

He tried to remind himself that Lady Celia's loyalties were unproven, that she could yet prove a threat to Nuvinland, but he no longer could give much credence to that thought, no more than Sorn had.

Sorn. The memory brought Dahleven up short.

Sorn was dead barely a day. Dahleven winced. He'd been lusting after the woman who grieved the loss of his sworn brother. The memory of her fingers, clasped with Sorn's played against the lightless back-drop, as did the image of his brother's cuff on her arm. Sorn had always drawn sisterly affection from the ladies, but Lady Celia's tender attention to him in his last hours spoke of more than that. It was a bitter irony that Sorn had finally found a woman who saw him as a man instead of a brother only as he lay dying.

He felt Lady Celia shiver beside him. Now that they weren't moving, the underground chill began to penetrate. "Are you cold? Let's wrap in our blankets," Dahleven said, suiting action to words.

"How old are these tunnels?"

Celia's voice was still tense, but the musical quality had returned to it. Had it always been so pleasant to the ear? Sorn must have thought so. "We made them a long time ago. We still use them sometimes, especially in the winter."

"So that's how you knew where it was. I thought we were trapped until you pulled us in here."

He was tempted to let her believe his sharp planning had saved them, but honesty prevailed. "I don't know where every tunnel opens to the outside. Luck smiled on us, and my Talent revealed a path of escape."

"What do you use them for, when you're not on the run?"

"For mining." *And sneak attacks. And hiding wealth.* "They're still in use, though far from here. No one uses these tunnels much any longer."

He remembered the last time he and Sorn had been down in the tunnels. *When was it? Five? No, six years ago.* They'd been long past the reckless age of daring one another to foolhardy challenges. But others weren't, and they'd come down to the tunnels in search of his young niece Aenid. The girl had gone missing and her mother, Dahleven's sister Ingirid, was frantic. Dahleven had been out of patience with his sister. After all, Aenid was twelve and not stupid. Sorn, on the other hand, had said all the right things to Ingirid, and then they'd gone looking for the wayward girl.

When they found her, Aenid had been leading young Ljot and Solvin back to the Knot, the meeting and parting of ways. No one had noticed the boys missing except Aenid. And that was when Aenid had known she was a

Pathfinder, too, just like her uncle. For all the good it would do her, since Ingirid hardly let the girl out of her sight. How a sister of his could be so tight on the reins, Dahleven would never understand. But then he didn't understand how she could choose Jon to marry, either.

Sorn had become Aenid's champion after that. And between him and Dahleven, they'd won his niece a measure of freedom. Dahleven imagined the tears his niece would shed when she learned of Sorn's death. His eyes stung. He might shed a few himself.

Dahleven pinched the bridge of his nose and cleared his throat. Sitting in the dark like this only made it worse. "Get your things together. We need to move."

Cele flinched at Dahleven's unexpectedly gruff tone. *What did I say? Are the tunnels a sore spot with him?*

Dahleven stood and quickly shrugged into his pack.

"Wait here a minute. I need to, um, go." Cele could almost feel Dahleven roll his eyes.

"Don't go far."

"I know, I know. I won't be long. I'll just step around the corner." Cele carefully climbed the five steps out of the alcove, feeling her way slowly along the wall. The further she went, the more the dark pressed on her. She barely turned the corner before she stopped. This was far enough. *He can't see anything anyway.*

As quickly as possible Cele returned to the alcove. Too quickly; she misgauged the second step and fell the rest of the way, her tumble stopped by Dahleven's feet.

"Ow! Damn it! Son of a—" Cele grabbed her shin and bit off the curse.

Dahleven knelt by her side. "Are you hurt?"

"Of course I'm hurt! Damn it, that smarts!" She clenched her teeth.

"Where are you injured?" Dahleven ran his hands over her head then down her arms, feeling for cuts and broken bones. His touch was firm and sure and warm.

"I'm okay. It's nothing serious, it just hurts like the dickens."

Dahleven's hands were on her legs as she curled to sit up. His hands found hers clamped to her shin, and gently pulled them away. The cool air stung as it hit the scrape.

"You're bleeding."

Despite his care, Cele hissed and pulled away from the pain. "Where's my belt-pack? I've got some first aid stuff in there."

Dahleven left her side for a moment. Then he was back, pressing her pack into her hand. "I've water here." He steadied her leg with a warm touch on her bent knee, then cool water splashed and stung over her new wound.

Cele sucked in breath sharply. "Damn. I'm not usually such a klutz—though you wouldn't know it from the last few days." She fished around in her pack until she found by feel what she needed. "Here, hold this." She put a square of gauze in place.

Dahleven's hands quickly found where his help was needed and gently held the bandage till she could tape it down. It was awkward, working blind, and their fingers bumped several times. The cloth of his long sleeve brushed lightly against her bare thigh as he passed one hand beneath her bent leg to hold the other side of the bandage without getting in the way of her taping.

By the time she finished, she had become acutely aware of Dahleven's nearness. His heat made her shiver. She couldn't help wondering what it would feel like to have him touch her because he wanted to instead of helping her with some injury.

Yeah, like that's going to happen. "Done," she said.

Dahleven pulled back a little as she re-packed her first aid kit, but he didn't move away. "Can you walk?"

Cele snapped her belt-pack around her waist. "Of course!" She might be clumsy, but she wasn't that badly hurt. Hadn't she proven by now that she wasn't some delicate little flower? "Just give me a second to get my stuff together." Her voice was sharper than she'd intended, and that made her even angrier. She gritted her teeth behind clamped lips. She'd been about to thank him for his help before he opened his mouth.

Cele felt around for the pack and waterskins. Crawling on the cold stone floor was awkward as she tried to keep her shin from touching down, and her discomfort didn't improve her mood. She was almost grateful for Dahleven's stupid question. It was a good reminder how really dumb it was to be thinking sexual thoughts about him. She ought to be glad for the dark, too, since it kept her from ogling his perfect ass and flat abs. Finally, she stood and shrugged into the pack she'd inherited from Lindimer with abrupt, angry movements. Dahleven didn't say anything when she indicated she was ready. He just groped for her left hand, brought it to his belt, and headed out.

He took the lead, and from the sound of metal scraping rock, Cele guessed he was feeling his way with his sword. Apparently, knowing the way didn't keep him from stubbing his toes. The blackness pressed around them, so thick that Cele thought it ought to have substance. With nothing but the steady ache of her leg to indicate its flow, time slowed.

She hated stumbling around in the dark. She wanted out of this musty hole in the ground. She wanted light. She thought of the clear, clean sunlight that shafted down through the pine trees on the mountain somewhere above and felt that odd *tug* that said, *This way.* Off to her left and above there was light. She knew it. But there was also who knew how many tons of solid rock. Cele shook her head and dismissed the peculiar sensation as Dahleven towed her through the inky blackness.

Twice she felt a change in the air, as though they walked by an opening on the right, but Dahleven never turned from the passage they followed. The third time it felt like the opening was on the left. The peculiar sensation flared. The pull was almost physical, and Cele turned toward it. *This is the quickest way to light.*

"What is it?"

Dahleven's voice distracted her. What could she say? The feeling she had didn't make any sense to her, so how could she explain it to him? And she certainly had no business suggesting which way to go. "I, uh, thought I felt a change in the air." She felt stupid for giving in to her imaginings.

"You *are* feeling fresh air. We're next to a ventilation shaft."

"Could we get out this way?"

"I suppose so. But it's steep and we have no climbing gear. It would take us longer in the end to get to Quartzholm."

With some surprise, she realized her feeling wasn't wrong, just impractical. She still wanted light, though. Any light. "Did you say something before about torches?"

"Yes. There's a store of them not too far ahead."

Cele thought about dancing firelight. Even the light of inconstant flame would be welcome in this void. Her odd certainty shifted. Now it pulled in the direction Dahleven had been headed. "Great! Let's go!"

They continued down the tunnel, each step the same as the last, but eventually the sound of their footsteps told Cele they'd entered a larger chamber. The air seemed a little fresher.

Dahleven dropped her hand. "Wait here."

Cele wanted to follow the tugging sensation that compelled her forward, but she did as Dahleven commanded. She could hear the occasional *ting* of his sword as he felt his way around the chamber. Then she heard him put his sword down and fumble with something. Bright, brief flashes of light made Cele wonder for a moment if she'd been staring into the darkness too long, but an instant later she realized Dahleven was striking sparks. In a moment the tinder caught, and a tiny flame flared to life, bright after so many hours of absolute dark, riveting her attention. Dahleven held a torch to the flame. The pitch caught, flaring with the scent of burning pine tar, and its brightness overwhelmed her eyes, long adapted to the dark. She squinted, blinking back tears of relief as the dark retreated. Dahleven put the torch into an iron wall bracket.

The light revealed a round chamber with three black openings cut into its walls. Wooden chests bound with iron rested against the stone between each doorway. A sconce hung at shoulder height next to each opening, with a bucket of sand beneath. The domed ceiling arched high overhead.

Dahleven returned the flint and tinder to the chest nearest him, then shucked his pack and rose, stretching his shoulders and arms until his chest cracked. He gestured at the stone floor. "Sit. Be comfortable," he said without apparent irony. "We'll rest here tonight."

The stone floor was cold, and they each sat crosslegged with the edges of their blanket-shawls tucked beneath them. Cele became aware she was ravenous and pulled the last of the dried fruit from her pack. Dahleven chewed his jerky. They ate in companionable silence, the only sound the soft sizzle of the torch.

Dahleven cleared his throat. "We honor our dead by telling their tales, that those we have lost may live on in our memories though they no longer live among us. May Bragi inspire my words." His speech had a ritual cant to it. Cele remembered he'd said the same thing before the men had started their stories about Sorn the night before. Tonight he talked about Lindimer first, telling how he'd once saved nineteen men from ambush by hearing one of the enemy scratch as they lay in wait to attack. Cele had heard Lindimer's Talent called Heimdal's Ear and understood he'd had sharp hearing, but Dahleven's tale seemed far-fetched in the same way Ghav's story about Sorn had. *It doesn't matter. The point is to honor a fallen friend, not historical accuracy.*

She watched Dahleven as he spoke. His eyes brightened as he related Lindimer's warning, and his face grew fiercely joyous as he told how Lindimer and his fellows turned the ambush into a trap for their enemies. She'd seen that kind of intensity on Jeff's face when he watched football with his friends. But Dahleven wasn't talking about a game. His story was about life and death, and the loyalty of comrades who depended on one another for their lives.

The achingly beautiful death song, sung by the men at Lindimer's cairn, repeated its melody in her mind. Dahleven was part of a tightly woven community, no thread of which could be pulled without affecting the whole. They held values and goals in common, supported one another in life, and honored each other in death.

That kind of belonging called to her, but the violence of the world it came in was frightening. In just a handful of days she'd been in two battles, seen a friend die horribly, seen another man die with his throat cut by a traitor, and a third man go down with an arrow in his back. The price paid for community was a high one here, and as Knut had proved, loyalty wasn't guaranteed.

Dahleven seemed to have followed her thoughts. "Knut's family will pay a high price for Lindimer's death. What could that cur have been thinking? What gain could be great enough?" His strong hands clenched till the knuckles whitened and his voice rose, edged with outrage. "The *wereguild* alone will near break his brother. Unless they find Knut first and execute the sentence for his perfidy, their family will forever be shamed by it."

Why should Knut's family suffer for his actions? "Will Knut be held responsible for the last attack, and for Halsten?"

Dahleven's attention snapped to her. "Halsten?"

Shit. He didn't know. She shrank from telling him that another of his men had fallen, but there was no help for it. "When we were running I saw Halsten go down...with an arrow in his back."

"Halsten, too." The muscles in Dahleven's jaw jumped. "Another good man." His eyes narrowed and his voice was tight. "The Council may not hold Knut accountable for Halsten, but I will."

Cele wanted to change the cold expression carved into Dahleven's features. "What was Halsten's Talent?"

"True Aim. I never met a man who could best him in archery or with thrown axes. But he'll be missed even more for his music." Dahleven's face relaxed as he related how Halsten had won competitions with his music, amused his comrades with his drinking ditties, and seduced more than one maiden with his melodies.

"Do you know any of his songs?" Cele asked. At his nod, Cele urged, "Sing one for me."

Dahleven didn't demur. Maybe he saw it as the best way to honor Halsten—to remember him through his music. He paused for a moment, then he smiled and cleared his throat.

The melody was a simple one, but Dahleven's rich

baritone brought it life. It told the adventures of a hapless hunter who returned home empty-handed time after time to an irate wife and vegetable stew. Cele started rocking to the song's rhythm and felt herself smiling in response to Dahleven's grin. It was a long song with lots of verses and an often repeated chorus. At the end, Dahleven gestured she join him.

Cele hesitated. Her voice was untrained, but she liked the song and she could hardly refuse to honor Halsten's memory. She sang softly at first, but she knew the words after so many repetitions, and by the end of the chorus, her voice was strong.

"Hot pot, what have you got?
Naught but a meatless stew.
A carrot, a turnip, a green tomato,
Is all I can offer you."

"That was one of Sorn's favorites," Dahleven said when they'd finished. "He liked to pretend to bare competence as a hunter, but he was nearly as good a shot as Halsten." Dahleven's face took light with affection as he talked about Sorn. "Sorn saved my life, but he never liked me to speak of it. His valor assured him of a place in Valhalla many times over."

Valhalla? Dahleven had sworn by Odin before, but somehow it hadn't clicked into place for her till now. *As in* Vikings? *But how would they get here?* Cele grimaced at the stupidity of the question and shook her head. *How did I get here?*

Dahleven misinterpreted her expression. "It can be painful to speak of those gone, but we honor them by doing so."

He was right. It hurt. The more she heard, the worse she felt about Sorn's death, and the more she wished she'd had a chance to know him better. But the only way to know him now was through the stories of his friends. "Please go on."

Dahleven gave her an approving smile. "Two years ago, a petition came before the Kon. The shepherds who run their sheep in the high pastures of the eastern range were losing their lambs to a mountain cat. They'd hunted her themselves, but the canny beast proved too elusive. Worse, while they'd been hunting her, she'd been hunting too, and she'd killed the shepherd left guarding the flock. So they sent a man to bring their need before Kon Neven.

"I asked for the privilege of ridding the high valleys of the cat, and Sorn came with me. We'd hunted together often, and we each knew the other's ways. So we begged Freya's blessing to hunt her cat and rode up to the high pastures. We left our mounts with the men who'd sought our help, and went forward on foot.

"We followed that cat for four days. We tracked her well, through bone-chilling streams and over the twisted rocky trails she took trying to evade us. We rested little, and she even less. Often we saw her on a distant ridge, grown sleek and fat on the lambs she'd stolen.

"Late on the fourth day she'd run enough. The summer sun on her coat no longer rippled like molten gold, and her movements were slow and tired. Sorn and I split, circling wide, knowing she was most dangerous now.

"The sun was in my eyes when I jumped down into a hollow, following her trail, and I came upon her suddenly, and alone. She was above me and leapt before I could knock arrow. Her spotted belly blurred in motion, but I saw clearly her teeth bared, her claws extended, reaching for me as if I was a helpless lamb.

"Sorn's arrow took her in mid-leap, clean into her eye. She fell, her full weight upon me. My ankle twisted as I went down, and her weight cracked two of my ribs. Sorn had to half carry me down the mountain."

His voice was thick as he continued. "He'd crept quietly around her with the breeze in his teeth so she never knew he was there. He'd been about to take her when I blundered in. And that is how I gave Sorn the chance to be a hero, saving with one shot both the flocks and me." He coughed and cleared his throat.

Cele peered at him. The torch flickered unsteadily, nearly burned out, the wavering light concealing his face with uncertain shadows, but she had heard the unshed tears in his voice. She blinked away the moisture that stung her eyes. "I'll miss him. I know we only just met, but he treated me with kindness." Dahleven would probably think her words sounded lame, but it was all she had to offer. "That may not be heroic, but it meant a lot to me."

"Freyr honors such things."

"Freyr?"

Dahleven raised his eyebrows, and his voice questioned her ignorance. "Freyr. Of the Vanir."

He peered at her in the dim light and must have seen her blankness. Hardly surprising, since she didn't have a clue what he was talking about. Apparently, he came to that conclusion, because he continued, offering explanation.

"The Vanir are the first gods, older even than the Aesir. We look to Freyr and his sister Freya to bless us with peace and plenty, as he did when he opened the way to this land for us, some eight hundred years ago. We may thank Odin for poetry, Tyr for law, and Thor for courage in battle, but it is Freyr who blesses the union of men and women with pleasure and children. He rewards those who show respect and courtesy to women."

"Sorn is dead. That's not much of a reward." She swallowed hard. "I'm sorry. That's not fair. I can't blame someone else for what I did."

"What you did?"

Cele looked down at her hands clenched in her lap.

"It's my fault he died. If I hadn't distracted him..."

Dahleven lifted her chin with two fingers and looked her in the eye. "Did you summon the Renegades to attack us?"

"No! Of course not!"

"Did you wield the club that pierced Sorn's belly?"

"That's not—"

"Did you not prevent two Renegades from taking him unaware?"

"I suppose so, but—"

"These things happen in battle, Celia."

"Sorn said something like that, too, but he was only trying to make me feel better."

Dahleven shook his head. "He spoke the truth. We do our best, but we have no say in when the Norns snip our life's thread. I am sorry to have lost my sworn brother, but his death was an honorable one. You bear no fault in this. You owe no *wereguild* for Sorn."

Cele looked into Dahleven's steady gray eyes. He meant it. He didn't hold her responsible in any way. He was far more familiar with combat than she was. Maybe she should trust that he knew what he was talking about. Maybe Sorn's death wasn't her fault.

But her heart still ached.

The light flickered wildly, casting erratic shadows on the walls. "The torch won't last much longer," Dahleven said. "I'll show you to the latrine."

"Latrine?"

Dahleven's tone was rather arch. "We don't usually relieve ourselves in the hallways."

Cele felt herself blushing and hoped he couldn't tell in the uncertain light.

They'd barely returned to the chamber when the last small flame of the torch finally died. Its light had been minimal, but the return of absolute blackness oppressed Cele by its stark contrast with the cheerful red flame.

She hadn't slept with a nightlight since childhood, but she'd welcome one now. The floor was smooth but hard and unyielding and the wool beneath her did little to insulate her from the cold seeping into her bones. She felt isolated in the utter absence of light, and as she huddled at the edge of the blankets, she listened for the sounds of Dahleven's breathing to tell her she was not alone.

She wished she could reach out to him, just for the relief of touching another person, but she didn't want to give him the wrong impression. It would only embarrass them both if he thought she was issuing an invitation. The memory of the first morning flashed into her mind, that moment when she'd awakened entwined with Dahleven, her head pillowed on his shoulder. Heat flooded her face—and other parts of her body.

They'd fit together perfectly. She'd felt comforted and secure until she realized he was awake. *I don't need this. I don't want this. Life is weird enough without me falling for some macho jerk of a Viking.* Maybe the dark wasn't so bad after all, since it hid her blush from his eyes. Cele groaned and covered her face.

Dahleven put a warm hand on her shoulder. "Are you unwell? Does your leg pain you?"

A macho Viking who worries about my welfare.

Cele managed to reply in a perfectly normal voice that she was fine, but when Dahleven withdrew his hand, she had a hard time not pulling it back.

Dahleven tried to ignore his frustration as he rolled away from Celia. Something troubled her, something beyond the wearing strain of the endless dark. He wanted to take her into his arms as he had after Sorn died, as he would one of his own sisters. Except that his feelings for her were not exactly brotherly. It was probably just as well that she kept her fears and troubles to herself. The concern he felt for her had uneven footing; it would be too easy to slide down that slope, out of control.

He lay on his back, staring at the ceiling. It could have been two or twenty feet away for all he could see. He'd never enjoyed exploring the tunnels, not the way Sorn had. It wasn't so much the dark—most of the tunnels had torches—but the thought of all that rock overhead.

He'd possessed no special advantage in their youthful tunnel adventures; his ordinary sense of direction failed him underground and his Talent had developed late. He remembered the year his younger brother's Talent bloomed. Ragni had never gloated over him, but he had a boy's natural excitement in exercising his new ability and learning how to use, or not use it, appropriately. Meanwhile, their elders had obviously begun to fear Dahleven's Talent would never Emerge. Even when it did appear, it had taken many months to master. Until he'd learned to concentrate, to commit to one path, his variable interest in first the most direct route, then the easiest, or the one with the best light or water had his Talent pulling him hither and yon.

He was master of his Talent now, confident in his ability after years of practice. He could give over his goal to one part of his mind so he could think about other things even as his Talent pulled him where he wanted to go. Which was a good thing, since he'd spent a fair amount of time of late thinking about the woman at his side.

The blanket quivered. Celia was shivering. Tentatively, half expecting a rebuff, he rolled to his side and moved a few inches until his back was against hers. He would rather wrap himself around her, but he feared she would refuse. *She needs the warmth*, he told himself, ignoring the foolish pleasure the slight contact brought. *We need to move quickly tomorrow. I can't afford for her to take a chill.* Slowly, almost imperceptibly, he felt her relax and lean back into his body's heat. She stopped shivering, and the rhythm of her breathing changed as she slipped into the realm of dreams. He was glad she could escape her troubles for a little while.

He should do the same, he knew, and closed his eyes.

It seemed like only a moment later when a sudden gasp and moan startled him awake. He was already reaching for his sword when he realized there was no threat. Celia lay on her back beside him, rigid and shaking. He reached out to her and found her hands covering her face. She was clammy with sweat. "What is it? Are you ill?"

She took a deep shuddering breath and sat up. "I'm okay. It was just a nightmare." She shivered.

Dahleven sat up and pulled the blanket they'd lain on over her shoulders.

It was no surprise that fear plagued her dreams after what she'd been through. For the moment, his desire for her was not an issue. All he wanted now was to comfort her. He rubbed his hand in slow circles over her back, just as he used to do for his little sister, Kaidlin. For some reason she'd always sought him out, rather than her nurse or their mother or sister, when some night terror had upset her.

Dahleven didn't ask Celia to relive her nightmare by recounting it, he just rubbed her back in slow, lazy circles until he felt her relax. Then he pulled her down to nestle against his chest. To his relief, she didn't argue or resist. She'd barely settled her head into the hollow of his shoulder before he heard her breathing deepen and slow in sleep.

Pleased by her trust in him, Dahleven slept.

When Cele awoke, she saw the same scene as when she'd closed her eyes the night before. Nothing. Only the feel of her lids moving told her that her eyes were open.

During the night, she'd curled around Dahleven, her arm curving over his waist, her legs tucked behind his. She was toasty and comfortable—except where the stone floor pressed an ache into her shoulder and hip. He'd been so gentle when she'd wakened from the nightmare. Was this the same man who'd barked at her just days ago? Reluctant to leave the warmth but needing to ease her bones, Cele gingerly pulled away, hoping he wasn't awake yet.

Stiffly, she stood and stretched life back into her sore muscles. The worst of the pain from their long climb had faded, but her muscles and joints felt like they belonged to an old woman after the night on the cold floor. She'd never thought of bare dirt as accommodating before, but compared to unforgiving stone, it was comfy.

Dahleven apparently felt the same way. He groaned as she heard him roll onto his back, then stand and make his way to one of the chests. A moment later, sparks flashed like fireflies and a torch flared and caught.

Cele blinked owlishly even as she welcomed the light. Her eyes weren't so bedazzled, though, that she missed Dahleven's half-smile.

"We'll move faster today, now that we can see where we're going. You won't have to hang onto my belt."

"That'll be nice."

"But don't take that as freedom to wander," he said. "Stay with me, and stay in the shaped tunnels. The natural caverns are dangerous."

Cele had no desire to go exploring on her own, but

she was curious. "Dangerous how?"

"The footing's treacherous; in some places the floor can drop right out from under you. And...creatures live in there, in the dark. Creatures you don't want to meet."

Creatures? She shivered. "I haven't seen or smelled any sign of animals so far."

"They avoid our tunnels." Dahleven spoke seriously. "You're safe as long as you stay out of the natural ways."

"Don't worry, I'll be right behind you."

Dahleven smiled. "We'll be above ground by midday. Does that suit you?"

Cele grinned. "Definitely!"

"Myself, also. Let's eat and take care of the necessities. Sooner begun, sooner done."

Before long they were on their way, each of them carrying a supply of torches. Dahleven led the way, holding one aloft. The flame danced, casting flickering shadows on the walls. A thousand questions flooded into Cele's mind. *How many of the others survived? What is Quartzholm like? Will the others be there?* And top of the list, *How the heck am I going to get home?*

chapter eight

when the floor started to angle upward, Dahleven felt some of the tension leave his shoulders. They were almost home, almost out of the tunnels. The rock walls on either side opened wider and they had space enough to comfortably walk abreast as they climbed the gentle slopes or shallow, widely spaced steps. He ignored the occasional narrow passageways that opened on either side of the wider tunnel. Some were ventilation shafts, others were bolt-holes from the private areas of Quartzholm above.

There had been talk off and on about sealing the various hidden passages, or at least locking them with iron gates as the main tunnel was, if only to keep the children from wandering down and getting lost. It had been a long time since the provinces had moved against one another with more than a minor raid; there no longer existed a need for a quick exit. Or so the argument went on the rare occasion the subject arose—usually after a brief search for an errant child.

Nothing ever came of it, though, and Dahleven was glad. He hoped the provinces never came to war again, but peace could never be guaranteed. Vigilance and preparation remained necessary, and that included maintaining the bolt holes. Besides, he wouldn't have missed the chance to explore them as a boy. Shadows dancing on stone walls had looked much more ominous when he was eight. A memory of eager apprehension tickled down his spine. No, he didn't support closing the tunnels. If a boy could find one of the hidden entrances, he should have the chance to test himself and challenge the Tunnel Trolls.

Dahleven grinned and shook his head. How long had parents been using that old tale to frighten children into obedience?

He wasn't leading Lady Celia through any of the private ways, though. Their route would take them through the storehouse and up into the courtyard. He wasn't going to give away the secrets of his home to this stranger, no matter how innocent she seemed or how lovely she was.

Dahleven's grin faded as his thoughts turned back to the business at hand and the grim news he bore. Outcasts and Renegades encamped together. Sorn, Lindy, and Halsten dead, and perhaps more. Knut a traitor.

It ground in his gut that he had trusted the whoreson, honored him by requesting him for his company. Memories of camaraderie, training on the practice field together, celebrations, and conversations played themselves out in his mind. Had Knut paused overlong in reply to a question? Should he have interpreted a particular look in Knut's eyes differently? He had thought before that Knut was merely private about a lady love, but now it was clear that Knut had been evasive about more than where he spent his free time.

Everything Knut had said and done seemed doubtworthy. Now.

Dahleven shook his head. Urd's view of the past was always clear. Verdandi's present was murky at best, and

Skuld delighted in keeping the future obscure. The three Ladies of Fate gave away nothing, and he was only mortal. That was small comfort when Lindy lay dead by the hand of a traitor that Dahleven had welcomed into his company. *The skalds will sing no songs in praise of my cleverness.*

And if all of that wasn't enough, there was the wholly surprising news he brought of Lady Celia's appearance, and the Lady herself.

She was a puzzle. Her presence alone was a mystery, and she could yet prove to have dangerous allies. She claimed innocence, and he was inclined to believe her. But he had trusted Knut, also.

Dahleven surfaced from his musings. Lady Celia had been walking by his side; now he realized she'd fallen behind. She was only a few steps back, but she was walking with her head down, favoring the leg she'd gashed in her fall yesterday. He remembered the feel of her leg, slick with warm blood, under his hand, and felt an echo of the concern that had washed through him then. He'd have Ghav look at her wound when they got to Quartzholm.

If Ghav still lives.

Dahleven clenched his teeth, bunching the muscles of his jaw. His entire patrol could be dead, thanks to that traitor Knut. *And my blindness.*

He slowed his steps till Lady Celia came even with him again. She was definitely walking more slowly. He could call a break, but they were very nearly home, and her leg would just stiffen in rest.

"What is this place you're taking me to?"

Was she worried? Did she have reason to be? "Quartzholm."

"That was informative." Her voice sounded wry—and tired. She paused a moment and shifted her pack. "What happens when we get there?"

"We get warm baths, good food, and"—he glanced sidelong at her—"clean, *appropriate* clothing. What did you think would happen?"

She considered at him closely, as though weighing his words. Then she nodded and straightened as if a worry had lifted from her. "I don't know what to think. *You* weren't too happy to see me. I thought others might feel the same. For all I know, they might lock me up or torture me or something."

"Do you deserve such punishment?"

"Of course not! But I don't know you, or your people! Who knows what could happen here?"

"Odin's Eye! What have we done that you would expect such treatment?" *Or what has she done?*

Cele took in a deep breath, ready to blast him. *The arrogant bastard. What had he done?* He'd shouted at her and menaced her with a knife. He'd run her over desert and mountain and dragged her underground. He had moved Sorn too soon.

What has he done?

Her emotions rebounded abruptly. He'd comforted her when Sorn died. He'd been gentle when she'd fallen. He'd shared his memories with her. He'd rubbed her back and taken no advantage after her nightmare. He and his men had saved her life three times.

Five days on the trail were taking their toll. Cele's fatigued thoughts spun with the emotional whiplash of outrage and gratitude. And, if she were honest, attraction. Jeff's betrayal had left her stunned and angry and numb. But she wasn't numb with Dahleven. He stirred up every feeling she had. *It's just a reaction to danger.* But she remembered wanting to curl up against him last night, and blushed, glad of the uncertain light from the torch.

"I don't know *what* to expect," she said in a tight voice. "Everything is different here. I'm trying not to *expect* anything—but that doesn't keep me from worrying."

Dahleven blew out a deep breath. "You should stop that. Worry is a waste of time and energy." He slanted a sideways glance at her. "Now planning, that's another thing altogether. Right now I'm planning on a bath, hot food, and rest. You should do the same. Beyond that, only the Norns know what the future holds, and they never tell."

Cele's anger ebbed. He'd done his best to reassure her, without promising anything. He was right. Worrying was a waste of time, especially since she didn't really know enough about the place to know what to worry about.

Eventually, they came to a halt before an iron gate, secured with a large boxy metal lock. The room on the other side of the gate was already lit with lanterns, but the area was so large and filled with barrels and sacks that they created more shadows than light. Dahleven handed the torch to Cele, shrugged out of his pack, and knelt, digging through it to pull a ring of keys from the bottom. He selected one shaped like a spatula with two holes of differing shapes cut in it. Dahleven reached through the bars and put the key into the slot and slid it upward. There was a metal on metal screech, then he jerked the lock off the curved hasp. In response to Dahleven's push, the gate swung open with a groan. *Just like a grade B horror flick.* Cele suppressed a shudder.

Dahleven waved her into the dimly lit storeroom, then locked the gate and relieved her of the torch. Holding it aloft, he led the way down a dim aisle formed by wooden boxes and hundreds of sacks of grain. The torchlight flickered across hollows and recesses; shadows wavered and jumped.

Suddenly, a blackness shot down from above, landing abruptly at Cele's feet. A spike of fear shot through her, and she shrieked. Breath jerked raggedly in her lungs, and she jumped back, banging against the boxes. Her eyes, adapted to the dim light, followed the shape as it streaked down the aisle.

It was a cat.

Dahleven swung around, sword drawn, just in time to see the mouser before it disappeared into another hidey-hole. Cele laughed shakily. Her eyes met Dahleven's in chagrined amusement, and his tight expression returned a crooked half-smile. He chuckled before sheathing his weapon.

Something tight released in Cele. A giggle bubbled to the surface. She shook with it, overcome by the absurdity of startling at a cat after what she'd been through in the last week. Laughter bounced through her, shaking loose from the uncertainty and fear, anguish and loss. Her breath came in gasps, and she propped one shoulder against the wall of boxes.

Dahleven's half-smile spread across his face, and his chuckle grew to full-throated mirth. He leaned on the boxes next to Cele, his shoulders quaking with the force of his laughter, then threw back his head and let it pour out of him.

It was a beautiful sound, delightful and rich, and it triggered another gale of merriment from Cele. Tears trickled from the corners of her eyes. The tension poured out of her. Gradually, the wildness of her laugh faded back to giggles.

Close by her, Dahleven's laughter subsided as he wiped moisture from his cheek. He faced her, left shoulder against the boxes, right hand holding the torch, and smiled into her eyes. He was barely a foot away, and the

closeness felt comfortable, bonded as they were by humor and the release of days of worry and fear. When he
leaned over and kissed her, she didn't pull away.

It was a brief and gentle query. Then he pulled back a
scant inch.

That small kiss wasn't enough. Cele turned her face
up, seeking Dahleven's mouth. That seemed to release
him, and he took her lips again, caressing them with his
own. He stood, pulling away from where he leaned
against the wall of boxes, freeing his left arm to slip
around her. His hand bumped into her belt-pack, then
collided with her backpack before he finally pulled her
close. She giggled, and Dahleven snorted his amusement, then bent to kiss her again. Cele's fingers gripped
his shoulders. Every point of contact sizzled over her
skin like a Fourth of July sparkler, and each spark
threatened to ignite a conflagration. He tasted warm
and salty and of something more that was ineffably
Dahleven. His beard was soft, and she sighed with
pleasure when he trailed little kisses down her cheek
and neck.

"Who's there?" A voice came from the other side of
the vast cavern.

Cele stiffened and Dahleven pulled back enough to
murmur, "That's just one of the thralls who works down
here." After a soft final kiss, he lifted his head and slowly
released his hold on her. He stayed close a moment,
tracing his fingers along her cheek before stepping away
with a rueful and chagrined smile. "We must go on."

Cele nodded, not trusting herself to speak. Her skin
still tingled. It had been a long time since she'd enjoyed
a kiss that much. She wasn't sure she trusted the feeling,
but it felt too good to turn away from. Bemused, she followed him through the maze of supplies.

The aisle opened onto a wide, uncluttered area. The
far wall was broken by openings of various sizes, five of

which appeared to be dumbwaiters. Two men were hauling on the ropes, lifting something to a higher level. Two others were wheeling handcarts while a third was striding toward them.

"You there!" he called out. "What are you doing down here?"

As Dahleven came closer, the man's expression changed from challenge to embarrassment. "My lord! I beg your pardon! I didn't—"

"Be at ease," Dahleven said. "I've just come in the back door; you couldn't have known."

The man bowed then straightened. His gaze drifted to Cele, obviously focusing on her bare, bruised legs. Cele could feel her lips tingling from Dahleven's kisses and she cringed inwardly, sure the man was drawing an unflattering conclusion from her appearance.

Dahleven spoke, drawing the man's attention back to him. "This is Lady Celia, whom I've rescued from the drylands. Send up a message for Ranulf to meet us in the courtyard." Then he turned away as though he had no doubt his command would be obeyed.

They went through one of two wide doorways bracketed by open ironbound wooden doors. A tall flight of stairs stretched above them. Cele climbed automatically, her mind floating back to Dahleven's kiss. *What did he mean by it*? Was it merely impulse? A reaction to the scare? Or something more? Did she want it to be more?

She shook her head. *It doesn't matter. I'm going home.*

It was a long climb; Cele felt it in the gash on her shin by the time they reached the first landing. There they found three sets of double doors. Dahleven led her through the set on the right. They continued to climb to another landing, the sound of their steps bouncing off the seamless stone walls. *How did they get it so smooth?*

As they neared the next landing, she saw glorious golden daylight spilling down from above through open doors on the left. The promise of sunlight banished her questions, and the ache in her legs almost vanished. Cele started climbing before Dahleven quenched the flames of their torch in a barrel of sand. Then he caught up with her quickly, taking the stairs two at a time.

A cacophony echoed down the steps. Laughter, shouts, and shrieks of children playing reverberated on the stone, mingling with faint music. When they reached the top, Cele stopped under a wide arch framed with a set of open doors, and gazed out into a huge courtyard filled with the colorful mayhem of a bazaar. The deep blue sky of dry mountain air arced from wall to wall, streaked with high gauzy clouds. Cele's heart suddenly felt lighter, without the weight of the mountain hanging over her head. Then Dahleven took her arm and propelled her forward, into chaos.

The crowd was thick, with people jockeying for access to carts and stalls displaying wares. Dahleven paused as a gaggle of children ran by, laughing shrilly, then hustled Cele forward through the throng. Her surroundings blurred into a mélange of bright colors and jostling bodies, broken by the occasional voice hawking wool or tarts, lifted to carry over the hubbub. The aroma of roasted meat wafted to her and made her mouth water. Cele pressed closer to Dahleven, overwhelmed by the riotous sounds of the market after the quiet of the tunnels. Halfway across the compound, Dahleven startled Cele by shouting, "Ranulf!"

A gray haired man, barely taller than Cele, separated himself from the crowd. He hurried over and nodded in an approximation of a bow. "Lord Dahleven! We've looked for you these last two days." Ranulf stared at Cele. His eyes widened as he took in her appearance, then he focused on Dahleven. "Your father is anxious to see you."

Dahleven ignored Ranulf's remarks. "This is Lady Celia Montrose. Give her a room in the west wing and fetch Thora to attend her. Show her all courtesy, and tell Thora to find her some new clothing." Dahleven turned to her. "Lady Celia, I leave you in Ranulf's expert care. If you have any concern or need, either Thora or he will see to it." Dahleven said the last looking pointedly at Ranulf under lowered brows, and the older man nodded again, deeper this time, but with his head cocked to the side.

Cele felt a surge of alarm, but Dahleven didn't give her any opportunity to protest. He was striding away before she could utter a word.

"My lady? If you will follow me?" Ranulf inclined his head respectfully, then paused. "I'll take your pack for you, my lady."

Cele remembered the appalled expression he'd flashed at her scratched, bruised, and bloody legs. He might not approve of her appearance, but he was all politeness now.

Suddenly, the style of clothing worn by the women in the crowd impressed itself on Cele's awareness. All of the women wore long skirts, or tunics over loose pants bloused at the ankles. Some of the market-goers were stealing glances at her, while others stared openly.

Cele pretended not to notice and handed Ranulf the pack. "Lead on." The sooner she was out of here, the better.

She followed Ranulf through the crowd in the same direction Dahleven had taken. He seemed to have the knack, or was it a Talent? for moving smoothly through crowds, because they quickly reached a clear space near a massive wall of pink granite. A set of steps wide enough for six men to stand abreast led up to a large arch, but beside the pair of sentries only two other people were on the steps. Or two and a half.

At the top of the stairs, a pretty, strawberry-blonde woman stood embracing Dahleven. Comfortably snuggled into his left arm, a one-year-old child patted his face. It was a beautiful, heart-warming, family tableau.

Cele felt sick.

chapter nine

the young woman and Dahleven turned, his arm around her shoulders, and disappeared beneath the arch.

Married. The son-of-a-bitch was married, with a child, and he had kissed her. He had kissed her, and she had enjoyed it and wanted more. And he was married.

Shock evaporated under the rising heat of righteous anger. *The bastard. The two-faced, sneaking, lying bastard.* No, not lying. He hadn't *said* he was free to kiss whomever he pleased. He'd just done so. And she'd allowed it. Welcomed it. She'd let her heart do her thinking for her. Again. Her stupid, impulsive heart.

"My lady?" Ranulf stood, one foot on the bottom step, waiting for her.

She'd stopped in her tracks. How long had she been standing there, staring? Cele returned to life and followed Ranulf up the stone steps. How obvious had her pause been? How much had shown on her face? Would Ranulf report her stunned expression? Would Dahleven be amused? Or frustrated that his plans for seduction were now spoiled?

Ranulf led her through wide hallways of polished

pink granite flecked with black. Shiny bits embedded in the stone sparkled in the light slanting through clerestory windows. They passed a huge rectangular room on the left, which connected to the hall through six arches. Wide ledges ran the length of the hall, ending in a broad dais. Three rectangular fire-pits split the hall in half lengthwise, still leaving a wide expanse on either side. Elaborately decorated fire-hoods flared high above them. Cele stopped to look, but Ranulf quickly urged her onward. Then he led her up a wide curving stairway of black polished stone.

The finials on the bottom newels seemed to bear no relation to those on the top posts. Carved of the same gleaming stone as the steps, a gilded boar and mountain lion seemed to leap upward. At the top a man and woman faced each other across the stair, beautiful and noble. Cele would have liked to admire the workmanship, but Ranulf didn't pause, leading her across a long curving mezzanine before climbing another flight.

She lost track of hallways and turns and stairs before Ranulf stopped in front of a round topped door, swung it inward, and stepped back to bow her in.

The room was narrower than it was deep. Wooden cabinets lined the far wall. An abstract mosaic on the floor disappeared beneath a tightly woven rug, and ledges ran along either side of the chamber, much like in the great hall downstairs. A thick feather bed lay on the deep ledges to the right, cloaked by heavy draperies. Thinner cushions upholstered in rich burgundy cloth softened the narrower window seats on the left side. High narrow windows cut the thick walls, letting in the afternoon light.

"Thora will attend you soon, my lady." With that prediction, Ranulf set down her pack, bowed himself out, and shut the door.

Alone for the first time in days, with no one hurrying

her along, the strain and stress of the last week finally caught up with her. She wanted nothing more than what that son-of-a-bitch Dahleven had promised her: rest, a bath, and food.

The feather bed looked plump and inviting. Cele ran a hand over the intricately loomed coverlet. It was soft and smooth, but her roughened skin caught on the fine threads. She looked more closely at her hands. They were dry and scabbed in many places—dirt and blood crusted her nails. She scratched her scalp and tried to think how long it had been since she'd washed. Too long. She couldn't climb into that fine bed as she was, so she lay down on the rug.

The floor was hard, but no worse than the ground she'd slept on for the last five nights, and it had the advantage of having no hidden lumps or stones. *I'll just lie down for a moment until Thora gets here.* Cele stretched out, luxuriating in the freedom to move without concern for implying an unintended, and unwanted, intimacy.

Dahleven clasped his father's arm in greeting before Neven pulled him into a hug and thumped him on the back with strong arms. The familiar aroma of leather and pipe smoke enveloped him. Dahleven returned the embrace with warmth.

"The sentries gave no warning of you, Dahl. Are they growing lax?" Neven asked when they pulled apart. He sat in one of the chairs by the cold fire grate and filled his pipe.

Dahleven sat before answering. The large, well-padded seat fit him perfectly, and the curved arms were polished dark and smooth by years of hands resting there. "I used the tunnels, Father. Once we were in, it was the quickest way, and I knew you'd want this news before you convened the Althing."

Neven's sharp grey eyes focused intently on him. When Dahleven was younger, that riveting gaze had made him want to squirm. Now, he returned it levelly. "The Tewakwe aren't raiding our caravans."

Neven's response was an eyebrow lifted in increased scrutiny, but he didn't interrupt.

Dahleven quickly outlined his observations of the combined camp of Nuvinland Outcasts and Tewakwe Renegades. "We're meant to believe that the Tewakwe have injured us, and I suspect the Tewakwe must believe we've attacked them." Dahleven's voice dropped slightly. "I couldn't tell whether it was Renegades or honorable Tewakwe who believed us to be Outcasts, that attacked us and killed Sorn."

"Sorn!" Neven pulled his pipe from his mouth. "He was a good man. His father will feel the loss sorely. And Aenid! She loved him as another brother, I think."

Dahleven saw the look of understanding in his father's eyes, and was grateful Neven's tact prevented direct sympathy. "Yes, she'll take it hard."

Neven stroked the ends of his forked and braided beard, then returned to the main problem. "This is too coordinated to be mere raiding for profit. There is a larger purpose in it."

"I am convinced of it." Dahleven's voice was harsh, knowing what he must say next. "We have traitors among us."

Dahleven would have smiled as his father's hand went unconsciously to the knife at his side, but his news was too grim. As he relayed Knut's betrayal and Lindimer's death, Dahleven's hand fisted on the arm of the chair.

"The Althing will cast him out. But he cannot be

alone in this." Neven's voice was tight. "Our troubles are deeper and darker than we thought."

"There is more."

Neven lifted both brows this time. In response, Dahleven cleared the unexpected nervousness from his throat, and spoke of Lady Celia Montrose, knowing that nothing escaped his father's acute perception.

"My lady!"

A sharp, fear-edged voice and firm hands jerked Cele to wakefulness. For a moment she didn't know where she was, or why this round-faced woman with coiled, graying braids was hovering over her, gently slapping her face.

Cele pushed the woman's hands away. "I'm awake, already." She sat up and tossed aside the light cover that had been put over her, but the woman hastily covered her legs again. Cele decided to let her have her way for now and stayed sitting. She knew where she was again. *I'm in Quartzholm. And this must be Thora.* She didn't know who the man standing by the door was though, the one holding a pitcher and basin and with towels draped over his arm.

"Fid, put those down." Thora gestured to the rear of the room.

Fid crossed the room, opened one of the tall cabinet doors, and disappeared inside. When he returned emp-ty-handed, Cele saw what the towels had concealed: Fid was missing the thumb and first two fingers of his right hand. The stumps looked red and barely healed.

"That will be all, Fid."

Fid nodded a bow to Thora and bent more fully to Cele.

She felt awkward in the face of so much courtesy. "Thank you," was all she could think to say.

Surprise flashed across the man's face, then was quickly concealed as he turned to go.

"My lady, you needn't thank him or even speak to him; he's a thief serving his sentence."

Before Cele could think what to say to that, Thora bustled on. "They told me you'd want to tidy up, so I had Fid bring water, but I can see now that won't do. You'll want more than just a freshening. A hot bath will do you good. Do you feel well enough to walk? Should I call the Healer?" Thora peered at Cele with sharp eyes.

"I'm fine. I was just resting. I didn't mean to fall asleep."

"On the floor?" Thora's tone was incredulous.

"As you noticed, I need more than just 'a freshening.' I didn't want to dirty the bed."

Thora gave Cele a quick, appraising glance. "That should not concern you. There are more than enough folk here to keep things clean and tidy, and most are in need of something to do." Thora's brisk manner suggested that she had little patience with idlers. "Now, let's find you a robe and we'll get you to the baths." She bustled to the back of the room. Her sturdy body moved with more energy than Cele would have thought possible, fluttering the edges of her long tunic over her ample hips and flapping the hems of her loose-legged pants. Several keys hung from chains pinned at her waist by an ornate brooch, jingling and chiming as she moved. She had just opened a closet when a sharp rap sounded at the door.

Cele started toward the door, but Thora hustled past her and reached it first. She gave Cele an admonishing shake of her head, then opened the door just enough to speak with whomever stood in the hall. Cele couldn't hear what the visitor said, just the low rumble of his voice, but she could tell Thora wasn't pleased.

"But the lady hasn't bathed yet!"

Another low rumble.

"Just a moment." Thora shut the door with an abrupt gesture that dropped the well-oiled latch into place with an audible snap. "My lady, Kon Neven requests your presence immediately."

With a gentle but firm pressure on Cele's back, Thora directed Cele into the alcove hidden behind one of the wooden doors, where Fid had left the water and towels.

"It's just as well I brought that water, after all. When Kon Neven says 'immediately,' there's no 'in just a moment' to it; he is the Master of the House and Jarl of Quartzholm, after all, not to mention Kon. But I think you may be allowed to wash your face, at least." Thora suited her actions to her words, pouring water into a basin, wetting a cloth, then combing Cele's hair and braiding it while Cele washed her face and arms.

The dirty brown of the water in the basin appalled Cele. *At least it's not on my face any more.*

Thora handed Cele a towel just as the messenger rapped impatiently on the door again. "There's no more time, my lady. Where are your clothes?"

"These *are* my clothes."

Thora looked appalled. "All of them?"

Cele was acutely aware of Thora's disapproving glance at her scratched, bruised, *bare* legs. Another sharp rap on the door forestalled any comment. Thora shook her head before hurrying to the door, but she opened it with elaborate dignity. "Lady Celia is pleased to attend Kon Neven."

Cele suppressed a smile at the consequence Thora tried to give her and joined the man waiting in the hall. He was dressed in cloth pants and a shirt with a banded collar and long, loose sleeves under a green suede tunic. Embroidered in red on his left breast, the stylized depiction of a hawk swooped head-on, as though the viewer were prey. A long dagger hung at the man's waist. His eyes widened a fraction when he saw Cele, but he didn't waste time indulging his surprise. He gave her the barest of bows, then turned to lead her through more hallways.

He didn't take her to the large audience chamber Cele had seen below, but higher, up two more flights of stairs. He stopped in front of a beautifully carved double door and rapped once.

Another man immediately opened the door. After a murmured exchange with her escort, the other man announced, "Lady Celia Montrose," and bowed her into the room.

The nearly square chamber smelled faintly of pipe smoke and was sparsely furnished. On one side two comfortable looking chairs were drawn close to the unlit fireplace; a long oval table of polished black stone filled the other side, surrounded by chairs. Several tall candelabra stood in the corners of the room. Two men stood near a deep window embrasure on the right wall.

The man facing the door immediately drew Cele's gaze. Even lounging against the green and blue draperies, the man had an alertness, a controlled power that warned Cele that she had just stepped into a lion's den. He didn't move from his seemingly relaxed posture, but she knew from his single lifted brow that he missed nothing of her dirty, bare-legged, bedraggled condition. She resisted the urge to squirm under his assessing scrutiny.

The other man didn't lean against the wall. He stood facing the first man, his hand lifted in mid-gesture, as though Cele's arrival had interrupted a vigorous debate. He turned deliberately and precisely, dropping his hand to his side. His body stilled to such an extent he removed himself from consideration. Cele's attention immediately returned to the first man.

He shrugged away from the wall and came toward her, moving his sturdy muscular frame with the same unconscious grace that Cele had seen in Dahleven. A flare of anger threatened to distract her as he surfaced in her thoughts. She wrenched her mind back to the present.

The middle-aged man who approached her was tall, with light brown hair braided down the back of his head to his shoulders. Wide streaks of gray swept back from his temples; more showed in his beard, which fell halfway down his chest and was braided in two forks. But his eyes were what captured Cele's attention. Pale blue, ringed with a darker grey, they were bottomless as a mountain lake and just as sharp and cold. Had she thought him a lion before? He was more like a hawk. His eyes missed nothing, and he seemed poised to swoop and attack.

Kon Neven, as Cele supposed him to be, stopped four feet from her and regarded her silently. The seconds stretched to a minute, then more. *Should I bow or curtsey or something?*

No. Not yet. She had never liked these sorts of games, but she knew how to play them. This guy reminded Cele of the Director of the Emergency Services Center. He knew his power and how to use it. He despised weakness and rewarded competence. She could deal with this. She lifted her chin, looked him in the eye, and waited.

Finally, he spoke. "Welcome to Quartzholm, *Lady* Montrose."

His doubt of an honorific she'd never sought didn't threaten her, so she ignored it. "Thank you, my lord." Cele wasn't sure of the correct way to honor someone who was the Kon and Jarl of the Province. A curtsey in shorts somehow seemed absurd, so she bowed, but not too deeply. Some instinct warned her not to give too much, too soon.

"This is Gris, my chamberlain." Kon Neven lifted his left hand and turned away. The other man rematerialized from his assumed obscurity by the window and came forward. He was taller than his master, well over six feet, but too thin for his height.

"Your presence here is quite an event," the chamberlain said.

"So Dahleven led me to believe."

"What else did *Lord* Dahleven tell you?" Gris's voice was smooth and mellow.

"Not much. You're having some trouble with the Indians here—the Tewakwe? Or Renegades and Outcasts. That much is obvious." Cele pushed down the grief for Sorn that tightened her throat.

"The trouble with the Tewakwe is obvious?"

"I was there when they attacked."

Gris nodded. "You called them...'Indians?'"

"That's what they're called where I come from. Used to be called. Now they're called 'Native Americans.'"

Gris paused, then asked, "What else did Lord Dahleven tell you of our situation?"

Are they worried that Dahleven blabbed State secrets? They didn't know him very well if they thought that. He might toy with a woman's affection, but even she could see his sense of duty wouldn't allow him to betray his people. "Not much. He was pretty tight-lipped."

Her interrogator changed the subject. "Tell me about your people."

"What do you want to know? They're people."

Gris shrugged. "Their customs, beliefs. Their Talents."

Talents. Cele's heart beat faster. She'd forgotten that Dahleven had told her about them. He hadn't acted like it was a secret, but now they might think she'd been lying. Cele looked for Kon Neven. He'd stepped to the window, his eyes intent as they watched her. She could pretend ignorance, but he would see the lie, she was sure. "That's a big question," she stalled.

Gris hadn't missed her glance. He moved closer, drawing her attention to him as he loomed over her.

Cele fought her inclination to take a step back. "The short answer is that we're a pretty independent bunch. We don't like people pushing us around," she said, pointedly. "Our customs seem fairly different from yours, certainly we dress differently," she spread her hand, indicating her shorts, "but I don't know much about Talents. Just what Sorn and Dahleven told me."

"Your people are Talentless then?" His manner had none of the embarrassed gentleness that had character-ized Dahleven's question. He stated his question more like a challenge.

"Yes, as far as I understand what I've been told."

"Where are your people? Are you here alone?"

Alone? Definitely. Friendless, too, since Sorn's death. And getting tired of this quiz show. She kept her voice cool. "Yes, I'm alone, and I certainly didn't choose to come here."

Gris took another step closer. "And how did you get here? Your Indians, did they open a portal to send you here?"

"I have no idea how it happened, and even less how to get back where I belong. Do you—"

"That's very convenient," Gris interrupted, "but hardly believable."

Cele's voice was controlled, but edged with anger. Her eyes didn't waver from Gris's as she thrust her an-swers up into his face. "I really don't care what you believe. Do *you* know what happened? Do you have any better answers? I'm not any happier about me being here than you are. I'd like nothing better than to leave."

Cele looked from Gris to Kon Neven. "Can *you* open a portal, or whatever you call it? Can you help me go home?"

Kon Neven pushed away from the wall. "Thank you for coming," he said, as Gris faded into the background again.

As if I had a choice. Clearly, she'd been dismissed. Just as clearly, she would get no help from him. She inclined her head in an ironic imitation of courtesy, turned her back on the Kon, and left.

Her escort was waiting. She followed him, fuming at the arrogance bred by power. She hardly noted how he led her through the maze of hallways and stairs to her room, where Thora welcomed her return.

"How did you find the Kon? He's a fine man, is he not?" Thora asked.

Cele couldn't share Thora's enthusiasm, but she did agree that Neven was a handsome man, even at his age. "And don't forget Gris." Cele said, failing to keep the sarcasm out of her voice.

"That man." Thora shuddered. "He's a fine chamberlain, with a good mind for detail, but I've never been able to warm to him." Thora had a floor-length robe in her hands. "Shall I take you to the baths now, my lady?"

"Yes, please. The sooner the better." Celia slipped Sorn's gift from her arm and set it on the table.

"Is that not Sorn Sevondsson's?" Thora asked.

"Yes. He gave it to me in thanks for saving his life." Cele grimaced as tears unexpectedly welled up. "I didn't do a very good job of it, did I?"

Thora nodded as if she now understood something that had puzzled her. "It's beautiful work, done by his father, at Lord Dahleven's request."

"Oh!" Celia examined the gold mountain cat embossed on the silver cuff. "He told me how Sorn saved his life."

"Yes, thank Baldur. But such a gift should be worn here," Thora lightly touched Cele's forearm, "not above the elbow. That's not the place for it. If the cuff is too loose, you can press the edges tighter."

"Okay," Cele agreed, thinking that there were probably a lot of odd customs she was running afoul of just by being here. "But don't you think Dahleven would want this back? To remember Sorn?"

"No. He won't need a cuff to remember his sworn brother, and he'd want you to keep what Sorn has gifted you. Now, let's get you into that bath," Thora said, then hustled Cele out the door.

The bathing room was at the end of the hall. Towels hung on racks by a large round tub carved into the floor. It was the size of an eight-person spa. A ceramic pipe came out of the wall to it. A smaller, free-standing tub stood off to the side in a depression fitted with a drain. Thora hooked a box-shaped, open-ended extension onto the pipe and pulled a lever. A bubbling rumble preceded a flow of hot steaming water. The sharp tang of minerals assailed Cele's nostrils. The extension diverted the flow, and in short order the smaller tub was nearly full. Another shift of the lever and the water trickled to a stop.

Thora pulled a miniature pitcher from a shelf and unstoppered it. She poured a sweet smelling oil into the water, and a scent like lavender rose on the steam, masking the smell of minerals. "This should suit you, my lady." Then she rolled up her sleeves and donned a smock. Cele was already shucking her clothes.

The water was almost too hot. Almost. Cele stepped into the tub gingerly at first, then sank down to submerge herself up to her chin. The knots in her muscles melted in the heat.

Cele groaned. She was in heaven.

The heat soothed her aches and scrapes. She leaned back against the gentle slope of the tub, closed her eyes, and pushed the unpleasant interview with Kon Neven out of her mind.

Her respite was short lived.

"My lady?"

She reluctantly opened her eyes. Thora stood by with a brush and a pot of soap. Cele couldn't deny it, she needed scrubbing.

"I'll wash your hair first, my lady."

"I can manage."

Thora stiffened, as though she'd been struck.

"But it would be lovely if you helped me," Cele said, thinking that in this case she should sacrifice her self-sufficiency. She was rewarded by Thora's satisfied nod.

It *was* lovely. Thora wet Cele's hair with water carefully poured from a dipper, without getting a drop in her ears. Then she twice worked up a lather with a gentle massage. Cele let her head rest on the rolled edge of the stone tub as Thora rinsed the soap and sweat and dust away.

Without comment, Thora moved on to apply a soft brush to her arms and legs. She clucked over Cele's scrapes and bruises, but her light touch barely stung until she got to the gash on her leg. Then Cele jerked to sit upright.

"I'm sorry, my lady, but there's no help for it. It must be cleaned." Thora sounded more businesslike than contrite.

Cele nodded. "I know. Do what you have to."

Thora made quick work of it while Cele clenched her teeth at the pain. The renewed bleeding stopped before it could tint the water pink. Then Thora moved on to scrub Cele's back. The brush felt wonderful, scratching itches that surfaced now that relief was at hand. Cele let Thora rub just for the pleasure of it long after she must have been clean. Thora would have washed her front for her, too, but Cele insisted on doing that job herself.

When the water began to cool, Cele stood while Thora pulled the plug. Thora poured warm rinse water over her shoulders and down her body. Then the woman poured a final rinse of clear, *cold* water over her.

Cele's heart almost stopped, and she shrieked and lunged away, almost slipping. "What did you do that for? That's freezing!"

Thora gaped. "It's not healthy to go about with your pores open."

"Well, I like my pores open, thank you! Don't ever do that again."

Thora opened and shut her mouth, shaking her head. Cele shivered and stepped out of the tub into a warm, oversized towel the older woman held for her. The shock of the frigid water faded as the heat penetrated and she relaxed. The last of the water swirled out of the tub and down the drain in the floor beneath, taking a week's worth of grime with it.

Dahleven's stomach rumbled loudly. It sounded, and felt, like rocks grinding in his belly, but he didn't have time to eat. He'd satisfy his hunger later, with a bit of journey bread. He needed to get out onto the trails to look for his men before the sun westered any further. He had to know if any survived. Were they struggling home wounded? He couldn't take his ease until they, too, were safe.

His steps echoed down the stone corridor, slowing as he neared Sevond's apartments. Before he could go, he had an unpleasant task to complete. Telling Sorn's father that his son was dead.

Cele hadn't been back in her room for two minutes before there was a knock at the door. Thora stopped combing Cele's hair to admit another woman carrying a large, cloth covered tray. The delicious aroma made Cele's mouth water. The woman put the tray on the table near the window seat and left, bobbing a curtsey to Thora and a deeper one to Cele.

Thora lifted the cloth to reveal sausages, roasted meat, turnips, bread, steaming cider, and stewed fruit. Cele crooned an appreciative "Ooh," and took a sip of the cider. It had an alcoholic bite, and she complimented it, murmuring "Hmm," as she reached for a knife and the loaf of brown bread. There was enough on the tray to feed three strong men. "Sit down and have some, Thora. There's far more than I can eat here."

"Oh, no, my lady."

"Oh, yes. Please."

Thora sat, sitting awkwardly on the cushions across from Cele. A moment later, another knock caused Thora to pop up from her seat. This time two men entered, bearing a chest at the behest of Kon Neven, they said. Cele continued nibbling a sausage speared on a two-pronged fork as they left and Thora inspected the contents.

Thora's surprised "Well!" brought Cele over to share the discovery.

The chest held clothes in bright blues, greens, reds, and whites. They were accented with intricate embroidery at the collars and cuffs and hems, and a buttery soft suede tunic had an insignia stitched on the left breast similar to those present on clothing worn by Thora and the various servants, only this one was detailed with gold thread. The tight, even weave of the fabrics spoke eloquently of the quality of the clothes. At the bottom was a cloak of short black fur, lined with red velvet and closed with a ruby-eyed hawk-shaped clasp of finely worked gold.

"Oh, my." Then Cele remembered the fork in her hand and set it aside before she knelt next to Thora. "This is beautiful," she said, reaching to slide her hand down the smooth, slick fur.

Kon Neven's generosity made no sense to her in the wake of his chamberlain's interrogation. Was this his way of apologizing? She looked at Thora, hoping for an explanation, but the older woman merely looked at her with increased respect. *Maybe this is part of Kon Neven's plan.* No one who saw her dressed in these clothes could doubt Cele's standing and importance.

Important to whom? She wondered. *What game is Neven playing?*

chapter ten

CELE APPROACHED the dark wood door and hesitated, twitching the long green dress that fell heavily to her ankles. She would have felt elegant if the extra fabric around her feet hadn't made her nervous about tripping, especially on the stairs.

She forced herself to stop fidgeting. She'd asked Thora to bring her here, to Sorn's father, but now that she was at the point of speaking to him, reluctance slowed her steps. *What if no one has told him yet that his son is dead? What if I'm the first one? He shouldn't hear this from a stranger.* She almost turned around. *But someone should tell him about his son's bravery. He should know Sorn died saving my life.* She straightened her shoulders.

"Thanks, Thora. I don't know how long I'll be, and you probably have things to do. I'll catch you later."

Thora looked at her doubtfully. "My duty is to see to your needs, Lady Celia."

"That's up to you, but you don't have to wait. I can find my own way back." Thinking of the twists and turns of their route, Cele hoped that was true. She didn't wait to see what Thora would do, but turned and knocked firmly on the door.

A teenage boy answered. His face had the stunned look that people got when tragedy struck, colored with a faint hope that Cele brought some relief.

He knows.

Suddenly Cele wasn't sure what to say. "I—I'm Celia Montrose. I've come to see Sevond, Sorn's father."

The boy stepped aside. "I'm Hrolf, Master Sevond's apprentice. I'll take you to him." He shut the door and led her down a hallway. "The news has overset him. Lord Dahleven did what he could, but he couldn't stay."

Dahleven. She gave him points for speaking to Sevond promptly, but her anger made it feel like swallowing stones.

"I was learning how to plate silver when he came—Lord Dahleven, that is. I've never seen him like that. Well, I've never seen him that much at all, really, but he looked awful. I think my master knew before he spoke. The tools just fell from his hands. They went into the other room then, so I don't know what he said, but Master Sevond hasn't said a word to me since, even when I asked him if he wanted something to settle his nerves. He just waved his hand at me, and now he just sits there with that bracelet and I don't know what to do."

They stopped in front of an arched doorway. Within the small parlor, a stocky white-haired man sat slumped, turning a silver cuff over and over in his hands.

Hrolf continued, barely taking a breath. "I'm no comfort to him; perhaps you—well, there's probably not enough words in the world to ease such a hurt, but maybe you can help. I'm just his apprentice—he might talk to a lady."

Hrolf was babbling, made talkative by his distress. Cele had heard it before on the phones with the 911 calls she'd handled. He needed something concrete to focus on. She put her hand on his shoulder and in a calm, firm voice, directed him. "Hrolf, get us something warm to drink." The boy nodded and ran back down the hallway.

Cele entered the room and pulled a chair up close to Sevond, off to the side and facing him. "Master Sevond, I'm Celia Montrose. May I sit with you?"

The old gentleman slowly raised his eyes to Cele's, then nodded to the chair she had positioned. She sat, her knees nearly touching the side of his leg. Sevond's pale eyes were dry. Despite his stocky build, he looked fragile.

"Sorn saved my life. He was injured defending me." She'd hoped that once she got started she'd know what to say. Now that she was here, it was even harder than she'd feared. "I'm so sorry for your loss."

Sevond nodded and looked Cele directly in the eye. "Lord Dahleven told me. My son died an honorable death, and feasts in Valhalla. For that, I am proud. He was a good boy, and a good man." He looked down at the carved silver bracelet in his hands. His voice became tighter. "But I'm selfish. I would rather he lived."

"Me, too. He was my only friend here."

"He was my only *son*. The last of the precious children given me by my Bera. He had no children. My line, my family, died with him. Where are the grandchildren to comfort me in my age? They're buried with him on the far side of the mountains."

Cele had nothing to say to that. Her stomach felt like a giant stone. When her mother had died by painful inches two years ago, Cele had wished a quicker end for her. A heart attack, an accident, *anything* would have been better than watching her slow, agonizing decline. Sevond had been spared that kind of ordeal. But his son was still dead. At least her mother's death had been in the expected order of things. A child wasn't supposed to die before the parent.

Sevond's face was a tight mask. He'd hoped for grandchildren that would never come, now. His large, thick-fingered hands rested in his lap, gently cupping the silver cuff.

Cele groped for something to say. "That's a lovely bracelet."

Sevond lifted it so the pattern caught the light. Stylized horses danced around the circle. "Sorn made this. Many years ago. He did fine work. See here?" Sevond's finger traced a short line of metal beading. "Even the blankets are detailed. Much better than most apprentice work. But his father's craft didn't make his heart sing. It wasn't his fate, he said. He was Lord Dahleven's, from the time they were boys."

She ached for Sevond. He didn't blame her, but she felt responsible despite what Dahleven had said. She might not have killed Sorn, but if he hadn't been protecting her, if she hadn't fallen into this violent world, he might still be alive.

A commotion in the hallway brought Cele's eyes to the arch just as a young woman rushed in. Wisps of her pale blond hair straggled around her face and neck, escaping intricate braids and sticking to her flushed, tear-stained cheeks. She knelt on the other side of Sevond's chair and hugged his waist, burying her face in his side.

"Oh, Master Sevond. Oh!" She wept, her words muffled against his clothing.

"Aenid! Aenid, my dear. Oh, dear, Aenid," Sevond murmured, patting the young woman's back.

Cele leaned forward instinctively to comfort the girl, then pulled back. She didn't know her, and the girl obviously wanted Sevond's touch now, not some stranger's. It was hard to watch her sob and do nothing, and Cele wondered if she should leave and allow Sevond and Aenid to share their grief in private.

Sevond continued crooning to the weeping girl. "You

cared deeply for him I know, little one. He loved you, too. You were like a little sister to him."

Aenid moaned and cried harder. Cele's eyes grew moist. Her own grief for Sorn seemed shallow, yet she didn't feel foolish weeping for a man she had barely known.

Eventually, Aenid lifted her damp face to Sevond's. Sorn's father seemed a little more at peace. Perhaps he had needed to comfort someone else. Then Aenid reacted to Cele's presence. She straightened and wiped her face, smearing the moist evidence of her grief.

"My apologies—"

"I'm Celia Mon—"

They spoke at once, and stopped. Cele smiled at the overlap. Aenid raised an eyebrow.

"You go ahead." Cele nodded encouragement to the younger woman.

Aenid almost looked offended. Her voice was thickened with weeping, but she spoke with composure. "My apologies for intruding upon you. My grief robbed me of proper behavior, I fear. How did you know Sorn?"

"He was my friend. He saved my life. I'm Celia Montrose."

Aenid's eyes widened, as though startled. "Uncle Dahben spoke of you." Her voice was odd.

"Dahben?" Who was talking about her already?

Aenid gestured impatiently. "Uncle Dahleven. He said Sorn died because of you."

So, Dahleven does *blame me, despite what he said.*

Sevond gently rebuked the girl. "My dear, he died of wounds won in honorable combat."

"Yes, that's what he said." Aenid's puffy eyes were cold.

Clearly, Cele had overstayed her welcome. "I'm very sorry for your loss," she said, standing.

Aenid stood to face her.

"He was a kind person," Cele said, trying to make up for whatever she'd done to offend. "Sorn was my friend, though I only knew him a day."

A change in Aenid's face made Cele pause; the younger woman's gaze fell to the cuff Cele now wore on her forearm. Aenid's expression turned surprised, then thoughtful.

Unexpectedly, Cele found it hard to speak, her throat tight. Her mind blanked; she couldn't think of anything adequate to say. "I'm sorry." She left, heading down the long hall to the door. The boy was nowhere in sight.

Aenid caught up with Cele as she reached for the latch. "Wait."

Cele turned.

Aenid's tear blotched face blushed red to the roots of her pale hair. "You...you said Sorn was your *friend*."

"Yes. He made being lost in a strange place a little less terrifying for me." Cele remembered Fendrikanin's teasing. "I guess he adopted me as another one of his 'sisters.'"

Something in Aenid relaxed. "He...he wasn't in love with you, then?"

"What? No! Of course not!" Suddenly, Aenid's question shifted into focus. "You were in love with him," she said softly. "And he loved you, too, didn't he?"

Aenid's red face blanched white, which sharply delineated a scatter of freckles across her cheeks and delicate nose. Sweat sprang to her brow and upper lip, her eyes lost focus, and she wavered. Cele steadied the girl as she started to slump, and helped her over to a bench, pushing Aenid's head between her knees.

"Take a deep breath and blow it out slowly. That's right. Another one," Cele directed.

A minute later, Aenid pushed herself upright. She was still pale, but some color had returned to her cheeks.

"How long since you've eaten?" Cele asked, the professional part of her mind clicking in.

"Not long. I'd just finished my midday meal when Uncle Dahben..."

It wasn't low blood sugar then. It was probably just the shock of the news.

"I suppose I've been anxious since Sorn left."

A little bell rang in the back of Cele's mind. "Were you and Sorn...? Could you be pregnant?" *It could be something else*, her professional mind said. *Just the shock of Sorn's death.* But her instincts said otherwise.

A light came to Aenid's face. "I've been hoping. It's been over three months since my last courses, but I've never been regular. I've prayed that Freyr blessed us, but I've been afraid to believe it."

Cele blinked, nonplused. The father of her unborn child was dead, and Aenid was happy and eager rather than afraid of the prospect of raising a child alone. "How long were you and Sorn lovers?"

Aenid looked down at her hands, clasped tightly in her lap. "Five months. But I've loved him forever, I think."

"Sevond doesn't know about you and Sorn, does he?"

"No. Oh! I should tell him!" Aenid jumped up. "He'll be so happy!" Then she paused, a shadow darkening her joy. "*If* I am truly with child. If not, it would be cruel to add to his sorrow."

Cele nodded. A lot of early pregnancies ended in miscarriage. "Why did you keep your relationship with Sorn secret?"

"We were afraid Grandfather wouldn't approve."

"Why? What could anyone possibly have against Sorn?"

"He was only a carl—a freeman— and he wasn't landed." Aenid's voice said she thought she was stating the obvious. "Being with him wasn't a problem—I'm of age after all. But we wanted to marry, so we kept to ourselves. We were afraid that if Grandfather found out, he might try to arrange a marriage for me. There have been offers aplenty. I'm the Kon's granddaughter after all. At least, until the next election." Aenid's voice was bitter.

Aenid is Neven's granddaughter? And Dahleven is her uncle. And Neven's son. Cele wrenched her mind away from that fact. It didn't matter what or who he was. "Election?"

"For the Konship, of course."

"I thought that was hereditary."

Aenid stared at her as though she were demented. "The Jarldom is hereditary, but the Jarls elect the Kon of Nuvinland from among themselves every five years. Grandfather has been Kon for nearly twenty. Jarls's sons and brothers and cousins and nephews who don't even know me have asked for my hand, just because I'm the Kon's granddaughter. Sooner or later, he'll say yes to one of them. Sorn and I were hoping for later."

"Would he do that? Marry you off against your will?"

Aenid looked down at the floor. "No, probably not. But I don't think he would have let me marry Sorn, either."

"Well, he can hardly pressure you to marry now."

"Why not?" At Cele's raised eyebrows she added, "Many men are happy to have proof their betrothed wife is able to bear healthy children. But he'll probably wait until the baby is born."

Cele nodded, suppressing a frown. Was that all Aenid was to Neven, a brood mare to be sold to the highest bidder? "Are you all right now? You probably want to spend time with Sevond."

"Yes, I'm well." Aenid laid a hand on Cele's. "You won't tell Grandfather? Not until I'm sure?"

Cele clasped Aenid's hand in both of hers. "Don't worry. I won't tell Neven anything."

Thora waited for Cele in the hall. Cele's shoulders relaxed a little. She was grateful the older woman hadn't accepted dismissal. She really didn't want to test her memory of the way back to her room just then.

She followed her escort? maid? guard? down the hall, trying to memorize the twists and turns of their route. *Two doors on the right before the left-hand turn, then a gradual curve to the right and a flight of stairs.* All the while, that odd sensation she'd experienced before insisted that her destination was above her, first to the right, then ahead, then to the left as she and Thora wended their way through the halls. The keys hanging from Thora's waist chimed together as she moved briskly.

They turned onto the mezzanine, where there were more people. Cele had lost track of how she got there. She tried to mentally retrace the last few turns in their route but a servant bustled by with an armload of linen and Cele barely stepped out of the way in time to avoid a collision.

"Watch yourself, Bergid! You nearly knocked Lady Celia off her feet." Thora rebuked the girl.

The young woman stopped and turned, her face tight and apprehensive. She bowed as best she could with her arms full. Another servant carrying a chest sidled past, hugging the wall.

"No harm done," Cele said. The girl's face relaxed. She bowed again, then hurried on.

"That's hardly the point, my lady. The girl should be more careful. We've a houseful of nobility gathered for the Althing. If she doesn't watch herself, the person she runs into next may not be so generous as you."

As they turned to continue, Cele noticed a tall, dark-haired man without the ever-present hawk crest on his shoulder observing their exchange with the servant. Cele felt self-conscious. Did she appear so out of place that she drew attention?

Cele ran her hand over her skirt and gathered a fold of cloth in her fingers, savoring the soft hand of the forest green fabric of her dress. Intricate embroidery at the hem gave weight and substance to the skirt. She was beginning to get the hang of walking in it. Thora had braided her hair and pinned the looped and swirled plaits in an elaborate pattern similar to the styles on the better-dressed women they passed in the hallway. Cele knew she looked good, but the man's gaze was more watchful than admiring as they passed him leaning against the mezzanine railing.

Thora seemed not to have noticed him. "Come, my lady. We've got to get you dressed for the Feasting tonight." Thora led her up a flight of stairs and down another hall. "It's fortunate we got you in and out of the baths already. There will be a press in there now."

A feast? "What are you celebrating?"

Thora's eyes widened. "Fanlon's Feast, of course." At Cele's blank expression, Thora looked incredulous. "You've not heard of Fanlon? How could that be?"

They stopped in front of a door Cele recognized as her own. The older woman unlocked it with one of the keys hanging from her waist and ushered her in. "How is it you've never heard of Fanlon, my lady?"

Cele shrugged and shook her head. She didn't want to go into the whole story about her transit to this world again. "I'm from a long way away. Why don't you tell me?"

"No need. You'll hear the story tonight; the bards always tell it." Thora went to the closet where she'd stored Neven's gifts, then withdrew a red gown heavy with gold embroidery around the low neckline and hem. Slit sleeves of gauzy white cloth with gold and red decorative stitching flowed from the shoulders nearly down to the floor. "*This* will do very well, indeed." Obviously, Thora was still impressed with the elegance of the clothes Kon Neven had sent.

Cele reached behind her neck to unfasten the buttons closing her dress, but Thora brushed her hands away after laying the red dress on the bed.

Cele hadn't been dressed by someone since she was three, but remembering Thora's expression of hurt when Cele had said she'd bathe herself, she decided to let Thora have her way. To cover her awkwardness, she asked again, "Please, tell me about Fanlon and the Feast."

Apparently, Thora had only been waiting for a little encouragement. "Well, it won't be as pretty as the bards tell it, but I can acquaint you with his story.

"As everyone knows, Lord Fanlon was born nigh onto two hundred years ago, heir to the Jarl of this very province."

"Like Dahleven?"

"Yes. Just like Lord Dahleven. In that time, the Jarls were a contentious and quarrelsome lot, long descended from the adventurers who had left behind the settlements of the First Families in Nuheimjord."

"The First Families?"

Thora paused in her unbuttoning and spoke as though to a dim-witted child. "Those who crossed the portal from Midgard, some eight hundred years ago."

Excited, Cele turned to look at Thora. "Your people came through a portal? Gris said something about that. Could I go back that way?"

Thora shook her head. "No one has ever returned to Midgard, my lady. Who would want to?"

Disappointment washed away Cele's excitement. "I would."

"I've heard no tales of anyone passing back over the bridge, my lady." Thora's voice was kind as she turned Cele and resumed her unbuttoning. "But I'm not privy to the deeper secrets and magicks. You should ask Father Wirmund, the *Overprest*. He'll be at the feast tonight. He would know."

Cele nodded. "Please go on with your story."

"Well, those Jarls had Great Talents back then, and they could do such things as shape stone, call the winds, or bring the mortally wounded back from the brink of death. But they used their Talents in endless bickering and war.

"To increase their holdings and keep the Talents of their children growing stronger, they married carefully, choosing their wives for the sake of their Talents as though they were breeding sheep or cattle. New and stronger Talents sprang up, but not the wisdom to use them well." The multitude of tiny buttons undone, Thora slipped the dress off Cele's shoulders. "When one young Jarl came into his Talent and used it to shake the earth so that all in his opponent's province was destroyed, Lord Fanlon decided he must act.

"He called the Jarls together under the truce of the Althing. Then, with his own hand, Lord Fanlon dosed the guests with a sleeping draught, sacrificing his honor to save all he held dear. The Jarls fell into a deep sleep, and then he and his brother Arn, a priest of Baldur, combined their Talents. Lord Fanlon had the Viking Talent: Borrowing. Keeping was his brother's Talent. In a Great Working, Lord Fanlon took all the Great Talents from the Jarls and their men, and Arn contained them in crystal, hidden deep within the mountains. But to make the Keeping permanent, Arn had to die in the Working." Thora held the red dress for Cele to step into.

Cele paused with one leg raised. "Die! Why?"

"I told you, my lady. To make it last." Thora used the dress to gesture that Cele should step into it. "Great magic requires a great sacrifice. Otherwise, the Working would have failed when Arn's attention faltered, and the fractious Lords would again have had possession of their Talents."

Cele slipped her arms into the sleeves. Her horror must have shown on her face.

"Lord Fanlon was no more happy with the idea than you, and almost put an end to the plan when Arn told him this, but Arn insisted on his right to serve the needs of their people. Seeing no better path, Lord Fanlon was persuaded." Thora began threading the gold laces on the front of Cele's gown.

Cele tried to ignore the awkward feeling of being dressed like a doll. "What happened?"

"When the Jarls awoke and learned what had happened, their anger knew no bounds. They declared Fanlon Oathbreaker for violating the truce. Even his father called him Outcast when he learned what his sons had done. The Jarls drew arms, and in the fighting, Lady Sigrid, Lord Fanlon's beloved wife, was mortally wounded." Thora paused again, pulling tight the gold ribbons.

Cele was about to urge her on when the maid continued.

"Seeing this, the Jarls expected Lord Fanlon to release the Talents, for all knew of his passion for her, and one of their number had possessed the Talent of Healing those near death.

"Fanlon held his beloved in his arms as her life slipped away, drop by drop. At first, they clamored for the release of their Talents, promising the restoration of his wife and forgiveness of his betrayal. He looked at them with dry-eyed grief carved on his stony face. 'No man has the right to buy his happiness with the sorrow of others,' he told them. 'Our people deserve the peace and safety we have taken from them with our endless wars. They shall have some measure of it now.' The Jarls fell silent, and when Sigrid released her last breath, the

Jarls were stunned by Fanlon's sacrifice."

Cele blinked away tears.

"One by one, the Jarls swore to support the Alliance, though it took some of them a year or more to come to it. And though he had violated the truce of Althing, none called for the Outcasting of Lord Fanlon. Within a year, he took his father's place as Jarl of Quartzholm, and then as Kon of Nuvinland.

"Lord Fanlon, realizing that eventually Great Talents might develop again, and that even normal Talents could be used to great harm, did another Great Working, his last. He poured his Viking Talent into another crystal and bequeathed it to the priests of Baldur to use for taking the Talents from those who misuse them. But he feared even a priest might be led astray by the power held in the single crystal, so he shattered it, and in doing so, died to make it permanent. The shards and the power were separated and shared among the priests.

"Now, when someone is judged by the Althing to be Outcast, a group of priests must gather and work together to take the Talent from the offender.

"And that is how Lord Fanlon became known as 'Fanlon the Great.' Since that day, the Jarls have married for political alliance, wealth, and love, but not to breed their Talents." Thora tied the golden ribbons and tucked the ends down between Cele's breasts.

Cele felt a little squeezed.

"Now bend over and plump yourself, my lady," Thora urged.

Cele did as commanded, lifting her breasts to fill the low neckline.

"The Althing is always opened, now, with a Feast of Fanlon, honoring him who brought us to together in Alliance," Thora finished, putting a drop of fragrance between Cele's breasts.

Cele felt like her bosom was being offered on a platter. "That's quite a story."

"It's a proud heritage. Lord Dahleven is heir to a great Family."

"Dahleven is descended from Fanlon?"

Thora looked at her as if she were pulling a poor joke. "Of course! Through Kon Neven and sixteen generations of Jarls."

No wonder Dahleven thought he had the right to play around with her. He was a prince, or whatever they called the son of a Jarl or a Kon. IIe thought he could get away with whatever he wanted. He probably could.

Cele turned in front of a mirror and the hem of her dress swirled around her ankles, revealing her matching red slippers. Though the clothing here looked strange compared to what people wore in Tucson, it certainly looked good on her. No one would look at her legs and think she was half-dressed now. Her breasts, maybe. *Dahleven, eat your heart out.*

"The red looks well on you, my lady," Thora said. "You'll not be left sitting when the music begins."

"Thank you." *Dancing? I can barely walk in these skirts.*

A brisk tattoo summoned Thora to the door. She opened it a modest amount, then wider as she curtsied the visitor in. "Lord Ragnar! Be welcome."

A young man about Cele's age stepped into her room and lifted Thora out of her curtsy. He wore an embroidered gray velvet tunic over a satiny gray shirt with a high collar and full sleeves. His dark gray pants were tucked into high gray boots. A small bag of rich purple velvet hung from a wide purple ribbon around his neck, the only color on his person. "It's Ragni, Thora, as you know all too well. I've told you often enough. You don't want to give Lady Celia the wrong impression of me, do you? 'Lord Ragnar' sounds so pompous."

The tall young man turned his smile on Cele. He was

slimmer, but something about the shape of his gray eyes and the cut of his high cheekbones echoed Dahleven's. He came forward and honored her with a slight bow. His gaze hesitated for a moment on Sorn's cuff, but then he focused his attention on her face. "Lady Celia Montrose, it is a pleasure to meet you. If I'd known there were such treasures to be found in the drylands, I would have gone there myself, rather than leaving such adventures to my brother." He lightly touched her right arm above the elbow.

For some reason Ragni's gesture felt suggestive. "Your brother?" Cele shifted, breaking the contact. Ragni withdrew his hand and she wondered if she'd imagined the feeling of familiarity.

"Dahben. Lord Dahleven, rather. I suppose I shouldn't call him by his childhood nickname."

"That's what Aenid called him."

"She's the one who gave it to him. She couldn't say Dahleven when she was little. 'Dahben' was the best she could manage, and the rest of us adopted it. We should drop it I suppose; he *will* be Jarl someday, and 'Lord Dahben' doesn't quite have the ring of authority, does it?"

Cele didn't have a response to that, but she found herself smiling at Ragni's breezy manner.

"When did you meet Aenid?" Ragni lifted a brow in an expression much like his brother's.

"This afternoon, when I went to visit Sevond."

Ragni lost his air of amusement. "That's a sad thing, for Sevond to lose Sorn on top of all his other losses. It was well done of you to go to him. And Aenid was there, too, you say? She was rather fond of Sorn. I expect she'll feel his death nearly as much as Dahleven will."

"More, I'd say," Cele said before she caught herself. It wasn't her place to allude to Aenid's situation, especially since Aenid's family clearly had no idea how far things between her and Sorn had progressed.

Fortunately, Ragni misunderstood. "You don't understand. Dahleven and Sorn were sworn brothers."

Cele thought back to Dahleven's stoic behavior. "He seemed to handle Sorn's death pretty well."

"He won't show it, of course. He can't." Ragni paused and shook his head as though shaking free of the unhappy subject. His smile returned. "I am here to escort you to the Feast, my lady. May I have the pleasure of your company?" he finished with a little bow and the offer of his hand.

The great hall had been set with two rows of tables down the length of the room, on either side of the fire pit. The setting looked like something out of a costume drama. Servants hurried up and down the aisles, replacing empty pitchers and carafes on each table with full ones.

A table with three chairs had been set up on the dais and another much longer one was below it, both crosswise to the length of the hall.

As Ragni escorted her into the chamber through an opening near the dais, a din of voices enveloped her. Cele scanned the revelers for Dahleven. Color flashed everywhere, but she didn't see him or his wife among the throng. She wasn't sure if she was disappointed or relieved. She knew she looked hugely better than she had the last time he'd seen her, with her scratched legs and dirty face, and wanted to show off a little, but she didn't want to confront him in front of all these people.

Cele became suddenly and uncomfortably aware that her entrance with Ragni was causing a stir. People glanced at her, leaned to speak to their neighbors, then looked back at her. Cele's blush made her feel warm, and she was glad only the center section of the huge tri-part firepit was aflame. Delicately wrought oil lamps hanging from tall stands added more heat. The smell of resinous wood burning overlay everything, despite the firehoods drawing the smoke upward. Cele took a deep breath and tried to relax.

Ragni gave her an encouraging wink and led her to the long table below the dais. He seated her next to a man dressed in green velvet. Cele remained acutely aware of the many eyes upon her and tried not to squirm under the scrutiny. They were probably wondering who the unknown upstart was, and why was she being seated so highly. Cele wondered the same thing.

Ragni made the introductions. "This is my sister Lady Ingirid," Ragni indicated an auburn haired woman just beyond the man in green, "and her husband, Lord Jon."

Cele smiled and nodded. "It's a pleasure to meet you."

"Lady Celia Montrose." Ragni finished the introduction.

Lord Jon tilted his head and cast a sideways glance at Ragni before taking another swallow of wine. "Still picking up Dahleven's castoffs, Ragni?"

Ingirid laid her hand on Jon's arm, but he twitched it off.

Cele flinched inwardly, stung by the volley aimed at her escort. *Is that what they think me? Dahleven's used-up mistress?* She felt Ragni stiffen beside her, but his voice was light as he addressed Ingirid. "You're letting his leash get a bit long, aren't you, dear sister?"

Jon turned sharply to Ragni and Cele leaned back in her chair between them. She didn't want to be here. Running battles with the Renegades was bad enough; now she was in the middle of familial warfare. She wanted to go home. *Where are my ruby slippers?*

Jon opened his mouth, but suddenly the hall fell silent and he swallowed whatever he'd been about to say. All attention turned to the dais. Ragni stood and pulled out her chair. Cele rose along with everyone else, as Kon Neven entered the hall.

chapter eleven

Cele wasn't sure what it was about him, but she couldn't help but admire Neven's confidence and authority. A woman of about his age walked beside him, her hand resting lightly on his arm, but Cele didn't notice what she looked like; she couldn't take her eyes off the Kon. Even allowing for the effect of standing on the dais, he seemed taller and more powerful than he had earlier in the afternoon. Gold embroidery accented the deep forest green of his tunic, seeming almost to glow with its own light. His appearance made the finery and jewels of the others in the hall seem shabby by comparison. Despite her anger at his bullying, when he looked at her, Cele felt eager to hear his words.

"Be welcome to this house," Neven said into the attentive silence. Though his words had the tone of ritual, Cele felt he really meant them as his rich, resonant voice flowed into her like warm honey. She felt whole and safe, as though she belonged and was truly welcome.

"We come together for the Althing, to fulfill our responsibilities in governing the Jarldoms and provinces of Nuvinland. But first, we feast. First, we share meat and ale. First we honor Fanlon and the Alliance, for which he sacrificed all he held dear, and which we come together each year to serve." Neven held aloft a drinking horn chased with silver and gold. "To Fanlon!"

"To Fanlon!" Everyone shouted, and Cele joined in, lifting her cup.

"The Alliance!" Neven drank again.

"The Alliance!" Cele took another swallow of ale, though the brew's bite was stronger than she liked.

Neven set his horn in its stand and poured a libation into the goblet at an empty space to his left, then he lifted his drink again. "To our hosts, unseen, but not forgotten."

Cele lifted her tankard again, though she didn't know who they were honoring.

"Now, be merry! Eat your fill, slake your thirst!" Neven lifted his drinking horn in salute to the assembly and drank deeply as the silence evaporated under the onslaught of shouts and salubrious toasts.

Ragni assisted Cele with her heavy chair as she once again sat with her back to the dais. No one faced her across the table, so she had a clear view of the people in the hall, and they had a clear view of her. She tried not to notice the covert glances of the other guests, but it was harder to ignore the occasional stare. She stared back, but the startled looks on the gawkers' faces made it clear that she was committing a social error. *Is everyone who sits at the high table on display, or is it just me?* She stopped returning the looks and tried to ignore them.

Cele opened her mouth to ask about Neven's last toast, but Lord Jon spoke first.

"He poured it out in full measure tonight, didn't he?" Jon's voice barely carried over the din, as servants began bringing in food. Though his face was puffy and sallow, Cele could see he'd once been a handsome man. His red-rimmed eyes held a combination of bitterness and admiration.

What's he talking about?

Ingirid put her hand on her husband's arm again. Jon left it there, ignoring her. She was still a lovely woman, but the tired, pinched look around her eyes and mouth marred her beauty.

"Kon Neven," Jon said to Cele's confused look. "His Talent is strong—and he doesn't stint in its use, does he?"

Jon's attempt at clarification didn't help. Cele looked at Ragni, who leaned forward to speak to the older man. His smile didn't reach his eyes. "He uses it to good purpose, does he not? As we should all use our Talents." Settling back into his chair, he added in an undertone, "Those who have Talents worthy of use, that is."

Lord Jon evidently didn't hear. He seemed to lose interest in the conversation and turned back to his drink.

Apparently Ragni didn't know she was Talentless. If some Talents didn't get much respect, how much less would he think of her for not having one at all? She remembered the pitying looks of Dahleven and Sorn. The thought chafed—she liked Ragni. She didn't want him to think less of her over something so unimportant.

Cele looked at him, and Ragni gave her an encouraging smile.

She noticed that the seat to the right of Neven's wife was empty. "Who's supposed to sit there?" she asked Ragni.

"That's Dahl's place. He should have been here, but he couldn't rest until he knew how his men fared."

Ghav. Falsom. Kep. Fender. In her mind's eye, she saw Halsten fall, an arrow in his back, and saw the blood pouring from Sorn's belly. Were the others dead, too?

Her thoughts must have shown in her face. Ragni touched her hand. "Don't worry, he'll find them. They are fine warriors all. They're probably strolling home even now, singing ribald songs off-key. Tonight is for feasting and celebration. You can't help them with your frown."

The servants arrived at the front of the hall with platters of meat and bread, spring vegetables, dried fruit and cheeses. The aromas of well-cooked food piqued Cele's hunger, despite her filling lunch. When the first platter, laden with succulent sliced meat, was held in front of her, her mouth began to water. She hesitated. Should she help herself before Ragni did? Before a prince? But he gestured for her to go ahead.

Just as she was about to place a thick red slice of meat on her platter, Ragni leaned close and spoke just loud enough for her to hear, "You should serve me first."

Belatedly she noticed that at all the tables, the women served the men on their left before filling their own plates. Some of them were staring, apparently shocked by her faux pas of slighting a prince. Cele's face burned. *So, women serve the men here. How delightfully archaic. What other charming customs do they have?*

"We do things differently where I'm from," Cele said, laying the meat on Ragni's plate.

Ragni winked, a smile in his eyes. "Different steps for different dances. You'll learn."

"That depends. I hope to go home before too long." Cele shrugged. "In the meantime, we have a saying: When in Rome, do as the Romans do."

"There is wisdom in that."

Cele cut and speared a piece of meat with her fork, then paused. "Do I have to wait until you eat first, too?"

Ragni chuckled. "No."

Cele took a bite. She didn't recognize the meat, but it

was flavorful and moist, tangy with spices. She was still feeling positive about Neven's address, but Jon's comment nagged at her. Speaking just for Ragni's ear, she asked, "What did Lord Jon mean about Kon Neven's Talent?"

Ragni paused, his lip curling in disdain. He replied in the same private tone Cele had used. "My esteemed brother-by-marriage is gifted with somewhat less Talent than most, and his lack distresses him—and those around him. Father's Talent runs strong. Such things cause Jon's bitterness to rise, I'm afraid, like scum on a cesspit."

"But what is Kon Neven's Talent? What did he do that upset Jon?"

Ragni looked at her hard. "Didn't you feel it? Father's Talent is Presence. When he chooses to use it, few can attend to anything but him, and all feel the truth of his words. Even when he doesn't consciously exercise it, he tends to draw attention. Few are immune to it, but those of us who live closest to him are least affected. Did you truly not feel it?"

"Oh I felt it, all right." *Mind control*? A skill every despot would love to have. The warm, welcome feeling she'd been enjoying suddenly chilled and frightened her. "I just didn't know what it was."

Ragni must have sensed the change in her. "He doesn't use it for ill. It's a powerful Talent, but he can't change the basic core of a person, or the way a person feels and thinks for long, especially since all know of it." He smiled at her. "He truly meant only to welcome his guests to the Feast. He had no darker purpose than that."

Except, perhaps, to lull everyone into a false sense of security. But if Neven was controlling her mind, how was she able to doubt him?

Cele searched Ragni's smiling face. He was telling

her the truth—as he knew it. At least *Ragni* wasn't lying to her. Not as far as she could tell, anyway. *Unless deception is his Talent.* She'd believed Jeff, too, when he said he loved her. Her track record in judging a man's character wasn't the best. She'd thought of Dahleven as a stand-up guy, too—before she'd seen him hugging his wife and child.

Ragni was still smiling at her. She couldn't help but smile back. She'd reserve judgment—for now.

The next platter held a dense white fish, and Cele pointedly served Ragni first—the best portion. She was intensely aware that other people in the hall were watching, waiting to see what mistake she would make next. She wasn't used to being on display like this and wanted to hide.

"Very good. You're learning," he said, a teasing gleam in his eye.

Cele relaxed a little. Ragni obviously wasn't too concerned about protocol.

When the third course arrived, with fancifully decorated roasted fowl, they made a game of it: she pretended to search for the choicest morsel while first offering him the tailings; he played at pompous refusal.

By the end of the meal, Cele felt replete and almost relaxed. She couldn't quite ignore her awareness of being scrutinized by the roomful of Nuvinland nobility, but for most of the meal, Ragni had distracted her from feeling too self-conscious. The information about Neven's Talent remained troublesome, but for the moment she had no sense of anything influencing her beyond the satisfaction of excellent food and drink, and Ragni's charm.

The bitter ale was replaced by flagons of sweet wine as portions of soft white cheese were offered with flatbread. The cacophony of conversation had dimmed somewhat during the meal. Now, with appetites sated, the noise level rose again. As servants cleared the tables of their empty plates, Cele spoke softly to Ragni, adopting a sincere expression. "I'm glad to see you have such a good appetite, my lord." She paused as Ragni looked at her curiously. "Thora told me the tale of Fanlon. I'll take your clean plate as assurance that *this* meal wasn't drugged."

Ragni's eyes widened for an instant, then narrowed as the joke struck home. In an exaggeratedly innocent voice he replied, "Well, *mine* wasn't."

Cele made a face and Ragni laughed.

A man with a rainbow of ribbons pinned by small golden brooches to his black tunic entered the hall and bowed first to Kon Neven, then to the second table, and finally to the rest of the assembly. The company hushed.

"Greetings to you all, Jarls and ladies, and ladies who are Jarls." The man bowed to a plump, middle-aged woman with a determined jaw.

Cele's attention increased. *So women can be Jarls.*

The man went on. "I am Eirik, skald and soothsayer. Tonight we sit full and satisfied at Kon Neven's table, but we gather to remember those who feasted here before, and the man who brought them together in Alliance."

The skald's silken voice drew Cele into his tale of Fanlon. His story captivated her, even though she'd heard the gist of it before. Eirik convinced her that no man had ever possessed truer vision or greater love for his people than Fanlon. No one had ever sacrificed so much. When he finished his tale, and paused to drink deeply from his tankard, the room seemed empty in the absence of his voice.

A moment later, Eirik compelled her attention again. "Now let us well remember Brynjolf Gunnarsson. Tall as a ship's mast, and as strong, he brought honor to his family and prosperity to his people. Generous was he, gifting good men well, though his meager stores were shrunken. By such good deeds a man assures himself of beloved companions when need arises.

"Long ago, the people of Greenland, in Midgard, suffered the whims of the false Kon of Norway."

Greenland? Norway? Cele's already keen attention sharpened.

"Few ships had they for the whale-road, and little means to find and trade the ivory. Loki's arts had taken the sun south, so that even in summer the ground remained barren, and ice choked the sea. Brynjolf's people hungered and brought their starving cattle within doors for shared warmth."

The skald's rich voice captured Cele's attention. She was *there*; she could *see* the people of Greenland struggling to survive.

"The people despaired," the skald continued. "The priests of the White Christ pronounced the unending winter a punishment because some of the people still followed the old gods. By this suffering, they said, the people would be purified and saved.

"But wise Brynjolf spoke against the priests. He remembered the tales told by his grandfather, of a rich land to the west where the wheat sowed itself and the grapes grew heavy on wild vines. Freyr would lead his people back to that land where harvests burst their storage sheds and game was plentiful, if only they would again honor the Vanir god.

"The priests denounced Brynjolf as mad for believing such tales.

"'Mad, am I?' said Brynjolf. 'The very beams of this house came from Vinland.'

"Then they pronounced him evil.

"'The only evil here,' said he, 'is the heavy hand of a false Kon who robs us of the means to feed ourselves, and the evil whisperings that turn us from the old, true gods.'

"Finally they announced him possessed.

"'Possessed, am I?' he answered them. 'Yes! Possessed by a hunger to make us a free people again!'

"But the lies of the priests turned the bones of some to water. 'Vinland is filled with savage Skraelings,' they said, 'who drove our fathers away not once, but three times.'

"Brynjolf roared, impatient with such faintheartedness. 'The Skraelings are on our own shores, and yet we live. Even if the Vinland breed is fiercer, would it not be better to live and die fighting than to starve here in the cold like old women and puling babes?'"

Cele shouted along with the rest of the audience as it erupted into shouts of approval of Brynjolf's words.

When the crowd quieted, Eirik continued. "Many vowed to join Brynjolf, but others did not, listening instead to the priests of the White Christ. 'This is but a test of our faith,' they said. 'Remain here, steadfast, and the White Christ will reward you abundantly. The ground will warm and the grasses grow again. Your cattle will fatten and increase.'

"Brynjolf bade the Geistlig, the seer of the true gods, to cast the runes, and the stones spoke true. 'The cold will grow, and the Frost Giants will take the land,' they said. 'Those who hunger now will starve, unless they follow the Bright Road.'

"The priests denounced the Speaking Stones and those who listened to them, but Brynjolf cared not. He gathered those of stout heart and embarked with the last of their cattle and sheep and geese for Vinland, bidding farewell to the priests and those who listened to them.

"Freyr smoothed the way, speeding their ships with a brisk wind over a smooth sea. On the fifth day, the brave-hearted folk with Brynjolf found Vinland just as he had promised, and there he cast his dais beams ashore." The gold brooches on the skald's black tunic winked in lamplight as he mimicked the gesture of casting the decorative panels into the water. "As they followed the beams aground, the truth of Freyr's blessing was proved. On a hill above a fertile valley, just beyond their landing place, they found an altar to Freyr awaiting them: a great round stone, balanced on three. Praising Freyr's gifting, they built their houses in the meadow below.

"That year their cattle grazed and fattened, their sheep grew more wool than could be spun, and fish jumped willfully into the Northmen's nets. The cheeks of the women grew round again, and their bellies filled with babes.

"When at last the Skraelings skulked from their hiding places, Brynjolf greeted them with gifts. These the Skraelings greedily accepted. The next season the Skraelings returned, wanting to trade for the strong blades and spears forged by the brave Northmen. Wise Brynjolf said them nay, but offered milk to drink. At the first taste the Skraelings delighted, and offered furs in trade for skins of milk. This Brynjolf accepted, and the Skraelings left with all they could carry.

"But the Skraelings in the new land were wretches indeed. Some weeks later they attacked Brynjolf's folk. Not facing them bravely in honest battle, but lurking in darkness and shame, accusing honest Brynjolf of black arts even as they died."

Cele cringed at the misunderstanding. Native Americans had no enzymes to digest milk. It would have tasted wonderful—and made them horribly ill. They would have thought they'd been poisoned.

"Thus began the season of fighting for the brave Vinlanders, always on watch for theft and fire and murder," Eirik continued.

"At the dawn of their third spring, as day and night

hung balanced, Brynjolf went to Freyr's altar alone. Though stout of heart, his people were tired from their long vigil against the Skraelings. Brynjolf longed to gift them peace as well as plenty. Thus, he petitioned Freyr, god of fruitfulness and peace, to lead them to a land free of strife.

"Three nights and days Brynjolf waited there for a sign. On the third dawn, he heard a loud crashing and saw a great boar rushing toward him. Though weak from hunger and sleeplessness, Brynjolf drew his mighty sword, but the boar didn't charge him. Instead, it leapt over the altar. In the instant the creature crested the stone it vanished, its bristling coat flashing gold. Then wise Brynjolf knew the beast was Gullinbursti, Freyr's steed.

"His petition answered, Brynjolf returned to his people and told them what he'd seen. 'Bravely you followed me to this land of plenty,' he said to them. 'Follow me once more, to the place which Freyr has shown me, where no Skraeling will challenge our peace.'

"Again, the brave Northmen heeded his words. They gathered their cattle and sheep and horses, took their new sons in their arms, and followed Brynjolf to Freyr's altar. Bold Brynjolf took his fair wife Groa's hand, and together they climbed over the altar.

"The world around them vanished, replaced by the rainbow colors of the Bright Road swirling about their feet."

"Oh!" Cele exclaimed softly, remembering the kaleidoscope of color when she'd fallen. This was the portal Gris and Thora had mentioned. Ragni glanced at her curiously, but she leaned forward, eager to hear what the skald would say next.

"With a flash of light, Brynjolf and Groa stepped into their new home. Behind them, no altar stood to Freyr, for this was Alfheim, and the Vanir needed none here.

In moments, all the brave Vinlanders had followed. Thus came our forefathers to this land, gifted us by Freyr's promise, and Brynjolf's boldness."

The attentive silence shattered into shouts and cheers and stamping feet.

Cele stared as the skald took his bows and left. Dahleven had sworn by Odin and mentioned Thor and the Vanir; she'd even thought of him as a Viking. Eirik's story had just confirmed it. *Norway, Greenland, Vinland.* By their own account, these people had come from her world. Or their ancestors had. *And they got here the same way I did.*

Distracted by her thoughts, Cele barely noticed when musicians entered the gallery above the arched entrance and began a lively tune, but she could hardly ignore the servants clearing away the tables. Neven and his wife rose and went to stand in an area opened by their removal. Guests of the highest rank formed two rows with the Kon and his wife at the head. The music slowed and the dancers began to move in a complicated pattern of traded partners and positions, with men and women weaving in and standing out of the pattern at various times. At intervals, everyone stamped or skipped, clapped their hands or clasped hands with another.

Cele stared, rapt with concentration, trying to follow the form of the dance. She thought she was beginning to understand the order of the figures when the last movement resolved itself once again into two rows, each dancer facing their original partner. They paid courtesy to one another and drifted back to their seats. No sooner had the floor cleared, when another, expanded group formed a huge ring.

Ragni pushed back his chair and stood holding out his hand. "My lady?"

The relaxing effect of the wine barely dulled Cele's alarm. "I don't know the steps!"

"This is an easy one. Just watch the other women and do what they do."

Cele started to shake her head.

"When in Rome...?" Ragni grinned, tossing her own words back at her.

She groaned and conceded, letting Ragni lead her to join the others. She tried to move gracefully in the unfamiliar long dress and ignore the fact that people were watching her with renewed interest and speculation. Then Ragni dropped her hand and bowed to her. All her concentration focused on imitating the other women, gathering and lifting some of her skirt in both hands, and moving as they did. She didn't want to look clumsy and ignorant of what was obviously a basic skill here. Fortunately, Ragni was right. The steps were simple, and after a couple of slight bobbles at the beginning, Cele found herself caught up in the pattern as she wove in and out of the line of men facing her, moving in the opposite direction. When the music ended, she was smiling and exhilarated. "That was fun!"

Ragni took her hand and held it close to his chest. "Dancing agrees with you." He brushed the knuckles of his other hand above her elbow as he had earlier.

It felt like a kiss and Cele blushed, enjoying Ragni's flirtation. Then a nasty thought surfaced. "You're not married, are you?"

Ragni smiled and shook his head. "I could hardly hide a wife from you here at the Feast!" He nodded at the dancers forming for the next dance. "Would you care to try another?"

Cele laughed, relieved her suspicion had proved groundless, and shook her head. "No, thank you. I was lucky this time." But she let Ragni retain her hand. She enjoyed his playful attentions; the admiring look in his eye buoyed her confidence. She felt a twinge of regret he wasn't his brother, then suppressed the feeling.

As they turned to their seats, a gray-haired man with a face deeply seamed by wrinkles called to Ragni. He was dressed in the same gray as her escort, and had a similar purple bag hanging around his neck. Cele felt Ragni's posture become more reserved, but he didn't release her hand.

"You must introduce me to your lovely lady, Father Ragnar," the older man said.

Father Ragnar! She'd been flirting with a *priest*?

Ragni nodded a bow and his tone became formal. "It would be my pleasure. This is Lady Celia Montrose. Lady Celia, may I introduce my sponsor and superior, Father Wirmund."

Somehow, Cele managed a normal tone of voice. "Father Wirmund." She offered her hand to him, using the gesture as an excuse to withdraw it from Ragni's grasp. "It's a pleasure." Then she remembered. *This is the guy Thora said I should talk to.*

The older man took her hand gently by the fingertips, not like a handshake, reminding Cele again that she was a fish out of water. His skin felt cool and papery. "Would you join me for this dance, my lady?" It was obvious despite his mild voice that Father Wirmund expected his request to be accepted.

Cele hesitated. Something about his gimlet gaze convinced her he didn't wish her well. She didn't want to insult him; he might be the only person in the place who could help her get home, but she didn't want to be around him any longer than she had to. Cele glanced at Ragni, unsure of how to respond.

"Lady Celia only just arrived in Quartzholm today, after a long journey, and is fatigued, I fear. She just refused me another dance, did you not, my lady?"

"Indeed, I did."

The look in Father Wirmund's mild brown eyes chilled Cele. "What a shame you used the last of your

strength before we met. You must sit and rest, my lady."
He bowed. "Father Ragnar, I would speak with you,
when you have escorted the lady to her chair." He inclined his head to Cele. "Until later," he said, and turned
away.

Cele relaxed as Father Wirmund removed his scrutiny. "Thank you. But I'm afraid you're in trouble now,"
Cele said softly to Ragni.

"It won't be the first time—or the last," Ragni said
with a smile tickling the corners of his mouth. "And I
only told the truth."

"Speaking of the truth—"

"Lord Ragnar, well met!" The tall man who'd hailed
Ragni had nearly white blond hair and his pale blue eyes
were startling in his deeply tanned face. "Pray introduce
me to your companion."

"Lady Celia Montrose, may I present Lord Ingdall,
heir to Lord Yngvar of Kyst-havn."

Lord Ingdall smiled and bowed his head. Cele returned him what she hoped was a passable curtsey of
the appropriate depth.

"You are the most exciting thing at the Feast, Lady
Celia. A new face at the high tables is a rarity for us. Did
you come from Nuheimland? Or one of Nuvinland's
daughter settlements?"

Cele had the feeling that Ingdall was asking more
than she understood, and glanced at Ragni. He just
smiled and made no move to intervene. *Honesty is the
best policy.* She smiled. "Neither, Lord Ingdall." *Guess
again.*

Lord Ingdall didn't seem upset by her obscure answer. "A lady of mystery. Doubly so, since you didn't
come through either Kyst-havn's port or Lord Ozur's.
How did you come to Nuvinland, my lady?"

I fell out of the sky. "I walked, my lord."

Lord Ingdall laughed, baring perfect teeth. "Very

well, keep your mystery. But you hardly need it to increase your allure. Would you dance with me, my lady?"

And let you continue grilling me? No, thank you. "I'm sorry, I'm quite tired, Lord Ingdall, and I've already declined Father Wirmund. Please excuse me."

Lord Ingdall pursed his lips in exaggerated disappointment. "Another time, then." He nodded a bow to them both. "Lord Ragnar, Lady Celia."

They made their way haltingly back to their seats, stopped frequently as more people sought to meet her. Each new person brought an assault of questions. Most of the questions were the same, just variations on the theme. Having answered them once, Cele had her replies ready, but she dreaded a query that she couldn't evade. She didn't want to broadcast that she was from out of this world; she was already uncomfortably the center of too much attention.

One of the curious was the plump, determined woman whom the skald had honored as the Lady Jarl. Her name was Solveig, and she spoke with more genuine warmth than the others seeking Cele's acquaintance. Most of her inquisitors made her nervous, though they didn't radiate the subtle hostility that Father Wirmund had. Instead, it felt as though they were quizzing her on a subject she'd skipped all semester. Lady Solveig, on the other hand, was friendly. As they parted, she said, "Please call upon me while I'm here in Quartzholm." And Cele felt the older woman meant it sincerely.

Though nonplused by her unexpected popularity, Cele had not forgotten what she'd meant to say to Ragni after parting from Father Wirmund, and her temper sparked to life. She stopped him as they came to their chairs. "How could you tease me that way?"

It was Ragni's turn to look perplexed. "What do you mean?"

Cele's temper flared hotter. *Is every man a jerk?*

"You flirted outrageously with me all night! And you're a priest!"

Ragni almost sputtered. "You're a lovely woman. This could hardly be the first time a man has flirted with you."

"It's the first time *a priest* has flirted with me!" Cele said in a sharp whisper.

"My priesthood could hardly be a surprise to you. I wear the sign of my office clearly." Ragni touched the purple bag lying on his chest. "And what objection do you have to priests?" He looked sharply at her, lifting one eyebrow in the same manner as his father and brother.

"I don't object to priests in general. Just to those who flirt when they're supposed to be celibate."

"Celibate!" Ragni spoke too loudly and a nearby couple turned to look. He lowered his voice again. "Where did you get such an appalling idea?"

Several awkward seconds ticked by as Ragni's words sank in. Cele felt her face redden as understanding blossomed and her anger turned to embarrassment. She'd assumed too much—again. She should have known, with everyone talking about Odin and Freyr and Thor, that he wasn't a *Catholic* priest. "Priests in my world have to be celibate," she said in a small voice. She remembered suddenly that there were Anglican and Episcopalian priests, in addition to Catholics. "Most of them, anyway."

"How unnatural! Baldur doesn't require his priests to be celibate. He's married himself. None of the honest pleasures of life are denied to us, Celia." His voice softened. "Not flirtation, nor what often follows." Ragni gently touched her upper arm again.

She shifted slightly away. She understood the situation better now, but the pleasure had gone from his touch. "I'm sorry I misjudged you." *I seem to be doing a lot of that lately. At least I didn't accuse him of attempted rape like I did Dahleven.* "You'd better go talk with Father Wirmund, before you get into any more trouble."

Ragni's expression was disappointed but resigned as he left her sitting next to Aenid. Ingirid and Jon were dancing. Jon moved with surprising agility. Cele could hardly believe he was the same man who had seemed well on his way to drunkenness.

"Lord Jon is quite a dancer," Cele commented to Aenid.

"Father's Talent is Grace," Aenid answered. "I think Mother fell in love with him on the dance floor."

Cele took a deep breath, relieved that in her ignorance she hadn't commented on Jon's drinking to his daughter. She made a mental note of the danger. She didn't understand anything here. Not the people, the customs, nor the relationships. She couldn't assume anything.

A hope burst to the surface of her mind, like an iridescent bubble. Maybe she had assumed too much about Dahleven. Maybe she had misinterpreted what she'd seen. Maybe Dahleven wasn't married, and he'd been free to kiss her after all.

But the hug? The baby? The three of them looked so natural together. Cele pushed the painful thought out of her mind. What did it matter? She was going home, as quickly as possible. Dahleven's marital status wasn't important.

Suddenly, as if summoned by her thoughts, she saw the strawberry-blonde that Dahleven had embraced twirling among the other dancers. Cele's breath caught. She was lovely. How could Dahleven cheat on her?

But Cele had learned her lesson, she wouldn't assume. She leaned close to Dahleven's niece and casually asked, "Who is that?"

"Who?"

Cele had to wait till the dance brought the woman back in sight. "There. That pretty woman in the green dress."

"Oh, her." Aenid said. "That's my aunt, Kaidlin."

Aunt Kaidlin. Uncle Dahleven. She hadn't been wrong.

Cele hated the way the bubble of hope turned into a stone and dropped into her belly. How could a foolish hope grow so out of control in just a moment?

"I need to get some air." Cele rose and headed for the door.

A petite young blonde with lots of curves intercepted her. "Welcome to Quartzholm, Lady Celia. I guess you've met the rest of the family by now." She glanced at Aenid across the room, then back to Cele. "I'm sorry Ragni didn't bother to introduce us. I'm Angrim."

Cele didn't want to endure another introduction and chat politely with another stranger. She couldn't help herself; she looked longingly at the door.

Angrim looked at her closely. "You've had too much excitement for one day, haven't you? The Feast can be a bit overwhelming." Angrim took Cele's arm familiarly. "Let me help you back to your room."

"Thank you, but—"

"It's no trouble, my dear. It will give us a chance to become acquainted." They left the great hall with its music and dancing and turned two corners. The stone walls blocked most of the sounds of celebration. After the noise of the gathering, the quiet seemed surreal. Angrim's companionable chatter was a welcome distraction from the mess Cele's thoughts and feelings had become.

"You're wise to retire early," Angrim said as they mounted the stairs. "The gathering will only grow more wild as the night goes on. Eventually, the young bucks will challenge each other to a fire-leap until one of them singes his rump. You're not missing much."

"They jump across the fire?"

"And they move the starting mark farther away with each round."

Cele could only stare.

"It wouldn't be a challenge if it was too easy, now would it? Who'd they impress?" The young blonde giggled.

Angrim turned the subject as she turned another corner. "Your trip through the drylands with Dahleven's men must have been quite an ordeal."

Cele didn't feel like talking. "It was hard."

"So I would think. Dirty and uncomfortable. And alone with all those men!" Angrim didn't miss a breath as they climbed another set of stairs.

"Actually, they were all kind, in their own ways. Sorn most of all." Her heart twinged at the name. Cele was relieved to recognize her own door as they turned onto yet another hall.

"I'm sure. Our Dahleven would never allow an insult to a lady."

Thinking back to Dahleven's grim-faced questioning, Cele wasn't so sure. Then Angrim's phrasing sank in. *Our Dahleven?* "You know Lord Dahleven well, then? Are you family?"

"Why, I thought you knew." Angrim smiled coyly. "Dahleven and I have known each other forever. We're quite *intimately* acquainted." Her meaning was unmistakable.

Married, with a mistress. That was clear enough.

chapter twelve

DAHLEVEN SHRUGGED, testing the fit of his new blue tunic. *Perfect.* He could draw a weapon if necessary while still looking fine enough as his father's heir.

He'd returned to Quartzholm with just enough time to bathe and dress before the Council of Jarls, the first meeting of the Althing. He was tired, but at least he didn't have the throbbing head that some of the Jarls would bring to the meeting. Knut's betrayal, and the deaths of Sorn, Lindy, and Halsten weighed on him, but they sharpened his focus. Finding Fender and Ghav had eased his concern. Except for Ghav's leg they were whole, and Falsom and Kep, though wounded, were being well cared for at the crofter's where Ghav and Fender had left them.

The decision to leave the two behind had clearly been difficult for the healer. Ghav had reassured Dahleven repeatedly that the two had been left in good care. His assurances had seemed as much for his own peace of mind as for Dahleven's. Ghav had followed his first duty, to help Fender get the information back to Quartzholm, despite inclination and his wounded leg.

I'll make sure Father knows. Ghav deserves recognition for that difficult choice. All his men deserved recognition, for that matter. Their scouting mission had proven far more challenging, and deadly, than expected.

Dahleven stretched again, clean for the first time in weeks, and slicked a hand over his still damp hair, braided close to his head. He was as ready as he'd ever be. He faced another challenge now: presenting what they'd learned to the ever-contentious Jarls. Fanlon may have created the Alliance, but its preservation was seldom smooth or simple.

Ragni followed his quick knock through Dahleven's door. "Greetings! Ready to face the dragons?"

"Someday you'll wish you had more respect for my privacy, Ragni."

"If such a day ever arrives, brother, feel free to bolt your door."

Dahleven rolled his eyes. "Let's move out. Delay won't make this any more pleasant."

Ragni grimaced and went back out the door. He might delight in stinging Dahleven's dignity, but they were of like mind on the pleasures of politics. Apparently, Ragni didn't want to dwell on them; his next remark jerked Dahleven's thoughts in a different direction. "Your little drylands flower was a pleasant companion last night," he said as they walked shoulder to shoulder down the wide corridor.

Dahleven felt like he'd missed a step, although his stride was smooth. "Oh?"

"Indeed. I quite enjoyed her company. Definitely one of the better assignments Father has given me."

Dahleven's temper warmed. Why had Father put Ragni on the task? He knew what his younger son was like. Ragni was a charmer, always had been. How far and how hard had he pursued Lady Celia? She was vulnerable now, so soon after Sorn's death. Though she'd known his sworn brother only a day, love could take a woman like that, and he didn't want to see her hurt by Ragni's dalliance. *She wears Sorn's bracelet, for Freya's sake!* How could his brother trespass on so fresh a grief?

A stab of guilt cooled his temper and tightened his shoulders. He'd kissed her himself, and it hadn't been a brotherly kiss. Far from it. A different kind of heat warmed him as his memory of that embrace tightened more than his shoulders.

"Speak, and she appears." Ragni indicated a figure at the end of the hall.

Lady Celia walked toward them, accompanied by Thora. His imagination hadn't prepared Dahleven for the sight of her in proper clothing. A gauzy viridian dress skimmed her body, draping gracefully to the floor under a darker green over-tunic nearly as long as the dress. With each step, the delicate fabric of the dress clung to her long muscular legs, their movement visible and tantalizing through the open front of the tunic. Even from this distance, Dahleven could see how the verdant colors of her clothing intensified the shade of her eyes. They were vivid, like the first bright meadow-grass of spring, and they flashed sparks as she recognized him.

"Lady Celia," Ragni said as they came together, "what a pleasure to see you again." He didn't touch her, but his posture suggested familiarity.

Dahleven wanted to step between them, but had no reason to.

"I trust you are well? Your early departure concerned me." Ragni's tone implied he had a right to ask.

Lady Celia flicked a brief glance at Dahleven, then smiled at Ragni. "I felt a little overwhelmed. It was rude for me to leave like that. I hope you'll forgive me."

"There is nothing to forgive. Such Feasts can indeed be over stimulating. I regret my time is spoken for at present, but I hope I may call on you again."

Dahleven's annoyance grew as Lady Celia smiled up into his brother's eyes and answered, "Please do."

Ragni bowed deeper than required by courtesy. "Lady Celia."

"Lord Ragnar. Or should I say, *Father* Ragnar?"

"Ah." Ragni lifted a warning finger. "Just Ragni." He delicately touched her bare arm above the elbow.

Dahleven's hand shot out and grasped Ragni's wrist. Ragni had no right to be so publicly intimate, and he doubted Lady Celia understood what Ragni was doing. A man touched an unmarried woman in the place where she'd wear the marriage bands as a confirmation of intimacy—or as an invitation. She permitted it, welcomed it, only if she agreed.

It was then he realized that Celia wore Sorn's cuff on her forearm now, rather than in the place of a betrothal band, as she had done before. Had he misunderstood her feelings for Sorn? Then he remembered her tears. No, her grief had been genuine.

Ragni and Lady Celia looked at him in surprise, and he released Ragni's wrist. "We're late. We must go." It sounded stiff even to his own ears, but he was angry enough he didn't care.

Without missing a step, Ragni smoothly took his leave a second time.

Dahleven bowed the appropriate degree. "Lady Celia."

She threw a glance sharp as shards of emerald at him and continued down the hall without speaking.

Ragni looked at him with wide eyes. "However did you earn such high regard from the lady, brother?"

Dahleven didn't answer for a moment. His desire to plant a fist in his brother's face warred with the impulse to kick himself. Was Ragni's behavior any worse than his own? He strode onward. Ragni kept pace.

The memory of Celia's glare cut like slivers of deep-winter ice. He'd brought this on himself. He'd given in to impulse and kissed her. She might have enjoyed it at the time, he was sure she had, but now, in clear reflection, she obviously resented his presumption. As well she might.

Dahleven cast a dark look at his brother. Ragni had always been smooth and glib and charming with women. *He*, no doubt, had said and done all the right things at the right time. He would slip into her regard without her notice, until one day she'd awaken and find herself in love with him. *He* would never blunder by pushing too far, too soon.

"Easy, brother. I'm not the one who cut you cold, nor did I speak against you last night. Indeed, I sang your praises as a fine warrior—when your name came up." Ragni looked closer at his face, and Dahleven wished his younger brother weren't so perceptive, or so Talented. Then Ragni dropped the false mockery and became the brother he trusted again. "What happened, Dahl?"

Dahleven saw no reason to hide the truth from Ragni. He said it in the fewest number of words. "Sorn caught her heart, and then she had to watch him die of a belly wound."

Ragni groaned softly and grimaced in sympathy.

"Then, yesterday, in the storeroom..." Dahleven ran a hand back over his braided hair. "Baldur's balls! I kissed her."

Ragni raised an eyebrow. He almost looked delighted. When Dahleven didn't continue, he said, "Aside from your blasphemy, I don't see the problem."

"She wears his band!"

"As a gift only."

"Now, perhaps. Not when I kissed her." Dahleven

shook his head. "It was too soon for her. You know how women are. She grieves for Sorn, and I took advantage of her. That's why she cut me. And why you shouldn't be presuming on her ignorance. She doesn't understand our customs, or what you imply when you touch her that way."

Ragni pursed his lips and rubbed his chin thoughtfully. Then he shook his head and sidestepped Dahleven's complaint. "You're right. I do know women. And you clearly don't. I don't know why she'd like to cut your heart out, but I'm pretty sure it's not because you kissed her, you dolt. She may be saddened by Sorn's death, but she doesn't act—or feel—like a woman lost in grief."

Despite his brother's Talent for Empathy, Dahleven knew what he'd seen pass between Sorn and Lady Celia. He would have argued, but they'd arrived outside the chambers where the Council of Jarls would convene. He gave Ragni a determined look as a servant opened the door and announced them. "Later," he growled, then smoothed his face to greet the assembled Jarls.

Ragni grinned and shrugged, and followed Dahleven into the hall.

Five of the seven Jarls were already present. Hafdan was missing, and their father, of course. As Kon, it wasn't appropriate that Neven wait on the others. He'd appear when the Jarls and their seconds were fully assembled.

At this, the first meeting, only the Jarls and their heirs gathered. At subsequent meetings of the Althing, lesser lords, their advisors, and prominent carls with significant holdings would attend, and the larger assembly would address and resolve any disputes that couldn't be resolved locally. Usually there weren't many. Most men settled their own disagreements directly, rather than bring their disputes to the Althing like children running to a parent.

An oval table surrounded by sixteen chairs dominated the room. Most of the Jarls stood talking, catching up on gossip, cementing alliances, and trolling for tidbits of rumor that might affect desired agreements. They turned and nodded as Dahleven and Ragni entered the room, eager to have one or both of the Kon's sons join them. Neither he nor Ragni immediately favored one over another, pausing first at a table set with refreshments. The Jarls resumed their conversations.

Dahleven accepted a tankard of ale from a servant and watched Ozur shake his wavy gray mane. The old Jarl disdained the fashion of braids, allowing his long hair to cascade over his shoulders and blend with his full beard. Combined with his ample girth, his hair made Ozur resemble a fuzzy gray ball, but Dahleven knew better than to underestimate the older man. Ozur was far from soft. He'd challenged Neven for leadership of Nuvinland since the two of them were young men. No, there was nothing soft about Ozur. He talked with Yngvar, the other Jarl with direct access to the sea.

Yngvar was another from his father's generation, but a very different kind of man. Easily swayed, he cared only for the peaceful continuity of his life. The people of his province prospered mainly due to the plentiful harvest of the ocean, not through great leadership. Yngvar hated contention, and Ozur would have had his vote on all matters, except that Yngvar voted his comfort and profit, and Ozur wasn't always comfortable. Despite his weakness, he would have been tolerable, if it weren't for his obtuse propensity for crude and tactless remarks. How Ozur tolerated it, Dahleven didn't know. He steered away from the two of them.

Ragni crossed the room to Father Wirmund, and Dahleven went to join the trio of Magnus, Solveig, and Ulf. Solveig thrust her jaw forward, obviously not pleased by something Magnus said, while Ulf laughed gently.

"Granted, Solveig isn't my neighbor, but you're too anxious, I think, Magnus. It's too early yet for the boy's Talent to emerge. The lady has ample time to plan for unfortunate possibilities."

This again. Magnus wanted Solveig to designate an alternate heir in case her son proved Talentless. She had taken on the duties of the Jarldom when her husband, Brand, had been killed by Renegades. Her son, Vali, was too young to inherit, especially since his Talent hadn't yet Emerged. She was within her rights to assume the Jarldom, and tradition supported her, but there were some who had spoken against the leadership of a woman. Magnus, though he didn't like the prospect of having a woman guiding a neighboring province, had spoken in her support. He observed the old ways, and by the laws of custom, a woman could and should protect the inheritance of her children. By all accounts she was doing well, and her people were behind her. She even had the support and aid of Brand's cousin Gunnar, who would most likely be Jarl if not for Vali and Solveig.

"You're right, Ulf, Solveig isn't your neighbor," Magnus said. "Nor do you share our burden of caravan losses and defending against Tewakwe raids. *Your* borders are safe. She has done well, but a strong man is always a better leader, especially in difficult times."

"No one knows better than I how difficult these times are," Solveig said tightly. "No one. You supported me a year ago, Magnus, when I was unproven. I wonder that you want to undermine me now."

"I don't want to undermine you, Solveig. You're right to protect Vali's place. But I've made it no secret that I think you should remarry. Gunnar is a fine man, after all." Magnus gestured at the warrior, who looked amused. "And you're still young enough. A man's hand on the reins would make everyone feel more secure. And should Vali prove Talentless—"

Talentless. It tripped off Magnus's tongue so easily. Dahleven knew what weight that word carried. He'd come into his Talent late, wondering each day after he turned twelve if every odd sensation was a portent of his Talent, knowing that his elders watched him for a sign and speculated on whether he'd grow up to be Jarl, or half a man. At least Father had had Ragni to fall back on. Dahleven glanced at Ragni talking quietly with Father Wirmund, and sent a quick prayer of gratitude to the gods for his brother. Ragni had never once gloated when he'd come into his Talent before Dahleven had. Vali had no brother, and the pressure for him was starting early, at only eight.

"Vali will not be Talentless!" Solveig interrupted. "Nor do I need to buy Gunnar's loyalty with marriage. It is precisely because he *is* a fine man that he should choose his wife for reasons other than power and politics. He knows I will not oppose his leadership of the jarldom, should Vali...not be able to inherit. Until that time, to proclaim him publicly as successor would weaken Vali's position. I will do nothing to harm my son. Not for any reason, nor for any*one.*" Solveig had kept her voice low and controlled, but the intensity of her words wasn't lessened.

Hafdan was announced and he hurried in, breaking the tension. A little younger than Dahleven, Hafdan stood tall yet relaxed, radiating self-confidence. He'd been a good choice to replace his cousin as Jarl, when Jorund's ambition had driven him to the crime of house-burning two years ago. Hafdan bowed his courtesies to the room at large. "My apologies for my late arrival."

"I've only just arrived myself, and we're all still slaking our thirsts." Dahleven said, pressing a tankard into Hafdan's hand.

Hafdan smiled and took a swallow.

"Too much ale last night, Hafdan?" Yngvar bellowed from across the room. "You young pups haven't enough experience in ruling or drinking to know your limits."

Dahleven cringed inwardly. *First one squabble, then another. Thank the gods the Althing brings the Jarls together only once a year.* The Jarls had been calm and well-mannered for a while after they'd voted to Outcast one of their own. The shock of Jorund's crime had subdued even Yngvar for a time. Apparently, that time was now past.

Ingdall, Yngvar's heir, winced ever so subtly and stepped away from his father as the Jarl continued. "Or did your lady wife detain you late abed? She's breeding again, yes? Women in her state are insatiable, aren't they? I remember my own wife, once her sickness passed, couldn't wait—"

Hafdan's face stiffened in a rictus of control. Dahleven knew that only the truce of the Althing saved Yngvar from immediate and serious harm. Enviably, Hafdan had a true union of mind and heart with his lady wife, and felt any lack of courtesy toward her keenly.

"Yngvar!" Magnus voice cut sharply across the other Jarl's. "Tell me about your new fishing fleet. I'm told you have five new ships." Magnus strode across the room and drew Yngvar aside.

Dahleven had never understood how such a spineless man could habitually spout the most tactless and offensive things. Perhaps because no one thought him worth the effort to call him on it.

He glanced at Ingdall, where the man stood expressionless, trying to ignore the fuss caused by his father. He was very fair and looked nothing like his sire. How would it be to have a father who inspired derision rather than respect? Ingdall was a hard man to know: quiet, competent in the games, but not flashy.

Dahleven turned back to Hafdan, whose face was still rigid with anger. Dahleven nudged the tankard upward, clutched forgotten in Hafdan's white-knuckled hand. "Drink."

Hafdan pulled his daggered gaze from Yngvar's back. He lifted his ale, took a sip, and swallowed tightly, his face relaxing a bit.

"Tell me about the new terracing of your fields," Dahleven said. "I hear your crop yields have increased."

Hafdan smiled grimly, as if to say, *Don't worry, I won't kill the old fool—today*, but he accepted the distraction Dahleven offered. "We decided to rotate the crops—"

"Kon Neven," a servant announced in stentorian tones. The Jarls fell silent as Dahleven's father entered the room.

Neven wasn't exercising his Talent, but every eye followed him to the table. His green brocade tunic flashed with gems sewn across his chest in the pattern of his emblem, a swooping hawk. By comparison, the other Jarls looked like minor lordlings. Dahleven made no effort to suppress his proud smile.

Neven rested one hand on the back of the large chair at the head of the table. "My Lords, throughout the long years we have come together to hear the needs of our people and make the land prosper." The ritual words were powerful, and sent a shiver up Dahleven's back. "Just as our fathers in Midgard gathered, so do we now. We have feasted together, as we have since Fanlon's day, and now we convene the Althing with this Council, to guide our future together." He gestured with open hand, inviting the others to sit, then did so himself.

Dahleven sat on his father's right. Father Wirmund took his place at the far end of the table, to Ragni's left.

Other than the four of them, no one had an assigned place, and no precedence was accorded any particular position. *Thank the gods. We hardly need another source of contention.*

After the usual shuffling and scraping of chair legs on the fitted stone floor, Neven regained the Jarls' full attention. "My Lords, we have a matter of importance to consider, one beyond our usual concerns. Though not in equal measure, all of our provinces have been affected by the raids on our trade caravans to the Tewakwe. In recent months, our borders have been attacked. We can no longer continue as we have been. Increasing the strength of the caravans and the numbers of our border patrols is not enough. We must face this threat to our peace and deal with it. End it. If we do not, it will continue to grow."

"It's clear what we must do," Solveig said. "We must take the fight to the Tewakwe Confederation. Give them a taste of the bitter draught they've been feeding us!"

"Are you proposing a combined force again, Kon Neven?" Ozur shook his wooly head. "I can't support that. I'll not ask the men of my province to fight and die for another's land with no hope of gain."

"If we sent you our men we would have too few to work the nets and leave our own lands undefended." Yngvar bared his yellow teeth in a poor attempt to smile. "And such a force would give you a great deal of power."

"In truth, Neven, are the losses really so serious? I've lost a few barrels of salt-fish, but that's to be expected in trade. I think perhaps you are making overmuch of this. There's been a bit of raiding and pilfering by Tewakwe Renegades going back as far as I can remember. That's not new." Ozur's reasonable and avuncular tone was only a step away from condescension.

"Assaults on our borders *are* new." Magnus slapped his hand down on the table. "Running battles on the ridges are new. The death of my son is new." Magnus drew down his bushy brown eyebrows and spoke with such vehemence that his dark braids shook. Ozur didn't meet his eyes. Magnus's son had been killed in a raid on his lands just after the thaw. His grandson, Magni, sat by his side now as heir. At seventeen, Magni had been a man for two years, but he still had the long, loose-limbed look of an unbroken colt.

"Lord Dahleven has just returned from the dry-lands." Neven's voice pulled everyone's attention back to him. He still wasn't using his Talent. Dahleven wasn't surprised. His father preferred to let reason prevail, when possible. He thought his father might be overly optimistic with this group.

"He went there to learn more of the threat we face." Neven continued, turning to Dahleven. "Tell them what you observed."

Dahleven saw no reason to lead into it slowly. "Tucked in a blind canyon near the Owlridge crest, this side of the Tewakwe holdings, we observed a camp of Renegade Tewakwe. They were living side by side with our own Outcasts."

"Outcasts!"

"Nuvinlanders?"

"It's hardly surprising that evil-doers flock together," Hafdan said mildly.

Dahleven, curious, turned to Hafdan.

"With no community, no family, a man must make what connections he can, or die alone," Hafdan said.

"Are you sure you saw clearly? Wouldn't they be more likely to prey on each other?" Ulf asked. "The nameless curs we've cast out broke our laws and shamed their families. It hardly seems possible that they could ally with anyone, let alone Tewakwe *skraelings*, when they betrayed their own." Ulf had only recently ascended to his Jarldom, but he had ruled in his father's stead for the last two years, since Koll had been crippled by fire in Jorund's attack. He had less patience than most with Oathbreakers and Outcasts.

"How do you know that they weren't just Tewakwe from the Confederation trading with the Outcasts?" Yngvar put in.

"We saw clearly enough, and heard more. Falsom has Heimdal's eyes, and Lindimer...Lindy had Heimdal's ears. They weren't trading. They were sharpening blades, crafting arrows and bragging to each other about their latest raids. While the Renegade Tewakwe have been raiding our trade caravans and testing our borders, our Outcasts have been attacking the Confederation."

"Truly? Perhaps the Tewakwe Confederation has joined forces with the Outcasts."

"No. The Tewakwe holdings showed signs of raiding, and there were no Outcasts among them. They have fortified, however. They've narrowed the entrance to the cliffs with bulwarks of shaped stone."

"What did they say about the raids?" Yngvar asked.

Dahleven gave Lord Yngvar a long look before answering. "We were in the drylands, in Tewakwe territory without an invitation, and not on the caravan trails, Lord Yngvar." Dahleven paused, but comprehension didn't dawn on Yngvar's features. "We were there to look and listen, not to talk. Even if we had chosen to, the Tewakwe were not likely to welcome unexpected visitors after being raided by the Outcasts."

"This isn't just raiding for greed and gain." Magnus said. "They're not impulsive; they're organized. They always attack in greater numbers, destroying what they can't take. Someone is leading them—but to what purpose?"

"It's obvious. Revenge. Every man stripped of his Talent and cast out is bitter and angry," Hafdan said.

"There's more to this, I'm confident. Bitter, angry

men aren't so careful," Solveig countered.

"I believe they mean to turn us and the Tewakwe against each other," Dahleven said.

"That's ridiculous. Who would profit from that?" Ozur waved his hand dismissively.

"You would, for one." Magni said hotly, leaning forward in this chair. "While we in the border provinces defend against raids, you and Lord Yngvar can profit by selling us the food we haven't the time and men to provide ourselves with—especially since you won't send any men to help us defend your fat ass."

"You young whelp!"

"Magni!" Magnus barked. "An apology is in order."

"I should say so!" Yngvar chimed in.

The muscles in Magni's jaw jumped as his face reddened and the cords in his neck stood out. Dahleven thought he might strangle on the words before he got them out. "Your pardon, my Lord Ozur."

Ozur nodded his acceptance. "Watch your tongue in the future, boy. Feuds have started for less."

Magni's eyes burned.

"Lord Ozur is right, Magni." Magnus growled to his furious grandson. "You should be more careful with your words. There are more graceful ways to state the truth."

Ozur started to rise from his chair.

"Enough!" Neven's voice cut clean and sharp, strengthened now by a surge of his Talent. "We should no longer be asking ourselves whether we should act, but what action is necessary. You ask what purpose these attacks would serve? The answer is here, at this table. Not only are we weakened by the slow, continual loss of lives and resources, we weaken ourselves further by our bickering. We must not allow ourselves to be distracted from the real threat. It's not the Tewakwe. We were meant to believe that, just as they must believe that we threaten them. Whoever planned this hoped we would throw our lives away fighting a profitless war against the wrong enemy. Knowing this, we are stronger, but not strong enough to fight on two fronts. Until the Tewakwe understand the deception, we face the possibility of war with them. They'll want to stop the predation on their people as much as we do. We must arrange a parley with the Tewakwe to join forces against our common foe."

"Lady Celia!" a familiar masculine voice called.

Cele startled and looked around. She'd been blindly following Thora back to her room after visiting Sevond a second time.

He'd talked about his son as he worked on a new piece of jewelry. "Sorn had a good hand with the files," he'd said. "The boy could have been fine craftsman, but he had no heart for it."

The gentle old man hadn't required any response from her, so she just listened. Over two hours, the jeweler's words had built a clear picture of the love between father and son. Though Sorn had chosen a very different path from Sevond, there'd been no resentment or rancor between them.

She'd had that kind of relationship with her mother, before she died.

Fendrikanin's voice pulled Cele from her reflections. "Lady Celia! Well met!" Fender caught up with them and came around to face her, pausing to nod an acknowledgment to Thora.

Cele knew she was grinning foolishly, but the last time she'd seen Fender they'd all been running for their lives. She was relieved to see his impudent face again, and find him well and whole.

"I'm glad to find you here and safe," he said, "but with Lord Dahleven as escort, I wouldn't expect otherwise."

Safe indeed! The memory of Dahleven's kiss intruded, and she pushed it away.

Fender looked at her, clearly admiring the benefits of the bath and her green dress. "I am sorry indeed now, that we didn't hurry back for the Feast last night. I would have liked to claim a dance from you."

Cele smiled at the compliment but focused on something else. "We? Are the others back safely, too?"

"Ghav is with me. A renegade arrow bit a piece of meat from him so he won't be dancing for a while. We left Kep and Falsom in the care of a crofter's wife."

"Are they badly hurt?"

"Oh no. The slug-a-beds will soon be well enough to return to Quartzholm." Fender smiled, but his face twitched and Cele knew he was more concerned for his comrades than he admitted.

"And Ghav? He's here? Would he like a visitor?"

"What man would decline a visit from a lovely woman?" Fender smiled with boyish charm at Thora. "I'll escort her safely back to her rooms and your care," he said, offering his arm to Cele.

Thora looked at them with skeptical amusement. "Don't lose her."

"You wound me, Thora. In all my days, I've not lost more than two or three young maids. And that was years ago." Fender winked at Cele and escorted her back the way she'd come, then turned down a new hallway.

After taking several more turns, climbing then descending four staircases, they passed through a corridor lighted by a series of tall, narrow windows. The door at the end led outside, onto a stone bridge that arched high above the courtyard to another tower. Birds perched on the parapets. They took flight as Cele and Fender stepped onto the apparently seamless span. Below, the hubbub of merchants hawking their wares blended into a noisy hum. The crowd swirled and eddied in front of the various booths, pooling and growing stagnant where performers juggled on a low stage at the near end of the courtyard.

Cele stopped and looked over the edge, taking in the maelstrom of color and sound that wrapped around the corner of the castle and out of sight. The smells of cooking meat, fresh bread, and roasted nuts made her mouth water. It reminded her of a county fair. "Is it like this all the time?"

Fendrikanin looked surprised. "No, of course not. We have a market once a week, but this is five times the size of that. This is the Althing Market. The merchants have come from all over Nuvinland to profit from the gathering of the Jarls and their folk."

The swirl of activity looked inviting. "Can we go down there?"

"I thought you wanted to visit Ghav."

"Afterwards, I mean."

Fender looked thoughtful. "Thora warned me not to lose you. Will you stay close? She'll have the skin off my back if I lose track of you in that crowd."

Cele laughed, recognizing capitulation when she heard it. "I'm a big girl, Fender."

"That's not the answer I want."

Fender's stern reply surprised her. Apparently, Fender had a touch of steel beneath his playful manner. Her laughter subsided to a smile. "I'll stay close. And if we do get separated, we'll meet here under the bridge. Fair enough?"

He relaxed and nodded. "Let's go visit Ghav."

The healer sat with his right leg propped on a chair, writing on parchment on a board in his lap. Shelves lined one wall, filled with an orderly assortment of scrolls, wood and leather bound books, boxes, and flasks. His bushy eyebrows rose in surprise when Fender pulled her into the room. "Lady Celia! You look well, I see. Better than well, in fact." He winced as he started to rise.

"No, don't get up," Cele said, putting out her hand to halt his movement.

Ghav settled back into his chair with a soft grunt. He looked tired and pale.

"Does it hurt very much?"

"Only when he's gone too long without sympathy," Fender said.

Ghav shot the younger man a dark look. "Please, be seated Lady Celia. I have a fine wine in the cupboard there," he said, indicating the direction with his hand. "Fender, be a gentleman for once and pour a cup for the lady. And bring me that pouch, too."

Cele jumped up from her seat. "I'll get it."

She handed Ghav the small leather bag. He drew a leaf from it and crumbled half into his cup. The herb looked the same as what he had dosed Sorn with. Cele's concern grew. Ghav had quelled her pain and much of Sorn's with just a touch. His wound must be more serious than they'd admit if he needed the herb to dull the pain.

Ghav looked up and caught Cele's worried look before she could clear her expression. "I can't ease my own pain as I can another's," he said, correctly guessing the cause of her concern.

How do Talents work, then? Too much had been happening for Cele to wonder about it. And if these people were descended from Vikings, where had these Talents come from? People from her world didn't have them.

A knock forestalled Cele's questions. Fender opened

the door to a man dressed in what Cele had come to recognize as Kon Neven's livery: a green suede tunic with the hawk embroidered on the left breast.

"Lady Gudrun invites Lady Celia to attend her in her chambers," the man announced.

Fender's eyebrows rose and Ghav sat up straighter.

Apparently, this invitation was something significant. "Who is Lady Gudrun?"

Apparently, she'd surprised everyone again. Even the messenger looked at her with a startled expression.

Ghav answered her question. "Kon Neven's wife."

chapter thirteen

CELE'S ESCORT BROUGHT HER to a narrow door and announced her to a small group of women, then stepped back so she could enter. The oldest woman in the room immediately drew her attention. Her face and figure were softened by middle age, but her calm dignity made her strength unmistakable. Light from tall slender windows highlighted threads of red, gold, and silver in the medium brown coil of braids on her head.

Dahleven's mother.

Cele saw the resemblance in Lady Gudrun's mouth when she smiled her welcome. *Not that Dahleven smiles much.* He had his father's eyes and brow, but definitely his mother's firm chin. Cele remembered seeing Gudrun on Neven's arm last night, though she'd paid attention only to the Kon. *Because of his mind control.*

I wonder what tricks she *has up her sleeve.*

The softly appointed sitting room showed a woman's touch. Flowers bloomed in pots with a black on white

Mimbres motif; the chairs, grouped in a circle around a low table, were well upholstered with soft cushions. Cele recognized Ingirid and Aenid. And Dahleven's wife.

Cele pushed the shock aside. *Of course she's here with the women of the family.*

Gudrun rose and came to Cele, taking her hands and drawing her into the group. "Welcome to Quartzholm, Lady Celia. We're about to enjoy a little afternoon refreshment. Please, join us." Gudrun indicated a chair next to her own. Ingirid sat on Cele's right, and Aenid sat just beyond her mother. She looked subdued, with dark circles under her eyes.

Cele broke away from Aenid's gaze and looked across the table—straight into the eyes of Dahleven's wife. They were the same smoky gray as his.

The young woman smiled warmly at her. "I'm Kaidlin. I regret we didn't have a chance to meet last night. My little one won't go to sleep without me, I'm afraid, and I arrived late to the Feast."

"My apologies," Gudrun said. "I knew you'd met Ingirid and Aenid already, so I assumed you knew Kaidlin, as well. We're not very formal when it's just family."

Cele smiled at Gudrun and then turned back to Kaidlin. The warmth in the young woman's face made it easier to return her smile than Cele would have expected. "I left early myself. I'd had a full day."

A servant came into the room and deposited a large tray filled with cold roast fowl, dried fruit, bread, and three kinds of cheese on the low central table. Gudrun herself poured a pale wine into a silver goblet and handed it to Cele.

Some afternoon snack.

"You'd had several full days, from what I hear," Gudrun said. "I hope you'll tell us about your experiences."

Gudrun's interest felt genuine, but Cele's track record of misjudgments made her wary. *At least Gudrun's approach is smoother than her husband's.* "I certainly found more adventure than I'd planned on when I left home—what is it now? A week ago?" *Has it really only been a week?*

"What happened?" Kaidlin leaned forward eagerly.

"I'm not sure. I climbed down a cliff to look at some amazing petroglyphs, probably Hohokam, and when I climbed back up—bam! I must have slipped or something, because suddenly I was falling. When I woke up, I was in a different desert than where I'd been, with no trail and very little water."

"The rainbow bridge, did you see it?" Gudrun asked.

Gudrun's question triggered a flash of memory, startling Cele. "Yes! I saw colored lights, anyway. Just like the in the story last night. Do you know what it is? How it works? Can you get me home?"

"I only know the old stories, and none of them tell of anyone returning to Midgard." Gudrun's regret sounded genuine. "Perhaps the skald or the priests could tell you more."

Cele's eagerness evaporated. Gudrun didn't sound very encouraging.

"Please go on with your story," Kaidlin said. "What happened next?"

Cele smiled ruefully. "For the next day I tried to find water, without any success. I was getting pretty desperate when your husband and his men found me." Cele was glad she'd said *husband* without choking on it.

"My husband?" Kaidlin drew back, startled. "My husband's dead, killed by raiders. Who do you mean?"

Cele felt her face grow hot. She'd done it again. "Uh, I thought Dahleven…"

Gudrun smiled and Kaidlin's short peal of laughter rang like a bell. "He's my brother. Why ever did you think we were married?"

Cele's face burned and her fingers tightened on her wine goblet. "I saw you together on the steps yesterday, with the baby."

Kaidlin looked confused.

Cele tried to explain. "Extended families, living close together like yours, aren't very common where I come from. Well, not unless you're Hispanic or Native American. It's usually just a husband, wife and their kids—when the man sticks around." *Why did I say that?* She rushed on. "That's why when I saw the three of you together on the steps...I thought you were married."

Kaidlin smiled gently. "He's been so good with Bjorn since Sven died." She chuckled. "How funny. I can't wait to tell Dahleven."

Oh, no. Cele put a hand up to her hot face. "I'm so embarrassed."

Gudrun patted Cele's knee. "No harm."

"So some men love their families and some don't," Ingirid said, bitterness edging her voice. "Midgard doesn't sound so very different from Alfheim, after all."

"Men are men. They're good and bad. Sven was one of the good ones," Kaidlin said softly. "So is Dahleven."

Cele noticed that no one disagreed. Of course, they were family. But with her misunderstanding cleared up, Cele felt the tight knot she'd carried under her breast begin to loosen. She felt a little freer now to listen to the whisper of her instincts, to believe what she'd known deep down: that Dahleven was an honorable man.

Then she remembered Angrim. *He wasn't cheating on his wife when he kissed me. Just cheating on his mistress.*

Dahleven stretched until his joints popped. The Council

had broken for the day, and only he and Ragni remained with Neven. The Jarls had voted six to two to send a delegation to parley with the Tewakwe immediately after the conclusion of the Althing. Ozur and Yngvar had thought it unnecessary and a waste of time, but fortunately, the other Jarls had more sense. Messengers would leave immediately for the Confederation to contact the Tewakwe to set up the parley.

Though he must have been tired, Neven still sat straight in his chair. Dahleven didn't think he'd ever seen his father slouch. "Did anyone jump?" Neven asked his younger son.

Ragni still occupied a chair at the far end of the table from Neven, but instead of his father's impeccable posture, he slumped deeply, eyes closed. The heels of his boots rested on the table, ankles crossed. Ragni answered without opening his eyes. "Not a one."

"Ozur?" Neven prodded.

"No one." His brother pulled his feet off the table and opened his eyes. "Ozur still hates you as much as he ever did, but he was just as surprised as the rest about the alliance of Outcasts and Renegades." Though it wasn't a secret, Ragni's Talent for Empathy wasn't widely known, and their father liked to keep it that way. Most thought Ragni's Talent was Truth Saying, which discerned only spoken lies. Instead, his Empathy revealed all emotions, including the intent to deceive. And though it worked only at very close range, it served him well with the ladies and made him a useful tool, especially during the Althing. Father Wirmund thought so, too. He'd chosen Ragni as his second with no encouragement from Neven.

"Which means we still don't know who our enemy is. I'm not sure if I'm relieved or not that one of the Jarls isn't the organizer of this," Dahleven said.

"I am," Neven said. "We've snapped and snarled our

way through the years, but we haven't fought a true war since Fanlon's day. That's what it would have come to if it were one of them."

His father was right; Dahleven had no wish to fight his own people, but men of his had died, and more would yet until they discovered who their enemy was and stopped him. "Who has power or persuasion enough to unify the Renegades and Outcasts?"

Neither Neven nor Ragni responded; there was no answer, yet.

"There is another matter I would have you consider, Dahl," Neven said after a moment's silence. "Magnus spoke to me last night about his daughter Utta."

Baldur's Balls. Magnus had wanted to ally his family with Neven's for some years. Given the friendship between the two men it was a wonder they hadn't handfasted him and Utta in their cradles.

Dahleven ignored Ragni's grin. Dahleven knew his duty. He must marry and provide an heir to the Jarldom, and he was late in pursuing it. He'd rejected several overtures from other lords and Neven hadn't quibbled. What Magnus proposed was a worthy and desirable alliance. The Kon had to give it due consideration.

"Utta is a fine woman, Dahl."

"I know, Father. But my feelings on the matter haven't changed. I will honor my duty to you and Quartzholm, but I would wed a woman of my own choosing."

"Then choose! The fairest maids of Nuvinland are here for the Althing. Pick one." Neven paused, then continued more calmly. "I'll not compel you. But you cannot delay indefinitely. The times are too uncertain to leave the succession in question." Then he turned to Ragni. "And you needn't look so amused. You, too, should be thinking of your duty to the family. You've never quibbled over an arranged marriage. Perhaps Magnus will accept my second son for his daughter."

Ragni stood abruptly. "I'm starved. Mother and Kaidlin said they'd wait dinner for us."

Neven smiled wryly and let the subject change. "Indeed. Your mother's spies will have told her the Council is recessed. We'd best not dawdle."

"Give her my apologies," Dahleven said. "I have another matter to attend to."

Both Neven and Ragni cocked an eyebrow at him, but didn't press for an explanation. Ragni started to grin. Dahleven glared at him. Wisely, his little brother said nothing.

Cele leaned back on the cushions of the window seat as the late afternoon sun suffused the room with a golden glow. The interview with Gudrun and her daughters had been surprisingly pleasant—despite her embarrassment—but it was still a relief to be away from their scrutiny. Gudrun was clearly an intelligent woman; Cele wondered what conclusions Neven's wife had drawn about her.

She'd told Lady Gudrun the truth, but she'd tried not to say too much about the long days—and nights— crossing over the desert and under the mountains with Dahleven. She suspected Gudrun was very good at reading between the lines, and she didn't want her to guess more about what she felt for Dahleven than she understood herself, especially since the question of his mistress was still unresolved. Instead, Cele had asked questions which the other women had answered freely. She'd come away with a slightly better understanding of the situation here.

The Nuvinlanders had traded with the Tewakwe for time out of mind. The Confederation's cliff-houses were over a week's hard travel away, over mountain passes that were closed by deep snow except in summer. Cele remembered the bite of the wind sweeping through the gap and shivered. She didn't want to think about what those steep tracks would be like in winter.

A little over a year ago, the trade caravans began to be attacked, and now the border holdings were being raided. Too many families in the northern provinces grieved for someone killed in the attacks. Sorn. Halsten. Kaidlin's husband.

Dahleven isn't married. Now that she knew Kaidlin and Dahleven were brother and sister, his embrace of Kaidlin on the steps looked different in her mind's eye. No longer a betraying seducer, he was an affectionate brother and uncle.

Cele cringed, remembering how she'd cut him. No wonder he'd been so brusque in the hallway with Ragni. He probably wanted to save his brother the bite of her tongue. Given her recent behavior, Dahleven probably regretted his impulsive kiss, and was glad to be rid of her.

She warmed, remembering the press of his lips. This time she didn't push the memory away in a wash of anger. He'd surprised her. He'd been so abrupt at times, so clearly impatient with the delay and complication she presented. But he'd also been gentle, giving comfort and offering glimpses of himself as he spoke of his dead friends.

When he kissed her, he hadn't pressured her; he didn't have to. From the first gentle brush of his lips, she'd wanted it, embracing the feelings so unexpectedly kindled. There'd been moments down in the tunnels, thoughts, glances, casual touches that had stirred feelings she'd tried to ignore. But she hadn't expected

Dahleven to feed the flame that raced over her skin even now, now that she let herself remember.

She gave herself a mental shake. *I have more important things to think about than Viking lust. Or lust for Vikings.*

And no matter how nice Dahleven's kiss had been, she'd shut the door on him. She hoped he would accept her apology, but she didn't expect more. Kaidlin would tell him about her misunderstanding and he'd probably get a good laugh out of it. Or maybe not. He might well be angry at being thought dishonorable.

A knock brought Cele out of her musings to answer the door.

Angrim, the curvaceous blonde from the night before, stood smiling in the hallway. Her greeting was light and airy, and she glanced around as she breezed into the room, almost as though looking for someone. "I'm so glad to find you unoccupied, Lady Celia!"

Dahleven's mistress—maybe. Some newly awakened instinct warned Cele not to take everything Angrim said at face value.

"Have you been to the market yet?" The petite young woman continued without a pause. "There's so much to see. The vendors have come from all seven provinces to sell their finest wares during the Althing, and the performers do the most amazing things! But I hate to go alone. Will you join me?"

Angrim didn't seem like the kind of woman who normally chose a woman's company over a man's. After what Angrim had implied last night, Cele wondered at her solitary state. "That sounds great, but wouldn't you rather go with Lord Dahleven?"

Angrim's eyes sharpened but were immediately softened by a smile. "I always enjoy his company, of course, but you know how men are about shopping. They begin pleasantly enough, but they lose patience so quickly. Before long, they're tapping their feet and sighing. Besides, Dahleven is otherwise occupied this evening. You'll be the perfect companion. Please say yes. I shall delight in showing you around."

What Angrim said was straightforward enough, and she offered a pleasant diversion. And Angrim was right about men and shopping. Though Fender had said he'd take her, he'd displayed a distinct lack of enthusiasm for the project. "Yes, I'd like that."

Angrim clapped her hands and gave Cele a quick hug. "Wonderful!" She swept Cele out the door and down the hall. "If we're to be friends, we must get to know one another better," she bubbled. "Tell me all about yourself. Is your father a landowner? Are your brothers warriors, or do they belong to a guild?"

The questions begin. Everyone was trying to figure out where she fit in. Now Angrim was assessing her status. Checking out the competition? Well, she didn't have anything to hide. "My mother owned property."

"Your mother! She held it for your brothers, then?"

"No, I'm an only child."

"Oh." Angrim's voice held a hint of caution. "You must be well dowered then."

Dowered? Another archaic custom. "I suppose so." She'd sold the property and invested the money. She'd never thought of it as bait for a husband. "And you? Do you have brothers?"

"One. And five sisters." Angrim didn't sound happy about the latter.

"I always wanted a sister. I thought it would be wonderful to have a built-in friend."

"Sisters aren't always so accommodating," Angrim said dryly. "I prefer to choose my friends." Angrim squeezed Cele's arm and smiled up at her as they turned to descend the stair.

Out of the corner of her eye, Cele caught a flash of

movement in the hall behind them, but Angrim drew Cele's attention back. "Tell me more about yourself. What's your Talent? I think I can guess. You have Ull's Shield, don't you? All that time in the drylands, and you're only a bit pink. The sun can't blind or burn you, can it?"

Cele laughed. "I wish. I'd save a lot of money on sunscreen and sunglasses, then." She hesitated, remembering Dahleven and Sorn's reaction when they learned she was Talentless. She didn't want everyone looking at her with pitying eyes, especially when she didn't need their sympathy. *There's nothing wrong with me.* "I don't have a Talent. No one does where I come from."

Instead of frowning in pity, Angrim smiled. "Really? I admire the way you say that straight out. No mumbling or embarrassment." There was only a hint of condescension in Angrim's voice. "I'm sure Dahleven admires that in you, too."

Ah, Dahleven. That's what this is about. And why she's so cheerful. She doesn't believe Dahleven could be attracted to a Talentless woman. "I have nothing to be embarrassed about."

He'd kissed her, even knowing she was Talentless. But her lack of Talent might be as big a barrier between them as a wife. *Good God! What am I thinking? It was just a kiss! I don't care about Talents or what Dahleven thinks. I'm going home. Somehow.*

"No, of course not," Angrim agreed. "Since your people don't have Talents, you don't feel the lack, do you?"

Cele was about to ask Angrim about her Talent, but she forgot her question as they stepped out into a swirl of laughter, music, smells of cooking food, and a press of bodies.

They stopped first at a food stall. Angrim dipped into a pouch hanging from her belt and drew out an irregularly shaped coin. It bought them two thick slices of fresh bread drizzled with honey. It smelled warm and rich. Cele's mouth watered, despite the large snack she'd shared with Gudrun and the other women. The merchant weighed the coin and clipped off a bit, which he returned to Angrim.

A slanting ray from the setting sun glinted on gold at Angrim's wrist as she accepted her change from the vendor and handed Cele the larger slice. Then she pulled Cele with her to watch a puppet show.

The puppets, painted in bright colors, enacted a fairytale-like story that seemed well known to the audience, judging from the shouts of encouragement and disapproval. Cele watched, licking honey from her fingers, and found the tale strangely familiar.

A Talentless young man, despised for his condition, left his home to seek his fortune. Along the way, he faced three challenges, which by his cleverness he met and overcame with courage, humor, and generosity. In fact, he was being tested by the three Fates, the Norns. For his good deeds, the Norns rewarded him by granting him a Talent for Finding Gold, and in the end, a Jarl gave his daughter to the young man in marriage.

Angrim pulled Cele away while the crowd was still stamping and shouting its approbation. A player thrust a long handled pan forward to receive more concrete expressions of their approval. As Cele glanced around, a tall man with a dark complexion looked quickly away. Then Angrim led her past a row of stalls, stopping at one to admire the fine cloth, at another to coo over delicately wrought jewelry.

Cele licked the sweet stickiness from her fingers, hesitant to touch the beautiful pieces. Some items were delicate: necklaces of silver wire intricately knotted and studded with polished stones. Others were more substantial stylized animal figures cast in bronze. The piece

Celia liked best was a brooch of dark polished wood inlaid with a design of silver and copper.

They moved with the crowd as though swept by the current of a stream, swirling along from one eddy to the next in front of each successive booth. The aisle turned back on itself twice, like a river snaking through hill country. Lanterns were lit and hung from poles as the sunlight faded, casting a yellow glow over the crowd, creating multiple shadows on the faces of the vendors and their customers.

The crowd was mixed. People Cele recognized from the feast of the previous night stood beside others not so well dressed, and laughed side-by-side with them at the performers. Sometimes a face stood out; a gap-toothed woman laughed loudly and drew Cele's eye. Lantern light danced off the bald pate of an old man. Twice more she noticed the dark man standing not far away. There was nothing unusual about him, and Cele wasn't sure why she noticed him at all. The third time he drew her gaze, she and Angrim were all the way across the courtyard from where they'd started.

She turned to Angrim. "Who is that man?"

"Who?" Angrim looked up eagerly. "Has a handsome face caught your eye?"

"No, over there, I think—" But he'd disappeared into the crowd. *Is he following us, or am I imagining things*? Her concern seemed baseless, but she couldn't quite dismiss it, and she searched the swirling mob for his face.

Angrim's shriek pulled Cele around sharply. "My bracelet! It's gone!" Angrim clutched her wrist where the bracelet had been and looked wildly around her at the ground, obscured by shadows and passing feet. "I've got to find it!"

The little blonde's hysteria triggered Cele's professional calm. "Take it easy. When did you last know you had it? Where were you?"

Angrim looked frantic, her eyes widened by panic. "I've got to find it! Help me!" She gripped Cele's hand painfully. Tears spilled down her cheeks.

The courtyard was huge, and they'd stopped at every booth. The bracelet could be anywhere. Hundreds of people milled in front of the stalls and the performers' platforms, and any one of them could have picked it up or kicked it out of sight. "What does it look like?"

Suddenly Cele remembered the flash of gold on Angrim's wrist, glinting in the lowering sun. Just as suddenly she knew, *knew*, where to find the bracelet.

It was like the peculiar certainty she'd felt when looking for water, or wishing for light in the tunnels, but much, much stronger. It drew her. She returned Angrim's tight hand clasp and headed off through the crowd, towing the smaller woman behind her. Unmindful of the annoyed looks cast at her as she shouldered past, she followed the direction of her certainty into one booth, through the back of another and beyond. The sensation was urgent now, like a cord tied to her diaphragm. Her breath came in deep gasps. It was *there*. *THERE!*

She stopped in front of a stall selling cloth and dove into the mounds of fabric, pushing aside stacked bolts and folded samples.

"Here now! What are you doing? Be careful there!"

Cele ignored the merchant's exclamation and withdrew the bracelet, still hooked to an ivory lace. Cele stared at the heavy gold circle in her hand. Rampant stags with ruby eyes butted heads around the circumference. The demanding need evaporated. *What just happened? How did I do that?*

"My bracelet!" Angrim snatched the bracelet to her breast. "However did you find it?" She freed her treasure from the fabric and put it back on her wrist. Then she looked at Cele more sharply. "How *did* you find it?"

With the bracelet found, Cele's single-minded focus no longer buffered the sights and smells and sounds of the marketplace. They flooded back, overwhelming her senses. It was hard to focus on any one thing when every sensation demanded her attention. Cele blinked, trying to reorient to her surroundings.

"Who's going to clean up this mess?" The vendor's indignant demand felt like a bludgeon and Cele flinched.

"Do you require assistance? Shall I fold your cloth for you?" A familiar deep voice spoke close over Cele's head.

"My lord!" the merchant sputtered. "That's not for *you* to do."

"Then we shall step aside and make room for your other customers," Dahleven said, drawing Lady Celia's arm through his own. He was pleased she didn't pull away; he didn't want to fight on two fronts.

"But my lord, this—this *woman* has overset my wares," the merchant protested.

Dahleven enjoyed correcting the man more than he should have. "This *lady* is a guest of Kon Neven."

For an instant, the merchant looked taken aback, then Dahleven's displeasure increased as a look of calculation replaced the outrage fading from the other man's features. He continued to bluster. "I carry the finest weaving in the seven provinces, my lord, but if the cloth is torn I can sell it only as remnants and rags."

Dahleven picked up the length of ivory lace from the rumpled and tumbled piles of cloth and held it next to Lady Celia's face. Her eyes looked a little glazed, but they focused on his own when he spoke to her. He was relieved to find no anger in them, though its absence surprised him. *Why the change?* "This goes well with your coloring, Lady Celia."

He fished a gold coin from the wallet at his waist and slapped it down hard on the counter in the only narrow space not covered with fabric. It was four times what the lace was worth. "This should cover it. Wrap it up."

Greed had already widened the merchant's eyes when Dahleven speared him with a sharp slicing gaze. "I shall tell my father of your patience and understanding, sir. I'm sure he will see you compensated *appropriately* if you've suffered any loss." Dahleven smiled, convinced by the man's stiffening expression that his message had been understood. Neven would cover any real damage caused by Lady Celia, but he was even less patient with this kind of calculating greed than his son. Ambition and profit were one thing, avarice another. Dahleven guessed the merchant would pocket the outrageous overpayment and count himself ahead.

Dahleven turned away while the vendor wrapped his purchase and tied the parcel with a ribbon instead of the usual string.

"Lady Angrim." Dahleven nodded politely to her. *What is* she *doing with Lady Celia?*

"Lord Dahleven. I'm surprised you have time for such amusements as the market." Angrim looked up at him through her thick lashes and gave him her best smile. "Will you join us?" She slipped her hand beneath his other arm, pressing against his side. A moment later, she had to relinquish her position as he reached for the wrapped lace and tucked it under that arm.

He smiled back, impervious to her flirtation. They'd answered each other's needs for a few months the previous year, but Dahleven's ardor had chilled when he realized Angrim's ambition was greater than her affection. "That was my intention from the first." He patted

Lady Celia's hand where it lay on his arm. It was too cold, and he placed his warmer hand over it.

Angrim's eyes narrowed ever so slightly, but she smiled sweetly. "However did you find us in this crowd?"

"I saw you from the steps as Lady Celia towed you through the merchants' stalls. What was so urgent?"

The tuning of instruments carried across the courtyard.

"Come! The dancing is about to begin," Angrim said.

A suspicion was bubbling to the surface of his mind. "I think food would be a better choice," Dahleven said. "Which would you prefer, Lady Celia? Sausage or meat pies?"

Lady Celia's glazed eyes brightened. "Meat pies!"

Five meat pies later, three of them eaten by Celia, Dahleven's suspicion was stronger. *She's in Emergence; I'd wager my sword on it.* He glanced at her; she was licking the last of the sauce from her fingers. The food had steadied her, and he was relieved to find the glassy look gone from her eyes. *Dazed and hungry. No—ravenous.* He remembered when his own Talent had finally Emerged. He'd been voracious for weeks.

He looked at Angrim and caught her considering Lady Celia with a thoughtful expression. Then she smiled at him and urged them toward the dancing. No sooner had they approached the gathering dancers, than a tall, broad-shouldered man asked Angrim to dance. She hesitated, glancing at Dahleven, obviously hoping he'd insist on escorting her.

He gave her a bland smile. "Enjoy the dance."

Angrim moved briskly away, hand in hand with her partner.

He turned to Lady Celia and bent close so he wouldn't have to shout and gestured to the two rows beginning to form. "Would you like to join them?"

"No, thanks. I got lucky with Ragni last night, but most of your dances are too complicated for me."

He frowned at her familiar mention of Ragni, but Celia didn't see, as her gaze had returned to the twining steps of the dancers.

She watched as Angrim disappeared from view. The men and women wove through the patterns, keeping time with stamping and clapping, always light on their feet. Eventually, Angrim came into view again. Celia pulled him closer and spoke into his ear. Her question surprised him. "Are you and Angrim...together?"

What in Freyr's name has Angrim been telling Celia? He could guess. "No."

"But you were."

It was a statement, not a question, but he decided to answer it anyway. "Yes. Last year."

She nodded. "I thought it was something like that."

The music ended and a different set formed. Angrim didn't return. Dahleven smiled to himself. *She always knows when to cut her losses.*

Celia pulled him close again. She looked embarrassed and serious. "By the way, thanks for not rubbing it in."

Dahleven looked at her curiously and smiled. "You're quite welcome. What are you talking about?"

Celia's mouth opened and closed. It was hard to tell in the dim light, but he thought she was blushing. "Kaidlin will tell you."

Dahleven was about to ask what Kaidlin had to do with it, when he felt Celia's fingers trembling through the fine weave of his sleeve. "Are you tired? Would you like to go in?"

She gave him a crooked smile. "Yeah. All of a sudden I'm wiped out."

Fatigue, too. She was definitely in Emergence. The delight he felt at the thought surprised him. *Of course*

I'm happy for her. But it went beyond the happiness one usually felt for another's new Talent. Dahleven grimaced, chagrined to realize that what he felt was akin to relief. *Why shouldn't I be relieved? The world isn't gentle to those without Talent.* And since Celia was in Emergence, she was not beyond consideration, after all.

Dahleven led her slowly through the thick crowd. A group of boys ran by, bumping Celia. She stumbled and fell against him. Dahleven steadied her with an arm around her waist.

The boys didn't stop. The first three had disappeared into the crowd but he recognized the last two. "Ljot! Solvin!" he barked. "Come back here!"

The boys stopped and turned around as if their reins had been jerked. At ten and eleven, they were still young enough for their eyes to widen with alarm when they saw his scowl.

"You nearly knocked Lady Celia off her feet. You owe her an apology." He wouldn't have his nephews growing up to be ruffians.

"I wasn't the one who hit her!" Ljot protested.

"Nor me! It was Han," Solvin added.

"If you keep company with ill-mannered louts, you must expect to pay the consequences," Dahleven admonished. "Apologize. Now." For an instant, he thought Celia might protest, but she kept silent.

"Please accept my apologies, Lady Celia, for myself and my friends. I hope you weren't injured," Ljot said, bowing.

"I'm sorry, too, Lady Celia." Solvin bowed.

Dahleven suppressed a smile, keeping his face stern. Ljot had done well; Solvin's apology was less polished, but heartfelt.

"Thank you, Ljot, Solvin. You're forgiven. No harm was done," Celia said solemnly.

"Are you supposed to be watching Ari?" Dahleven

asked. Their five-year-old brother was a mischief-maker and needed constant supervision.

"No, Uncle Dahben. He's with Aunt Kaidlin," Ljot said.

"Very well, then. Off with you. And watch where you're going."

The boys bowed again and escaped into the crowd like rabbits into a burrow.

"They're good boys," Dahleven said.

"I can see they are. They're very polite."

"With a little reminder."

"Like most men." Celia smiled but her voice was dull with fatigue.

They climbed the stairs to the broad doorway slowly. Dahleven kept his arm around Celia, enjoying the way her hip rubbed against his with the sway of her stride.

The long hallway was empty and relatively quiet. The door guards' attention was on the courtyard and the crowd. Everyone not required for some task was out enjoying the cool summer night and the carefree atmosphere of the Althing market.

"I don't understand this. I don't usually crash so early in the evening." Lady Celia ran a hand over her forehead, then let her arm fall limp to her side.

His last lingering doubts about her evaporated. Those doubts had grown weaker as he'd come to know her in the field; now it was clear she was no spy from the Outcasts. No one could fake Emergence, and he could not imagine a Nuvinland woman her age concealing her delight in finally developing Talent. Only someone just from Midgard would be so ignorant and unconcerned. "It's Emergence. It affects everyone a little differently, and you're going through it later than most."

"Emergence?" Lady Celia's first step up the staircase was slow and labored as she half pulled herself up by the railing.

Dahleven kept a hand on her back, guarding against a fall. "Your Talent is Emerging. It usually peaks over a two-week period. You'll be hungry after you've exercised it, like you were tonight, and a little tired—until you get used to it. Then it will be like any other sense. It'll be part of you. You'll take it for granted."

"A little tired?" Lady Celia chuckled weakly. "I feel like I've been hit by a truck." Then she paused on the second step and half turned to look at him. "I don't want to get used to it. I don't need a Talent. I'm going home. I'm not staying here any longer than I have to."

Even a step below her, Dahleven was still taller. He gazed down at Lady Celia, disturbed by her vehement desire to leave. He shook his head and smiled. "Whether you will it or not, your Talent is Emerging. You should practice so you learn control, and your limits...What Talent have you developed?"

"How should I know?" She turned and pulled herself up another step.

"What were you doing when I found you?"

Lady Celia rested on the third step. "Searching for Angrim's bracelet."

"And you found it among the cloth? How did you know where to look?"

The surprise on Lady Celia's face was almost amusing. "I just knew. It pulled me. And the closer I got, the stronger I felt it. It was sort of like when we were short of water, only much stronger. I couldn't help finding it."

A Finder, then.

Lady Celia turned and started to pull herself up the next step.

It will be dawn before she climbs these stairs—if she doesn't fall and break her neck. Dahleven swept Celia up into his arms. She went rigid and tried to push away.

"What are you doing? Put me down!"

He had to lean against the stone balustrade to keep

his balance while he shifted her weight to carry her comfortably. "Forgive my presumption, Lady Celia, but each of your steps was slower and more difficult than the last. Speak the truth; do you truly have the strength to climb three flights of stairs?"

She opened her mouth, then shut it with a snap. When she sagged against his chest, he knew he'd won—this skirmish, anyway.

He remembered how she forthrightly admitted her misjudgments in the field, and apologized for whatever it was that Kaidlin would tell him. *Her own honest nature defeats her.* He suppressed a grin and accepted her concession sober-faced.

"You're right, I'd never make it." Her voice sounded limp, now that the outrage had drained from it. She waved a hand toward the stairs without much energy. "Home, James."

chapter fourteen

cele awoke in her room, cocooned in the warmth of the featherbed. The light cascading through her window told her it was early afternoon. She didn't remember getting into bed. But she did remember Dahleven carrying her up the stairs.

Then she realized she was nude under the sheets.

Someone had removed her clothes.

She scrunched down, pulling the covers up tight under her chin. *What happened last night?*

Thora sat on the window seat, sewing and talking with Ghav. She looked up when Cele moved. "Awake at last! And ready for food, too, I'll wager." With her usual briskness, she opened the door and spoke to someone just outside, then went to the closet.

At the mention of food, Cele thought of the meat pies Dahleven had fed her, finding Angrim's bracelet, and Dahleven carrying her up the stairs. She'd liked the strength and safety of his arms. Cele blushed, embarrassed to admit to herself how much she'd enjoyed it. *But what did we do after that?*

With a moment's reflection, she knew the answer. Nothing. She'd been nearly comatose when he picked her up. Dahleven wouldn't take advantage of her that way. She knew it as surely as she'd known where Angrim's bracelet was last night.

Her stomach rumbled. It felt hollow and crampy, as though she hadn't eaten for days. "What's happening to me?"

Ghav hobbled over to her bedside, supporting part of his weight on a cane. "Nothing to worry about," he said. "Your body is merely adjusting to the Emergence of your Talent. It's normal for you to be hungry and tired after Finding something. That should only last for a couple of weeks, until you become accustomed to its use. And you should practice. Developing your Talent is best done early."

"I think Dahleven said something like that last night."

"You should listen to him. He also came into his Talent later than most—though not this late."

"Was he this wiped out?"

Ghav shook his head. "Emergence may hit you harder, or last longer than usual. Or you may have an easier time of it, overall. I can't predict with any certainty. The experience varies, and I've never heard of a Talent Emerging this late. But then, I've never known someone from Midgard, before." Ghav smiled crookedly. "Even the Sagas aren't much help. When Brynjolf led our people to Alfheim, Talents Emerged only in the children."

"Well, it's all new to me." Cele clenched the sheet under her chin. "Maybe we could continue this conversation when I'm up and dressed."

"How do you feel? Any headache? Nausea?"

"No, I feel fine. Just a little fuzzyheaded from sleeping so long. And hungry."

"Very good. There's no reason for you to stay abed, then." He held out his hand to help her up.

Cele looked at his hand. "Uh, I know you're a Healer, but I'd prefer a little privacy."

Ghav lifted his thick graying eyebrows in surprise, but he turned and hobbled back to the window seat, keeping his back to her.

I guess it's the best I'm going to get. Cele slid out of bed, wrapping and draping the sheet around her like a toga.

Thora already had clothing ready for her. She didn't seem concerned about Ghav's presence. She slipped a floor-length, light blue dress over Cele's head, followed by a low cut tunic of darker blue panels that fastened only at the shoulders and waist. The tunic was heavy with embroidery, but the cloth of the dress was soft against her skin. Cele liked the freedom of not wearing a bra, but she wasn't sure she would ever get used to not wearing panties. *Maybe I can get some made.*

Dressed, she felt better. "You can turn around, now. I'm decent."

Ghav turned and smiled. "I can't imagine you otherwise, my lady."

Cele felt awkward. "Thanks."

He waved a worn brown glove. "I've lost one of my gloves. Will you help me look for it?"

Cele's discomfort vanished; she tilted her head and tucked her chin, peering at him skeptically from under raised brows. "My training begins immediately, I see." She felt like she was participating in a parlor trick. "What do I do?"

Ghav shrugged. "Most Finders find just one thing, like Fender. He Finds water. He says he imagines the sounds it makes, and how it feels sliding down his throat. What did you do before?"

What *had* she done?

"Let me see your other glove."

It was an ordinary, well-worn brown leather glove. *Where? There!* Without any doubt, Cele walked to the cabinet and pulled out the third drawer. There was the glove.

What just happened? When she turned her mind to it, she'd *known* where the glove was. It had drawn her, but the sensation wasn't quite physical. *What's going on?* She stared at the glove. Whatever it was, it was kind of weird—and fun.

Finding Angrim's bracelet wasn't the first time she'd felt the peculiar certainty, the odd *knowing* of where to go. She'd been thirsty when she'd felt the pull of the water. Underground, she'd been anxious for light and open air when she felt drawn to the ventilation shaft, then she'd imagined torchlight and *known* that it was ahead. When Angrim became hysterical, she had wanted to calm her, wanted the bracelet, and suddenly, without hesitation, she'd *known* without question what direction to go to find it.

Cele lifted the glove from the drawer and laughed with delight. "This is great! What's next?"

"Nothing for now. Practice is necessary, but don't over-do it. Emergence Exhaustion is a serious danger," Ghav said. Thora nodded.

Cele's stomach rumbled. "Well, then, what about lunch?"

Food. It was close. Cele crossed the room to the door and stepped out into the passageway. There at the end of the hall, just turning the corner toward her, was a servant carrying a tray. *Bingo!*

The Great Hall buzzed with a multitude of conversations. Dahleven stood to one side talking with a crofter of substantial holdings. The Althing had broken for the noon meal, and now, afterward, the Jarls and their heirs moved among the carls and freemen, maintaining good will with the men of their provinces. Servants passed quietly along the sides of the room, removing the remains of the meal from the tables and refreshing the pitchers of ale.

Dahleven wondered if Celia was awake yet. He'd never seen someone hit so hard by Emergence. The memory of her in his arms tingled along his skin. He'd liked the weight of her nestled against his chest. When she'd fallen asleep with her head tucked into the hollow between his neck and shoulder, her trust had felt like a greater gift than any Jarl could bestow.

"What can we expect, my lord?" the crofter asked.

What had the man been saying? Dahleven cursed silently; he'd lost track of the conversation. *Ah yes, the pasturage.* "Kon Neven has decided not to open the high range this year. It needs time to recover from the past few years of grazing." *And we need time to make the borders safe again.*

The crofter looked sour, but took his leave politely. Dahleven turned and saw Jon up near the dais, draining his tankard. Again.

His sister had made no bargain with that one. Ingirid had married for love, but Jon had married for position. Neither of them had gotten what they'd hoped for. He watched Jon lean back and hook his elbow on the empty table on the dais, then casually turn and switch his tankard for the full one Neven had left behind.

Dahleven had seen Jon do it before. There was plenty of ale to be had from the pitchers kept full on the sideboards, but this was one of the ways Jon puffed his ego. Neven had never given Jon the power he'd expected would come with marrying Ingirid. His father had seen too clearly what Jon was. So Jon took his petty revenge and pretended to himself that he had somehow bested Neven.

Dahleven clenched his teeth and turned so he wouldn't have to look at his brother-by-marriage. He and Ragni would have taken Jon aside long ago for a "talk," but Neven had forbidden it. He supposed Father was right. Nothing would change what Jon was, and that kind of "conversation" would only have made Ingirid unhappy.

Instead, he turned his anger to better purpose, rehearsing in his mind the petition he would soon make to have Knut declared Outcast.

Cele awoke the second time in early evening. Ghav had tested and teased her to Find things for half the afternoon—when she wasn't wolfing down everything on the well-laden tray. Eventually she'd hit the wall, or the wall had hit her, and he'd called a halt.

"You must respect the fatigue," he'd said.

She sat down heavily on the edge of the bed. "I don't think I can do anything *but* respect it," she'd said short minutes before falling into a deep sleep.

Cele stretched and sat up. At least this time only a few hours of sleep had restored her. Having a Talent would be pretty useless if she passed out for nearly a day every time she used it. *I wonder if I'll still have it when I get home. I'd be a natural for Search and Rescue.*

Home.

How long had she been gone? Eight days? They would have called off the search for her by now. Her boss might already be interviewing for her replacement; Elaine and her other friends would be thinking of her as dead, rather than missing. She was moving further and further away from her life as she'd known it. She felt like she'd taken the wrong turn onto an L.A. freeway and couldn't find an exit ramp.

Her heart pounded. *I might never get home.* She'd avoided the thought until now. *Marooned.* In a place where nothing worked the way she expected it to and she kept making the wrong assumptions about what was going on. A place where people killed each other with swords and arrows and could control your mind just by thinking about it.

Cele hugged her knees and hid her face in her arms. The terrible thought that she might never get home weighed on her, crushing her silently, paralyzing her thoughts, grinding in her chest like the ache from a deep, unhealing bruise.

She had to find a way home. Where she understood the rules. Where she belonged.

Hope flickered. Could she Find a way back? Cele opened herself, focusing on the comforting safety of Home. She held the picture of the little adobe cottage she shared with Elaine in her mind's eye, and imagined snuggling into the overstuffed leather couch in the wood-floored living room.

She didn't feel a thing.

She squinched her eyes shut, imagining herself leaning against the headboard of Elaine's bed while her friend tried to decide what to wear on a date.

Nothing.

Not a tingle, not a tug, not a whisper.

Everything familiar and comforting suddenly seemed even farther away and more out of reach than ever. She felt small and alone in the wide expanse of the feather-bed, tiny and lost in the cold stone labyrinth of Quartzholm, cut off from everyone who'd ever cared for her. When her mother had died, when Jeff left, there had been Elaine and others offering the comfort of friendship. Here there was no one.

Except Thora.

She sat there, aching, as the last light from the setting sun crept up the wall.

And Fender, and Ghav.

Her stomach felt like it was full of rocks. She was stuck here. She was foolish to keep hoping.

Ragni. And Dahleven.

Cele sighed and flopped back on the bed. *Okay. So I'm not quite alone. But I'm still stuck here.*

Being miserable won't solve anything. She'd learned that after Jeff had left. She had to do something, and helping someone else was the best way she knew to push aside her own grief. The only people who were more unhappy than she was were Sevond and Aenid. Cele slipped into her shoes. *Misery loves company.*

She made her way through the twists and turns of the hallways and stairs to Sevond's door. Servants bowed or bobbed curtsies to her as she navigated down the long halls, and higher-ranking folk nodded to her in passing. Cele acknowledged the courtesies, surprised at how easily she was adapting to her position in Nuvinland society. A position she enjoyed, she reminded herself, only because Neven had granted it to her, and could easily take away again.

As she turned a corner, Cele thought she recognized a tall, dark-haired man following her. She wasn't sure if he was the same man she'd seen at the market or not. *I'm tired of this. This is one mystery I can solve.* Cele slowed her step, waiting for him to catch up. He didn't, and when she stopped to look behind he turned down a different way.

She started to follow him, then remembered Sevond. It was already late in the day. Vowing that next time she saw her dark-haired stalker she'd get some answers,

Cele returned to her original path.

Sevond was alone, except for his apprentice Hrolf. "Ah, my dear, I'm glad to see you again," Sevond said. "I'd begun to think you might not come today."

"I've been asleep most of the day. Ghav and Lord Dahleven say my Talent for Finding is Emerging."

The overlay of grief vanished for a moment from Sevond's face as he smiled broadly. "Congratulations, my dear! How wonderful! I have a fine little wine set aside. We must celebrate." He reached into a dusty cabinet and pulled out a hand-blown bottle, then bellowed down the hall. "Hrolf! Bring three cups!"

A moment later Hrolf appeared, followed by Father Wirmund. "Perhaps you can make it four?" the priest said.

Cele stiffened at the sight of the gaunt old man.

"Father Wirmund!" Sevond bowed deeply. "What brings me such unexpected honor?"

Father Wirmund smiled gently. "Should a priest not visit a man so recently deprived of his only child? I've come to offer my condolences, and praise Sorn for the fine man and warrior that he was."

Sevond lost his smile. "Thank you, Father. He was that. No man had a finer son, and it makes me proud that others know it...Hrolf! Four cups!"

The apprentice was already returning with four goblets on a tray. The glass bowls were set into silver stems, beautifully detailed like flowers on a vine.

"I'm rather surprised to find you in such good spirits, Master Sevond. What are we drinking to?" Father Wirmund asked.

The Overprest's rank didn't spare him a sharp look from Sevond. "My grief is beyond speaking, my lord. But when a young woman's Talent Emerges, she deserves a toast." Sevond pulled the cork and poured three small portions.

Wirmund bowed graciously to Cele, letting Sevond's rebuke slide by without comment. "My congratulations, Lady Celia. May I ask your Talent?"

She didn't want to share it with him, but had no good reason not to. "I find things."

The priest's brows lifted. "You are most fortunate. Most who have the Finding Talent can locate only one or two kinds of...*thing.*"

"So I've been told."

"I should keep you close, my dear," Sevond said, smiling ruefully. "I'm forever misplacing all sorts of items. My lady wife was in despair of me."

"You never lose your jewelry tools, master," Hrolf volunteered.

"That's right, boy. Never my tools. I might lose my head, but never my pliers and files." Sevond lifted his glass. "Congratulations, Lady Celia, on the Emergence of your Talent. May it serve you well."

The others lifted their goblets to her, then downed the wine in one gulp.

It felt strange to be congratulated for something she wasn't sure she wanted and didn't fully understand. "Thank you."

Sevond refilled the goblets, filling the fourth this time for her. Cele sipped the thick amber liquid. It was intensely sweet, and not to her taste, but she finished it anyway. She wouldn't be so rude as to refuse Sevond's hospitality, and it was something to do while waiting for Father Wirmund to conclude his courtesy visit.

Unfortunately, Father Wirmund didn't leave. He talked with Sevond about the jeweler's current commission, complimented him on the golden mistletoe he'd crafted for Baldur's altar, and drank a second glass of wine.

Cele finally decided she wasn't going to get her cozy chat with Sevond, and in a break in the conversation, she rose to leave. "Master Sevond, Father Wirmund, please excuse me. I guess I'm still a little tired."

"Of course, my dear. Practice, eat, rest. That's the way of it during Emergence," Sevond said.

"I must take my leave as well, I fear. Thank you for your hospitality, Master Sevond. And accept my heartfelt sympathy for your loss, and my blessing on your son's valorous death." Father Wirmund turned to Cele. "May I escort you, Lady Celia?"

She really didn't want to remain in his company any longer than necessary, but she smiled anyway. "That's kind of you, but you probably have much more important things to do. I'd hate to take you away from your duties." She wondered if he could see how insincere her expression was.

"Nothing could be more important than escorting a lovely lady." He nodded to Sevond and took Cele's arm.

She cringed inwardly at Father Wirmund's dry, papery touch, but didn't pull away. She turned to Sorn's father. "Thanks, Master Sevond. May I visit you tomorrow?"

"Of course, my dear."

They hadn't taken three steps from Sevond's door when Cele became sure that Wirmund had come to find her, rather than to visit Sevond.

"Tell me, Lady Celia, is the belief in Baldur strong in Midgard? Or do they yet exalt His servants, Odin and Thor?"

Cele knew he wouldn't like the answer, but she didn't care. "Neither. The dominant religion is Christianity, but Islam is gaining on it. Buddhism is popular too."

Father Wirmund looked both alarmed and confused before he adopted a neutral mask. "The White Christ is still followed in Midgard?" His voice was mild.

Cele had to admire his control. The people they passed in the hall would never know he was upset, but she wasn't fooled. *Wirmund is worried.* "Yes. All over the world." She couldn't resist adding, "I'm afraid no one believes in Odin and Thor anymore, except maybe the Icelanders. And almost nobody's heard of Baldur." She probably shouldn't yank his chain, but she didn't like the condescending way he'd treated Sevond.

Wirmund's face didn't change, but Cele felt his fingers tighten ever so slightly on her arm.

"And what do you believe, Lady Celia?"

Now we come to it. "My beliefs are my own, Father Wirmund." She smiled a little to take the slap out of her words. *Let him chew on that for a while.*

She didn't let him chew too long. As they turned down a familiar hallway, Cele remembered Gudrun's suggestion to query the priests about a homeward path, something about a rainbow or a bright road, and she kicked herself for baiting him. *Maybe it won't matter.* If she guessed right, he'd be only too happy to get rid of her. "You know, I'm glad we met today, Father. Lady Gudrun suggested I speak to you. I'd like to know more about how your people got here. Do you know of any way for me to go home?"

Father Wirmund remained silent as they climbed the long staircase. Then he turned and leveled his cool, assessing gaze on her. "There are no altars to Freyr here in Alfheim, except those we have built to him as Baldur's servant."

Cele knew he was telling her something, but she didn't understand what.

He must have seen her confusion, because he added, "The altar shown to Brynjolf was not built by human hands, and there are none such here in Alfheim. There is no path back to Midgard. Those who follow Baldur know that." He wasn't above a dig of his own. "Nor do we wish to leave. Why would we? The earth is fertile, the winters mild in the valleys, and Baldur himself led us here through his servant Freyr."

Wirmund's words chilled her. As he'd meant them to, she guessed. Cele looked at him closely. Did he mean what he said? Was there really no way back? Or was he punishing her for her lack of respect?

Wirmund's face gave away nothing.

They walked in silence for a few steps, before Wirmund asked, "Tell me about your own passage, Lady Celia. I gather it was rather different from Brynjolf's."

"I thought Neven must have filled you in." The other lords didn't seem to know as much as Father Wirmund.

"*Kon* Neven trusts me. But I hoped to hear the tale from your own lips."

The blow to her hopes made her answer sharp. "I told Kon Neven the truth, and Lady Gudrun, too, so you won't catch me changing any details. I was climbing past the petroglyphs when I fell, and woke up here."

"You saw no altar? No golden boar?"

Cele shook her head. "No." Then she remembered something. "I saw colored lights. Lady Gudrun said I should tell you about them."

Wirmund seemed to relax a little, though it was hard to tell, he was so tight and dried out. "Ah," was all he said.

"Does that mean something?"

Wirmund nodded and patted her hand. "Only to a follower of Baldur."

Cele wanted to scream, but she managed to remain silent. Wirmund had been playing these games for a long time by the look of him. She wouldn't get anywhere by pushing him.

Ragni, on the other hand, might be more informative. Cele made a mental note to talk to him. And it wouldn't hurt her to be more pleasant to Father Wirmund—not too much, anyway. "Maybe I should learn more about Baldur, then."

Father Wirmund smiled thinly. "That would be wise, Lady Celia." He stopped in front of her door and took her hand in one of his, then touched the purple bag that was the symbol of his office with the other. He spoke in a ritual tone. "May Baldur's blessings be upon you, may He guide your Talent, and give you joy." He released her hand and nodded to her. "Good rest, Lady Celia."

Surprised at the blessing, Cele watched him walk down the hall and turn the corner before she went into her room.

There was a visitor waiting for her.

"Fender! I hope you haven't been waiting long. Did you come to take me to the market? I'm afraid I went last night with Angrim."

"That one." Fender made a face. "No. I've come to continue your lessons." He looked her over. "You seem to have recovered well from Ghav's tutorial. That's a good sign. Now it's my turn."

Fender didn't give her a chance to wonder about his opinion of Angrim, since he started to challenge her immediately. Cele had hoped that since he was a Finder of water, he'd be able to tell her more about her Talent, but he quickly reinforced what Ghav had said: everyone was a little different; it was misleading to draw conclusions from someone else's experience. The only way to understand one's Talent, he affirmed, was to use it until it was second nature.

Fender tried to stump her, and suggested items to find all over two floors of the castle, but Cele found them all. He seemed impressed, especially when she found something he'd only described to her. "You've never seen one of these before?" he said after she'd Found the bootjack shaped like a small animal.

Cele shook her head. "Is that important? I never saw Angrim's bracelet, either, and she was too hysterical to tell me what it looked like. I knew it was gold, though."

Fender whistled softly. "You're good. Very, very good."

When they returned to her room after two hours, Cele was ravenous.

Thora had a tray waiting for her. Cele barely managed to invite Fender to join her before falling on the food.

"No, thank you, my lady," he said. "Thora, the fatigue will hit her soon. Make sure she's in bed before she falls on her face."

Thora directed an affronted look at Fender. "This is not *quite* the first time I've tended someone in Emergence, Lord Fendrikanin."

"*Lord* Fendrikanin?" Cele said around a mouthful of cheese.

Fender waved his hand dismissively. "A second son of a second son. Thora just drags it out when she wants to put me in my place." Fender made an elaborate bow. "Good rest to you, Lady Celia," he said, and swept out the door with a wink to Thora.

Fender was right; she started to crash as soon as the worst of her hunger was sated. She felt like she was sleepwalking as Thora prepared her for bed. Between the blessings of Father Wirmund and Fender's good wishes, Cele slept through the night and awoke refreshed midway through the morning.

Cele ate a nearly normal amount at breakfast, still dressed in her nightgown. When she'd finished eating, Thora prepared to dress her.

Lord Neven's gift of clothing included a pair of wide-legged pants in a soft flowing fabric. Cele chose to wear those along with the same tunic she'd worn the day before. It was blue and knee-length and fastened front to back only at the shoulders and waist with gold brooches.

She donned the white loose-sleeved blouse that Thora handed her. The delicate fabric was covered with white embroidery, and several narrow ribbons closed the throat. *Where do they find the time to decorate their clothes like this?* The generosity of Neven's gift struck her again, even more forcefully now as she considered these "everyday clothes."

Neven must have his reasons. But they were unknowable, so she turned her thoughts elsewhere. "What's on the agenda today, Thora?"

Thora turned a blank look at her. "Naught that I know of, my lady. What do you wish?"

That brought Cele up short. With nothing planned or scheduled for her, she was free to choose. Kaidlin had asked her to visit, or she could see Sevond again. And Solveig, the lady Jarl, had invited her to visit as well.

None of those options immediately appealed. She felt on display and under inspection with everyone except Sevond and Dahleven. What she really wanted was to get outside, away from the massive weight of the stone palace, somewhere where she didn't have to mind her manners and worry about offending against customs she knew nothing about.

"Where's my belt-pack, Thora?" No sooner were the words out of her mouth, than Cele knew where to Find it.

Her face must have betrayed her chagrin, because Thora gave her an amused look. "It takes time to get used to, my lady."

As Cele retrieved her pack from the cabinet, Thora asked, "What are you planning?"

"I'm going for a walk. This is a lovely place, but I need to get outside for a while." Cele peered at Thora. "That's not a problem, is it?"

Hesitantly, Thora said, "No, but—"

Cele flashed on the attacks she'd survived. "The fields beyond the village look so peaceful." She gestured to the window. "They're safe, aren't they?"

"Yes, of course! But you don't know your way around, my lady. You should take an escort."

Cele smiled. "I'm a Finder, remember? How can I get lost?"

Thora shrugged, defeated. "As you wish."

"Great! Can you get me some nuts and dried fruit? And I'll need to fill my water bottles."

Dahleven sat on a long bench near the back of the great hall, trying to pay attention as yet another crofter discussed the need for increased pasturage.

No, that was the last man. This one wants to divert more water to his fields.

How did his father manage to look interested through all of this? The other Jarls on the dais with him weren't so successful in looking concerned. Solveig and Magnus were attending to the proceedings, but Yngvar was digging in his ear and inspecting the results. Ozur looked bored, and Hafdan and Ulf looked like they'd rather be anywhere else. He knew how they felt.

Another crofter jumped up to interrupt the first. "And in the dry years, what will become of my flocks and fields downstream? Will you enrich him only to beggar me?"

This is more interesting.

Hafdan, in whose province the second man held land, answered. "Build the sluice high enough that it will divert water only when the stream is full. In dry years you'll still have water."

All the Jarls nodded or shrugged their agreement, but the crofter wasn't satisfied. "But will he build it as you say? He would have built the sluice without discussion, but I discovered him."

The first crofter's land was in Neven's province. "You will build it together," Neven said. He looked at Hafdan for agreement as the crofter opened his mouth to protest. "So speak we all. The matter is settled."

The crofters glared at each other and sat down. Another stood to bring forward his petition. Dahleven felt the room settle in for renewed tedium after the brief flare of excitement. Yesterday, the atmosphere had been more tense, as the Jarls had answered claims and complaints pertaining to losses from the raiding of the borders and caravans. The lords were responsible for paying *wereguild* to the relatives of men killed in their service. When a man was killed in a joint venture like a caravan, the matter could be muddy. Multiple lords and crofters had to sort out the responsibility.

Even the matter regarding Knut had been clouded. Knut's brother Hegg hadn't fought the Outcasting of his brother once Dahleven told the story, but he'd disputed the levying of Lindimer's *wereguild* against him. Dahleven could hardly blame Hegg; the fine would be a terrible hardship for him. Hegg petitioned that Dahleven share the burden, because Knut had been under his command.

Hegg's petition had been voted down. A man's actions were his own burden or glory, and his family's. But Dahleven couldn't help feeling there was some truth in Knut's brother's words.

Dahleven hadn't liked the disposition of another petition either.

A young woman, with babe in arms, had accused a lord in Ozur's Jarldom of subverting the law to his own ends. "My Harald was an honest man," she said. "He worked hard in our fields, that's why they grew green and rich. But Braga said Harald used dark magic to steal the life from *his* fields to enrich our own. He lied! Braga is a lazy pig! That's why his crops are spare and brown."

"Why accuse Lord Vestar then, rather than Braga?" Magnus inquired.

"Because it was he who put Braga up to it." The woman's voice was shrill. "He wanted under my skirts, but I wanted Harald. Vestar banished Harald for a year. He asked no questions of our neighbors, nor anybody. They would have told him how hard Harald works, but he didn't ask. And when Harald was gone, Lord Vestar gave Harald's lands to Braga and took me into his great house and kept me there."

"Why didn't you turn to your family, or Harald's?" Magnus asked.

"What chance did I have? He swept me up that very day. And what could Harald's family do against a lord? Their son was branded a criminal, and worse."

"And your family? What of them?"

"My father thought me foolish to refuse Lord Vestar from the first. I think Father hoped I would please him and bring some favor upon the family. He was no more made happy by Lord Vestar than I. Vestar no longer wanted me when his seed took root, and I grew large." Her voice started to thicken with tears. "And Harald didn't return at the end of his year."

"Why are we listening to this here?" Ozur demanded. "This is clearly a matter that should have been brought to me. I am Jarl over Lord Vestar. This isn't a matter for the Althing. There is no conflict here between Jarl-doms."

"Very true," Magnus said and looked at Neven.

"Do all agree this matter is for Ozur?" Neven asked, looking at each Jarl in turn. All nodded. Lady Solveig most reluctantly.

Dahleven watched his father. Only someone who knew him well would notice the slight tightening of his jaw, a sign of Neven's extreme reluctance to leave the matter to Ozur. Unfortunately, it was the law.

"Well then, since I have at last heard the case, I will give judgment," Ozur pronounced.

"You haven't heard from Lord Vestar or Braga or Harald's neighbors," Neven pointed out.

"It's hardly necessary. She's clearly a scorned woman, unhappy with the loss of her position as a lord's bedmate. But I do agree Lord Vestar must take responsibility for his child." Ozur's voice took on the tone of official pronouncement. "The child will be given into the care of Lord Vestar, to be raised in his household. You woman, are hereby banished from Skipsheim for six months, for bringing false accusations against a lord."

A ripple of unhappy murmuring had swept the room and Neven had to call for order as the babe was taken from the shrieking woman's arms. Dahleven had left soon after she was led away. She wouldn't starve, homeless and alone. He'd made arrangements for her to live and work the six months in Quartzholm, but the matter had left a sour griping in his belly.

The current session of the Althing addressed more common matters, and from the number present, the crofters and minor lords had had more trouble than usual settling their own disputes this year. Dahleven wasn't required to be present, but it was wise for an heir to attend these sessions at least part of the time, to show respect for those he would one day govern and lead.

Dahleven was trying to follow the rambling of the current petitioner when a light touch on his shoulder drew his attention. Tholvien bent his tall, lean frame to crouch next to him, bringing his dark head near enough to whisper. "The lady intends to leave the castle, my lord. Do you want me to prevent her, or merely follow?"

Leaving? Curiosity energized Dahleven's muscles. "No. I'll handle this." He stood and walked out with Tholvien, relieved to have a good reason to quit the Althing. "How is she provisioned?"

The gates to the huge courtyard stood open, allowing the market to spill out into the village that nestled around the castle walls. Cele had no difficulty leaving, and no one but merchants hawking their wares accosted her. She'd wondered if anyone would follow her, but she saw no sign of it. The village spilled downslope from the stone ramparts surrounding the bailey. Many of the larger buildings were built of the same rose quartz and granite that formed the walls.

Cele turned left after leaving the gates and followed a wide street that wrapped around the base of the wall. Long ago, someone had cleared the nearby forest, leaving large meadows between the town and the forest. She didn't have to use her new Talent to know that the fields were closest in that direction; she'd seen that from her window. The road narrowed as she got further away from the main thoroughfare, then stopped in a dead end next to a broad building with tables and benches out front. A few men sat drinking, hunched over their tankards.

Cele slowed and came to a halt. The only way out was the narrow path running along one side of the tavern. She hesitated, looking down the claustrophobic alley as far as she could. It curved to the right, behind the building. She thought about back-tracking to find another way out to the green fields she'd seen from her window, but she didn't want to spend half the day looking for a way out of the village. She *knew* the open fields she wanted were close, she could feel them just beyond the tavern, but there was no guarantee the alley would get her there. *So much for never being lost again.* The idea of walking down the blind passage made her skin prickle, but the sun was at her back, brightly lighting the narrow space between the buildings and the broken crockery in it, making it less frightening than it would have been in shadow.

One of the early drinkers called to her while she was considering her options, rising on muscular legs to approach her. Cele turned nervously to face him.

The breeze carried the scent of beer to her as he lifted a huge tankard. "Care for a sip, girl?" His face was half shadowed from the morning light. What she could see, and smell, suggested he'd been drinking since the night before. He looked surprisingly steady on his feet despite that, and still quite capable of giving her a hard time.

"No, thanks." She took a half step away, putting a little more distance between them. The first rule of self-defense: avoid trouble in the first place.

The man shrugged, not offended, then gestured to the alley with his tankard, slopping some of his ale to the cobblestones. "A tumble, then?" He stepped closer, leering eagerly.

Cele shook her head as her fear notched higher, and backed further away, up the street.

The light was full in the man's face now, making him squint, but he still didn't look angry. "What do you want here then? You lost? Looking for someone?"

"Not for you, Finlig!" The man's companion called out.

Cele cringed inwardly, fearing the effect the razzing would have. *Why didn't I ask for directions at the gate? I could have avoided this. So much for the first rule of self-defense.*

But the man waved aside the catcall like a troublesome fly.

Cele took a chance. "I'm looking for a way out, beyond the village, to the fields."

The man turned, his movement somewhat slow. "That'll get you out." He pointed down the alley, more careful this time not to spill his drink. "Sure you don't want company?"

"Not yours!" his companion said.

Cele managed a half-smile. "No, thanks." Then she sprinted past the man and down the narrow path, staying to one side to avoid the dirty trickle that ran down the center.

Dahleven followed the perimeter of the village further upslope, wishing his Talent was Tracking or Finding. He could Pathfind his way anywhere, and find the fastest or easiest or safest route. But that wouldn't help him follow a person or know where she was. For that, he had to rely on ordinary skill.

He left the village by the first street that led directly out to the open fields, but Cele was nowhere in sight. He should be able to see her, unless she'd left the city by the alleyways nearer the castle. Then she could already be on the upper slopes near the forest.

Dahleven increased his pace. He didn't like the thought of Celia picking her way through the noisome alleys. Her clothing would proclaim her status, and that status might protect her from some of the less polite freemen and thralls—or it might attract their attention. He pressed on. If he didn't find some sign of her exit from the town soon, he'd go back and recruit the aid of a Tracker.

There! A smeared footprint of a lady's slipper where she'd slipped in the muddy drainage. There was another. The length of her stride said she was running. *From what*? Dahleven clenched his jaw and swallowed the surge of fear that rose in his throat.

He hurried.

Dahleven scrambled to the top of a rocky outcropping where he could survey more of the land. A flash of blue, high upslope near the edge of the forest, drew his eye. He could just make her out, sitting like a large bluebonnet among the other wildflowers.

She wasn't hiding, or curled into a frightened ball. Relief almost stole his breath. *She's all right.*

Anger followed on its heels. What was she thinking? Surely even someone fresh from Midgard should recognize a less savory area, and understand what that could mean. Anything could have happened to her! If she didn't know any better than that, he'd teach her quick enough. He'd spell it out clearly for her—she'd think twice before acting so foolishly again.

He could tell when she noticed his approach. She must not be able to recognize him at this distance because her posture changed, as if alarmed. *She must have had some trouble after all.* He didn't raise his hand in salutation, but let her stew. *A little worry may make her more cautious next time.*

As he continued toward her, she got to her feet. She didn't run, but took a defensive stance. He had to admire that, even as his anger pricked him. *She shouldn't put herself in a position to be so afraid.*

Then she recognized him, waved, and sat down again.

"It's a beautiful day to be outside, isn't it?" Celia said, smiling when he came close.

Dahleven forgot the sharp words he'd rehearsed all the way up the slope.

He looked down at her. She seemed hale and whole and none the worse for taking the alleyways out of the village. Her long legs stretched out in front of her, swathed in voluminous light blue pants. Celia leaned back, next to her belt-pack, propped on straight arms. The day was warm and she'd undone the laces at the top of her blouse, nearly all the way down the deep V of her tunic. Sweat glistened on her throat. He could just see the curve of her breast inside, and glanced away. "Yes it is." Then he looked back.

She was still smiling at him. "Sit down. Enjoy the day." She drew her legs up and leaned forward, resting her arms on her bent knees, blousing her tunic and shirt even more.

Dahleven busied himself for a moment pulling his scabbard from his belt. He laid his sword beside him as he sat down on her right. When he looked again, he found he could see the pink bud of her left nipple. His groin tightened delightfully, painfully, and he shifted his weight to find some comfort, though he knew the quest was futile.

Then she turned a more serious face to him and he shifted his gaze to her eyes. "Have you talked to Kaidlin?" she asked. "Did she...?"

"Yes, she told me."

"I'm sorry about the other day, with Ragni," she said softly. "I misjudged you. Again."

He smiled at her blush, and took mercy on her. "You drew no blood."

Kaidlin had been so full of laughter that she hadn't noticed his anger at first. Celia had thought him a seducing betrayer of a young wife and mother of his son. The idea that she would believe him so callous as to kiss her practically on his wife's doorstep had burned like a hot coal in his throat. Fortunately, she'd been sleeping away her Emergence fatigue at the time, giving him time to see the matter through her eyes.

There were Lords aplenty who flaunted mistresses in their wives' faces, after all, not having the decency to take but one as an *elskerinne*. And Lady Celia hardly knew him well enough to know which kind of man he was. It rankled that she would assume the worst of him when he'd given her no cause, until he remembered what she'd said of her father. Her experience of men had taught her distrust. Perhaps it was righteous anger that had prompted her frosty manner in the hall, not offended modesty and grief. Ragni might be right about Celia not grieving Sorn as a lost love.

He hadn't quite been able to hide his delight at that realization, piquing Kaidlin's curiosity. He hadn't explained. His nosey little sister could speculate all she wanted.

"And thanks for getting me upstairs," Celia added.

He nodded a bow, smiling. "It was a pleasure to be of service." He tried without success to push away the thought of how soft and warm she'd felt in his arms.

She rewarded him with a deeper blush and looked away.

He wanted to stay here with her, enjoying the glow in her cheeks and the sweet smells of the meadow, but he had duties to attend to and she should be resting. Reluctantly, he said, "You're in Emergence now. You shouldn't be wandering off alone."

"I'm fine. Ghav said so."

"Nevertheless, we should go back."

Celia shook her head. "Wouldn't you rather be out here than inside those old stone halls?" She jumped up and threw her arms wide. "It's a glorious day! We're healthy. We're safe. There's no one chasing us. Let's play."

"Play?"

"Play." She removed her tunic, then bent and did five somersaults down the hill.

Dahleven sprang to his feet as she started rolling, but it was clear she was in control. When she reached a level place, she stopped and sat up, laughing. Bits of stem and flowers clung to her hair and shirt. She turned around and looked up at him. "Your turn."

Somersaults? The only tumbling he'd done since childhood had been in training, when he'd been more focused on avoiding the sharp sting of a practice sword than on fun.

"Don't worry. No one's watching. No one will catch the heir to Quartzholm being silly."

Did she see him as being so grim? Had he become so? "Is that a challenge?" He lifted an eyebrow at her.

"You bet." She grinned back at him from below.

"What shall we wager then?"

She made a show of considering. "If you do don't do the somersaults, you have to walk back to Quartzholm on your hands."

"And if I do?"

"Then I'll teach you how to do one-handed cart-wheels."

He suppressed a smile. She offered a Loki's bargain: Yea I win, nay you lose. But he didn't care. "You have a deal." Then he dropped and rolled down the hill.

He came to a stop not far from where she sat, laughing and clapping her hands. He found himself grinning back at her. "I win. Pay your forfeit."

"Gladly." She jumped up. "What you want to do is look ahead. Don't look down."

As she threw herself slightly forward, legs swinging over her head then back down to the ground in a clean arc, the wide legs of her pants slipped, giving him a glimpse of her knees. He felt an unexpected rush of heat. Why should her legs affect him now, when he'd had a clear view of them the entire time they were on the trail?

"Now you try."

"Show me again first." He felt a bit wicked teasing her into exposing herself, but it was harmless enough.

She demonstrated again and he got another look at her shapely limbs.

He stood up. "Very well. You've taught me the way of it. It's time to go." He started up the slope.

"Dahleven! We can't just go! You haven't done one yet." She hustled up the hill behind him.

He pressed his lips together and ignored her protests until they reached the flat space, then let his laughter out. While she stood there gaping, he did three perfect cartwheels in a row.

"You sneak! You let me go on and on while you already knew how to do it!"

"Yes."

She shook her head, grinning. "Who would've known you could be so rotten?"

"My sisters, no doubt."

"No doubt." She plopped down and lay back into the wildflowers, releasing their sweet fragrance. She crossed her arms behind her head. Dahleven noted where he'd left his sword, then sat beside her, no longer in a hurry to return to Quartzholm. Her sheer embroidered blouse lay lightly on her breasts, hinting at their pink nipples and soft curves. She stared silently at the high, thin clouds overhead.

Dahleven forced himself to look away from her, willing his cockstand to subside. He shouldn't allow himself to become too attracted to her. Though he no longer thought her an enemy, she was still a cipher, her role in Alfheim uncertain. Though he didn't look at her, he remained aware of her nearness, and of all her small movements. He was concentrating so hard on not noticing her that she startled him when she spoke.

"When I look at the sky, I can almost imagine myself back home." Her wistful tone reminded him she'd lost her whole world.

He looked at her face. It was calm, her eyes staring upward into the infinite pale blue sky. "Is your home so different, then?"

Celia turned a crooked smile on him. "Amazingly different. I couldn't begin to tell you."

"Try."

She rolled to face him, pillowing her head on her bent arm. "Where I come from, people can get on a plane and fly across the country in a few hours. We can pick up the phone or get on the computer to talk to someone on the other side of the world, and almost everyone has a car."

He didn't know what a plane or a phone or a car was, but they sounded like miracles. Or Great Talents. *No wonder she misses Midgard.*

Celia frowned. "And almost everyone knows someone who's been hurt in a crash, or died of a drug overdose, or mugged. That's what I used to do, answer calls and send help to people who'd been hurt, or shot, or..." Celia shook her head.

"It sounds as though you paid a high price for your wonders," Dahleven said.

"We could have airlifted Sorn to a hospital, given him IV antibiotics. We might have been able to save him." Her voice was soft.

Sorn. To have his sworn brother back by his side again. But death was a part of life, and Sorn had died honorably. You moved on. You had to. What would Sorn think of the oath he'd made to Sevond? Would his sworn brother be pleased Dahleven had promised his second son to Sorn's father in his place? Would Celia?

Dahleven lay on his side looking at her with his head propped on his hand. Midgard was so different. He couldn't guess her reaction. What kind of place had this beautiful woman come from, where men flew, abandoned women who carried their babes, and saved the lives of men with belly wounds?

He plucked a grass stem and rolled it in his fingers. "When I was young, I was afraid I would be Talentless, and I wondered what a world without Talent would be like. If the people would be very different." Why had he told her that? Then he realized it didn't matter, he wanted her to know. He traced her jaw line with the stem.

She twitched at the tickle and brushed it away. "Now you know." She grinned. "We're just the same."

"And marvelously different." The bracelet he'd once gifted Sorn, that Sorn had given Celia, glinted on her forearm now, not where a betrothal band would rest. He dropped the grass and ran his knuckle gently over her arm above the elbow. She didn't pull away. *Does she understand?* Their faces were only a foot apart. He imagined leaning over her, pressing his lips to hers. He remembered their softness and warmth and the heat of her body against his, and his cock grew full again. He hesitated, knowing their ways were different, remembering her hand clasped with Sorn's, wondering if Ragni was wrong after all.

Celia leaned over and kissed him. She tasted sweet and warm and smelled of wildflowers. Then she pulled away and searched his face. He didn't want her to doubt. He cupped her head, pulling her lips back to his, then kissed and nibbled his way down into the open collar of her shirt.

Her response removed the last of his reservations. She arched her neck, laughing deep in her throat, almost like a purr. Then she pushed him onto his back and followed him over. Her blouse hung loosely, revealing a glimpse of her breasts before she pressed their roundness against his chest and lowered her lips to his again.

Celia's tongue teased the corners of his mouth, and he opened to her tentative foray, then penetrating her warmth in turn with his bolder thrusts. He rolled her under him without breaking the kiss. Only the thin fabric of her blouse came between his hand and her breast. Her nipple rose, hot and hard against his palm, and his cock throbbed with single-minded desire to be in her. Dahleven's breath came deep and rapid and his blood raced, sped by Celia's soft moan as she arched and pressed into him.

A fragment of his warrior instinct shouted a distant warning. Dahleven lifted his head. It was almost too late. Three men charged toward them, running downslope from the nearby forest, swords drawn.

chapter fifteen

"what–?" cele protested as Dahleven abruptly rolled away, almost flinging her aside as he jumped to his feet. He landed in a crouch, and Cele's heart jolted as he swept his still sheathed sword up from the ground just in time to block an overhead blow from the first of two attackers.

Two fair-skinned men bracketed Dahleven with drawn swords. Cele scrambled to her feet and someone grabbed her from behind. A thin, hairy man pulled her back against his chest, his left arm across her throat. He had a knife in his other hand, a big knife, but he held it out, as though he expected little resistance from her, and defended instead against Dahleven. He began dragging her toward the tree-line.

Instinct and two years of self-defense classes took over. Instead of pulling away from her captor, Cele leaned back into him and turned, jabbing her right elbow hard into his diaphragm while holding his knife away with her left. The arm across her throat loosened; Cele spun out, still holding the wrist of his knife hand, and slammed her other palm at his nose.

He saw it coming and swept her blow aside, then grabbed for her, getting only her blouse. Cele went limp, dropping to the ground as dead weight, her grasp still tight on his wrist. The delicate fabric of her embroidered shirt ripped as she fell. The fragrance of crushed wild-flowers rose around her as her attacker lurched forward, off balance, trying to regain control of her.

Cele pulled her legs up and punched them forward with all her strength, into her attacker's unprotected groin. He screamed and doubled over, crumpling to his knees, retching. Scrambling closer crab-like, she axe kicked his neck. His gasp of pain was cut off as he collapsed.

Cele stared at the man's motionless body, not trusting that her battle was won.

A short scream brought her head around in time to see Dahleven pulling his sword out of one of his enemies. The man fell to his knees and toppled over as the steel, slick and red, was withdrawn. The other man already lay still on the ground.

Breathing heavily, Dahleven kicked his foe's sword out of easy reach and rapidly scanned the forest. Then his focus snapped to Cele and he ran to her, kneeling by her side. "Are you injured?" His hand was gentle as he cupped her face, her shoulder.

Cele shook her head, then noticed the blood sprayed across his chest and staining his sleeve. "You're hurt!" She reached for his arm, but Dahleven drew her to her feet and away from her downed attacker.

"It's not mine. Not most of it, anyway." He fumbled with her ripped blouse, trying to cover her exposed breasts, but the cloth wouldn't stay.

"Never mind that. Let me see." She tried again to

look at his bloody arm, but he pushed her hands away.

"Celia, I'm fine. It's you I'm worried about. We have to get you out of here."

She began to shake.

"Where's your tunic?" he muttered. He scanned the ground, then bent and pulled the bloodstained and crumpled fabric from under one of the men he'd killed. He grimaced. "You can't wear this." He tossed it away as he stuck his blade in the earth. Then he pulled off his dress tunic and handed it to her. It was stained with blood but was still better than letting her return to Quartzholm bare-breasted. She fumbled with it, unable to make her fingers do what she wanted. Dahleven took it from her and helped her put it on. She felt like a child, unable to manage the simplest of tasks, grateful for his care.

Her trembling increased and she wrapped her arms tightly around herself. "Who are these guys? They're your own people! Why'd they attack us? Do you know them?" A tiny part of her mind knew she was overloaded with adrenaline. She tried to clamp down on it, but the words continued to pour out. "Are you sure you're all right? You really should let me look at that."

She paused just long enough for Dahleven to repeat, "I'm fine." Then her babbling rushed on, tumbling out with no control as she looked at the man who'd attacked her. "Is he okay? He just grabbed me. I had to kick him; he had a knife." She knelt abruptly next to him, rolled him as carefully as she could to his back, and put her ear to his mouth, watching his chest. "He's not breathing!" She tilted his chin to improve the airway. Nothing. The man's chest remained still. "Oh, God!"

Cele wiped the vomit from the man's lips with the hem of Dahleven's tunic and exhaled a breath into the man's mouth before Dahleven pulled her away.

"What are you doing, Celia? Stop that! Come away."

"No! He needs CPR!" Cele shrugged violently out of Dahleven's grasp.

She felt the man's neck for a pulse. Her hand shook visibly; all she felt was her own trembling. "I can't find it!" Cele moved her fingers and still couldn't find the pulse. She pressed her ear to his chest. All she could hear was her own blood rushing in her ears. She bent to give another rescue breath, but Dahleven pulled her away again folding her into his arms.

"Leave him. He's dead."

"No!" Cele struggled, pushing hard against Dahleven's chest, trying to writhe out of his grasp. "I might be able to save him! He doesn't have to die!" She couldn't get away. Dahleven held her tight. "You don't understand!" she sobbed. "Too many are dead already! I have to try!" She saved people, she didn't kill them.

The unyielding warmth of Dahleven's hard muscles slowly penetrated Cele's frenzy. She stopped struggling, but her heart still pounded wildly and her breath came in rasping gasps.

Slowly, gradually, her pulse slowed. She became aware of Dahleven rubbing her back and stroking her hair. His deep voice kept rumbling, "It's all right. You did well. It's all right." His soothing tones calmed and steadied her, and she clung to his strength until she regained a measure of balance.

"I've never killed anyone before," she said at last, her voice muffled by Dahleven's shoulder.

"And I hope you never need to again." Dahleven set her back from him just far enough to look into her eyes and gently stroked a stray tendril from her damp face. "But you did need to. You protected your life, and possibly mine as well. You did what you had to do." He gave her a little smile. "Few women could have done so well. I'm proud of you."

Cele let his words sink in for a moment, then she

said, plaintively, "I might have saved him, though."

Dahleven looked at her, doubt wrinkling his brow. "How? Even a Great Talent couldn't bring a man back from death."

Cele turned to look at the man. She'd trained for two years to learn how to defend herself, and now she'd used her knowledge. Fatally. Dahleven was right, she had performed well. A man was dead because she had done well what she had trained to do.

She didn't like the way it felt.

But it was better than being dead.

Dahleven kept his sword in hand as they walked down-hill, alert for the possibility of another attack, though he didn't really expect one. Celia was calm now, silent, and he watched her scramble over a rocky ledge with some-thing like wonder. There were tales of women in the past who'd taken up the sword to defend their lands and loved ones. The women of his own family were certainly strong-willed enough to do so, but he'd never seen a woman defend herself bare-handed against an armed opponent. Celia might not have the skill with a blade necessary for full battle, but she'd done very well today, her hysteria notwithstanding. That was an entirely nor-mal reaction, especially for a woman. And he'd known young warriors who hadn't stood up as well as she had to her first kill.

And her last.

Dahleven ground his teeth. She would never have to kill again because she would never again be in that kind of danger. Never before had he experienced the terror he'd felt when he'd looked up to see those men almost on them. He'd fought for his life before, and was familiar with the tense excitement that accompanied battle. This had been different. Celia had been at risk. She'd been the target. He never wanted to feel that kind of fear again.

Someone wants her taken, alive. The thought chilled him. *For what purpose?*

He'd increase the guard assigned to her, but would that keep her safe? There'd been no reasonable way to predict the attack they'd just survived. *Who would expect it, so close to Quartzholm?* Which raised the next question. *Who ordered it? Who would dare?*

They entered the alleys and Dahleven followed Celia through the twists and turns, guarding her back. The late morning sun heated the drainage and the sour smell of refuse mingled with the bitter tang of ale. Ahead of him, Celia stepped into the street.

A male voice called out, "Come back for a sip, sweeting? Looks like you had that tumble after all."

Celia stiffened.

Dahleven stepped out of the alleyway, the shine of his sword still marred by streaks of dried blood. With extreme satisfaction, Dahleven watched the expression of the lout who'd spoken change from a leer to fear. The man backed a step and sat down hard.

"Did he trouble you before?" Dahleven asked Celia.

Celia shook her head. "No. He tried to push his friend into it, but he was all talk."

Another day, Dahleven might have reminded the lout of the virtues of courtesy, but at the moment he was more concerned with getting Celia to safety. He urged her onward.

Three turns and two hundred yards later, they entered the gates and stepped into the hubbub of the market. He would not sheath a bloodied sword, so he held it high, and clasped Celia's arm with his free hand. The crowd parted, opening a path for them across the courtyard.

By the time they reached the stairs leading up to the open arch, ten warriors waited to escort them. Dahleven spoke in the voice he used to command. "You, Jeger, take Lady Celia to her room and remain outside her door. You others, there are three men dead on the western slopes near the edge of the forest. Get Tracker Talents to follow their backtrail. Bring their bodies here." *Someone at the Althing should know who they are.*

He turned back to Celia. Her fingers had tightened in his when he'd given direction for the guard to take her to her room. Her face was tense. He'd much rather escort her himself, but Neven needed to know as soon as possible that even the fields surrounding Quartzholm were no longer safe from Outcasts. "You'll be all right, Celia. Jeger will keep you safe." He pulled his hand from hers and turned back to the guard, giving him a look that promised mayhem if he failed. "Go. Tell Thora to give her some spiced mead."

Less than an hour later, the events of the morning were still chasing themselves through Cele's mind, but her body was more relaxed, thanks to the warm mead Thora kept pouring. The older woman had wrapped her in a blanket as thick and warm as a hug, but Cele wished for Dahleven's arms around her again, instead. She'd finally stopped trembling, but she couldn't rid herself of the thought that a human being lay dead on the hillside because of her. She wondered at her inconsistency; the two Dahleven killed didn't bother her. They'd been trying to kill him. But she kept seeing the slack features of the man whose neck she'd broken.

She knew she hadn't used excessive force. She'd learned in her training that real life shouldn't imitate the movies. Too many women on TV ran away the first time their assailant stumbled, leaving him to follow and catch and kill. In a real life and death struggle, you made sure the bad guy was down, really down, and would stay down long enough for you to get away. The groin shot hadn't been enough.

She knew that was true. But it didn't make her feel better.

Thora bustled back into the room. "I've drawn a bath for you, my lady, nice and warm." She took the empty cup from Cele. Men's voices spoke just outside, then a sharp rap drew Thora to open the door.

A clear male voice said, "Lady Celia is summoned to an audience with Kon Neven."

Cele noted the lack of polite veneer. Not "requested" or "invited." She was *summoned*.

"A moment, please," Thora said.

"Now." The door was pushed open and the guard addressed Cele directly. "Come with me, Lady Celia."

Cele stood and took off the robe, revealing her torn blouse and Dahleven's too large tunic. It covered just enough to satisfy modesty, but Cele noted with grim satisfaction that Neven would have a clear view of the bruise rising on her collarbone. The guard's eyes widened, but he didn't flinch, only gestured to the door. Cele walked with what she hoped was a dignified pace. "Let's go, then."

Just outside the door, Jeger fell into step beside her. "I'm sorry, my lady. It's by the Kon's order."

She gave the guardsman half a smile. "Not your fault, Jeger."

She was taken to a chamber she hadn't been to before. Jeger was forced to remain outside. Kon Neven sat in one of two massive chairs in front of a large, intricately woven tapestry. Gris met her at the door. Neither of them offered her a seat, but kept her standing.

The chamberlain loomed over her, dressed in grays and blacks like an undertaker, his thin arms clasped behind his back. "You attract trouble wherever you go, don't you, Lady Celia?" Gris began without preamble.

Cele wasn't interested in playing games. She'd had a bad day, and it wasn't getting any better. "Is this blame the victim time?"

"What makes you such an attractive prize, my lady?" Gris sneered. "Are your friends trying to steal you away from us?"

"What are you talking about?" Cele stood her ground.

"The attack this morning was clearly for the purpose of getting you away."

"Me? Don't you think it more likely that Dahleven was the target?"

"Why would *Lord* Dahleven be attacked?"

She looked at Neven when she answered. "He's your heir, isn't he? That makes him important. You may have a spare, but wouldn't Dahleven's death throw a monkeywrench into things?"

Gris shifted his body so she had to look at him. "But he wouldn't have been there, if not for you."

"You think it's my fault? How could I know he'd follow me?"

"Why did you enter Alfheim in Renegade territory?"

"What?" Gris's change in direction threw Cele off balance.

"Did Lord Dahleven find you before your friends could?"

"What friends?"

"Did Sorn die because they attempted to rescue you?"

The question landed like a slap. Had someone *brought* her to Alfheim? Had those people been trying to get to her, when Sorn was wounded? If she hadn't been here, would Sorn still be alive?

Cele shook her head. This was all twisted. She couldn't let Gris and Neven distort the truth this way. She wasn't responsible. Someone else had torn out Sorn's belly, not her. "Why are you doing this? I was the one attacked out there this morning!"

"No one has come to Alfheim from Midgard for six hundred years, my lady. Why you? Why now, when our borders are threatened?" Gris sneered. "Do you truly expect us to believe you *tripped* and *fell* into Alfheim, when it required the act of a god to bring us here?"

The mead and her frustration made Cele reckless. With her torn blouse trailing nearly to the floor from under Dahleven's too-large tunic, she ducked past Gris and stood in front of Neven, hands on hips. "Why are you setting your dog on me? Do you think I *wanted* to come here? Do you think I want to stay? I had a life, before. It might not have been much, but it was *my* life. If you don't like me being here, find a way to send me home."

Neven met her eyes. Her outburst had elicited no visible emotion from him. His voice was cool and calm. "We're looking into it."

Gris came close, poised to resume the attack, but Neven lifted two fingers and Gris remained silent.

"You may go," Neven said to Cele.

Cele stood for a moment, almost strangling on her anger, then turned and stalked to the door. Neven's voice stopped her with her fingers on the latch. "Lady Celia, a bit of advice, if you'll take it. Know well who your friends are."

She turned angry eyes on Neven. "I know, at least, that you are not among them."

The door had barely closed behind Celia when Dahleven swept out of the tapestry covered alcove where he'd hidden with Ragni. "Was that necessary?" he demanded, his voice grating in an effort not to shout. Neven had wanted him to leave, but when he'd refused, his father had insisted he remain out of view. Keeping still had been a severe test of his will and loyalty.

Neven's voice was stern. "Are you questioning my plans?"

"Since you haven't yet seen fit to share them with me, yes, I am."

"We both are," Ragni added, his voice tight.

"You should know by now, both of you, that governing the Jarldom is seldom a case of following well-laid plans. More often it's a matter of adapting to circumstances and taking calculated risks." Neven glanced at Ragni before looking straight into Dahleven's eyes. He didn't use his Talent, but Dahleven felt the intensity of the contact. He didn't flinch from it.

"What are you playing at?" Dahleven demanded. "What 'calculated risks' are you taking with Lady Celia?"

"You found the camp of Renegade Tewakwe and Outcasts, Dahl. *You* pointed out that someone has organized them, that their actions are coordinated. Yet we still don't know who our enemy is, or what his goals are. At the very least he threatens disruption of trade, and possible war with the Tewakwe."

It was true. Their caravans and borders had been attacked time and again, always from surprise, always with superior numbers. Somehow their enemy had information about their plans while they knew nothing of him, or who was acting on his behalf.

Dahleven wasn't deterred, but his voice was a fraction calmer. "What has that got to do with Celia? What purpose did it serve to abuse her?"

Neven's voice was cold. "In war, individuals must sometimes be sacrificed to the greater good. Lady Celia is the only new tool we have to lure our enemy into possibly, hopefully, revealing himself. If she hates me, she'll be more receptive to another's offer."

Dahleven stiffened. He'd stood near the seat of power long enough to recognize the truth of his father's words, but they chilled him nonetheless. He'd lost men in his command, friends, but always as a consequence of battle, and they each and all had understood the dangers they faced. This was different. "She has no part in this," Dahleven argued.

"Hasn't she?" Neven challenged. "How many have traveled the Bright Road in the last six hundred years? It's no coincidence she's here now. She has a purpose here, but whom does it serve? When it comes down to where steel meets skin, what do we truly know of her?"

"She is innocent," Dahleven insisted.

Neven glanced at Ragni, who nodded. "Anger, frustration, no deception." Bitterness edged Ragni's voice and his face was tight. "She's an innocent, just as I told you before."

"Good. Let's hope she stays that way. That innocence may be all that saves her."

"From our enemies, or from you?" Dahleven growled, and stalked from the room.

"My lady! What happened?" Thora exclaimed as Jeger opened the door and Cele stalked into her room.

"I am sick to death of bullies! I used to work for one, but he couldn't hold a candle to Neven. At least back home I could change jobs. Here, I'm stuck with the arrogant bastard." Cele sat down on the window seat, then stood again to pace the room.

"He's a good Kon, Lady Celia."

Thora's tone was a gentle reminder that Cele was in Neven's house, talking to Neven's servant. She softened her voice, but she wouldn't lie about her feelings. "I'm sorry, Thora, but I can't share your high opinion of your lord and master. He's a bully, despite having Gris say the words for him. He all but accused me of being in league with the outlaws, tricking Dahleven into an ambush, and getting Sorn killed!"

"Oh, no!"

"Oh, yes."

Thora was silent for a moment. "You'll feel better after a warm bath. Then we'll get you something to eat." She poured another cup of mead for Cele. "Drink this, while I make sure there are clean towels for you."

Thora was gone much longer than Cele expected, but she supposed the water had cooled and Thora was drawing another tub. It was after lunchtime when Thora returned, and Cele was beginning to feel hungry.

"Come, my lady." Thora held out her hands. Cele obediently rose and let Thora undress her, then wrap her in the robe and lead her down the hall. When Thora opened the door to the bathing room, they were greeted by the sound of feminine voices, which quickly fell silent.

Three women sat in the larger tub, submerged to their shoulders. The scent of honey-suckle rose from the steaming water. The eldest of the women spoke, her brown eyes warm and welcoming. "Greetings, Lady Celia. Join us."

Thora was already pulling the robe from her shoulders, so Cele stepped into the small pool. The water was just right; hot, but not scalding. An involuntary sigh escaped her lips as the water's warmth eased her stiffness.

"That's a nasty bruise you've got coming up on your shoulder, my lady. Did you get that this morning?" the youngest asked.

"You know about that already?" Cele asked, then glanced at Thora who stood with her back to the door. Thora just gave her a small smile.

"News travels fast in the castle. You defended yourself well, we hear," the third woman said.

"Who is 'we?'"

"Forgive us," the oldest said. "Please, call me Alna. This is Osk," she said, indicating the middle woman, adding, "and Saeun." She inclined her head toward the youngest.

Cele nodded to the three and glanced again at Thora. This obviously wasn't a chance meeting, but she'd play along for a while. The water felt too good to leave yet, anyway. "Nice to meet you."

"Are all the women in Midgard so able to defend themselves?" Saeun asked.

Cele shook her head. "No. But it's not uncommon."

"Were you reviled for learning such things?" Osk asked.

Cele cocked her head, surprised and amused. "No. A lot of women take self-defense classes. Some guys think it's sexy to go out with a strong woman." *I wonder how Dahleven feels about it.*

Saeun was tentative. "Were you required to forswear marriage?"

"What? No, of course not!"

"Were no restrictions at all laid on you for the acquisition of your skills?" Osk demanded.

"Just that I follow the directions of my instructor. To use my skills only for my own defense and the defense of others. What is this all about?"

"So you could teach us?" Saeun asked eagerly, leaning forward so the water lapped at her breasts.

Cele looked at the young woman. "Yes, I suppose so. As much as I know. I'm not that advanced."

The conversation took an abrupt turn. "Do women own property in Midgard?"

"Yes, of course." The light dawned. She was getting slow; the morning's excitement must have dulled her wits. "We vote, we choose our own professions, and we marry whom we please, if we marry at all. Is that what you were wondering about?"

Alna nodded. "You understand us well, Lady Celia." She looked at the others, who nodded. Alna lowered her voice. "We are members of the Daughters of Freya. We seek to end the limitations placed on us by our brothers and sons and fathers and husbands. Freya stands beside her brother Freyr, she doesn't sit at his feet. So should we stand beside men. Do you find fault with this?"

Cele grinned. *Viking feminists!* "I think it's wonderful."

Alna smiled, revealing two missing teeth. At Cele's glance she said, "My first husband had a temper, and my brothers depended on his good will for their living."

"I'm sorry," Cele said. "Wasn't there anyone who could help?"

"She might have appealed to the Lord of the holding—but her husband *was* the Lord, and third cousin to the Jarl," Osk said.

Thora spoke from the door. "Her husband wasn't a lord in Kon Neven's province. The Kon wouldn't condone such behavior."

"That's not the point!" Osk said sharply. "It should not be accepted *at all* that a man can act as he will, unless there's a more powerful *man* to stop him."

"You need the power of the law to protect you," Cele said.

"That may be," Osk said, "but what power do laws

have when lords may ignore them for their own gain? I know of women who have been sold into thralldom to cancel their husband's debts, and that's outside the law."

"Thralldom? Do you mean slavery?" Celia's voice rose in shock.

"Indentured service," Osk replied. "But for some it might as well be slavery as their husband's debts are so great."

"That's horrible!"

"Women must stand together if we are to find the strength to make men hear," Alna said.

"We need a leader who stands apart, who isn't afraid to speak and act." Saeun leaned forward looking Cele in the eye meaningfully.

"Whoa. I was with you until that last bit. I'll teach you self-defense, but I'm not the person you want as a leader. You need one of your own. I'd be seen as an outsider by the men, a troublemaker. Even some of the women would reject me, and reject you because of me. You need to define your own freedom. Your leader should be someone that everyone knows, that everyone respects. Not me."

Alna nodded as though Cele had come down on her side of an earlier argument. "She's right."

Saeun and Osk looked rebellious.

"Besides, I won't be here long enough to be of much help, if I can find a way home," Cele added.

Alna looked at Cele closely. "Has anyone held out such hope to you?"

Cele sighed. "No," she conceded. "The best answer I've gotten is 'We'll look into it.' The worst is that there isn't any way."

Alna's eyes were sad. "The skalds tell no tales of anyone returning to Midgard."

"That could be so no one knows they have a choice." Osk said, bitterly. "Our masters couldn't control us so

292

well if we had an escape."

"That may be," Alna said. Then she lowered her voice still further. "We have seers among us, Lady Celia, though the priests of Baldur and the Skalds' Guild forbid it. I'll ask them to throw the stones for you."

"Seers? Is that a kind of Talent?"

"No. Even women are allowed to use their Talents. I speak of casting the runes. At present, the skalds alone are allowed to read the augury of the futhark. For a woman to do so is against the Law of Sanction, never mind the use of ritual magic."

Cele wasn't sure what Alna was promising, but thanked her anyway, adding, "If you can arrange a time and place, I'll teach some women some defensive moves." The water had cooled. Cele stood and Thora wrapped the warmed robe around her. "Good luck to you."

Back in her room, Cele slipped into a long-sleeved, cream-colored dress and the green tunic. It was mid-afternoon and Cele's stomach was reminding her that a lot had happened since she'd last eaten. Thora spoke to the guard in the hall, ordering a meal, then unpinned Cele's braids. Having a maid help her dress still felt strange, but she loved having her hair brushed and braided for her. Her mother had done that when she was little.

Tendrils were still curling damply around Cele's face when the guard knocked and announced Lord Dahleven. Thora dropped a brief curtsey as the Kon's heir entered the room. He too had bathed, and no longer wore his bloodied clothing.

He peered at Cele closely. "You look well. Are you re-covered from this morning?"

"From the fight, or from my meeting with Kon Ne-ven?" Cele grimaced. "I'm sorry. He's your father. I shouldn't have said that." *Not to you, anyway.* "Yes, I'm fine. Just a bit hungry. Would you like to join me for lunch?"

Dahleven smiled ruefully. "I've already—"

A knock on the door interrupted him. Thora opened it to a breathless messenger. "My apologies, Lord Dahleven. Lady Ingirid sends for you. Ari is missing."

"Again?" Thora asked.

Dahleven rolled his eyes. "I assume you've looked in all the usual places?"

"Yes, my lord. We think he followed his brothers down into the tunnels."

Dahleven's attention sharpened. "How long has he been missing?"

"Masters Ljot and Solvin returned a candlemark ago. Several groups are searching already. Unfortunately, the Tracker Talents are all out following the backtrail of those men who attacked you."

"Who's Ari?" Celia asked.

"My nephew," Dahleven said. "He's five. He's not the first boy to get lost in the tunnels, but he is one of the youngest. Ingirid is probably out of her mind with worry. He's her baby. I've got to look for him."

"Of course. Let's go." Cele moved briskly to the door.

"Wait," Dahleven said. "You should rest. This could take a while. After this morning—"

"I'm a Finder, and a good one, or so Fender tells me. Let me help you Find Ari."

Dahleven hesitated.

"Come on," she urged. "The sooner we start, the sooner Ari will be back in Ingirid's arms."

"All right. But the tunnels are too cool for those clothes. Thora, a cloak."

The servant hastily brought the black fur cloak. Dahleven raised his brows as he took the luxurious garment from her and draped it around Cele's shoulders, then urged her out the door. In the hall, Cele started to turn toward the main staircase that she'd always used, but Dahleven stopped her.

"This way." He led her in the opposite direction, to the bathing room. For an instant, Cele wondered if they'd be walking in on the Daughters of Freya, but the bath was empty. The humid air of the room made Cele's cloak feel heavy and oppressive. *What are we doing in here?* She soon got an answer. Dahleven opened the doors of a wide, shallow closet stacked with shelves of towels and linens. He reached in and released a catch, then pushed on the center portion until it swung away, revealing a shaft with a ladder.

Cele raised her eyebrows. *A secret passage. Cool.*

Dahleven lit the oil lamp hanging just inside and hung it from his belt. "This way is quicker," he said. He almost sounded embarrassed. "You'll have to tie up your skirts."

Cele knotted the cream dress up above her knees and swung onto the rungs after Dahleven. Innumerable steps down, the ladder ended. The air had grown much cooler and Cele was glad of her cloak. Her hands were sore from grasping the rungs and she flexed her stiff fingers.

Dahleven turned to her. "Can you Find him? I'm sorry I have no likeness of him. He's about this tall," his hand indicated the height, "very blond, very blue eyes."

Cele smiled. *That probably describes half the five-year-olds in Quartzholm.* "Anything that makes him special? What was he wearing?"

Dahleven ran his fingers through his hair. "I don't know. But you don't have to pick him out of a crowd. There aren't that many children down here."

Dahleven looked away, then back. "My apologies, Celia. I know what I'm asking is difficult." Dahleven looked intently into her eyes. The dim lantern light made his dark gray eyes seem nearly black, but Cele could see the urgency in them, leashed and controlled, but there. Cele touched him lightly on the arm. "It's okay. That's why I'm here."

She fumbled around in her head for a moment, remembering what she'd done the day before with Fender and Ghav. They'd given her examples and descriptions of the things they'd wanted Found, and she'd had fun Finding them. She'd wanted to do it. Wanted to show off a little too, after a while. It had been easy, as long as she held the *wanting* of the thing in her mind.

Cele tried to build an image of a little boy in her mind. She imagined how he might look right then: dirty, frightened, tear-stained. She tried to reach out, to *want* that child, to feel where he was.

Nothing.

She shook her head. "I'm not getting anything."

Dahleven caressed her arm above the elbow. "Take it easy. Reach out. The little adventurer could be quite a distance from here."

"Adventurer?"

Dahleven flashed a crooked smile. "Ari is the bane of Ingirid's life. He's fearless. Ever since he could walk he's been getting into one mischief or another. Last year he split his lip falling out of the storage-lift." Dahleven touched his own mouth.

I've been looking for the wrong boy. Cele revised the image she'd created in her mind to include clear, curious blue eyes, and a scarred lip. She wanted that boy. *Where—*

The strange certainty began immediately, though faintly. "That way, I think." She pointed at the wall. "This doesn't help much, does it?"

"How far?" Dahleven asked.

"I don't know." Cele covered her face and concentrated. "Farther than Angrim's bracelet. Not as far as the spring from where you found me."

"Good, I think I know where to go then." Dahleven concentrated a moment, then took her arm, urging her down the tunnel on the left.

They walked a long way, further than Cele would have expected a five-year-old to go by himself, but the sensation of being drawn continued, and grew stronger. They came to a four way branch and stopped.

"Which one?" Dahleven asked.

Cele hardly needed to concentrate. The peculiar certainty pulled her surely into the second tunnel from the left. She half expected Dahleven to question her, but he merely held the lantern aloft to light their way. The stone walls grew moist and dampness thickened the air.

The feeling grew stronger and Cele picked up her pace. "He's close."

"Ari!" Dahleven's shout reverberated off the stone walls, making Cele jump.

"Uncle Dahben?" A boy's high-pitched voice came back faintly. He sounded nervous, but not frightened.

"Stay put! We're coming," Dahleven shouted again.

Then, faintly, they heard a splash.

"Is there standing water down here?" Cele asked.

"Yes!" Dahleven started to jog, then run. Cele nearly kept up, only slowly falling behind.

A minute later Cele nearly ran into Dahleven's back. The tunnel opened to a wide cavern, filled with dark water. The light glinted gold on the still surface.

"Ari!" Dahleven's voice echoed.

Nothing.

"Answer me! Ari!" Dahleven's commanding voice should have made the five-year-old jump.

The silence was broken only by their own ragged breathing.

Cele's Talent pulled her gaze to the right. Fear froze her heart. There was something in the water. "Look!" She pointed.

Dahleven held the lantern high. "No!"

He thrust the light into Cele's hands, then waded into the lake. A moment later he carried Ari's limp, sodden body out of the water, clutching the boy to his chest, his fists clenched in the child's clothes.

chapter sixteen

"put him down!" Cele used her professional voice, the one she used to get people on the phone to listen in difficult situations.

Dahleven's head bent low to the boy's shoulder. "I told you to stay put, you little fool." Grief strangled his words.

"Dahleven! Put, him, down!" She put the lantern on the ground and pulled at Ari, and her professional demeanor slipping. "Now, dammit!"

Dahleven raised an angry, anguished face to hers, but let Ari go. Cele took the child and laid him on the smooth damp floor. She adjusted his head, clearing the airway, then put an ear to his mouth and watched his chest.

Nothing. No motion.

Cele felt like she was replaying a horrible nightmare.

Carefully, she sealed the boy's mouth and nose with her lips and exhaled, twice.

Dahleven dropped to his knees on the other side of the child. "What are you doing?" He demanded. "Leave him be!"

Cele ignored him. She felt Ari's neck for a pulse. *Yes!* It was there, a little slow, but there. Two more breaths, and suddenly Ari coughed, took a deep breath, and vomited lake water all over her dress. Cele turned him on his side until he finished retching. And then the little adventurer began to cry.

Dahleven pulled Ari into his arms and looked at Cele with wonder-widened eyes. "What did you do? Are you doubly Talented?"

She shook her head. "I learned that back home. It's called CPR. I can teach you—later." Cele's stomach cramped in hunger and she winced. "Let's go. We need to get him warm and dry."

Dahleven led the way, carrying Ari wrapped in Cele's cloak, while Cele carried the light. Ari's wails quickly subsided to whimpers that echoed loudly off the tunnel walls. Cele didn't think they returned the same way they came, though it was difficult for her to tell. A fog of fatigue enveloped her; the details of the tunnels' twists and turns faded into unimportance. Even the chill bite of the cold tunnels became indistinct. All that mattered was putting one leaden foot in front of the other fast enough to keep up with Dahleven.

Finally, they came to a narrow staircase that rose steeply into the wall. Dahleven told her to go first; he followed close behind.

She was taking too much time. They'd only climbed ten steps, and already Cele felt like she faced Everest. "I'm slowing you down. You should go on ahead," Cele said as they approached a tiny landing. "I'll hook the lantern to your belt."

"No. Keep going," Dahleven said shortly.

"I'm not afraid of the dark. I can feel my way up or

wait for you to come back for me. You should get Ari back."

Dahleven looked stubborn. "Ari is fine now. It's you we need to get back."

Ari did look fine. He stared around him with large, blue, curious eyes, just as Cele had imagined. *He still should be examined by a doctor, or a healer at least.* There was no urgency for her. She was just tired and hungry and moving too slowly. Cele turned and pushed upward. She could be stubborn, too, but an argument would delay Ari's return even more. She saw Dahleven nod, apparently pleased with her compliance, and that sparked her annoyance. *The prince of Nuvinland must have his way.*

Her irritation distracted Cele from the difficulty of the next three steps. She forgot why she was angry, but held on to it for strength. *Oh, yeah,* she remembered. *Dahleven. Macho jerk.*

A voice echoed up the narrow stair. "Hello! Have you found him?"

Dahleven turned and shouted over his shoulder. "Tholvien? Yes, we've got him." Dahleven turned carefully in the confined space and descended.

Cele collapsed to sit on a shallow step. What was going on? She couldn't think.

A moment later Dahleven returned, empty-handed. "Come on, we're going to go a different way now."

"Why? What did you do with Ari?"

"Tholvien's got him. Come on."

Descending the fourteen steps was easier than climbing them, but she was still moving slowly and her legs felt wobbly. Dahleven backed down the steps in front of her until she made the bottom. Then he swept her up in his arms. This time she didn't protest.

"What's wrong with her?" The tall, dark-haired man holding Ari asked. He looked familiar.

"She's in Emergence, and I don't think she's eaten since this morning. Do you have any food on you?"

"Emergence! What were you thinking, then, having her climb that stair? My lord."

Cele was vaguely surprised to hear Dahleven sound defensive. "It was the quickest way, and she didn't seem so bad when we started."

Cele lost track of the conversation and let her eyes close, her head resting on Dahleven's shoulder.

The next thing she knew she was in her room and Thora and Ghav were pressing a cup against her lips.

"You must drink, my lady! Swallow!" Ghav shouted.

Why is he shouting at me? The liquid was warm and fruity and vilely sweet, but Cele swallowed, just to get rid of it. The bed was tilting sideways, but her tormentors still held the cup to her lips.

"More! Another little bit, that's it," Thora said.

Why won't they leave me alone? Cele tried to turn away, but Ghav held her head in place until she swallowed again.

"That's it, finish it off."

They let her lie down then, on the blessedly soft featherbed, where she fell into a dreamless sleep.

Dahleven shifted in the chair he'd had brought to Celia's room. He'd spent all night and most of the morning watching her sleep. Exhaustion marred the skin under her eyes with dark circles. He shouldn't have accepted her offer of help. She didn't understand Emergence. He'd been careless with her, deceived against his own experience by her apparent strength. And she'd Found Ari just in time, and breathed life back into him. Without her, Ingrid would be mourning her son. But Celia suffered because of his inattention.

Every time she stirred, he hoped she'd wake to set his concerns to rest, to give him a chance to apologize for his careless treatment of her, but her breathing barely varied. She remained deeply asleep, in the fatigue brought on by use of her Talent. He wondered if she'd drunk enough of the *sterkkidrikk* before she'd slept. What if she never woke? It had happened.

He could have brought serious harm to Celia. After surviving a battle, killing a man, and enduring his father's interrogation, he'd asked her to use her Talent when she hadn't had a bite since morning. Ghav and Thora had barely been able to force the restorative liquid down her throat, giving her some reserves before she passed out. It wasn't safe for someone in Emergence to yield to the fatigue without eating first. It could be especially bad for women. In one case, the girl had never reawakened.

Celia dreamed on. He wanted to shake her, to relieve his concern, to know she could wake, but Ghav had told him to leave her be. Her body would heal itself if left alone.

So Dahleven sat and watched her sleep, and waited for her to wake. He wasn't happy when Thora shooed him out to join the Althing.

Dahleven tugged his wrinkled tunic straight before stepping into the room full of Jarls and heirs, crofters and carls. His attention was demanded immediately by Lord Yngvar.

"Nice bit of excitement yesterday, wasn't it, Lord Dahleven?"

Dahleven hedged, not sure which "excitement" Yngvar referred to, or how much he knew. "Indeed. Though I would hardly call it 'nice.'"

Yngvar ignored the implied rebuke. "How is young Ari? I imagine Jon gave the sprat a lesson he'll not soon forget."

That excitement. "I hope nearly drowning is all the lesson Ari needs."

Fortunately, Jon had been too drunk to know Ari was even missing, sparing the boy and his brothers from their father's temper for a while. Ari had followed his older brothers Ljot and Solvin down into the tunnels. When they'd discovered him, they'd given him a torch and told him to go back. They should have known better. They certainly did once Dahleven had gotten through with them.

"Lord Ragnar's lady, Lady Celia, she helped Find him, didn't she?"

Ragni's lady? Is that what the rumor mongers are spewing? "Yes, Lady Celia helped."

"Guess she overtaxed her new Talent, though. Heard you had to carry her out of the tunnels. Is she going to be all right?"

Dahleven winced inwardly. "Yes, she's quite well." He hoped it was true.

"I hope Lord Ragnar doesn't find fault with you for sneaking about the tunnels with his lady, let alone carrying her through the halls of Quartzholm. It's a sad thing when a woman comes between brothers," Yngvar said.

The first thing Cele did when she awoke was eat. Thora had fruit ready and waiting, and sent out for bread, roast fowl, and cheese while Cele demolished it. By the time her hunger was sated, it was nearly mid-afternoon and the fog that had clouded her mind had begun to lift.

Thora picked up the tray and gave Cele an approving nod. "I'm glad you ate more willingly than you did last evening, my lady. The best thing for you now is to sleep again." Cele yawned and Thora nodded in satisfaction before she swept out of the room with the tray.

A few minutes later, a knock made Cele abandon Thora's advice. It was the servant she'd met the first day, bearing water and fresh towels. It struck her as odd that Thora would have called for them when she wanted Cele to sleep, but the idea of freshening up appealed too much for her to question it. She thanked the man as he left, eliciting the same startled nodding bow from him as the last time, and she remembered Thora's casual dismissal of the mutilated man as a convicted thief.

Cele poured water into the basin and splashed her face. When she pulled a towel off the stack, a small rolled note fell from the folds.

"A friend would like to meet you in the bathing room," the scroll read. The note was signed, "A."

A? Aenid? Angrim? Alna? The first two would have come directly to her. It must be Alna, whom she'd met in the bathing room before.

Cele gathered up the towels and stepped out into the hall. The guard posted outside her chamber followed her, taking up a position to one side of the bathing room door. She acknowledged him with half a smile as she slipped inside. She felt strange having someone watch her all the time, especially when she wasn't sure if he was protecting her or protecting others from her.

There was no one in the bathing room. She'd have to wait, then. Cele paced back and forth for a bit, growing concerned. Had she misread the note? She looked at it again. *Meet a friend in the bathing room. Okay, I'm here. Now what?*

Cele thought about the guard outside. *Maybe that's the problem.* She wasn't sure how much Jeger could hear, but she thought he might become curious if there were no sounds of bathing, so she started running water into the small tub.

A hand came from behind, sealing her mouth and nose with an aromatic cloth.

Whatever was in the cloth didn't knock her out, but it left her limp as a rag doll. Cele tried to pull at the assailant's fingers, tried to turn, to twist out of his grasp, to kick backward. Nothing happened. Her mind was clear, but her body wouldn't respond. Her heart pounded frantically, urging her body to fight or flee, but she couldn't move so much as a finger. Two men tied her into a sling and lowered her down the ladder shaft. It was a jerky descent, and she bounced against the walls several times, feeling every scrape and bruise with unusual and excruciating intensity, adding injury to insult since she couldn't protect herself. At the bottom, another man took charge of her, rolling her in an old carpet. Then she felt three pairs of hands lift her and carry her away.

"You really should be more circumspect when you carry my lady through the halls, brother. Someone might get the wrong idea." Ragni grinned and pressed a tankard of ale into Dahleven's hand at the mid-afternoon break of the Althing.

Dahleven glared at his younger brother, but Ragni's grin just grew broader. Dahleven grimaced and relaxed. Ragni knew exactly how tightly his emotions were knotted with regard to Celia. Probably better than he knew himself. "You've been enjoying Yngvar's company, I see."

"'Enjoying' may be stating it a bit too broadly. But it served its purpose. He had nothing to do with the attack on you yesterday."

"I didn't really think so. He's not subtle enough to hide something like that."

"Nor did any of the other Jarls," Ragni added.

Dahleven's frustration sharpened his voice. "Then who?"

Ragni shook his head and spread his hands. "I'm an Empath, not a Seer."

"Then maybe—"

A shout interrupted them. "Get a Healer! Lord Jon is down!"

Dahleven pushed his way through the knot of people surrounding Jon, closely followed by Ragni. *He's probably just had too much to drink. Again.*

His brother-by-marriage had fallen at the base of the dais, and was sitting on the floor in front of Neven's place. His chest heaved and his neck muscles stood out as he struggled to take in air. The wind whistled in his throat. Jon's eyes were wide with terror, pleading for help. He had no breath for words. Then the whistling stopped. Jon's hands went to his throat.

Magnus thumped Jon powerfully on his back. "Breathe, man! Breathe!"

Jon's lips started to turn blue.

Dahleven grabbed Ragni's arm. "Get Celia!"

Ragni took off, plowing through the crowd. He knew how Celia had saved Ari, and didn't waste time with questions. Dahleven had told the whole family. Ingirid and Kaidlin were so grateful they would have adopted Celia immediately if she hadn't been insensible.

A long minute dragged by. The crowd shouted suggestions.

"Raise his hands over his head!"

"Get him some wine!"

"He's had enough wine, that's the problem."

"Turn him upside down!"

Magnus continued to shake and thump Jon. Then Jon's eyes rolled back and he slumped to the floor, unconscious.

What's taking so long? What had Celia done to Ari? Dahleven knelt by Jon and blew into his mouth. He felt air puff against his cheek from Jon's nose and pinched it off before he exhaled again. Around him, the Jarls and lords exclaimed and questioned what he was doing.

His breath wouldn't go in. Dahleven's lips began to feel numb and swollen.

Poison!

He turned his head and spat. Then he saw Neven's spilled tankard under the dais. Jon had been up to his old tricks, and this time it had gotten him killed.

Dahleven looked up into his father's gray eyes. "Kon Neven, gather your guard. There has been an attempt on your life."

CHAPTER SEVENTEEN

CELE'S FINGERS TINGLED and she realized she could wiggle them. She'd never known such a tiny action could bring so much satisfaction—until she'd been unable to do it. The carpet was rolled so tightly around her she still couldn't move her arms and legs, but at least now she *could* move.

If she got the chance.

Cele's heart pounded. *At least they didn't kill me outright. That's a good sign.*

"This is far enough." a muffled voice said as they put her down. "We can do her here."

She and the carpet were dropped abruptly. With the drug fading from her system, the impact as she hit the floor was only normally uncomfortable instead of magnified. Another blow landed on her hip through the heavy weave as what seemed to be a foot gave her a shove. Then she was rolling. Rough shoves kept her moving. In a moment she was free, and she drew in a deep breath of chilly underground air. It tasted sweet after the musty smell of the carpet.

Cele blinked in the dim lantern light, trying to focus. There were three men. "Who are you? Why did you kidnap me?"

One of the men tightened a fist in her hair as he drew a long knife and placed the point against her throat.

"No! No! You don't have to do this!" Cele panted as terror stole her breath.

One of the other men lifted a hand. His hair fell lank around his face and his filthy beard overgrew his mouth "Wait a minute, Mord. Let's not be hasty."

No, let's not!

"What do you mean, Harvener?" A third man in a blue shirt asked. "Our order was to make her disappear."

"And we will, Orlyg. But waste not, want not, I always say. She's a pretty piece. Let's do the deed before we do the deed, as it were. Shall we?"

Cele felt bile rise in her throat.

"Aye!" Mord released her and slid his knife back into its sheath.

"You don't have to do this! I can pay you!" It was a desperate lie, and the men clearly knew it.

"Not enough," Harve sneered, stepping forward.

Cele spun on her butt and punched upward into Mord's groin with both feet. He doubled over with a startled scream. Orlyg grabbed for her, but she was already rolling away. All he got was the edge of her robe. Her momentum ripped half the ribbon ties off the front. Then he hauled her back. She tried to slip out of the arms, but he was too fast. He had her.

Harve laughed.

"A little spice just seasons the broth, *my lady.*" Orlyg put his hand inside her robe and roughly squeezed her breast.

Cele ignored the pain, sweeping her elbow backward at his nose. She only landed a glancing blow, but it was enough to make him grunt and loosen his hold. She feigned a knee to his groin. As she hoped, he twisted away. She shoved, pushing him off balance, and he fell over Mord. Harve grabbed her wrist, but she broke his hold and spun, landing a kick to the side of his knee. He screamed as the leg collapsed, but he managed to grab a fistful of velvet, his nails scraping high on the inside of her thigh. His yank tore loose the remaining ties.

Her robe fell open, but Cele didn't care. She grabbed his thumb and twisted, lifting his arm so she could plant a kick in his armpit. Harve's arm went limp and she dropped it. She ran.

Within moments, she realized her mistake. *I should have grabbed the lantern.* She had no light, and no idea where she was. *No way I'm going back for it.* She kept running, trailing one hand along the wall. After a few minutes, she stopped and listened. The only sound was her own ragged breathing, echoing off the walls. No sound, no light betrayed pursuit. But she couldn't relax. Not yet. Harve's knee might keep him from catching up, but Mord and Orlyg might still come after her.

As if summoned by her thoughts, she heard running feet echoing. Wildly swinging shadows appeared in the tunnel behind her. Cele ran, but the dark slowed her. The footsteps came closer and closer, the light brighter. At the last moment, Cele spun to defend, but Orlyg's momentum slammed her into the stone wall, trapping one arm and knocking the wind out of her.

"You bitch!" His forearm was against her throat.

She tried to gouge Orlyg's eyes with her free hand, but he blocked her.

"I'll not die for failing an order!" Mord drew his knife.

Cele's chest strained to expand. Blackness curled into

her vision.

"No. You'll just die," someone said.

Suddenly her captor was gone. Cele sagged to her knees, coughing.

Mord screamed, "No!" then fell silent.

She shuddered, desperately sucking precious air into her lungs.

Gentle hands pulled her upright. "Let me help you." A man's voice, rich and mellifluous as a classical radio station host's, sounded close to her ear. Strong, long-fingered hands supported Cele under her elbows as she got shakily to her feet, wobbling as she found her balance.

Her rescuer was of middle height and his clothing was of fine quality, though fraying at the collar and cuffs. His beard was neat and close-cropped beneath startlingly turquoise eyes, one of which peered at her through a hard leather mask that covered the left half his face. Despite the Phantom of the Opera look, the sharp edge of Cele's fear dulled, easing the hammering of her heart a little.

"Are you steady, now?" His hands withdrew slowly along her forearms, lingering a moment on her fingertips. He had an air of self-possessed arrogance and virility.

Cele shivered, not entirely from the cool air, and pulled her robe tightly closed, uncomfortably aware it was all she had on.

"You're cold, of course." He took off his cloak and wrapped it around her. It was warm from his body, and smelled faintly like cloves. He fastened it with a gold brooch set with a red stone and his touch tarried intimately on her shoulders. "Better?" He paused, smiling warmly into her eyes, then dropped his hands before Cele felt uncomfortable with the contact. He turned to one of the other men she hadn't realized were there.

"Bring me another, then go ahead and prepare a meal." He flicked a gesture at the bodies of Orlyg and Mord. "And take these with you."

In an instant, another cloak was draped on his shoulders, and they were alone except for the blood stains seeping into the stone.

"Come with me, Lady Celia. You've had a terrible ordeal."

"Did you catch the other one?" Cele hated the way her voice quavered.

"I saw only these two."

"Who are they? Why did they kidnap me?"

"That's a complicated question. I'll do my best to answer, but first you need warmth and food."

He's right. That's exactly what I need. With a light touch on her shoulder, the man guided her into a side passage and she didn't resist. "How do you know who I am?"

"Everyone in Quartzholm knows of you, my lady. And with the way you evaded your captors, who else could you be?"

"How did you know to find me? For that matter, where am I? Somewhere below Quartzholm, obviously." Cele trembled and her mind raced. "But why are you down here? Were you looking for me? Are you part of a search party? Does Dahleven know where I am?"

Her escort smiled and guided her with a light touch on her back. "Calm yourself, my lady. You're safe now. Soon all your questions will be answered."

He was right. Cele clamped her mouth shut. Her speeding pulse slowed a little. *I'm safe now.* At least no one was trying to kill her.

It seemed only a few minutes before they entered a chamber lit by lamps that had no flame and made no smoke. By the time they'd arrived, Cele had marshaled her scrambled thoughts into a semblance of order, but she was still full of questions. "Who are you?"

"Besides being your rescuer?"

Cele felt herself blush. "I'm sorry. You saved my life. Thanking you doesn't seem like enough."

The man by her side inclined his head in a slight bow. "No thanks are necessary. I am Jorund, my lady. Lord of all you survey." He swept out an arm.

The small, well-lit room held several brass-bound chests and a pallet covered with folded blankets. The chamber had only two entrances. One was the smoothly finished arch they'd entered through. The other was a natural fissure, like the one she and Dahleven had squeezed through to escape their attackers on the mountain. No daylight showed beyond this one, however. Jorund gestured to the only real furniture in the room, a pair of well-upholstered armchairs drawn close together near a table. Two pewter steins and a steaming pitcher of *sjokolade* awaited them.

Cele sank into one of the seats. Jorund took the other and filled a mug for her. She shivered and wrapped her hands around the tankard, huddling within Jorund's heavy cloak. The spicy sweet chocolate steadied her.

"Neven doesn't trust you, does he?"

Cele stared. She didn't know what she'd expected Jorund to say, but this wasn't it. He must have read her face.

"Of course he doesn't. He doesn't trust anything he doesn't control. And he doesn't control you, does he?" Jorund smiled and she felt absurdly pleased by his approval. "Neven doesn't know how you got to Alfheim, or why you're here, and that makes him nervous. He sees you as a threat." Jorund shook his head and took a sip of the chocolate. "He sees everyone he doesn't control as an enemy. If he knew we'd met, he'd throw you in the dungeon. *If* he was feeling generous."

Jorund was the first person she'd met who was openly critical of Neven. Ragni had dismissed her concerns about Neven's mind control, and even Thora, who'd arranged the meeting with the Daughters of Freya, was loyal to her Kon. "Why? Why wouldn't he want me to meet you? He hasn't stopped me from talking to anyone else."

"Hasn't he? How would you know?" Jorund paused, while the implications of his question sunk in.

Would she know if Neven had kept people away from her? And Dahleven had posted a guard outside her door.

"Neven doesn't tolerate opposition," Jorund continued. "He strangles everything he touches, uses his Talent to bend everyone to his will." His hand fisted on the arm of his chair.

"But not you."

"I tried to build a coalition to unseat him as Kon in the last election, and was careless in my choice of allies." He smiled ruefully. "I failed, and he had me Outcast. He would have killed me outright, I think, but he was afraid of making a martyr of me."

Cele thought of the servant's missing fingers, and what the Daughters of Freya had said about debtors being sold into slavery. Judgment, such as it was, could be brutal here. "Why are we talking about Neven?"

Jorund smiled with half his mouth. "You asked who those men were. Why you were abducted."

She felt herself gaping. "Are you saying Neven arranged the attack?"

"It would have been an excellent strategy, would it not? You disappear, and he blames his enemies for it."

Cele leaned back in her chair, stunned. "But Dahleven and Ragni would never go along with something like that."

"Are you sure?"

Cele paused for a moment. Her track record with men wasn't great. She'd trusted Jeff, too, and he'd blindsided her. She could imagine Neven scheming against her, but she just couldn't bring herself to believe Dahleven or his brother would willingly hurt her. "Yes."

Jorund lifted one shoulder in a shrug. "Well, Neven has been weaving his schemes since before they were born. I doubt he consulted them." Jorund leaned forward and laid his hand on Cele's. The warmth of his touch was welcome against her cool flesh. "I think we can assist one another. You want to return to your home, don't you? I'll wager Neven hasn't been very helpful in that endeavor, has he?"

Cele remembered Neven's bullying and his bland, *We're looking into it*, and shook her head.

"I thought not. Neven controls the priesthood, and they control the ritual magic that can send you home."

Father Wirmund's assertions sprang to mind. He obviously didn't like her any more than Neven did. "But if they wanted me out of the picture, why not just send me home instead of killing me?"

"Neven and the priests keep that magic secret from the people. They say it doesn't exist. That's how they maintain their control. They could hardly do that if they sent you back to Midgard with a Great Working. I've searched for many long years and I've learned a great deal. I know how to send you home. But for magic to work, I need something only your Talent can Find."

Home!

Was it really within her reach? Jorund's thumb stroked the back of her hand. His confidence and smooth elegance were persuasive. She didn't pull away. "Go on."

"You heard the tale of Fanlon at the Feast. Eirik tells it well. You know how Neven's ancestor stole the Great Talents and hid them away. But the story never mentions the Staff of *Befaling*. That's one of the secrets Neven and Wirmund keep from the people. Without it,

Fanlon and his brother-priest could not have succeeded."

Jorund met her eyes with his clear turquoise gaze. "It will take a powerful magic to return you to Midgard. I can use the strength of the stolen Talents to send you back, but I'll need the Staff to do it. "

Cele sipped her chocolate. "How does this help you?"

"Neven stole my Talent when he had me Outcast, just as his ancestor Fanlon stole the Great Talents. I want it back." Jorund's hand fisted on the arm of his chair. "I want to restore my family's name to honor. And I haven't forgotten my people. Neven still holds Nuvinland in thrall. I want to put a stop to his corruption. I hope that returning the stolen Talents to the people will break Neven's stranglehold."

Cele's heart leapt at the fervor in Jorund's voice, but her eyes strayed to the leather covering half of his face. "That's not all there is to this, is it?"

His head dipped, and half his mouth tilted in a grim smile. "No. There is this also." He untied the strings that held his mask in place and slowly pulled it away. Where his high cheekbone should have been, the flesh sagged in twisted ropes down to his jaw. "Wirmund did this to me with but a touch. It is progressive. Soon it will make its way down to my chest and my loins, and inward to destroy my heart. I need the healing power of one of the Great Talents to stop it. Neven did not kill me outright, where others could witness it, but he insured my eventual death nevertheless. Unless you help me."

The gawking Jarls and crofters were dispersed to their rooms quickly by the arrival of the Kon's guards. Three of the thirty-six stood near Neven, the rest Dahleven positioned in and around the Great Hall. Though the guards were quite competent, they were there as much for effect as for Neven's protection. The attempt by poison wasn't likely to be followed by a direct assault, but the other Jarls and Lords needed a reminder of Neven's strength.

Father Wirmund stood off to one side while Helbreden, the Kon's Healer, knelt over Jon's body.

"*Kveletepp*," Helbreden said. "They put strangledrops in your drink, Kon Neven. It kills within minutes, quicker if you're already in your cups as Jon was." The healer's Talent was Diagnosis. He looked closely at Dahleven. "And you? You're well? It doesn't take much to kill a man, you know. No, of course you're all right. It would have killed you by now. What were you doing, kissing Jon that way? What did you hope to do?"

Dahleven took a deep breath. Helbreden was a knowledgeable man, an excellent Healer, but he nattered on so much that Dahleven thanked the gods he was healthy and didn't require the man's services. He'd much rather have Ghav tend him on those rare occasions an injury demanded attention. "I'd hoped to imitate what Lady Celia did for Ari."

"Did you? Did you? And just what did the Lady do? I'd hoped to meet with her today to discuss it. Is she awake yet? You know, Kon Neven, I would have been pleased to tend her myself. Ghav is quite competent, but Emergence Exhaustion can be quite serious. I doubt a warrior-healer has much experience with it."

Eirik entered the room and waited until Kon Neven's gesture told the guard to let him proceed. His thin sandy hair was in five braids, each hanging to his waist, ringing and clacking with bells and beads. Dahleven suspected he wore his hair so long to make up for the wispiness of his beard.

Father Wirmund had sent for the skald to cast the

runes. Too many people could have poisoned Neven's drink in the open, informal period between sessions of the Althing. It could have been anyone, Jarl, carl, or thrall. In addition to his skill with a tale, Eirik's training with the Skald's Guild included learning to throw and interpret the rune stones. His auguries hadn't revealed who was behind the attacks on the caravans, but apparently Father Wirmund hoped they would give some clue to the murderous traitor.

Dahleven stood by, silent and watchful. Sometimes the gods chose to share their knowledge with men, but more often not. Even when they did so, the message was frequently so cryptic as to be nearly useless. He had more confidence in the strength of his sword arm than he did in the stones.

An acolyte arrived bearing a sprig of mistletoe. Father Wirmund took it and inscribed a circle of protection around Jon and Eirik and the poisoned cup, intoning the blessings of Baldur. Eirik spread a ragged-edged piece of leather on the floor next to Jon's body. It was roughly circular, as wide as the length of a man's arm, and inscribed around the perimeter with the twenty-four runes of the Futhark. He shook his doeskin bag three times, rattling the stones.

Neven spoke the question in the indirect way tradition demanded. "Jon is dead by an unseen hand. We seek and welcome the gifting of knowledge."

Eirik stood and again shook the bag three times, rattling the contents like old bones. Then with three more shakes, he emptied the bag, casting Odin's Prize onto the leather.

Nine lay face up on the field of interpretation. An auspicious number, as far as Dahleven understood such things. Nine was whole and complete, a perfect number, a reflection of the nine worlds.

Eirik knelt to interpret the stones. He spoke in the

odd monotone used by skalds when they looked into the void revealed by the runes. "He who poisoned Jon is hidden among you. He is a liar, but soon the uncertainty and confusion will be resolved. Someone will change the old ways and the change will bring danger, but these problems may prove a blessing in disguise. Old friendships may prove false, but with strength to follow through, harmony will be achieved." Eirik took a deep shuddering breath and slumped, his Seeing complete.

That was useful. Dahleven looked away to hide his grimace.

"Hidden among us? What does that mean? Here in Quartzholm? Or in all of Nuvinland?" Helbreden asked.

Eirik stood and bowed shakily to Kon Neven. "The stones have spoken. I speak what the gods reveal."

Neven acknowledged the skald's service. "Our thanks, Eirik. You may go."

Eirik was at the door when Ragni hurried in. Alone.

Ragni gave the skald a hard look before continuing over to the small group by Jon's body. "Lady Celia is missing."

Ragni's words stopped the air in Dahleven's chest.

"Missing?" Kon Neven's voice was deceptively mild. Dahleven knew that tone. Father wanted answers—now. So did he.

His brother knew the tone too, and quickly provided them, such as they were. "Lady Celia awakened well and hungry, according to Thora. She ate heartily, and shortly after Thora left, Lady Celia received towels and water. Soon after that, the Lady decided to bathe. The guard escorted her, and that's where I found him. Standing outside the bathing room. He—"

"And the guard didn't think it odd that Celia would go to bathe after receiving towels and water?" Dahleven asked sharply.

"What was the man supposed to do, brother? Question the Lady's commitment to cleanliness?" Ragni looked sympathetic and annoyed at once. He went on. "Inside, I—"

"You walked in on her?" Dahleven interrupted again.

"Dahl," Neven warned.

Dahleven clamped his mouth shut.

Ragni cleared his throat. "The room was empty. Water was running over the tub and down the drain in the floor. Jeger didn't hear a thing. I summoned the guards and they're searching the tunnels, but so far there's no sign of her."

"There's a passage from that room. You revealed it to her yesterday, did you not, Lord Dahleven?" Father Wirmund asked. "She must have used it to escape her guard."

"I think not," Ragni said. "At least not of her own will. I found this dropped at the bottom of the ladder." Ragni held out a cloth still faintly aromatic with a sharp tangy smell.

"Let me see that," Helbreden said reaching for the cloth. He held it some two feet from his nose and wafted the vapors toward his face with the other hand. "*Gelemuskel.* Let's hope they know how to use it. Too much of this could stop her breathing and her heart."

Dahleven's shoulders tightened. He had to do something. "I'm going to look for her." He turned to leave, but his brother called him back.

"Where?" Ragni asked. "I've already got Tracker Talents searching. Let them do their work. They'll find her."

Dahleven hesitated. Ragni was right, but he was going to go anyway.

"Lord Dahleven, come to my chambers. I have a task for you." Neven turned and left, escorted by his guard, fully expecting compliance.

Dahleven stood rooted to the spot for a moment. His father knew full well his command was at odds with

Dahleven's will. *Odin's Eye!* The Kon had spoken. Dahleven gritted his teeth and followed, anger and worry knotting his stomach. He hoped he didn't look as sick as he felt.

"Tell them you escaped your abductors," Jorund said as he helped Cele to rise. He'd put his mask back on. "It's the truth, after all. You did escape them once." His lips curved and his eyes were clearly admiring. Then he turned grim again. "You must be convincing. Neven already distrusts you; he'll imprison you at the least provocation. Or more likely, he'll have you attacked a third time and use it as an excuse to increase his stranglehold on Nuvinland."

"A *third* time? Are you saying the attack on the hillside was arranged by Neven?" The image of the man she'd killed rose in her mind. Had the Kon arranged that? Would he put his son and heir at risk to kill her? *Had* Dahleven been at risk? They could have had orders not to hurt him, and he, not knowing, had used lethal force to defend himself, conveniently leaving no one to reveal Neven's plan.

Jorund merely shrugged. "My man will escort you away from here, to a place where those who search can find you. I regret the need for it, but I must insist you go hooded."

Cele's heart stuttered at the thought of traveling blind. "I won't tell them how to find you."

"Thank you, my lady, but Neven has Truth-sayers, and I will not put you at risk with too much knowledge. You can honestly say you could see nothing of where you were taken or the way you returned. And don't suffer Neven's anger for my sake if he tries to force you to Find this place. Do as he asks. I'll move on as soon as you depart. He'll not be able to track me." His hand tarried on Cele's arm above her elbow. "Please, be careful."

She felt the warmth of his touch even through the cloak, and the low, rich caress of Jorund's voice calmed her. If what he'd said was true, returning to Quartzholm could be dangerous, but if she was going to make it home, Jorund needed the Staff. His story was certainly compelling. *And there's no doubting the truth of his face.*

"Excuse me for a moment." He left her to speak in low tones with a man he called from the tunnel. By his curt hand movements, it looked as though Jorund was giving the man very specific instructions. He was obviously used to being obeyed. *It must have galled him terribly to have lost to Neven.*

Jorund and the other man returned together. "This is Asolf. He'll take you to a place where you'll be found by those searching for you. When you've found the Staff, drop a note down the shaft in the bath. Do not try to retrieve it yourself. That will be another's task. When all is in readiness, I'll contact you." He touched her chin with one fingertip and smiled. "Keep thinking of home." Then he held out a black hood.

Reluctantly, Cele put it on. She could always take it off later, when she was well away.

Suddenly her hand was grasped by a hard, calloused one.

"Let's go," Asolf growled.

The trip through the dark was nothing like the one with Dahleven. Asolf moved briskly and took little care that Cele couldn't see. She stumbled more than once before she thought they'd gone far enough to risk taking off the hood.

The way she walked must have changed and alerted her escort. He looked back almost immediately. "Put that back on!"

Asolf didn't look as if he'd tolerate any disagreement. Cele did as she was told.

He grabbed her hand again and dragged her down the corridor. Cele used her other hand to lift the hems of her robe and Jorund's cloak.

Many twists and turns and minutes later, Asolf dropped her hand. "You can take off the hood now."

Cele did, and blinked in the light from the lantern that he'd put on the floor.

"You're to give me the cloak." He reached to take it.

Cele stepped back, out of his reach, and unfastened the cloak herself. Asolf snatched it out of her hand and turned on his heel.

Fear flared. "Wait! Aren't you going to leave me a light?"

"And how would you explain it to your rescuers?" Asolf sneered, then he left.

Soon the darkness and the silence were complete. Minutes crept by with no way for her to gauge their passing.

Someone will come looking for me. Eventually.

How long had she been missing? How long had she been waiting? Even if people were searching for her, how would they know where to look? Jorund seemed confident that someone would discover her, but there were miles and miles of tunnels cutting through the mountains.

Maybe I can Find my way out of here.

She clutched her robe shut with shaking hands and concentrated. She wanted to be back in her room, warm and safe. The feeling came quick and easy this time. Cele knew with absolute certainty that her room was above her, to her left, and quite some distance away. *That's a big help.*

The best she could do would be to take the tunnels

that tended in that general direction. Or she could stay put and wait for the searchers to find her. Cele put a hand on the wall and started to walk.

It was only a few minutes before she saw a glimmering around a bend in the tunnel.

Relief zinged through her like a jolt of electricity. "Here! I'm here!" She hurried toward the flickering lantern light.

A man came limping into view, a twisted grin on his face and a sword in his hand.

Terror stopped her breath.

"Miss me, sweetheart?" Harve asked.

Cele turned and ran.

chapter eighteen

"what did the skald say?" Ragni asked Dahleven, pouring ale.

They were in Dahleven's rooms. After Dahleven had finished with Neven, Ragni had persuaded him that word of Celia would reach him quickest if he stayed where the guards could find him.

Neven had assigned Dahleven the task of organizing increased security throughout Quartzholm against spies and assassins. The job had required several hours of close conference with the Warden of the Guard, and all his attention. Now he had nothing to do but wait. Dahleven didn't like remaining idle, and he paced across the room. The search was taking far too long.

"Nothing of much use. 'Our enemy is among us.' 'Change brings danger.' 'Harmony will be achieved.' The usual dung." Dahleven looked closely at his brother. Ragni wasn't asking just to distract him. "Why?"

"When I passed him at the door, I felt something

strange from him. Not deception, exactly. Something more like...amusement."

"Maybe he didn't like Jon any better than we did," Dahleven suggested, pacing back across the room to stand in front of his brother.

"Probably not," Ragni agreed. "But that's not quite what I felt."

Dahleven cocked an eyebrow at his brother, but a knock forestalled his question. "Enter!"

It was Fender. "We've found her, my lord. They're taking her to her room."

Relief flared in Dahleven's breast like a torch, along with the need to see her safe with his own eyes. He pushed by Fendrikanin on his way out of the room, with Ragni only a step behind. "What took so long?" he demanded.

Fender continued his report on the move. "The Trackers only just picked up her trail, my lord. It started up clean at a nexus of tunnels. Before that they couldn't find a thing."

Fender hesitated and went on. "She's in bad shape. Exhausted. Apparently, she tried to Find her way out of the tunnels after she escaped from her captor. We gave her some *sterkkidrikk*, though, so she's safe, even if she's spent."

"Well done," Dahleven said.

Fender cleared his throat. "My lord..."

The younger man's awkward pause caught Dahleven's attention. He stopped and looked at him, demanding an answer with his eyes. "And?"

Fender met Dahleven's stare briefly, then looked past his shoulder as he went on. The younger man's mouth was tight with emotion. "She hasn't said much, about what happened. But her robe is torn and...she's bruised..."

Dahleven's gut twisted.

Ragni put a hand on his shoulder.

Dahleven turned and stalked down the hall. Whatever had happened had happened. There was nothing he could do to change that. Just as he couldn't change the fact that he'd failed to keep her safe, despite posting a guard. "I'm going to kill Jeger."

Cele opened her eyes on near dark, and for an instant she thought she was still in the tunnels, listening for Harve to pounce on her. She jerked as a hand touched her shoulder.

"You're safe," a familiar deep voice said from very close.

"Dahleven?" Cele asked, clasping his hand with her own.

The light grew, the wick turned up on the wall lamp by Thora, who said, "You gave us quite a scare, my lady."

"Leave us," Dahleven said.

Thora balked. "My lord!"

"Thora, leave us—please."

Thora still hesitated and Dahleven turned to Cele. His face was half shadowed, but she heard the hesitation in his voice. "Do you will it? That she go?"

Dahleven's question surprised her, but not as much as the tone of his voice. He sounded worried, tentative. *What could he have to say that he wouldn't want Thora to hear*? She'd spent too much time uncomfortably alone with men lately, but she had no reservations about Dahleven. Whatever he had to say, he could say it in private if that's what he wanted. "It's all right, Thora. Only..."

"Yes, my lady?"

"Could you send food? Enough for two, please."

"I'll see to it." Thora smiled at her, then glowered at Dahleven as she sailed out the door.

Cele was nude under the sheets again, but warm. She didn't remember much about returning to her room. She'd tried to Find her way back, but the tunnels kept veering off in the wrong direction, away from where she wanted to go. Crushing fatigue had nearly brought her to her knees, but the fear that Harve would catch her kept her going. She'd still been stumbling forward when she'd heard the footsteps of the search party echoing in the dark. At first she'd thought it was Harve, and she'd drawn back as the light of the lantern fell on her. Then she'd recognized Fender's voice and collapsed from relief. After that, her rescuers made her drink that vile, sweet liquid. She vaguely remembered being carried before she passed out.

Now here she was talking to Dahleven while wearing even less than she had during her interview with Jorund. At the thought of the Outcast lord, Cele looked away from Dahleven, unable to meet his eyes. She couldn't tell him about Jorund. Jorund probably hadn't told her everything, but what he had told her was very convincing. And the Outcast Jarl was the only one offering a way home. She couldn't risk that by saying too much to Neven's son. Dahleven would have to tell the Kon. She couldn't expect Dahleven to take sides against his own father.

"You needn't turn away. I deserve your censure." Dahleven said in a voice full of sorrow.

Cele's gaze snapped back to him, surprised. His face was rigid, but his eyes were full of grief. "What are you talking about? I'm not angry."

Dahleven's brows drew downward. "I let you be taken. My guards failed to keep you safe. How could you not blame me for...for what you endured?"

"Dahleven!" She couldn't talk lying down like this.

She struggled to sit up, holding the covers up against her chest, wincing as her sore muscles protested. *I can't tell him it was probably his own father's men who took me, not without betraying Jorund.* "What were you supposed to do? Send a guard in to wash my back for me? You can't think of everything."

"I'm *supposed* to think of everything!" Dahleven stood and took a step away from the bed before turning and spreading his hands. "I can't keep my people safe if I don't. As I've proven far too often, of late." His hands clenched.

"Stop it! That's your grief talking. If Sorn were here, I bet he wouldn't let you get away with that crap. You can't anticipate everything. You can only do your best and learn from your mistakes."

"I have a lot to learn from, don't I?" Dahleven's voice was bitter and angry. "And what do you know of what Sorn would say? He'd be the first to condemn me for letting you be kidnapped and raped."

"Raped!"

Dahleven knelt beside the bed and took her hand in both of his. "I'm so sorry, Celia. I—"

"I wasn't raped. I got away."

"But..."

Her voice was as firm as she knew how to make it, even as the memory of the men's hands on her made her shiver. "I got away."

Dahleven sat on the edge of the bed, cradling her shoulders with a gentle touch, searching her face with anxious, hopeful eyes.

She couldn't let Dahleven carry the responsibility and the guilt for something that hadn't quite happened. "I'm okay."

Dahleven groaned and pulled her against him, burying his face in her hair. She hadn't realized how much she'd needed his arms around her. She melted into the warmth of his embrace with a sigh and let go her hold on the covers to pull him closer.

She felt safe and protected, nestled against the hard muscle of his body, wrapped in his strong arms. Nothing could hurt her. Not Mord or Orlyg or Harve. A flash of terror swept over her and a sob escaped her throat. She blinked away tears. *What's the matter with me? I escaped!* But the tears wouldn't stop and she shook with uneven, shuddering breaths.

Dahleven swallowed hard on the lump of anguish in his throat as he felt her tremble in his arms. He couldn't believe her words. He'd ordered Ghav to tell him about her injuries. He knew about the bruises on her arms and breast and back, the scratches on her thigh. Those, combined with her torn robe and how she clung to him now—weeping with great racking sobs—told him all he needed to know of what had happened.

He wanted to kill whoever had done this to her, and crawl into a pit for letting it happen.

But at the moment there was nothing he could do but hold her. He stroked her silky hair and rubbed her bare back, murmuring whatever he could think of to comfort and reassure her. "You're safe now. I'll never let you be harmed again. Be still. You're safe."

Gradually her breathing eased. She sniffed and hiccupped, pulled a hand from his back to wipe her cheeks. "I'm sorry. I don't know what came over me."

He forced a tight smile. "I'd be surprised if you did not weep."

Celia held the sheets to cover her breasts as she pulled back to glance up at him, then she looked away again as if embarrassed. "It *was* a little traumatic."

Dahleven's chest constricted. He lifted her chin with one finger so he could look her in the eyes. "You have no need of shame, my lady. That is all mine."

Her eyes widened, then narrowed. Her lips pressed together.

He recognized that look of exasperation. He'd seen it on his sisters' faces often enough.

"Do I have to knock you upside the head to get you to believe me? Read my lips. I wasn't raped. I. Got. Away." And then she kissed him.

The touch of her soft lips and tongue made him instantly hard. He didn't believe her words, but her body...Celia pressed herself into his arms freely, without reservation. Could she have been raped and still forgive him? Still want him? Dahleven leaned back just enough to search her face. He saw no shame or fear there, just desire. Relief jumped in his veins. He kissed her back with all the joy flooding his body. She'd been through an ordeal, but at least she hadn't suffered that. She would be worth no less in his eyes if she had, but rape was a violation he was beyond glad she'd been spared.

Celia's mouth opened and her tongue stroked his. His body tightened and his hands slipped to just above her elbows, massaging the flesh there with his thumbs. Celia tightened her arms around him and he leaned forward, laying her back into the softness of the featherbed.

His heart threatened to choke him. In but a few candlemarks he'd been terrified for her, relieved, and ridden by guilt. Now she was safe and whole and opening her arms to him. Dahleven tenderly kissed his way down her shoulder. Celia lowered the covers to her waist and he continued to her breast, encouraged by the way Celia arched as his tongue laved her nipple.

"Yes." Celia's fingers threaded through his hair as he kissed his way over to her other breast. She wriggled against him and his cock throbbed, anxious to be free.

A knock at the door brought his head up, then he lowered it to rest his forehead against her shoulder in frustration.

Celia groaned, then huffed a small chuckle. "At least this interruption is less violent than our last one."

He was amazed she could find humor after all she'd been through.

The second knock was more forceful. He sat up, and Celia pulled the covers to her shoulders, but not before he glimpsed the bruises marring the tender flesh he'd just been kissing. He had just enough time to think about killing the whoreson who'd hurt her before a third, more demanding knock drew an answer from him. "Enter!"

Thora came in with a servant bearing a laden tray and a scalding expression on her face. Dahleven almost felt like he was fifteen again and caught with his sister's maid. The girl had been willing enough, and older than he, but the event had precipitated a stern lecture from his father about not abusing the privilege of his position. Thora looked like she wanted to do more than lecture.

The servant put the tray on the table by the bed. There looked to be enough food for six instead of two, even if one of them was in Emergence.

Thora's manner gave the impression she intended to stay. Dahleven was about to invite her to leave again when she said, "Kon Neven wants to speak to Lady Celia after she's eaten."

"Now?" Celia exclaimed.

"It's nearly midnight!" Dahleven protested.

"I can tell time, Lord Dahleven. And so can your father," Thora snapped.

What is Father thinking? "Celia, I..." What could he say? He couldn't, wouldn't, undermine his father's authority, even if he didn't agree with his methods. "I regret I can't join you at supper. Take your time, eat your fill. And don't let my father upset you."

Dahleven shut the door gently behind him and strode purposefully to Neven's chambers. This time he'd be present and visible during the interview.

Cele stepped into Neven's chambers, trying to look more confident than she felt. The heavy embroidered skirts of her green gown swished around her ankles. She'd chosen the dress because she knew it brought out the color of her eyes. She might be going back into the lion's den, but she'd go with her head held high. The ivory lace that Dahleven had bought for her was draped over her head and shoulders like a mantilla. She'd worn it to give her a little extra courage, and when she saw Dahleven's eyes widen in a subtle smile, she was glad she had.

As usual, Neven sat far from the door.

Gris spoke for him. "Your *ordeal* doesn't seem to have harmed you seriously, Lady Celia." Gris's tone turned his comment into a provocation. "I'm sure we're *all* grateful for that."

I can show you my bruises if you'd like. Cele glanced at Dahleven, who stood behind Neven. He nodded his encouragement almost imperceptibly.

Although she would just as soon have spit as speak to Gris, Cele answered civilly. "Thank you. I know how much that means, coming from you."

Ragni, standing beside Dahleven, suppressed a smile, but not before the corner of his mouth twitched upward.

Gris scowled, but continued in a neutral tone. "We're concerned for your safety, Lady Celia, and the safety of all who live in Quartzholm. Tell us *everything* that happened today, so we can prevent its recurrence."

Jorund had warned her to expect questions, but she thought she'd have a little longer to practice her story. Overnight, at least. But Neven hadn't granted her that time, so she told the truth. Most of it. Beginning with her abduction from the bathing room. *Neven must know most of it already, unless his men were too afraid of him to report their failure to kill me.*

Gris interrupted almost immediately. "How many men did you see after you climbed down the ladder?"

"I told you, they lowered me with a sling and ropes. I couldn't move."

"Yes, of course. How uncomfortable. It's just as well you couldn't feel anything."

"On the contrary. I felt every bump and scrape quite distinctly. I just couldn't do anything about it."

She reported her experience straight through, until she got to the part where her muscles returned to normal and the three men put down the rug she'd been rolled in. "They started talking about...about what they were going to do to me. That's when I got away."

"They just let you go?" The sneer wasn't far beneath the surface of Gris's question.

"No, they didn't just let me go." Cele stopped and looked away. The feel of their hands grasping her, the sound of her robe ripping suddenly flooded her senses.

Her stomach roiled, and she swallowed convulsively. Up until this moment she hadn't really understood why rape victims could feel ashamed for being attacked. Fear surged as she smelled Orlyg's foul breath again and felt his rough, dirty hand on her breast. She didn't want anyone to know how he'd touched her. She didn't want anyone to see in her eyes how he'd made her feel. In that instant before her training had kicked in, she'd felt terrified and helpless. She felt that way again now. Sweat pricked under her arms and her heart raced.

Not an hour ago, she'd reassured Dahleven that she wasn't angry. But she was. She was furious. Not at Dahleven. At the world, at fate, at all men, for making her feel that fear, for letting this happen at all.

But she was also proud of herself for having the skill to stop them, even if Jorund had saved her in the end. "I had to hurt them first. Then they let me go."

"There were only three of them? Where were their friends while this little dance was taking place?"

Only three? Cele forced herself to look Gris in the eyes. "I don't know. They didn't confide in me."

Gris turned away from her for a moment, blocking her view of Neven and Ragni. Dahleven's face was tight, but he gave her another small nod and Cele used that to steady herself. It was just as Jorund had said, Neven didn't trust her, and he was using Gris to trick her into a mistake.

The chamberlain turned back to her. "And in all of this, no one said anything about why you were taken?"

"Other than wanting to rape me? No, they didn't."

"Are we to believe you were kidnapped only so a few men could dally with you? You're quite beautiful, Lady Celia, but that's a lot of trouble to go to for a tumble, even with you."

Dahleven jerked and drew in a sharp breath, but held steady where he stood, clenching his fists. Ragni scowled.

"How did you really get those bruises?" Gris continued. "Did you put them there yourself to make your story more convincing? Or did your fellow conspirators help you? Did your lover get too rough?"

Involuntarily, Cele covered her breast. The memory of Harve's nails scraping her thigh as he tore her robe open stabbed through her. Her stomach soured on the food she'd eaten. There were no words sharp enough to reply to those accusations, or lay the sick feeling in her gut to rest.

Is that what Neven believes? How could he, if the men were his? Or was this just his way of diverting suspicion? The Kon's face was impassive; she couldn't read it. Would he throw her in the dungeon? Would Dahleven let him? Could he stop it? A hundred movies provided cold, dark images of damp and filthy prisons. Cele shivered.

Ragni glowered, and Dahleven looked like he was going to break a blood vessel, but neither one spoke in her defense. Apparently, Neven's control was absolute, just as Jorund had said. Still, Cele felt some comfort that she apparently had friends, even if they wouldn't, or couldn't, act on her behalf.

"Did your friends attempt to poison Kon Neven?" Gris asked, changing direction. "Or was Jon their intended target?"

Cele stood stunned, uncertain she'd heard correctly. "What?"

Neven rose smoothly from his chair. His voice was resonant and powerful, but Cele didn't think he was using his mind control. "Thank you, Lady Celia, for helping us understand what happened. Please accept our regrets that any of this occurred. Go now, and rest."

That was it? He wasn't throwing her in a cell? *After all of that badgering and bullying, he just says, "Thanks for coming, see ya later"?* Cele stared for a moment, speechless, then slowly she turned to leave. She didn't perform any courtesy. *I'll be damned if I curtsy to that bastard.*

"One more thing." Neven's voice stopped Cele as she neared the door.

She faced Neven again, half expecting the dungeon after all.

"Thank you for saving my grandson. I am in your debt." Neven bowed deeply.

Cele gaped. *He certainly has a strange way of re-paying it.* Then shut her mouth and straightened her shoulders. Neven's behavior made no sense to her, but in this instance, it didn't matter. "You're welcome, Kon Neven, but I didn't do it for you. I was only thinking of Ari." Cele paused. "Is he all right?"

As Neven answered his face softened, and Cele saw that the bully loved his grandson. "He's well, to the delight of his mother and aunt and grandmother. They'll call on you tomorrow, no doubt, to convey their thanks to you personally. Goodnight."

Anger and frustration gave Cele strength as she started back to her room, but after a while, the adrenaline that had kept her going during her audience with Neven drained away, leaving only fatigue and confusion. Her feet were dragging and her head was spinning as she returned to her room, escorted by not one, but two guards. She tried to make sense of her situation, but nothing lined up. Gris had grilled her at Neven's request, and then Neven had graciously thanked her for saving Ari. Neven treated her like a welcome guest, then accused her of attempted murder. Thora sang his praises, but belonged to a secret organization, and Jorund claimed Neven was a tyrant and had the scars to prove it.

Dahleven treated her like she was precious, stirring her to passion, yet he stood by while Neven's lackey ravaged her.

By the time she reached her room, Cele's head ached and her thoughts and feelings were thoroughly tangled. She barely spoke two words as Thora helped her to bed.

Gris faded into the background as his Talent allowed

him to do, and Dahleven had to concentrate to continue glaring at the chamberlain. He flexed his fingers, wishing he could wrap them around Gris's neck. The Kon's servant took too much pleasure in his work, in Dahleven's opinion.

Neven broke Dahleven's focus, and Gris faded from his awareness, but not his memory. "What of the lady's story, Ragni?"

His brother unclenched his jaw. "As you've probably already guessed, she's telling the truth about her abduction. If she were lying, she probably wouldn't have got that bit right about how the *gelemuskel* would feel. I felt no deception from her about that."

"Will you back off now, Father? She needs our protection, not this persecution," Dahleven demanded.

"Dahl—" Ragni hesitated. "She *was* kidnapped, but she wasn't quite straight about everything."

Dahleven looked at his younger brother. "What are you saying?"

"I think she left something out. It was all tied up in the questions about her escape, but it was clouded by a great deal of fear and anger."

No. Oh, gods. She said she got away. Before or...after? Dahleven's gut twisted tight. She'd been adamant that she hadn't been raped, and come willingly to his embrace, but she'd also sobbed brokenly in his arms. *What happened?*

"What else?" Neven asked.

"I think she knows more about why she was kidnapped than she's saying. But when Gris mentioned the attack on her again, fear washed out everything else. Whatever happened, her terror is real."

"And?" Neven prodded.

"She had nothing to do with Jon's death. She was completely bewildered by the question." Ragni rubbed his eyes. "Father, she's angry with you, but she doesn't hate you. Not quite. Not yet. Your gratitude for Ari surprised her, touched her. She isn't closed to you. You could make her an ally."

Neven shook his head. "I can't. Not yet."

Cele couldn't move. Filthy, distorted hands grasped at her while her muscles refused to respond. She couldn't breathe. A voice grated in the dark, "Miss me, sweetheart?"

Cele jerked awake, heart pounding. Twisted shadows cast by the lantern Thora had left burning loomed on the wall, then slowly resolved to their normal shapes. She stared at the ceiling as her pulse slowed.

I wish Dahleven were here. Then she pushed the thought away. It wasn't a good idea to get more involved with him, no matter how good he made her feel. He was Neven's son, and she was going home. Even so, she wished he were here with her, making her feel safe.

Cele was dressed and finished with breakfast when Thora pressed a small drawstring bag into her hand. "Here, my lady. You'll be needing this."

The bag crunched slightly, and when Cele looked within, she found it full of dried flowers and leaves. It made her think of the sachets some women put in their lingerie drawers, only she didn't have any lingerie here. She looked curiously at Thora. "What for?"

Thora looked at her sternly, then her face softened. "You don't know, do you? It's to stop the babies from coming. If you've been with a man, make a tea from this for three days just before your monthly is due. It'll keep the seed from taking root."

"Thank you, Thora, but I don't need this. I told you before. I wasn't raped." Cele held out the bag to the woman.

Thora pinned Cele with a sharp look and didn't reach for the bag. "I'm relieved to hear it. But I think you run a greater risk from another quarter, do you not, my lady?"

Cele looked at Thora in surprise. She should have thought of this before, considering the way things were going with Dahleven. "Does this really work?"

"Usually. Sometimes the tea is too weak or the seed is too strong, but it works for most—as long as you remember to use it."

"I will." While her mom had done a fine job of raising her alone, and while Nuvinlanders seemed at ease with single motherhood, Cele didn't want to repeat her mother's experience. And if she did get pregnant, would she still be able to return to Midgard if something of Alfheim was growing within her? Would she still want to?

chapter nineteen

A knock startled them both. Cele set aside the pouch of herbs as Thora opened the door.

"My lady!" Thora exclaimed, then curtsied very low.

Gudrun entered the room like a ship at sail, followed by Ingirid, Kaidlin, and Aenid. They all wore gauzy gray veils framing their heads and shoulders. Cele stood, surprised, and did her best to curtsey. "Lady Gudrun, welcome. Please, be seated." Cele gestured to the cushioned window ledge and pulled forward the chair Dahleven had brought. "Thora, perhaps you could arrange some refreshment for our guests?"

"No, my dear, we didn't come to put you ill at ease," Gudrun said. "We know you are barely recovered and not prepared to entertain visitors."

Thora hesitated by the door. Cele weighed her etiquette options. Lady Gudrun was the ranking woman present, and Quartzholm was her domain. Yet this was Cele's room and Thora, ostensibly, was her servant. In this small environment, she decided, hospitality was her obligation. She waved Thora on, and the older woman slipped out the door.

"Prepared or not, I'm honored by your visit. Won't you make yourself comfortable?" Cele gestured toward the chair and window seat again, and Gudrun and Ingirid sat down.

Kaidlin came forward and took Cele's hands. "Enough of this formality! You must know why we're here. There's no way we can thank you enough for what you did!" Then she hugged Cele and kissed her cheek.

Ingirid rose. Tears shimmered in her reddened eyes. "Dahl told us how you put yourself at risk to save Ari. I'd have been lost myself if he'd died. He's my baby, you know, and now with Jon dead, he's my last." The tears spilled down her cheeks.

"Dead!" Cele exclaimed. "Lord Jon is dead? I'm so sorry, I didn't know." Cele laid her hand on Ingirid's. What had Gris said? About Jon being her target? "What happened? He seemed quite well at the Feast." *Maybe his liver gave out. No, that wouldn't be so quick.*

"He drank a poison intended for my husband," Gudrun said quietly.

"Oh, no!" Neven's harassment made more sense now. "And you haven't caught the person who did it yet?"

"No, but the Skald has been consulted. The stones have spoken."

Cele shook her head, confused.

Gudrun explained. "Eirik's skills include casting the runestones and interpreting their oracle. When the gods choose, they can reveal much that is hidden in the Norns weavings.

"But we came for a happier reason," Gudrun went on. She rose, smiling and stepped closer. "Because of you, Ari is still among us—getting into mischief, no doubt, even as we speak." Gudrun kissed her more formally than Kaidlin had, on both cheeks. "We are in your debt, my dear, though I can't imagine how we could repay such an amazing act."

Aenid stepped forward and added her own kiss to Cele's cheek. "Uncle Dahben said Ari was dead."

Cele shook her head. "He just looked that way. He wasn't quite gone. He'd just stopped breathing."

"'*Just* stopped breathing?' Can everyone in Midgard breath life back into a child?" Gudrun asked.

Cele felt herself blush. "No. I have special training. But we were lucky, too. We got to him quickly. The water was cold and his heart was still beating. I could teach you what I did, if you'd like."

Thora returned with a servant bearing a tray, interrupting the conversation. Gudrun and her daughters accepted steaming cups of the dark, spicy-sweet *sjokolade* and sipped enough to be polite before rising to leave.

"You are as generous with your hospitality as with your Talent, Lady Celia. Thank you again," Gudrun said as she stood by the door, held open by a guard. Then she spoke to the others. "Go on. I have something yet to say to Lady Celia." She looked pointedly at Thora, who followed the rest into the hall. The guard closed the door.

"I meant what I said about being in your debt, Lady Celia, but that does not extend to giving you my son." Gudrun paused, letting her words sink in.

Cele said nothing, speechless with surprise.

"I can see he's taken with you," Gudrun continued. "You're generous and open-hearted and brave. But Dahl will be Jarl one day, and possibly Kon. His wife must understand the duties associated with that responsibility, and he would be wise to make an alliance with the house of another Jarl. But you could bring him great happiness as his *elskerinne*. Be his mistress. Don't reach for more."

Cele could not have been more surprised if Gudrun had donned a clown nose and capered around the room before slapping her. She stared for a moment, at a loss about which point to respond to, hoping that Gudrun would choose to make a dramatic exit after her astounding and offensive offer. But Gudrun waited, expecting an answer.

Cele was drawn to Dahleven. She couldn't deny it. He was both safe and dangerous, and integrity oozed from every pore in his body. And Lord, the man was sexy. But she had no intention of marrying him. She'd known him less than two weeks, for goodness sake. And she certainly wasn't going to be his mistress. She was going home. But when she opened her mouth, she said, "Don't you think this should be Dahleven's decision, at least in part? Since he hasn't asked me to be either his wife or his mistress, I think this conversation is rather premature."

Gudrun wasn't put off. "And when he does? What will your answer be? Will you be sensible, and become his *elskerinne*?"

Cele reminded herself that the cultural expectations must be different here, but that didn't make them any more attractive. "Where I come from, having an affair with a married man is, at best, considered stupid. I'm not stupid."

Gudrun looked at her oddly, as though Cele had missed the point. "You're no longer in Midgard, Lady Celia. It's an honor to be the *elskerinne* of a Jarl, and your sons, though they could not inherit, would be powerful men."

The memory of seeing Dahleven on the stairs with Kaidlin hovered in Cele's mind for a moment, then she shook her head. "I won't share a man I'm in love with."

Something like approval flashed in Gudrun's eyes, but was gone too quickly to identify. "So you'll injure him then, by marrying him?"

Despite her bruised pride and Gudrun's prejudice, she answered honestly. "No, Lady Gudrun. While I'm sure I could learn what I need to know to be his wife, I want to go home. This isn't where I belong."

Gudrun nodded. Cele thought she saw some respect in her eyes as the older woman said, "Though Dahleven is beyond you, I do hope you find some happiness here—if you can't find your way back to Midgard."

"Thank you, Lady Gudrun. I'm sure I will; I'm pretty resourceful." Then a perverse impulse made her add, "After all, there's still Ragni."

Gudrun looked at Cele from under lowered brows. "Good day, Lady Celia."

chapter twenty

Cele stared at the door after Lady Gudrun left, thoughts and feelings swirling in her mind like debris in a dust devil. She didn't want to listen too closely to some of the thoughts, like the whisper that suggested it wouldn't be so easy to leave Dahleven when the time came to go home.

He was a good man. He loved his nephews, and he cared for the men in his command. And his kisses were world-class—in both worlds. She smiled as the memory of last night's caresses sent heat skating through her body. Dahleven wasn't like her father or Jeff. He took his responsibilities seriously. He took *her* seriously. And he obviously wanted her as much as she wanted him. But what was she to him, really?

What did she want to be?

Thora knocked and came in, interrupting Cele's thoughts. "You have another visitor," she said, opening the door wider for Angrim.

Angrim's smile looked a little pinched, but her voice was as light and bantering as ever. "You're quite the heroine! Let me add my congratulations. First you survive being lost in the drylands, then you save Kon Neven's grandson, and you manage to escape from kidnappers not once, but twice! No wonder Lady Gudrun honors you by coming to your chambers."

"Is that unusual?" Apparently, Gudrun's visit meant even more than Cele thought.

Angrim looked at Cele as though she'd made a bad joke. "I'm glad your adventures haven't robbed you of your sense of humor, my dear."

Cele glanced at the barely touched tray, at Thora in the back of the room, then back at Angrim. She was starving, and she would gladly have eaten what was there, but she couldn't offer a guest leftovers. "Would you like something to eat? Thora could get us something fresh."

Angrim accepted enthusiastically. "Yes, that would be lovely, thank you." As soon as Thora left, the small blonde pulled Cele to the window seat and leaned forward eagerly. "Tell me what happened! Was it romantic, like a skald's tale?"

Cele pulled back a little, dismayed. "No! It was terrifying."

Angrim seemed doubtful. "Your kidnaper wasn't handsome and dashing?"

Jorund's rich, melodious voice echoed in Cele's mind, rippling over her skin like his casual caress of her arm. He *was* handsome, despite the mask, and his bright eyes had teased more than one smile out of her, but she could hardly tell Angrim that. The memory of Harve's foul breath made it easy for Cele to answer, "No. He was awful."

Angrim's brow furrowed.

Cele had met girls like Angrim before, who confused

348

real life with romantic notions. "It wasn't like a puppet show or skald's tale. It was painful and frightening. You shouldn't imagine otherwise. Don't envy me. Be glad you were safe at home. I wish I'd been."

Angrim pulled back, surprised, but she quickly recovered her composure. "I'm so sorry. I wish I'd been there with you. I'd have given him a piece of my mind."

If you had any to spare. But the image of Angrim shaking her finger in Orlyg's face was so ludicrous that Cele chuckled.

Angrim seemed pleased with the effect. "That's better. If you can laugh, the wound can't be too deep." She stood. "I'd better go now. I'm sorry I can't stay, after all. I've just remembered an appointment with my dressmaker."

Thora returned with a fresh tray of glazed fruit and a pot of steaming *sjokolade* not long after Angrim left.

"I'm sorry your trip was for nothing, Thora. Angrim's gone already. Why don't you sit down and have some with me?"

Thora hesitated, and Cele remembered her first day when the older woman had seemed so uncomfortable joining her meal. "You needn't if it goes against protocol, but I'd enjoy your company." Cele didn't wait for Thora to be persuaded. She bit into a large sugared berry and had to slurp to keep the juice from running down her chin.

It was just as well that Thora declined her invitation, Cele realized as she popped the last berry whole into her mouth. The large assortment of fruit had been just enough to take the edge off her hunger. Her eyes were drooping as she finished the last of her drink.

"Is this the way Emergence usually works?" Cele asked as she lay down.

"You've been harder hit than most, but it's come on you late." Thora said. "And you've Exhausted yourself twice as well. There's nothing to worry about. It won't be long until this will all be past."

Cele slept until late afternoon. She hadn't been awake long when another visitor arrived. It was Eirik, the skald.

Eirik was less impressive without his beribboned tunic. He was thin and his beard scraggly, but when he spoke, Cele hung on every word.

"I've heard a little of your adventures, my lady. Indeed, who has not? As skald to Kon Neven, I'm charged with keeping the histories and telling our tales. I've come hoping you'll tell me your story and allow me to keep it alive." He bowed and stepped into the room. He seemed taller and broader than just a moment before.

Going over it all again was the last thing she wanted to do, but she found herself thinking this might be a good idea. Then she remembered Gudrun saying something about Eirik interpreting stones and knowing hidden things. It sounded like superstitious mumbo-jumbo, like Ouija Boards and tarot cards, but then again, a week and a half ago she would have thought Talents were impossible, too. "Actually, I'm more interested in another of your skills," she said.

Thora looked unhappy. "Do you feel you need an augury, my lady?"

"I think I need all the help I can get." She felt foolish asking to have her fortune told, but life here was becoming more and more complicated, and her feelings more and more tangled. Gudrun and Dahleven. Jorund and Neven. If she could find a way home, she wouldn't need to sort through the mess. The Daughters of Freya had promised to throw the stones for her, but a second opinion couldn't hurt, could it?

"I'm gratified by your confidence in me, my lady, and honored to be of assistance. Tell me what knowledge you seek, and I shall read the gods' reply."

"I want to go home," Cele said.

"Of course you do. But your desire for knowledge must be spoken indirectly. The gods are not pleased by demands. They prefer gentle requests. Then they may share that which pertains to our mortal concerns."

Eirik's smiling explanation soothed away Cele's last lingering embarrassment about consulting the soothsayer. "What should I ask then?"

"The mind drives the cart, but the heart is the axle upon which the wheel turns, is it not? And the heart is a lady's natural home." Eirik smiled, and Cele felt truer words had never been spoken.

The skald produced a soft leather bag and shook it three times. The contents clacked and rattled. "We welcome the gifting of knowledge. Lady Celia seeks the path to her heart's home." He opened the bag. "Draw out a handful of stones and slap them on the table, my lady."

Cele did as directed. There were five flat, irregular stones of various colors. Four lay face up, revealing angular runes.

Eirik put down the bag. "The gods have favored you, my lady, with a clear answer." He stood close behind her with a hand on her left shoulder, pointing at the runes with his right. "A new friend offers a gift that will lead to happiness and a breakthrough. Perhaps to Midgard." His breath tickled as he murmured in her ear.

"Really? When? Which friend?" *Does he mean Jorund?* Cele turned to look at Eirik. His face was very close, but she didn't mind.

"Alas, the gods say no more than that. But you'll know him when you meet. You'll recognize your opportunity. You're a most perceptive woman."

"Indeed she is," Thora said, coming forward.

Eirik smiled at Thora. "And a lucky one, too, to have you caring for her."

Thora continued forward and touched Cele on the

arm. "Would you like to send for some refreshment for the skald, my lady?"

Suddenly Cele became uncomfortably aware of how close Eirik was. She stepped away from him to a comfortable distance. He looked faintly surprised. Cele was surprised too, that his nearness hadn't bothered her before. "Yes, please, Thora."

"Thank you, my lady, but I can't stay. Perhaps another time." He gathered his runestones back into his bag. "Thank you for allowing me to serve you. Please consider my request. I would be honored to tell your tale." He bowed and slipped out the door that Thora held for him.

Cele blinked as the door closed behind Eirik. "He's quite amazing, isn't he?"

Thora frowned and narrowed her eyes. "You could say that, my lady."

Eirik's interpretation of the stones ran through Cele's mind again. Their meaning had seemed obvious just moments before, and she'd felt lucky that they'd spoken so clearly. But now, as she turned his words over and examined them, doubt that the gods, or Eirik, had said anything useful crept in. Her feeling of foolishness at consulting little bits of rock about her future returned in full force. She was surprised she hadn't questioned Eirik more closely, but at the time everything he'd said made sense.

Thora touched her shoulder tentatively, piquing Cele's curiosity. She'd never seen Thora hesitate. "My lady, I—"

A knock at the door made her break off.

It was Ragni. Thora dropped a shallow curtsey as she let him enter.

"Was that Eirik I saw leaving? What did he want with you?" He paused, then added with a bit of chagrin, "If I may ask? I'm not *usually* so rude, Lady Celia."

Cele returned Ragni's infectious smile, but she felt

heat rising in her face. What would a priest think of her seeking answers from runes?

Ragni's grin faded a little around the edges, but his voice remained light. "A secret assignation, my lady?"

"No! Don't be absurd," Cele exclaimed. "He came to get my story, and, well, I asked him to tell my future. I hoped he might shed some light on how to go home. It sounds stupid, now."

Ragni's smile returned in full force, easing her embarrassment. "Not so stupid. Priests and Jarls have consulted Eirik. Did he say anything helpful?"

"I thought so at the time, but now it just seems like the usual vague stuff carnival fortune-tellers spout. 'A friend will help me break through to Midgard.' Or something like that."

"That doesn't sound vague at all. It's much clearer than the stones usually speak," Ragni said.

"Do you think it's true?" Cele asked.

"That's not what the stones said," Thora interrupted.

Ragni's brows rose high. "No?"

The older woman knelt in front of Ragni with folded hands. "Father Ragnar, I am a loyal servant of Kon Neven. You know this to be true." She looked up into his face. Her expression was anxious and urgent.

At the invocation of his priesthood, Ragni shed his surprise and assumed a formal posture and tone. "Yes, I know that."

"Thora—" Cele began.

Ragni silenced her with a lifted hand. "Go on, daughter," he encouraged Thora.

"I have a gift for scrying, Father. Against tradition, I have learned to read the runes. I tell you truly, Eirik misread the stones."

Ragni ran a hand over his close-cropped beard. "This is a serious matter, in many ways. Who taught you to interpret the stones?"

FRANKIE ROBERTSON

"A woman long dead, Father."

Ragni was silent for a long moment, his brow furrowed. Cele wondered if he would ask about Thora's friends. She had a feeling that if he asked, Thora's loyalty to Neven would force her to reveal the Daughters of Freya.

"What did the runes say?" Ragni finally asked.

"The way the stones were grouped, there were two parts. One stone stood apart, and urged caution in a new association, a reminder that action carries responsibility. The other three stones promised partnership, and new beginnings. A gift of harmony and transformation." Thora took her eyes off Ragni and looked at Cele. "I'm sorry, my lady. The stones said nothing about travel or departure."

"That doesn't sound so different from Eirik's interpretation," Cele protested. "He talked about new friends, and gifts and a breakthrough. That's like a transformation."

Ragni answered. "A soothsayer's skill lies in his, or her," he cocked an eyebrow at Thora, "understanding of the nuances of prophesy. If Eirik accidentally, or deliberately, misinterpreted the stones, his skill and integrity are in doubt." He looked again at Thora. "This is an extremely serious accusation." He paused, considering. "Did he use his Talent of Persuasion?"

"Yes, Father." Thora nodded.

"Is that why his prophesy was so convincing?" Cele asked sharply. She felt stupid and gullible. "He used some kind of mind control?"

Ragni ignored her question. "How is it you resisted Eirik's Talent, Thora?"

To Cele's surprise, Thora blushed a deep red. "I...I have an amulet, Father," she stammered.

Ragni sucked in a breath through his teeth. "You *are* in deep, aren't you?" After an instant's pause,

354

he asked, "Is it fixed and sealed?"

"No! Of course not. No one died in its making."

Cele opened her mouth and shut it again, too confused to ask an intelligent question. *What has death got to do with an amulet? What has an amulet got to do with resisting Eirik's Talent?*

Ragni blew out a deep breath. "Thank Baldur for that. I had not thought amulets so common that huscarls wear them casually."

"They aren't, Father. I know of only two others."

Ragni was silent. Again, the right question could expose the Daughters of Freya if he demanded to know who had them.

Then he asked, "Is your amulet specific to Persuasion?"

"And Presence, Father." Thora winced.

She looked startled when Ragni chuckled. "My father will no doubt be happy to know it's his personality and position alone that inspire your loyalty." He sobered and stared down at Thora for what seemed like a long time before he spoke again. "By your own admission, Thora Kannesdattir, you have violated tradition and the strictures of the priesthood by reading the runes and practicing unsanctioned magic. Rise and receive your punishment."

The older woman moved stiffly after so long on her knees, and Ragni reached out to help her. Once standing, Thora stood calmly without fidgeting.

Ragni closed one hand over the symbol of his office, the purple bag that hung from his neck by an embroidered ribbon. He held it away from his chest, toward Thora. "I declare as a priest of Baldur, that in penance for your transgressions, you must relinquish your amulet...to Lady Celia."

Thora's surprised expression mirrored Cele's emotion, and then the older woman's lips curled in a sly smile. She turned her back to Ragni and untied something from underneath the loose leg of her pants.

Cele shook her head, nonplused. "What's going on?"

"Take this, Lady Celia," Thora said. She held out a small black bag tied with a long ribbon and sewn with silver runes. "It will prevent the Talents of Persuasion and Presence from affecting you, and allow you to hear the words of those who use them without being swayed any more than your own reason permits."

Cele remembered Neven's overwhelming Presence at the Feast of Fanlon, but it didn't seem likely that Ragni would be arming her against his own father. It must be Eirik's Persuasion he wanted her safe from, but she couldn't see the skald as much of a threat. Nevertheless, she took the amulet from Thora and started to tie it around her neck.

"No, my lady," Thora stopped her. "Someone will see the ribbon there. Tie it around your waist, under your clothes, or some other hidden place."

"It will serve you better if people don't know you have it, Lady Celia," Ragni said. "It will protect the clarity of your thoughts, and by their failed efforts, you will know who has attempted to influence you. If others suspect you have such an amulet, they may not reveal themselves."

Cele nodded. "Turn around then," she said to Ragni.

It made too large a lump at her waist. Cele tied the amulet around her thigh as Thora had, so it could dangle among the folds of her skirt. "What did you mean about someone dying in its making?"

"No one died, my lady, as I said. The amulet isn't fixed or sealed," Thora protested.

"It will become no more than a cold lump of crystal at the passing of the one who worked the ritual, Lady Celia. As you heard in Fanlon's Tale, a death is required for permanence—to fix the magic and seal the crystal to its purpose," Ragni said. "Baldur frowns on such things, except in dire need."

That reminded Cele of Wirmund's admonitions about her ignorance of Baldur. Thor and Odin had only been names out of mythology to Cele before, and she'd never heard of Baldur at all. But Thora behaved like someone who took her religion very seriously. "Ragni," she began when the amulet was secure, "or should I say Father Ragnar? Tell me about Baldur. I'm so ignorant, it's a miracle I haven't offended someone."

"You mean, besides Father Wirmund?" Ragni asked, his eyes crinkling at the edges.

Cele felt herself reddening yet again. "Besides him. It's just that he was so pompous with Sevond, I couldn't help baiting him a little."

Ragni's reply was more stern than Cele expected. "He has some right to be pompous. He has risen through many years of service to Baldur to become the *Overprest*. His authority extends over all the priests of Baldur, and he votes in the Althing as a Jarl." Then his manner lightened. "And as it happens, you have Father Wirmund to thank for my visit today. He too, thinks you would do well to learn more of our ways."

Cele smiled, embarrassed yet again. "Great. Then let's start with why nobody talks much about Thor and Odin. I'd never heard about Baldur and Freyr before I got here."

Ragni shook his head, eyes wide. "Father Wirmund told me that Midgard must have fallen into darkness, but it still astonishes me to hear you speak so. Our eyes were opened to the true order of things only after we were shown the way to Alfheim, but Baldur and Freyr were well known even before we crossed over."

"So what is the true order of things?" Cele asked.

Ragni drew Cele over to sit on the window seat. "As you heard in Brynjolf's tale, in the dark days in Midgard, many were seduced by the false priests of the White-Christ. Those who remembered the old ways worshiped Odin, the All Father, but many also gave equal honor to the Thor. Freyr was honored also, but even his worship became twisted, and some sacrificed their children to entice his favor and assure the fruitfulness of their fields."

Cele jerked, shocked. "Human sacrifice? I never thought the Norse did that!"

"It wasn't widely practiced, but when hunger threatens, men can fall prey to twisted beliefs if they're desperate enough."

"So what happened?"

"When Freyr led us to Alfheim, we understood our first duty was to him, and to Baldur whom he serves, though we still honor Odin and even Thor."

"You're losing me. Where does Baldur come in?"

"Baldur is Odin's son. His radiance blessed all who saw him and inspired those in his presence to good will. We honor his spirit and await his return."

"His return? From where?"

Ragni looked surprised. "From Niflheim." He assumed a teaching voice. "Baldur's twin, Hoder, was tremendously strong, but he was blind, and dark in spirit and body. Yet Hoder loved his brother, and that proved his redemption.

"Baldur was skilled in healing and reading the rune-stones, and he learned that a terrible fate awaited him. This alarmed the gods, who all loved him. All except Loki. To allay their fears, his mother, Frigga, extracted a promise from all things in earth and heaven to never harm Baldur. But she overlooked the mistletoe, because of its lowly state, and Loki learned this secret.

"Knowing Baldur was invulnerable, the gods paid tribute to him by casting spears and rocks at him. This saddened Hoder, because his blindness prevented him from honoring his brother as the others did. Loki saw this and laid his evil plans. He fashioned a dart of mistletoe and gave it to Hoder. Jealous of Baldur, Loki offered to guide Hoder's hand, and with Hoder's strength behind it, the mistletoe pierced our bright god's heart. A single ruby drop of Baldur's blood fell from his death-wound. At the sight of it, the mistletoe's red berries paled in shame, and they remain white to this day."

"Poor Hoder!" Cele exclaimed, even though it was just a story.

"Indeed," Ragni agreed. "At first the gods all blamed him, but they saw his grief and the trick was discovered. When they sought a reprieve from Niflheim for Baldur, Hel promised to release him if every living thing wept for him. Soon the world was awash in tears. All things in earth and heaven wept for Baldur except one old woman, who was Loki in disguise. And so Baldur remains in the land of the dead with his wife Nanna, who could not bear to be parted from him."

"So did Loki get what he deserved?"

Ragni nodded. "Loki received his punishment, and Hel, knowing of her father's trickery, promised Baldur's release when the nine worlds pass away. After Ragnarok, Baldur will create a new order where all will live in harmony, just as he inspired good will in his first life. Until that time, Freyr acts in his stead." Ragni spoke earnestly. "It was Baldur who led us to Alfheim, through Freyr."

Cele was silent, taking it all in. Ragni obviously believed everything he'd said about the mythological, comic book, characters. Her mother had taught her that Spirit could take many forms. Truth could be found in many traditions, like light reflected from a faceted gem.

Ragni watched her intently. One thing he'd said still bothered her. "Do you still practice human sacrifice?"

He recoiled. "No! Of course not! Only the misguided

and desperate did that. We broke from that heresy long ago. Baldur's innocent blood is enough."

Cele relaxed. She couldn't imagine Ragni participating in something so gruesome, but what did she really know about these people? "Why is this place called Alfheim instead of Baldurland, or something like that?"

Ragni's expression said he thought the answer was obvious. "Because this is the home of the Alfar, the Elves."

"Elves!" Things kept getting stranger.

"They have little to do with us, but we still show our respect—as Father did at the Feast."

"Your unseen 'hosts'?"

"Yes. The Light Elves serve Baldur and let us share their land. The others, the Dark Elves, don't deal kindly with men. Fortunately, there's little contact with either race. Light or Dark, no one deals with the Elves and remains unchanged."

"No, I don't suppose they would," Cele agreed.

"To Jon," Dahleven said, lifting his tankard, "and his *graceful* entrance into Niflheim."

Ragni snorted and took a deep draught from his own ale.

Neven shook his head but completed the salute. "It ill becomes us to sneer at the dead," he said, "but I never met a greater waste of flesh."

"He sired strong sons," Ragni said.

Neven smiled. "That he did. To Jon's sons." He drank deeply.

"To Ljot and Solvin and Ari," Dahleven echoed.

"And Aenid," Ragni added. "I regret I've seen little of her of late. She's a daughter any man would be proud of."

"Any man but Jon. He never looked at her twice once Ljot came along," Dahleven said.

"I suppose I should find her a husband soon," Neven said.

"There's time enough," Ragni suggested. "Let her finish her grieving first. And Ingirid will need her help with the boys."

"True enough. Ari's a handful by himself." Neven raised his tankard again. "To Ingirid. May she have peace, at last."

Dahleven raised his ale in salute, knowing his father had long regretted giving in to Ingirid's desire for Jon. Now that mistake was laid to rest.

They were silent for a moment, then Neven rose. "We must rejoin the Althing soon, so they can tell complimentary lies about Jon and drink his honor."

"Such as it was," Ragni said, grimacing.

Neven shook his head, but didn't rebuke his son. "Don't dawdle," he said, and left.

Ragni took another swallow of his ale and said, "Lady Celia's conversation with Eirik today was illuminating."

Dahleven looked over at his brother. "So you said." He paused, then added, "Father's reaction to your news about Thora was interesting."

Ragni made a face. "What reaction?"

"Exactly." Neven had always kept a few things to himself, even after his sons were of an age to be allies. "He already knew about Thora's scrying and the amulet."

Ragni nodded. "He must have."

Dahleven still wondered at the news about Thora. He'd known the woman all his life. She'd cared for them when they were lads. Had she been throwing the stones while they napped?

Father knew about it all along. It made sense that

Neven wouldn't tell Ragni. As a priest of Baldur, he might feel honor bound to tell Wirmund about her use of unsanctioned magic. Dahleven was less sanguine about being kept in the dark himself.

"Will you tell Wirmund?" Dahleven asked.

Ragni stared into his ale for a long moment. "A priest has already heard her confession and pronounced her penance," he finally said. "I see no reason to trouble the *Overprest* with a matter already resolved."

Dahleven nodded, relieved. Wirmund's compassion wasn't as dependable as Ragni's.

"Thora was sorry to disappoint Celia, but the stones didn't say what she wanted to hear." Ragni returned to his earlier observation.

Dahleven let himself be diverted. "I never had much confidence in them."

"If our skald wasn't either false or foolish, you might have a higher opinion of scrying. It worked for Baldur."

"He's a god. And it didn't save him, did it?"

Ragni made a face.

This was a well-worn conversation for them and Dahleven was glad his brother didn't pursue it. "Wasn't it Father Wirmund who called Eirik to serve Father?"

Ragni understood his meaning. "Father Wirmund is loyal. He may be narrow-minded and hidebound, but he'd never work against the Kon. That would violate tradition, after all," he said with a wry smile. "The Skald's Guild selected Eirik in response to Wirmund's request. It wasn't a personal choice."

Dahleven shrugged. He hadn't really doubted Wirmund. He was just turning every possibility over in his mind, trying to make the pieces fit.

Ragni pulled him out of his pondering. "Celia *said* she wanted Eirik to find a way home for her."

Dahleven looked sharply at his brother, not pleased with his casual use of her name. "And didn't she?"

Ragni stretched his legs out on the low table between them and crossed his ankles. "In part. Her emotions were in a bit of a muddle. Not surprising, considering all she's been through. But she shows a great deal of interest in our ways for someone who's anxious to leave."

Dahleven tried to clamp down on his feelings. Celia had often stated her desire to return to Midgard. Her warm, sweet kisses notwithstanding, he had no reason to believe she might change her mind. Ragni was just prodding him again. Sometimes having a brother who could read him so well was a pain in the ass.

"It's unlikely she'll find a way home, anyway. I know of none," Ragni added.

"Did you tell her that?" Dahleven sat up straighter."No. Father Wirmund had already said as much to her. She wasn't convinced."

Dahleven leaned back his chair, relieved for Celia's sake that her hopes hadn't been crushed, but unhappy that she was still hoping to leave.

"Sooner or later, she'll accept Alfheim as her new home, brother. And then she'll want someone beside her," Ragni said.

Ragni was right, but what difference did it make? Dahleven might want to be the one lying at her side, but as heir, he was expected to marry for the benefit of the Jarldom.

His brother knew right where to jab him. He jabbed back. "So you've abandoned your concern that she knows why she was taken, and concealed it?"

Ragni shook his head, his lip curled in affectionate disgust. "There is no darkness in her, only confusion and doubt. If you can't see she's a prize, I can."

Dahleven's pulse picked up with a possessive surge. "You can't afford to compromise your position as Wirmund's second with a 'questionable marriage.'"

"More so than you can," Ragni replied. "Besides, who

spoke of marriage? I'll take her as my *elskerinne*."

chapter twenty-one

DAHLEVEN HESITATED BEFORE turning the corner to approach Celia's room. Jon's wake was still going on. He'd stayed only long enough to satisfy propriety, and even that had been too long. Jarls and crofters still drank to Jon's honor down in the great hall, gifting him with every virtue under the sun.

If only Jon had been half that good in life.

Away from the wake, Quartzholm lay quiet. It was late, long past time when he should be calling on a lady, but the next day would be fully taken up with preparations for the delegation to the Tewakwe. He'd have no other chance to speak to Celia.

Their messengers would be over halfway to the Confederation by now. If all went well, in a week's time Neven would be planning with the Tewakwe leaders how to crush their mutual enemy.

Dahleven stiffened as one of the sentries he'd posted to guard Celia rounded the corner to confront him, alert and at the ready.

"My lord!" The guard stepped back, his posture easing. "I heard someone loitering. I mean—"

"You did well, Vakter. I've come to check on Lady Celia. Has she had any visitors?" Dahleven strode onward as though he had no doubts of his reception at this hour. *I must be crazy.* He didn't usually let Ragni's barbs get to him.

"Not since Lord Ragnar, my lord."

"And Thora?"

"She retired an hour ago, my lord."

The other guard stood to one side of Celia's door.

"Take a few minutes for yourselves," he said. If Celia threw him out, he didn't need to have his men witness the event.

"Thank you, my lord."

His men were well trained. Neither smirked within sight of him.

No point in waiting. He tapped a knuckle briskly against the smooth wood.

Celia opened the door. She wore a new robe of soft cream-colored velvet in place of the one that had been torn and bloodstained. It skimmed her body, barely giving a hint of the curves beneath.

Her fine brows lifted in surprise. "Dahleven! Is anything wrong? Ari isn't lost again, is he?" Then she frowned. "Or does Neven want to see me?"

"Nothing's wrong. You can rest easy. My father has other things to do this night."

"That's a relief." She gestured to the room's interior. "Come in. Have a seat."

Dahleven stepped into the room, wishing he could say more, but he couldn't apologize for his father's actions. To do so would undermine Neven's authority. But perhaps he could ease her concerns, at least a little. "You did well last night."

"That's nice to know. Does that mean Neven is going

to call off his dog?" Celia's voice was bitter.

He couldn't blame her. But angry or not, she should be more respectful. "*Kon* Neven will do what he must to protect Quartzholm and Nuvinland," Dahleven rebuked her gently. "Ragni and I have given him our best advice on the matter, but it's his will that governs." There, that was as close as he could get to telling her that he didn't agree with what his father had done. Dahleven hoped she understood.

"How does badgering me protect Quartzholm?" she asked sharply. Then she took a deep breath and blew it out slowly. "Does he think I tried to kill him and got Jon instead?" she asked in more even tones.

"No. Not anymore." He wasn't giving anything away by admitting that.

"Good. I'm glad he's got that much sense." She nodded and sat down on the window seat, gesturing again for him to sit also. Then she looked up at him and smiled ruefully. "I'm sorry. He's your father. I shouldn't put you in the middle like that."

Dahleven sat down. His knees nearly brushed hers, but he didn't try to touch her. "The lace looked well on you."

Celia's face cleared and she smiled. "Thanks. I wore it to give me courage."

Her answer surprised and pleased him, like an unexpected gift. "It must have worked, though I can't imagine you needing more. You have enough courage for five women."

"Me? I just do what I have to." She smiled, and Dahleven was glad he could please her. Then she frowned and looked down.

"What troubles you?" He tilted his head to better see into her lowered face.

"I'm not so brave," she said flatly, shaking her head. Her tone was disgusted. "I had to sleep with the light on last night."

Dahleven's heart clenched, remembering her bruises and the way she'd sobbed in his arms. It wasn't surprising she needed a light to sleep after what she'd endured. "So?"

"So? So I'm proud of getting away from those slimy bastards!" Celia stood up and turned, gesturing broadly. "But at night, in my nightmares, they paw at me and I can't move." Her voice lowered and she looked down as her hands spread in a futile gesture. "I just lie there in terror as they clutch and press down on me in the dark."

Dahleven stood, yearning to fold her in his arms, comfort her, to shield her from the fear and self-doubt, but he stopped. With any other woman that might be appropriate, and it might be what Celia wanted, but that wasn't what she needed. Sympathy would weaken her now. He tilted her chin up with the knuckle of one finger. "And so they defeat you anyway? Raping your mind, if not your body?"

Celia's eyes widened in shock. "What?"

Dahleven adopted the no nonsense tone he used when training his men. "A good warrior fights his enemies, not himself. He must acknowledge his weaknesses or he becomes a liability to himself and his fellows. You're human. Fear is part of that. Accept it. Use it. Don't waste your energy fighting yourself for feeling what is natural and normal. Don't let fear become a barrier to moving forward."

Celia's eyes widened as if he'd slapped her, then her face clouded in anger. "You son of a bitch! How dare you lecture me! I fought them, and got away, and I'm proud of that. But they were going to gang rape me! You have no idea what that's like. Of course I was afraid. I know that better than anyone. And you have the gall to stand there telling me not to fight *myself*?"

Dahleven kept his face impassive, concealing his

pleasure at her change in attitude. "A warrior doesn't make excuses for herself, either."

Celia opened her mouth and shut it, apparently too furious for words. Dahleven was glad, once again, that there were no weapons ready to her hand. She glared at him, green eyes flashing, emotions racing across her face like clouds chased by a storm-wind. Eventually, her shoulders settled, giving him a clue that she'd regained a measure of calm.

He spoke gently this time, as a man to a woman. "Fear does not diminish you. You are still strong and able...and beautiful."

Celia obviously still wasn't happy with him. She wouldn't make peace so easily. "What did you come here for?"

"I came to say goodbye," Dahleven said. "We'll be leaving at dawn the day after tomorrow to meet with the Tewakwe leaders. I doubt we'll speak again before I depart."

Cele felt her anger recede a little as a new thought occurred to her. "Have the Tewakwe always been here?"

"No. They have tales like ours of coming from hardship to this new land. Though why Freyr brought them is a mystery."

"When did that happen?"

"We started trading with them some hundred and fifty years ago, but their sagas say they've been here longer."

Cele strove to keep her excitement contained. Archeological evidence in the southwest spoke of various lost tribes like the Anasazi and the Hohokam. Despite plenty of speculation about what happened to them, no one knew for sure. *Maybe some of them came to Alfheim just like the Greenlanders. Just like me.* Memory flashed. *The petroglyphs.*

Maybe they know a way home.

"I want to go with you." She wasn't sure why she liked this idea better than Jorund's offer, but she did.

Dahleven's eyes widened. "Absolutely not!"

"But their shamans may know things your priests don't."

"No. This is no casual trading mission. This parley is to avert a war. We cannot distract from that to satisfy your personal desires."

Dahleven's tone left no room for negotiation, but Cele refused to let it lie. "This isn't some whim of mine. We're talking about my life here."

"I understand, Celia, but it's your life I wish to preserve. It's too dangerous."

"How could I be safer here than I would be with you?" Cele paused, surprised that she'd so openly stated her trust in Dahleven. She couldn't take it back, but she could ignore it, for a little while longer.

Instead of smiling at the compliment, Dahleven stiffened and frowned, but he answered calmly. "Perhaps when peace is assured you can explore this, but not now. Kon Neven will not allow anything to put this parley at risk."

"But—"

"Enough." Dahleven lifted his hand sharply. His words were soft, but hard as stone. "You will not go."

He's as bad as Neven! But a rill of panic followed her anger. He was leaving her only one choice for getting home. She'd have to Find the Staff.

Everything Jorund had said made sense. He'd saved her from being raped. He'd offered to help her, as no one else had. So why the cold feet? Maybe it was because Dahleven would see helping Jorund as a betrayal.

Cele set her jaw. What else could she do?

Dahleven went to the door and laid his hand on the latch. "Stay well while I'm gone." Then he left.

She stared at the door after it closed behind him, fuming at his dictatorial manner. Then she sighed, wishing his visit had taken a different turn.

Why couldn't the jerk have just put his arms around her instead of baiting her? He'd been kind to her before, so why not tonight, when she really needed it? And now he was going off to meet with the Tewakwe, who might know how to get her back home, and he wouldn't let her go. He had no understanding whatsoever of what she was going through.

In the haze of her frustration, Dahleven's earlier words floated back to her. *Don't let fear become a barrier*. Her mother had been strong and had raised Cele to be independent. "You don't need to be afraid of anything," she'd said more than once. But maybe what she'd meant was, "Don't let fear stop you."

So maybe Dahleven had a point. But that didn't mean it was right for him to go off and leave her behind in some misguided attempt to keep her safe.

Safe from what? They're going to a parley! To share information. But she knew things didn't always go as planned. Misunderstandings occurred. Sorn's bloody belly, Lindimer's cut throat, Halsten's cry as the arrow took him in the back flashed through her mind.

Suddenly she felt cold. What if they couldn't avert the war? What if the Tewakwe and Nuvinlanders fought instead of talking? *Dahleven could be killed.*

"What do you mean, I'm not going?" Dahleven tried not to shout. It was just after dawn, and he'd come to this meeting with his father and Ragni expecting to plan their strategy for the delegation.

"I thought I was fairly clear on the matter," Neven said. "It would be foolhardy to risk both of us, you know that. And I need someone here I can trust."

"You need someone you can trust to guard your back, too," Dahleven protested. "Mother can hold Quartzholm for you."

"Not while we have traitors among us. *You* have established the additional security, and it is *you* who will hold Quartzholm one day. You are *not* going."

Dahleven glanced at Ragni, who wisely remained silent. *He* was going. Neven needed his Talent for the parley.

Dahleven ran his hand over his beard, stretching the tension out of his jaw. There was no arguing with his father—with the *Kon*—when he used that tone. "All right. I've already dispatched the advance guard to secure the parley site. Is there anything *else* I should know or do here while you're gone?"

Cele knew it was petty, but it took some of the sting out of being left behind to know that Dahleven couldn't go either. She had to admit, but only to herself, that she was relieved, too. Dahleven wouldn't be risking whatever dangers the delegates faced.

The delegation of Kon Neven and two other Jarls had left before dawn, along with their retainers and enough servants to carry their gear. She'd thought about sneaking away and finding her own way to the parley with the Tewakwe—for about five seconds. One glance at her guards and the determined set of Dahleven's jaw had persuaded her of the impossibility of it.

Jorund's offer kept replaying in her mind. He seemed to think she'd have no trouble Finding the staff he wanted, even though he'd only provided a vague description of it. And even if she could, how was she going to explain wandering all over the castle to the guard that would inevitably tag along?

Cele spent most of the morning with Sevond. They pretended he was teaching her the skills of jewelry making, but they were really taking comfort in each other's company. Sorn's father was a gentle teacher, and he complemented her efforts even though she was all thumbs. She'd never known her grandfathers and she wondered if they would have been like Sevond. *Probably not, since Mom's dad practically disowned her.* Being with Sevond soothed her heart. While she listened to his quiet instruction, she couldn't worry about making difficult choices in a dangerous world with confusing customs.

At noon, her guard escorted her back to her room. Dahleven dropped by to share her midday meal, and they talked without a single sharp word between them until Fender arrived to drill her on the use of her Talent.

"Don't work her too hard," Dahleven told the younger man, but his gaze met hers and his hand rested lightly above her elbow. It felt more intimate than it was, and for that moment, nothing else existed. She leaned toward him, wanting to move into the circle of his arms, to run her hands over all that hard muscle. His eyes held hers and a smile played around his lips. Cele was about to stretch up on tiptoe to kiss him when Fender cleared his throat.

Cele blushed as Dahleven stepped back. Then he left, leaving the room feeling a bit empty.

Amazingly, Fender didn't utter a single teasing remark. He just matter-of-factly put her to work.

After half an hour of practice, Cele had an idea. "Can

we go outside? Up high, on the what-you-call-its? The battlements?" You could ask me to Find things you know are in the various towers."

Fender gave her a searching look. "An excellent idea," he said slowly. "And it would allow you to get some fresh air at the same time. That's what you're really after, isn't it?"

Not exactly. But she smiled and said, "You caught me. Dahleven doesn't want me wandering about alone outside, not after what happened in the meadow." Which had the virtue of being the truth.

They climbed to a high walk midway between the two tall central towers. Wind whipped loose strands free of her braids. Cele leaned against a parapet, trying to take it all in. On three sides, forested mountains loomed. Below the castle, she could see the town wrapped around the base of the walls, and beyond that a combination of meadows and tilled fields. Far in the distance, a river flowed away around a ridge of hills. "Wow! You can see the whole valley. It's beautiful!"

"You should see the sunrise from up here." Fender swept out his arm, pointing to the east. "In the winter, if you care to brave the Frost Giants' breath, the sun comes up over the ridge there..."

Cele barely heard his words. Instead she concentrated, imagining a staff about a yard long, with a clear purple crystal set in a copper collar. A dim, muffled sensation pulled at her from the left. It was so faint she barely felt it. She turned, taking a step closer, trying to focus—

"Lady Celia?" Fender's voice shattered her concentration.

Damn! Just another second or two and she would have had a lock on it. "I'm sorry. What did you say?"

Fender frowned, studying her. "I asked if you're ready to begin."

"Of course!" She smiled. "Sorry. I was daydreaming. What would you like me to Find?"

She'd have to try again to Find the staff, but Fender was watching her closely now. Belatedly, she wondered if she got a peculiar look on her face when she used her Talent. One that Fender would recognize? If she did, there was only one way to hide what she was doing from him.

"Think of a stone table. About so high and so wide," Fender shaped the air with his hands. The stone is gray, speckled with black and silver, and the pedestals are plain except there are stretching mountain cats carved into them." He stretched his arms above his head.

Cele held the image in her mind. The sensation of tugging was immediate, pulling her attention to the right hand tower, then to a floor halfway down. The table was there in a room on the other side of the stone column.

But she didn't give her answer right away. Instead, she pictured the Staff. Her first attempt had seemed to come from the tower to her left, now she gave it her full attention. If her expression betrayed her, Fender would just think she was still working on Finding the table.

Cele felt guilty deceiving him, but pushed the feeling away so she could concentrate. She wasn't hurting anyone. She might not know all of Jorund's motives, but he had Nuvinland's best interests at heart.

The pull was fainter than usual, and she closed her eyes. The sensation was diffuse, like a muffled sound, or a whisper, and it kept shifting out of reach as if she were grasping at fog. *Why is it so hard to hold on to?* Gradually it coalesced, calling to her from somewhere near the top of the left hand tower.

Yes!

Now all she had to do was pinpoint the room. She'd have to get closer for that. Without Fender.

Cele opened her eyes and pointed to the tower on the right. "The table is there, on the far side."

Fender considered her thoughtfully. "Perhaps we should suspend your training today. I think you must be more tired than you admit. You took much longer than usual that time."

She couldn't meet his eyes. Fender been nothing but kind to her, and she was deceiving him. She didn't like how that felt, even if no harm would come of it. "Maybe you're right."

Fender leaned against the parapet and crossed his arms over his chest. "Lady Celia, you have a remarkable Talent. In all our sessions I haven't posed a challenge yet that you've failed to meet."

She smiled, enjoying the praise even if it was for something she didn't have much control over.

"Finding isn't a Talent that lends itself to misuse, and you're a grown woman, not a young miss, so I needn't caution you to use your gift wisely."

Cele's heart stuttered. Did he suspect something? She forced a smile of irony to her lips. "Even if you just did."

Fender grinned wryly. "I'm glad you're paying attention."

He hadn't forgotten her distraction earlier. Did he doubt her explanation? Cele cringed inwardly. She liked Fender. She didn't want him to distrust her.

He shrugged away from the wall. "Shall we go down?"

She'd rather have stayed up on the heights for a while, but she didn't want to lie to him again, so she nodded. "Yes. Let's."

As they entered the tower, the birds perched on the peak took flight with a flapping of wings. A lone raven flew north.

Cele was relieved that her hunger was less intense

than it had been in the past. It took only a short nap afterward to ease her fatigue.

"You see, my lady," Thora said when she woke, wagging her finger, "I said you'd come into your own soon. Your body's adjusting, just as it ought. You're on the easy side of the slope, now."

Cele nodded. Her Talent was becoming easier and more automatic. Using it no longer felt like a party trick—not when she was lying to people about Finding a long hidden artifact.

Fender's words about using her Talent wisely kept surfacing like a persistent dog begging to be fed. She felt guilty about deceiving him, but she didn't have a choice. If Jorund was right, Neven and Wirmund probably wanted her dead. Was he right? Had he told her the whole truth?

What was she thinking? He'd *saved* her, for goodness sake! He was the only person offering any hope at all of going home.

All he'd asked in return was that she Find the Staff of *Befaling* for him, so he'd have the power he needed to help her, and the people of Nuvinland.

She just wished she didn't have to lie to people she liked in order to help him.

chapter twenty-two

ANGRIM DROPPED BY after the evening meal. Cele heard her flirting outside with the guards for several minutes before a knock sounded at the door. While Angrim was obviously a woman who enjoyed male attention, she also seemed like the sort who aimed as high as she could. Cele thought the guards would seem a waste of time to someone who had once hoped to catch Dahleven. But Angrim was smiling coyly at them when Cele opened the door.

"Let's go for a stroll," Cele proposed before Angrim could enter. She smiled at the guards. "Which one of you gets to come along with us?"

The shorter one bowed. "Both, my lady."

Angrim hooked an arm through the taller man's and almost batted her eyelashes. "Come along, then."

Cele nodded at the other guard but didn't take his arm. Behind them, Angrim was chatting merrily. Cele couldn't help wondering if Angrim had come to visit *her* or the guards. She felt awkward walking in silence.

"What's your name?"

"Bergren, my lady."

Cele smiled. "It's nice to meet you. I'm sorry I haven't asked before. And Angrim's friend?"

The corners of Bergren's eyes crinkled. "Isolf."

Cele was quiet for a moment. She directed her steps gradually to the bridge that spanned between the two central towers, but not too directly. She didn't want to seem as if she had a destination. "Where's Jeger? I haven't seen him since...for a couple of days."

"He's been scrubbing shi—uh, latrines, my lady." Bergren's expression was grimly satisfied. "And grateful for it."

Cele's eyes widened. "But it wasn't his fault!"

Her guard's expression grew hard as granite. "It's better than he deserved. He failed in his duty. Another lord might well have exiled him."

Cele's heart flinched. *Like Jorund was exiled?* Justice in this world was harsh. If Jorund failed, if her part in stealing the Staff was discovered, what would Neven do to her? What would Dahleven say? She could imagine the look in his eyes. Disgust. Anger. Betrayal.

A niggling doubt suggested that Jorund had been a little too smooth, but she dismissed the worry. Of course he'd do his best to convince her to help. And how else was she going to get home?

They continued strolling through the winding corridors. She guided them indirectly to the other tower, asking questions about how old the castle was and how it was built. Sometimes they stopped and looked out of narrow windows onto the dark. Torch and lantern light twinkled below, but it was nothing like the blanket of diamonds Tucson's electric lights would have spread across the valley. Bergren told her that Quartzholm was one of the last holdings built, since it was furthest from the sea. Great Talents had carved it out of the mountains four hundred years ago, moving huge blocks of quartz and granite, flowing the stone into seamless perfection. The glass in the embrasures was actually quartz that had been shaped by Talents no longer in existence.

"It would be a much more difficult task today," Bergren said. "Fortunately, it isn't necessary."

Cele smiled, then returned an acknowledgment from a passing noble. The halls were much emptier now that the Althing had ended. Most of the lords and ladies and merchants had departed for home. "So Fanlon stole all the Great Talents, even the useful ones, just because of a few rotten apples."

"Rotten apples?" Bergren frowned, then his expression cleared. "No, the sagas say there were more than a few misusing their Talents. And while honor may be won in battle, many died in the endless conflicts. Lord Fanlon's solution had the virtue of being equitable. No one Jarl was left with an advantage over another."

He has a point. But that didn't change what she had to do.

She fell silent, but Angrim kept up a merry chatter, sharing gossip about men and women Cele didn't know. They'd climbed high in the tower, near where she'd sensed the Staff earlier. It was time to try again. Hoping that the others wouldn't notice, Cele reached out with her Talent. Instead of the crisp, clear tug she was growing accustomed to, the sensation was muddy and vague, just as it had been that afternoon. She focused her desire, holding the image sharp in her mind. Angrim's voice faded into the background. It was still above them, but she still couldn't tell where.

She stumbled, jerking her out of her concentration.

Bergren caught her arm. "My lady!"

I guess I can't walk and chew gum at the same time. She smiled up at the guard. "Thanks. That's what I get for letting my mind wander."

Bergren released his hold on her, but stayed closer, as if afraid she'd topple over. "Perhaps we should go back now, before you grow more fatigued."

No! She was too close to stop now. It would look suspicious if she came back here a second time.

He must have seen the refusal on her face. "We can't go much further in any case, my lady. This corridor leads only to Father Wirmund's chambers."

Wirmund! Cele nodded. She'd get no closer than this. She couldn't visit Wirmund; his sharp eyes saw too much. She'd never fool him about what she was doing. Not with as much concentration as it had taken earlier to Find the Staff. Bergren might not have noticed, but the *Overprest* would spot her using her Talent and suspect something, without a doubt.

She'd have to try again. Here. Now.

She wavered a little. "I think you must be right. The day is catching up with me. Is there a bench nearby?" She didn't have to fake the trembling of her fingers as she reached for Bergren's arm, though it was from nerves rather than fatigue.

Her escort looked faintly alarmed. "Up ahead. There's an antechamber where those seeking Father Wirmund's aid may wait. I believe there may be seating there." They made their way slowly down the hall, then turned a corner into a small chamber. Two doors and another staircase broke three of the walls. A pair of guards bracketed the stair, dressed not in the Kon's ubiquitous green, but in priestly gray, though they wore no purple bags around their necks.

"Have you come to see the *Overprest*, my lady?" One of the men asked.

"Lady Celia needs to rest," Bergren said. "Is there somewhere she may sit?"

"She's in Emergence," Angrim offered as she fluttered to Cele's side. "We shouldn't have let you tire yourself."

"Only in the *Overprest's* chambers. I'll inquire if he's accepting visitors."

Damn! "No! Don't trouble him. I'm just a little tired. Could I just sit here on the steps for a bit?"

The two gray-garbed guards looked at each other and shrugged. Bergren frowned, but held her elbow as she turned her back on the guards and sat on the second step.

Angrim sat beside her and put her arm around Cele's shoulders. "Just lean against me, Lady Celia."

"Isolf, get some *sterkkidrikk*," Bergren ordered the other guard. "Go."

Cele shuddered at the thought of the vilely sweet drink. Angrim patted her hand. Bergren hovered in front of them with the other guards.

It's now or never.

Cele closed her eyes and pictured the Staff as Jorund had described it: a carved wooden shaft surmounted by a purple gemstone as big as her palm. Again, instead of a clean solid tugging, the answering sensation was dull and indistinct. It wavered in and out of focus as if a barrier stood between her and what she sought. The sensation made her stomach dizzy, and she was glad she was sitting down. She forced herself to hold on. Then, for a moment, the mists cleared. The Staff was above and off to her left. She lifted her head, turning to face that direction. The focus blurred again and the room tilted.

"Are you all right?" Angrim patted Cele's shoulder and sounded genuinely concerned.

Cele straightened and pinched the bridge of her nose. She'd try again, as soon as her head stopped spinning.

"Lady Celia?" The *Overprest* spoke from behind.

Cele lifted her head and turned to find Father Wirmund standing a few steps above her. Adrenaline jumped through her veins. How much had he seen? Did he know she'd been trying to Find something?

The *Overprest* finished descending the wide stairs and stopped in front of Cele. Angrim rose and curtsied to him, but he barely acknowledged her.

"Are you unwell? Shall I summon a Healer?"

Cele forced a smile and pushed herself to her feet, then curtsied awkwardly. "No, thanks. I'm fine. Just a little tired. I wanted some exercise, but I guess I overdid it."

Wirmund frowned. "That was rather foolish of you, after your recent difficulties. Your escort should have known better than to indulge you." He speared Bergren with a sharp glance. "Won't you come into my chambers where you can rest in greater comfort?"

Where you can interrogate me? No thank you. "I don't want to disturb you."

"Nonsense." He took her arm as he considered his guards coldly. "You should have sent for me rather than allowing a Lady to crouch here on the steps."

"But you—" The first man started to protest, but the other cut him off.

"Yes, my lord."

Angrim nodded. "I was getting rather tired of sitting on this cold stone step."

Isolf barreled around the corner, skidding to an abrupt stop when he saw Father Wirmund. He bowed, breathing hard.

"Is that the *sterkkidrikk*?" Bergren pointed to the flask the other man clutched, forgotten.

Isolf nodded and held it out.

Cele took it, glad of an excuse to withdraw her arm from Wirmund's. "Thank you." She took a couple sips of the intensely sweet liquid and grimaced. She'd never liked the energy drinks back in Midgard, either.

Wirmund urged the flask upward again with a firm

touch. "All of it, my lady. We don't want you falling victim to Exhaustion again."

Cele suppressed a grimace and drank. When she'd finished, she said, "I'd like to go back to my room now."

Bergren nodded.

"Do you feel well enough?" Wirmund asked. "You may rest in my rooms."

"That would be lovely," Angrim chirped.

Cele fought the urge to clap her hand over Angrim's mouth. *I'm not going to get a second try at the Staff. Not with Wirmund watching.* "No. Thank you. I'm fine now. Let's go back."

The next day Aenid was with Master Sevond when Cele arrived, and the three of them spent a companionable morning together.

Cele and Aenid left at the same time, Cele's guard trailing along a little distance behind. "Is that something you wear in mourning for Lord Jon?" Cele asked, indicating the gray veil that Aenid wore.

"Yes. The women of the family wear these for six months. Then we'll burn them to symbolize the passing of our grief." Aenid smiled sadly. "I wear one for Sorn, too, beneath my clothes. But six months won't bring an end to my sorrow."

Cele nodded, not commenting on the difference of sentiment Aenid had for her father and Sorn. "How're you feeling?" she asked in a confidential tone. "Are you still fainting and getting sick?"

"No, it was only those few times. I feel quite well, actually."

"You haven't told Sevond yet."

"No. I will soon. When I tell him, I'll have to tell everyone. I want to be sure before I share it."

Cele nodded. "Don't wait too long. Better you tell them before they guess."

Aenid put her hand to her middle and spoke softly. "Do you think my belly is rounding?"

Cele looked at the younger woman critically. "Maybe, but no one will notice it in that loose gown." She cocked an eyebrow at Angrim. "Unless you keep walking around with your hand on your tummy."

Aenid colored and dropped her hand.

Cele laughed and changed the subject. "How's Ari?"

"He's well. Baldur smiled upon you that day. One would never know he came so close to Niflheim." Aenid grew more sober. "He's too young to really understand about Father, though he knows something's wrong and keeps asking for him. Ljot and Solvin feel it more."

"And your mother?"

Aenid shook her head. "She wept for a day afterward. But now she almost seems happy."

That Ingirid might feel some relief at Jon's death didn't surprise Cele, but she couldn't say that to Aenid. "Grief is different for everybody."

Aenid nodded. "We say, 'Grief travels a twisted road.' Aunt Kaidlin is staying with Mother and helping with the boys. I don't think she would follow Nanna's Path, but we're not leaving her alone for a while."

"Nanna's path?"

"Baldur's wife," Aenid's tone became instructional. "She killed herself rather than live without him. There's an old tradition of women joining their husbands in death. It's not much done anymore."

"Thank goodness!"

"Come visit soon," Aenid said as they parted ways at the top of the stairs. "Ari would like to thank his rescuer."

Cele doubted Ari remembered her, but she said, "I

will."

Dahleven and a covered tray awaited her in her room.

"You look well recovered from your jaunt of last evening." His voice was tight.

Of course the guards would tell him. "I'm fine."

He shook his head. "Emergence Exhaustion is nothing to flirt with, Celia! Surely Ghav has told you that."

"I wasn't that tired!"

"That's not what I heard. You collapsed on the stair for nearly half a candlemark!"

Cele frowned. Had she spent that much time trying to Find the Staff? "I was just resting."

"You needed *sterkkidrikk*!"

"Only to make the guards feel better! Isolf ran halfway across the castle for it. I had to drink it!"

Dahleven shook his head and pressed his lips together. When he spoke, it was in a softer voice. "I'm sorry. I should have thought to show you Quartzholm myself."

She would have liked seeing Quartzholm through his eyes, even if it completely prevented her from Finding the Staff. The tension sizzling between them transformed into something else. It surged, fluttering in her breasts and lower.

"I would have taken care that you didn't tire yourself." The heat in his gaze suggested he would have made sure she'd saved her energy for other activities.

Cele felt a little breathless at the thought. "I just overdid it a little. I really didn't need that sterkki-crap."

Dahleven's lips twitched. "It *is* vile, but it has saved your life more than once."

Cele smiled. "I know. And drinking it was better than resting in Wirmund's chamber, like Angrim wanted to."

Dahleven frowned at the mention of Angrim, but didn't say anything about his former lover. Instead, he changed the subject and poured them a pale amber wine. "I'm glad you felt well enough to visit Sevond this morning. Other duties have claimed so much of my time that I've not been able to see him as often as I'd like. He doesn't have anyone else now."

Cele thought of Aenid and Sorn's baby, but kept quiet as she took the goblet Dahleven handed her. "I like him. He asks me to Find things he's mislaid and then praises me as if I've worked a miracle."

Dahleven smiled. "He has a generous heart."

Cele nodded and sipped the wine. "Much better than *sterkkidrikk*."

Dahleven laughed and gestured toward the tray. "I, ah, had something special made for your midday meal." His eyes glinted with anticipation, and something else.

Is he nervous? "What is it?" Cele reached for the tray's lid and hesitated. It looked like Dahleven was holding his breath. "Is a snake going to jump out at me?"

"I hope it will be a more pleasant surprise than that."

Cele lifted the cover cautiously, peeking under the edge at first, then lifting it off completely. On the tray was a disk of flat bread spread with a green sauce redolent of spices, goat cheese, and covered with chunks of sausage.

Dahleven shifted from one foot to the other. "It's supposed to be a *peetsah*. You said it was your favorite food."

"Oh!" Cele laughed as tears fill her eyes, and she brought her hands up to her mouth. He'd remembered a silly remark from weeks ago and tried to please her.

Dahleven's brow furrowed. "I'm sorry. Is it very awful? It must be very different from the *peetsah* you remember."

"Yes. No! It's not awful at all! It's wonderful!" Cele flung herself at him, hugging his neck. "Thank you." She kissed his cheek.

Dahleven drew her closer, returning the kiss.

She'd wanted this, to feel his arms around her again since their time in the meadow, since he'd kissed her in her bed. Her nerve-endings sizzled as his caresses trailed down her back, lingered on the swell of her hips.

"Maybe you should you try it before you declare it wonderful," Dahleven murmured against her lips.

"It's wonderful. You're wonderful. Thank you." She punctuated each statement with a kiss, then kissed him again, savoring the taste of him. His lips were warm and his beard tickled her chin. She might have forgotten the pizza altogether if her stomach hadn't rumbled loudly.

They pulled apart, laughing.

Cele turned to the tray and cut a piece, serving Dahleven first, then herself. It didn't smell like any pizza she'd ever had. He waited until she took a bite. It didn't taste like any pizza she'd had before either. But it was still good. She smiled.

A satisfied grin replaced the anxious expression on Dahleven's face.

"Have some." Cele gestured to his plate with her slice. Dahleven intercepted her hand, raising the piece she held to his mouth. Her heart sped as Dahleven's eyes locked with hers as he bit into the bread and sauce.

"Delightful," he murmured, then lifted the slice from his plate and fed it to her in turn. Then he gently swept a finger along the corner of her mouth, lifting a dab of sauce and placing it between her lips.

Cele licked and sucked his finger longer than necessary and was rewarded when his eyes grew dark and his breath quickened. She knew it wasn't the wine that made her feel so warm, and his gaze was as hot as she felt.

They'd come close to sex twice before, and God knew she wanted him now, too. It would be so easy to just let it happen. Her body was clamoring for it. And she could see that Dahleven wanted it.

He answered her stare by licking the corner of her mouth, then kissing his way along her jaw.

Yes. Cele groaned and arched her neck, their meal forgotten. *No.* She cared for him too much to just jump in the sack. It wouldn't be "casual" or "just sex." It would be making love. For her anyway. *He* was destined for a dynastic marriage, and she was going home. If they made love, it would break her heart to watch him marry someone else. It would break her heart to leave.

Somewhere, Cele found the strength to pull out of Dahleven's arms. She gulped down half a goblet of wine, and her dazed mind searched for some distraction. "Is—is this the first time you've been left in charge of Quartzholm?"

Dahleven shook his head as if to clear it. "No. But it's the first time Father has left me behind while going into real danger. He's a capable warrior, but I would far rather face an enemy myself." He stroked her upper arm. "Do you really want to talk about this now?"

Cele shivered at his touch, hungry for more, but she moved away to sit on the window seat. Dahleven's hand dropped to his muscular thigh. No, she didn't want to talk about this. But she didn't know what else to do. Didn't know how to stop the longing ache in her chest. "Now you know how women feel."

Dahleven gave her a confused look.

"Women have always been left behind with nothing to do but worry until someone comes riding back to tell them 'we won, prepare a feast,' or 'we lost, you're a widow, your life has changed.'" She didn't want to think about what it would be like to have a stoic-faced warrior tell her that Dahleven was dead.

"How else could it be? I'm amazed and impressed at your skill in unarmed combat, Celia, but against a man with a sword or a bow, you'd be vulnerable."

"You could teach women how to fight with weapons."

He shook his head. "Even properly trained, a woman's lesser strength would put her at great disadvantage against a man with a sword. And if women joined men in combat, most warriors, the good ones anyway, would be too distracted by protecting them to fight well."

His words jolted like a splash of cold water. "You mean like Sorn was."

"Unfortunately, yes. The majority of wives and mothers and daughters don't belong in battle."

"But some would do very well."

Dahleven frowned, then surprised her by conceding, "A few."

She felt herself wanting to slide back into his arms and focused instead on the bigger picture instead of the lingering sensation of Dahleven's hands on her body. "That's not really my point. Women would rather be out doing things and managing their own lives than waiting to find out what some man has planned for them."

"Some women, perhaps. Most women are content with their children and homes."

"Argh!" Cele warmed to the topic. "Of course women love their children. So do most men. That doesn't keep us from wanting some control over our lives. What alternative does a woman have if she wants to marry a man her father disapproves of? Or doesn't want to marry the man he picks for her? What if he beats her? What if he's a drunk?"

Dahleven lips stiffened with anger, his voice grew cold and level. "Ingirid chose Jon against my father's will, yet Neven let them marry. When Jon's weak nature became worse, Father told Ingirid he'd settle a rich holding on Jon to release her, if Ingirid willed it. She refused. Baldur only knows why, but she loved him. Neven didn't force Jon on her, she *chose* him."

Cele winced. She didn't like having Dahleven angry

with her. And this was a side of Neven she hadn't expected, even if he was a doting grandfather.

She spoke softly. "I admit, I *was* thinking of Jon, but he's not really what I'm talking about. You're saying your father *let* Ingirid make a mistake, he let her chose. I'm saying it was her mistake to make. I'm glad Neven is a generous father, but all women should have the *right* to choose their husbands. And it goes beyond that. Women should have some way to live, apart from the good will and generosity of their husbands and fathers if they choose to. How does a woman support herself here if she's not raised in a trade? If she goes against tradition?"

"You've been talking to the Daughters of Freya," Dahleven accused.

Cele hesitated, surprised. *He knows about them?* "These are issues that are important to all women, even those in Midgard."

"It sounds much like what the Daughters espouse."

"Who are they? What do you know about them?"

"I know it's not wise for you to associate with them. They have a poor reputation."

"Because they want women to have rights?"

"Because many believe them to be whores and witches."

"Believed to be. By you?"

"What I believe isn't at issue. Your reputation will suffer if you meet openly with them. There's nothing wrong with a young woman taking her pleasure with a man before marriage, but the Daughters are rumored to think wives and mothers should be free to visit any bed as they will. That they bespell men with unsanctioned magic to get their way."

That didn't jibe with what Alna had said. Nor did Osk and Saeun and Thora strike Cele as being interested only in sexual freedom. Cele's fist closed for a moment on the amulet hanging under her skirts. "Why do people think that about them?"

Dahleven shrugged.

"Have you talked to a Daughter of Freya?" *Could I be wrong about them? God knows, I've been wrong before.*

Dahleven answered slowly. "No woman has ever told me she was one of them."

"That's not surprising."

Dahleven shook his head and took her hand. "Let's talk about something else."

Cele pressed her lips together, frustrated. He was right, in a way. She wasn't going to change this world by lecturing people. *I'm not going to change it all. I'm going home.* And for her to get home, Jorund needed the Staff.

She wasn't sure why she hadn't yet dropped a note down the shaft in the bathing room, as he'd asked. She'd meant to do it this morning. The information she'd gathered last night was probably the best she'd get. But when she'd thought of doing it, she'd hesitated. Jorund had saved her, but he *was* an Outcast, a criminal in this world, as Knut had become for killing Lindy. Or was he just a political exile? Jorund *said* he'd been Outcast because he'd opposed Neven, and from the way the Kon had interrogated her, she could believe that.

On the other hand, Neven had also treated her like an honored guest. He'd been grateful to her for saving Ari. Dahleven and Ragni supported him. Would they do that if he were really a tyrant? *Or do they support him just because he's their father?*

Of course, even if deep down Neven was really a nice guy, Jorund was still the only one offering her a way home. It was a no-brainer. Wasn't it?

Yet for some reason, when it had come time to set pen to paper, visiting Sevond had seemed much more urgent. There was no time limit on Jorund's request, after all. But the sooner she told him where the Staff was, the sooner she could go home.

"Celia?" Dahleven squeezed her hand.

"You're right. Let's change the subject. There's something I wanted to ask you." Dahleven lifted his brows, and Cele continued. "Do I really need to have guards on me at all times? What harm do you expect me to do?"

His eyes widened in what looked like genuine surprise. "They're not protecting Quartzholm. They're protecting *you*. You've been endangered *four times* while under my care! *Twice* here at Quartzholm!"

"Well yes, but...it didn't make any difference before."

Dahleven stiffened as if he'd been slapped.

"I'm sorry! That didn't come out right. It's just that I'm not used to being followed everywhere I go."

"No, you are quite right in faulting our security." His voice was stiff. "That's why you'll not be left unprotected until this threat is resolved." Dahleven rose and went to the door. "I will do all in my power to keep you from harm, Celia." He took his leave without trying to embrace her again. The door clicked shut with sharp finality.

"Damn it!" Cele slammed a fist into the pillow beside her. That hadn't gone as she'd wanted at all. He'd brought her pizza and all she'd done was insult him. *What's the matter with me?* She wouldn't blame him if he never wanted to kiss her again.

chapter twenty-three

cele still hadn't written the note for Jorund when Angrim showed up again long after dinner. She heard the little blonde laughing and bantering with the guards for several minutes before Bergren finally announced her. Cele saw a servant carrying away a tray when she opened the door.

"I hope I'm not calling too late, Lady Celia, but things are so dull now with everyone gone home from the Althing. You're the only interesting person left to talk to."

"I'm glad you think so."

Angrim apparently missed the irony in Cele's voice. "Absolutely. Most women only want to talk about foolish things; you're different."

"How did your appointment with the dressmaker go the other day?" Cele asked with deliberate innocence.

"Oh, wonderfully. She has a new blue fabric with the most delicious hand. It feels like warm honey sliding over the skin. And the color brings out my eyes. She's going to make up a new dress for me by the end of the week."

Their conversation continued in that vein for nearly an hour. Cele was trying to think of a way to encourage

Angrim to leave when the other woman stood up. "It's time to go."

Cele stood too, surprised at Angrim's abruptness. "I don't feel like another walk tonight. You go on without me."

Angrim smiled without her usual coyness. "We're both going, my dear, but not on a stroll. Lord Jorund is waiting. You should get your cloak—it's chilly down in the tunnels."

Cele stared at the petite woman waiting impatiently for her. She'd never have guessed Angrim would be the one to summon her back to Jorund. "But I haven't sent him the information yet!"

"I did. Last night. You weren't very circumspect. Fortunately, the guards were too worried about being blamed for your Exhaustion to pay attention. I gleaned enough from your careless glances to tell him where to search. Someone will retrieve the Staff tonight."

How many other agents does he have hidden in Quartzholm? And what's her stake in this? Angrim didn't strike Cele as an altruist, so bringing greater freedom to the people of Nuvinland probably wasn't her motivation. More likely it was because Jorund was a Jarl, or had been. He'd be one again if his plan succeeded, and Angrim was ambitious.

"Come along, Lady Celia. We need to hurry," Angrim said impatiently. "The *soven* I gave your guards won't last forever."

"*Soven?*"

"It makes them sleep. Now hurry."

Cele's steps slowed as she thought of going back down into the tunnels. Her hands grew clammy and her stomach tightened painfully. Would Harve still be down there? "Maybe we should take weapons," she suggested.

"That won't be necessary," Angrim snapped. "Come along!"

Cele stopped altogether when she got to the closet where her cloak hung. Dahleven would hate her for this. She wouldn't blame him. She knew what betrayal felt like.

Is Neven really as black as Jorund painted him? But the Outcast Jarl was the only one offering her any hope of returning home. Neven certainly hadn't, and Father Wirmund had as much as said there wasn't one. It could be months, or even years, before she had a chance to talk to the Tewakwe, and there was no guarantee *they* could help her either. Jorund did, and his dedication to his people was admirable. She had to go.

She thought of Dahleven again. She respected the way he looked out for his men and for her, even when he didn't trust her. He'd listened to what she had to say even when they'd been arguing. And when they hadn't been arguing...Cele pushed the seductive memory of Dahleven's strong arms and gentle lips away. She didn't want to feel the way her body softened at the thought of melting into his embrace. How she hungered to welcome him inside.

No. I can't stay. I can't be his wife and I won't be his mistress. People are trying to kill me. There's no future here.

She thought of how they'd argued that afternoon. She couldn't leave it that way. Couldn't go without a word.

"I need some paper. And a pen."

"Why?"

"I need to leave a note. So Dah—so Thora won't worry."

"We have no time for this. Lord Jorund is waiting."

"Look, if this works, I'll never see him, or anyone here, ever again. I have to say goodbye. And I want to thank them, too. A lot of people have been very kind to me." It was true, she realized, even as she said it. Almost everyone had been kind to her. Sevond treated her like a daughter, Fender's teasing flattered without threatening, and Ragni made her laugh. Thora behaved like a doting aunt. Gudrun's warning had been kindly meant, and her gratitude for Ari's life had been genuine. Even Neven had treated her like a princess—when he wasn't accusing her of murder.

Angrim gave her an exasperated look, then sighed as though she realized that it would take less time to agree than to argue. "Oh, very well. I'll be right back."

A few minutes later, she returned bearing a thick sheet of paper and something resembling a pencil. Celia thought for a moment then wrote:

Dahleven,

Please forgive me for leaving without saying good-bye. I have come to care for—

Cele stopped. She cared for him more than she wanted to admit. Leaving him was going to tear an aching hole in her heart. It didn't matter that they hadn't made love. But it didn't seem right to say it now, to write it in a letter that might be read by anyone.

I have come to care for so many here, but I've found a way home and must go. Thank you for—

She couldn't thank him for the kisses that made her blood race, for the caresses that set her afire, for the respect in his eyes when he looked at her.

—for your many kindnesses, especially the pizza.
Take care of Sevond for me, and keep an eye on Ari.
Celia

Cele folded the paper and left it tented on the table, then stood and swung her cloak over her shoulders. "Okay, I'm ready." She had to take this chance. It might not work, but if she didn't try, she'd never forgive herself. "Let's go."

In the hall, the two guards sat slumped against the wall. Cele knelt and pressed her fingers against the vein in Bergren's neck. It was very slow. "Are you sure they're all right?"

"They'll be fine," Angrim answered, still inside the room. Then she emerged and ushered Cele down the hall.

Dahleven jerked awake at the sound of violent pounding, his hand instinctively reaching for his sword.

"My lord!" an urgent male voice called.

Nude, sword in hand, Dahleven yanked open his door. One of his guards stood there, fist raised to pound again. "Report."

The man who'd summoned him so peremptorily from sleep hesitated an instant, fear flashing across his features, before he answered. "Lady Celia is missing, my lord. Her guards were dosed with *soven*. The next duty of guards discovered them near death in the hall."

"Who did it?"

"They weren't coherent, my lord. They kept saying Lady Angrim—"

"Angrim!" Dahleven turned back into his rooms and began donning his clothes. "How long? When did she dose them?"

"Thora says she left Lady Celia some four candle-marks ago, at the last change of duty."

What could have happened to Celia in that time? Dahleven's gut tightened, remembering what she'd suffered before. Celia's words echoed in his ears. She truly hadn't been any safer in Quartzholm than she might have been on the trail.

"Roust the Trackers from their beds," Dahleven barked. "Raise the Warden of the Guard. Tell him to establish double watches." He would find Celia, but he wouldn't let the search distract him from Quartzholm's defense.

"Go." Dahleven pulled a shirt over his head, donned and belted a leather jerkin. "Tell the Trackers to assemble at the base of the west wing ladder."

Cele followed Angrim through the cold tunnels. The little blonde insisted on holding her hand, and Cele wondered which of them her clasp was meant to comfort.

They seemed to walk for hours, with Angrim pausing only long enough to refill the lantern with oil from jars they found along the way. Cele's feet ached; she wore only the thin slippers that matched her dress. It had been late when they'd started this trek, and it was even later now. Had Dahleven discovered she was missing yet? Had her note made any difference to him? Doubt and worry sapped her energy. Cele licked dry lips and tugged free of the other woman's hand. "Angrim, stop."

The hem of Angrim's cloak swirled outward as she turned around, sweeping the ground. Cele thought again, as she had when Angrim first donned it at the base of the ladder, that the cloak looked like Jorund's. The gold brooch, with its distinctive red stone glowing like an ember in the dim light of the lantern, was the same.

"How much farther do we have to go? It's got to be nearly dawn by now."

"We can't stop yet, Lady Celia. We're almost there."

Angrim didn't wait for Cele to agree, she just turned and went on. Apparently, she didn't feel the need to hold Cele's hand any longer. The previously shallow young woman was all business now.

Cele had to follow or be left alone to Find her way in

the dark. She shivered as the memory of the last time she'd had to do that loomed like an ominous shadow. At least moving kept her feet from freezing. She hurried to catch up.

The cold stone floor slanted downward and sometimes they descended deep, gently sloping steps. The smooth walls changed as they continued. At first they had been the same pink of the walls of Quartzholm, then they became gray, with striations of darker rock. Now, as they descended still further, the walls sparkled with crystalline inclusions.

When she first saw the tiny sliver of light ahead, Cele thought her tired eyes were playing tricks on her, but it remained constant as they drew closer. Angrim confirmed her hope that it signaled the end of their journey. "There!" She pointed and hurried her steps. "We're here at last!" They rounded a corner and slipped under a curtain into a room filled with light. Angrim killed her lantern.

Jorund came forward, smiling, with arms spread wide. He wore a glove on one hand now, and Cele wondered if his disfigurement had progressed. "Ah, Ladies," he said in a voice that was sexier than the best FM deejay, though now it didn't seem as compelling as it had before.

Cele shivered uncomfortably as a stinging sensation rippled outward from the amulet tied to her leg. *He's using Persuasion on me? I thought he'd lost his Talent.*

"Come, rest and eat. You're safe at last." Jorund put an arm around each of them, guiding them toward the table with a light touch.

Cele sank gratefully into a soft comfortable chair. Angrim lingered for a moment, standing close to Jorund, yearning toward him as he ordered a meal for them. Jorund casually slid his hand up her arm, bending close as she sat in the chair he held for her. A connection sizzled between them, and Cele suddenly knew they were lovers, long comfortable with one another.

Dahleven ran a hand back through his loose hair. He hadn't had a chance to braid it, and he doubted he would for some time. The Warden of the Guard stood rigid, as unhappy with the news he brought as Dahleven was to hear it. The Trackers had found no trace of Celia. It was the same story as the last time she'd been taken. She'd descended the ladder from the bathing room and then had vanished, as far as their Talents could determine. Whoever had taken her must have used an unsanctioned amulet to conceal their trail, just as they had the first time. The Warden had search teams out scouring the tunnels in all directions from that point, but he had little hope they'd find anything. The smooth, Talent-shaped tunnels revealed no tracks.

"My lord?" Thora spoke from the doorway.

Dahleven looked up. "Yes?"

"I would speak to you." She glanced at the Warden. "Alone."

"And I would speak with *you*, also. In a moment." He needed to know how many unsanctioned amulets existed, who had them, and where they were now.

"This cannot wait, my lord." Thora spoke firmly.

"What then?" Dahleven turned, tapping a finger restlessly on his sword hilt.

"I found this on the hearth in Lady Celia's room." Thora handed him a scrap of paper, the edge burned, a single word upon it: *Dahleven*—

Gods! Dahleven's heart skipped a beat. She'd tried to tell him something, perhaps where she was going, and now her words were ash. Someone had burned her let-

ter—a letter she'd had time to write. She'd gone willingly. But whomever she'd gone with had betrayed her by
burning her words to him.

"The danger is greater than you understand, my
lord." Thora's words drew him out of his dark thoughts.

Dahleven looked at Thora more closely. "Speak."

Thora looked pointedly at the Warden of the Guard.

Dahleven sighed. He could command her, and she
would obey. But his instincts were telling him to humor
her. He knew from long experience that Thora didn't
overreact or behave hysterically. "Very well. Warden,
leave us. But don't go too far."

When they were alone, he raised eyebrows at Thora.
"Well?"

"I believe Lady Celia was taken to Find the Hidden
Talents."

Despite everything, Dahleven barked a startled
laugh. Then he sobered. It would be funny, if Celia
weren't missing. The Great Talents had been hidden for
nearly two hundred years. Generations of young Finders
had tested themselves against Fanlon. Not one had
Found a whisper of the Talents. Wherever they were
hidden, they were safely beyond reach. "On what do you
base this amazing conclusion?"

"I have a gift for scrying, my lord, and the runes have
shown me fire and ruin. But first, something hidden
must be revealed. It's all tied to Lady Celia and deception."

For an instant, Dahleven was surprised Thora spoke
so easily of her skill with the stones, but she'd already
revealed her forbidden knowledge to Ragni, and she was
no fool. She must realize his brother would share that
information with him and Neven, and that she wasn't
telling him anything he didn't already know. She didn't
seem the least bit ashamed of violating the Traditions of
Baldur's priests.

"I've heard of your unusual *gifts*. But why should I give your reading any more value than you gave Eirik's?"

Thora was urgent, forceful. "Lady Celia is a Finder of the like not seen since Fanlon's day, as I'm sure Lord Fendrikanin has told you. Even if *you* don't believe she can Find the Talents, whoever took her *does*."

Fender had indeed waxed eloquent on Celia's Talent. She'd succeeded at every test. She'd Found Ari, thank Baldur, though she'd never before laid eyes on him. Still, it was ridiculous to think she could Find the Talents.

But she *could* be pressured into trying, and Exhausting herself to death. The thought chilled him.

"It does me no good to know this. We can't find her trail. Could one of your friends with an unsanctioned amulet be concealing her tracks?"

Thora shook her head. "No one I know would have reason to use Lady Celia so. But we can help you find her."

"We?"

Thora hesitated, taking a deep breath. "The Daughters of Freya."

Dahleven snorted in disgust. This shouldn't surprise him after everything else. "You're involved with *them*, too?"

Thora ignored his tone. "There are ways of seeing afar that those who perform *sanctioned* magic have ignored."

A guard rapped, then opened the door. "Father Wirmund, *Overprest* of Baldur," he announced.

Thora's face tensed.

Dahleven turned to the door. *She* ought *to be nervous, considering what she's been up to.*

Like a storm cloud roiling over the mountains, Father Wirmund entered the small room Dahleven was using as his center of command. "Lady Celia is leading you a merry chase, I understand."

Wirmund's implication sent a hot surge of irritation through Dahleven's veins, but he kept his voice and face impassive. "Good morning, Father Wirmund. You're up with the dawn. Will you break fast with me?" Dahleven clenched his teeth and smiled. Fencing with Wirmund was a waste of time, but religion and politics would continue their dance long after Celia was found. It was best to keep Wirmund as an ally.

"I shall," Father Wirmund answered tightly.

"Thora, arrange something for us." Dahleven hesitated an instant, then, despite his doubts, added, "And attend to that other matter, as well."

Thora nodded and left.

Dahleven gestured to a chair, but Father Wirmund ignored it.

"You must find Lady Celia immediately!"

Wirmund's vehemence surprised Dahleven, but he merely lifted a brow. "We are doing all in our power to do so. Why such urgency? I did not think you particularly concerned with the lady's welfare, *Overprest*."

"I'm not!" Wirmund kept his voice low. "She has stolen the Staff of Befaling!"

Dahleven would have laughed if the implication weren't so grave. "That's ridiculous. Your rooms are guarded, and the Staff is warded with ritual magic."

"Nevertheless, the Staff is gone, and your *lady* was near my rooms only yestereve."

"Yes, I know. And she was accompanied by two guards and Lady Angrim. Are they all accomplices?"

"Then what conclusions do *you* draw from Lady Celia's *latest* disappearance?" Father Wirmund asked. "This cannot be coincidence."

"We have hostiles acting within Quartzholm." Dahleven kept his voice from sounding like he was schooling an idiot. "It is they who are most likely responsible for the theft."

Wirmund's jaw worked. "And Lady Celia?"

"Is in danger."

"Are you besotted? She clearly left under her own power! Lady Angrim is hardly able to carry her away. And your own brother stated the woman lied about her ignorance of why she was taken the first time."

Dahleven didn't wonder how Wirmund knew so much about Celia's disappearance. The *Overprest* had his spies, as all powerful men did. "Ragni also said there was no darkness in her."

"She wouldn't seem dark if she believed her actions were just. It's obvious that whoever took her the first time persuaded her to his cause. She's taken the Staff and gone to join him, and has used an unsanctioned amulet to keep her movements secret."

"And how did she, or anyone, take the Staff without being observed?"

"Who knows what Talents her patron has?" Wirmund paced the length of the small room, then stopped in front of Dahleven. "You don't seem to appreciate the danger we're in, my lord. Whoever has the Staff can release the Great Talents. And Lady Celia has given it to him."

The Hidden Talents. Just as Thora said. Gods, what has Celia done? "You have a low opinion of Lady Celia if you believe she'd ally herself with those who tried to rape her. But then, you never have believed her story despite what Ragni said, have you?"

"She believes her story, and so Father Ragnar believes. She is likely deluded, but that makes her no less dangerous. It makes no sense that Freyr would bring one lone unbeliever across the Rainbow Bridge. It's not as if she is a hero and there is some great task to perform." Wirmund grimaced. "But Loki might."

"Loki was stripped of his powers," Dahleven protested. "He won't rise till Ragnarok."

Wirmund shrugged.

Finding the Hidden Talents would be a heroic task. But would Freyr want them found? Enough to bring Celia over the Bright Road?

"Wake up, Lady Celia." Angrim shook Cele's shoulder.

Cele awakened with a start, heart pounding. For a moment she didn't recognize the dimly lit stone room or understand why Angrim was here, rousing her after too little sleep. Then it all came rushing back. Jorund. Home. Her betrayal of Dahleven's trust.

Cele clenched her teeth on the pain that thought caused. *I had to do it.*

She crawled from the thin feather bed and pile of blankets that Jorund had provided in an alcove off the main room. He soon arrived, striding in through the narrow archway.

"I trust you slept well, Lady Celia?" Jorund gave her a half bow and smiled warmly into Cele's eyes.

She hadn't. Her dreams had been troubled by ominous shadows, and she'd awakened once to see Jorund speaking with a dark figure she couldn't make out.

"I've had a small breakfast prepared for you." He glanced at Angrim and back to Cele. "I regret I must urge you to hasten. We must be away ere long." He drew Cele's arm through his and escorted her to the table at the far end of the room. Angrim hooked her hand through his other elbow and he turned to smile briefly at her before returning his regard to Cele. He didn't seem upset that it had been Angrim who'd told him where to find the Staff rather than Cele.

The table was laden with several dishes. Cele stared

at the distinctive black on white Mimbres-like design. The style was typical of certain southwestern tribes in the eleventh through fourteenth centuries. *Is this Tewakwe pottery?*

Appealing aromas made Cele's mouth water, pushing all other thoughts aside. Jorund led her to a chair near the head of the table opposite Angrim's. She was about to sit down when a familiar face caused Cele to draw a sharp breath and tense in alarm.

"What is it, my lady?" Jorund asked.

Cele's arm was pointed like a lance at Harve. "What's he doing here? I thought you said he was one of Neven's men."

"My lady?" Jorund's voice was beautiful, even when shocked.

"He's one of the men who kidnapped me!" She started around the table toward Harve. Cele wasn't sure what she intended to do when she reached him, but she was sure he wouldn't like it.

Jorund put a light restraining hand on her arm and stepped forward. "Is this true?" His outrage reverberated in the stone chamber. "Have you betrayed me to Neven? Did you try to harm this woman?"

Harve's eyes widened and he stepped back, limping. "No, my lord. I would never! I didn't hurt her!"

"How can I believe you when this Lady accuses you to you face?"

"I did just as you said!"

Cele's anger boiled over at his lies. "He tried to rape me! He was going to kill me!"

Jorund turned to Cele. "I deeply regret what happened, Lady Celia. He will be punished."

"But I only did what you told—"

"Silence!" Jorund roared, backhanding Harve into the wall.

Cele jumped at Jorund's sudden violence to the lying

coward, but didn't lament it. She wanted to do the same, and more.

"You." Jorund gestured to two of his guards. "Take him out of my sight and deal with him." They each grabbed an arm and dragged Harve into the tunnel.

Jorund turned to Cele. "Do you wish to witness his punishment?"

Cele's anger urged her to say *yes*, but then she remembered the servant with the missing fingers and something in her quailed. "What are you going to do to him?"

Jorund shrugged. "For betraying me, he deserves death."

As much as Harve deserved it, the summary judgment shocked her out of her fury. "That's...extreme."

"It is the same as his accomplices received."

Cele remembered their bodies lying still on the floor. She hadn't felt a shred of regret for their deaths, and Harve had come after her a second time. It was a miracle she'd escaped him. Who knew how many women he'd attacked in the past, or would in the future? "Do I have any say?"

Jorund inclined his head. "Would you have me show mercy?"

"If he'd attacked *me*, I'd have his balls!" Angrim declared.

The other men had been caught in the act, killed in the heat of battle. There was no doubt in Cele's mind that Harve had meant to murder her after making her suffer. "I don't know."

Jorund's eyes softened. "You have a woman's natural delicacy. Would it be better if I merely make him wish he were dead?" he asked without apparent irony.

Cele grimaced. "No."

Jorund turned to the guard waiting by the tunnel where Harve had disappeared. "Flog him."

What little Cele knew of flogging came from movies. She feared the reality would be even worse, but at least a man wouldn't die by her choice.

"You never answered, my lady. Will you witness his punishment?"

"No, I don't want to watch." It was enough to know Harve would get what he deserved. She didn't want to feel any squeamish, softhearted sympathy for him.

Dahleven followed Thora though a narrow door. She led him down servants' corridors and up winding steps and back down steep staircases to a remote part of the castle. With every step, he felt time slipping away. He wasn't sure he'd ever been in this part of Quartzholm, even when he'd explored the hidden corners as a boy. If not for Ragni's assurance of Thora's loyalty and the fact that she'd cared for him in the nursery, he might almost wonder if she were leading him into trouble.

Of course she's leading me into trouble. And he was going with his eyes wide open. He was going to meet someone who would perform unsanctioned magic for him. He was looking for a witch to help him find a woman who may have had a hand in stealing the Staff of *Befaling*. *If that isn't trouble, I don't know what is.*

How did he get to this point: the heir to Quartzholm, the son of the Kon, sworn to protect his people and uphold the teachings of Baldur, seeking to use forbidden arts?

I must be mad. But it was the only way to find Celia.

Wirmund was right. She was dangerous. If anyone had told him two weeks ago that he'd be conspiring with a Daughter of Freya to flout traditions guarded by the priesthood, he'd have laughed himself sick.

But Celia had changed everything. He'd failed to protect her; he couldn't abandon her while there was a still a chance.

Wirmund had said he had no magic that could help in this situation. He could break the power of the amulet if he had it, but the *Overprest* had no ritual to find the trail that the amulet had concealed. Thora offered him a tool and hope, and Dahleven couldn't refuse it. He might be mad, but his heart compelled him forward, following Thora through obscure passages.

The room he stepped into was sparsely appointed, holding only a table, a few chairs, a few boxes, and a cot. A pretty, dark-haired woman sat at the table. She rose when he entered.

"This is Lady Saeun," Thora said. "She can show you what you need to know."

He didn't recognize her. *She must be the daughter of a minor Lord, here for the Althing.* "Lady Saeun." He nodded his head slightly, showing the minimum of courtesy.

She curtsied deeply, and said, "Thank you for coming, my lord. Please be seated."

Lady Saeun didn't fit his expectations of what a witch should look and act like. Feeling somewhat churlish, Dahleven sat at a plain wooden table in a high-backed chair. He searched Saeun's heart-shaped face. "How can you help find Lady Celia?"

Saeun smiled nervously and glanced at Thora before answering. "I can show you where she will be, my lord...I can try to, I mean."

"How?" Dahleven demanded.

Saeun flinched. Thora put her arm around her and said, "Don't let Lord Dahleven unsettle you, dear heart. You can do this." She looked sharply at him. "Let her do her work, my lord. Ask your questions later."

Saeun brought a large box to the table. From it, she

withdrew a hairbrush bearing strands of Celia's yellow hair, her waist-pack, and the torn, bloodstained robe she'd worn during her first abduction. Dahleven's jaw tightened at the sight of it. Saeun set aside the box and put a shallow obsidian bowl in the midst of these items. Runes decorated the inside lip of the smooth, black vessel. Then she unstopped a glass bottle and poured its contents into the bowl.

Dahleven gaped as a small treasure in quicksilver rippled in the vessel before him. Saeun closed her eyes and lifted her head, stretching her arms out to her sides, palms outward. Then she began to chant in the priests' tongue.

A tingling raced over his skin in time with the rhythm of Saeun's words. Dahleven jerked and almost moved to stop her, a woman, from speaking the words reserved to the priests. Thora caught his eye and he stopped. What had he expected would happen here? Of course Saeun was breaking with tradition—and so was he. He listened and waited as the air grew thick, charged with the magic Saeun called upon.

Saeun turned her palms inward and swept them toward her breast three times, as though gathering something in over the bowl and its liquid treasure. The prickling of Dahleven's flesh pulsed and grew with each sweep of her arms. Then she bent and blew on the surface of the quicksilver. Dahleven felt a rush of cold wind, and the liquid metal smoothed like glass.

Saeun startled him by speaking a word he understood. "Look," she commanded.

Dahleven peered at the surface of the silvery liquid. It no longer reflected a distorted image of the room in which he sat. Instead, he saw a long, narrow cavern, unshaped by human hands or Talents.

Dahleven almost looked away. Danger lurked in such places; they were the province of the Dark Elves, and who was to say they couldn't somehow reach across this scrying? But his need was too great. He peered into the bowl.

The vision opened onto a larger space where the floor was smoothed by Talent, but the walls and ceiling had been left unchanged. No single point of light illuminated the space, yet he could see the rough walls glittering with crystals. Round and oblong orbs of rough stone protruded from the walls or lay on the floor. There were hundreds of them, of various sizes. A few of them were broken, their crystals dark. *Is this where the Great Talents are Hidden?* To one side of the image, Fender slumped against a wall, blood slicking the side of his face.

Dahleven grimaced. Was this the place as it would be, or might be? He'd already lost several good men. He knew he would lose more; it was inevitable—such was the nature of battle. But he didn't want the surety of it.

In the background, shadowed figures wavered indistinctly in a way that made his skin crawl, but closer stood a man with his back toward Dahleven, and with him was Celia, her face contorted with pain.

"No!" Dahleven hardly knew he spoke aloud.

The image flickered. He memorized the room, taking note of details. A moment later the image grew dark and the natural reflective surface of the quicksilver returned.

Dahleven blinked and looked up at Saeun. Her face was sweaty and gray. Thora helped her to sit, then poured her a cup of red wine and held it to her lips, wisely not trusting the young woman's shaky hands to hold it steady.

In a moment, Saeun pushed the cup away and looked shyly at him. "I hope you saw something helpful, my lord."

"You don't know what the magic revealed?"

"No. The image was for you alone." Her voice was

breathy and weak.

"You said this is where Lady Celia *will* be? Why not where she is now?"

"Lady Celia is some hours ahead of you, is she not? By the time you Pathfind your way there she will be gone again, where no Tracker may know. With this knowledge, you may find her, perhaps even get ahead, if your Talent shows you a shorter way than she travels."

"How long do I have? How far ahead did this vision look?"

Saeun's eyes fluttered and she slumped sideways. Thora kept her from falling to the floor until Dahleven came around the table and lifted the young woman in his arms.

"The visions seldom see more than a day ahead," Thora said.

Less than a day, then. Not much time. Dahleven laid Saeun on the cot and looked at Thora. "Does she need a Healer? I can summon Ghav. By my order, he'll not reveal her."

He saw approval in Thora's eyes and felt perversely pleased by it.

"No, my lord. She knows her limits; she's only tired. But ritual magic is not undertaken lightly."

Dahleven nodded. Reflexively, he said, "Perhaps that's why it's reserved for the priests."

Thora's lips tightened. "If we'd left you to Father Wirmund's offices, you'd be no wiser. The priests know many things, my lord, but they cling to *Tradition* like some women cling to husbands who beat and bloody them, afraid to free themselves. The priests are afraid to choose their own way, so they let Tradition do it for them. It keeps them ignorant and they call it virtue, and they try to keep others ignorant as well. It's time to move forward." Thora laid her hand on Dahleven's arm. "With the Kon's approval, and the sanction of the priesthood, we could do so more safely."

Wirmund's approval of this kind of magic was as likely as an open pass at mid-winter, and Neven's support could never be open and unreserved, not and remain Kon. He apparently knew of and tolerated Thora's covert use of the runestones, but he couldn't afford to support unsanctioned magic.

Dahleven remembered the fear on the face of the woman Ozur had banished for six months. Neven needed to remain Kon if he was to bring about the kind of changes necessary to protect woman like her. He had to maintain respect and goodwill among the Lords, Jarls, and priests to do that, even if doing so meant making compromises that left a vile taste in his mouth.

"Tradition isn't imposed only by the priests," Dahleven said. "It binds us all. Beliefs can't be changed so easily." He held up a hand to forestall Thora's angry retort. "But your assistance today will no doubt help. Have patience. And hope that what Lady Saeun revealed to me makes a difference."

chapter twenty-four

A MAN BROUGHT TRAYS of fruit and cheese and
bread to the table. Cele wondered if she was supposed to
serve Jorund, but Angrim was sitting to his right and
did that task with an air that it was her right to do so.
The food smelled delicious, but Cele no longer had an
appetite. *What did Harve mean, "I did as you said?"*

He was just trying to save his skin, she answered herself.

The sudden crack of the whip against flesh and
Harve's muffled cries echoed back into the chamber.
Cele flinched but refused to feel pity for him, using the
memory of his grasping hands ripping her robe to block
out his screams. She chewed a bite of the bread that had
smelled so wonderful just a moment before. It tasted
like dust now, settling in her stomach like a stone.

Eirik bustled in. Cele stared. *He's part of this, too?*
The tall, slender skald strode into the room, bowing
deeply to Jorund and again to the two women, setting

the beads in his long, thin braids to clacking. "Well met, my lord! And well timed." He looked pointedly at the trays of food until Jorund gestured for him to take a seat. An empty place waited for him at the table; obviously he'd been expected.

Cele remembered Eirik's Talent for Persuasion and Thora's doubts about his reading of the runestones. She tried to keep her face neutral, though she was wary.

Eirik poured himself a cup of pale wine and smiled at Cele across the table, apparently unconcerned by the sounds of Harve's punishment. "I see you recognized your opportunity when it came, Lady Celia. Lord Jorund will be a good friend to you."

Cele's skin tingled with a sensation similar to circulation returning to a limb that been asleep. She nodded slowly, distracted by the feeling. "He's offered to help me get home."

"And so he will," Eirik said. "Lord Jorund is a man of honor."

Again Cele's skin tingled. Was that the effect of the amulet Thora had given her? Was Eirik trying to use his Persuasion on her? *How much is his endorsement worth, if Thora's right about him lying*? Cele tried to ignore the thought. Jorund's offer of help had nothing to do with Eirik's truthfulness.

The cutting crack of the whip ceased. Harve moaned and wept.

"Hasten your meal, Eirik," Jorund said. "We must be away soon."

"Why such haste, my lord?" Eirik protested. "The search for Lady Celia is frustrated. The Trackers have found no trace of her. Lord Dahleven—"

"Lord Dahleven is a clever man, and will do all in his power to pursue his father's will. And Neven will not be pleased to lose his grasp on Lady Celia." Jorund rose. "Come, we're going."

Dahleven and his eight men moved briskly and quietly, their leather byrnies creaking softly. Moccasins, worn in place of their usual boots, muffled their footfalls. They'd been on the march for eight hours or more, with only two short breaks. Dahleven carried a lantern turned low to conserve oil and minimize the risk of discovery by those they sought.

He'd left Quartzholm in able hands. Gudrun commanded everyone's respect and loyalty, and the Warden of the Guard would do her will without question. Even Gris and Father Wirmund would obey her, if reluctantly. He regretted the need to abandon his charge, but his choice had been clear: the potential threat of the Hidden Talents being Found was more serious than whatever Quartzholm might face.

When had he begun to take Thora's scrying seriously? When he'd seen the vision Saeun showed him? Or was it earlier than that? Ragni would be amused to learn it was unsanctioned magic that had finally convinced him of scrying's usefulness. Or did he believe because it allowed him to do what he wanted: to go after Celia?

Was there really any danger to Quartzholm? Celia couldn't possibly do what generations of Finders had failed at. Even if she did succeed, her abductor would still need a priest to release the Talents.

Or would he? It had just been made very clear to him that the skill and knowledge of ritual magic was not restricted to priests.

Dahleven's jaw tightened as he remembered the bruises on Celia's breast. Whether she found the Talents or not, the danger to her was very real.

His men moved in near silence behind him. He hadn't explained where he was leading them, but they followed him nevertheless. Like him, they were glad to be taking action at last.

Jorund pulled Cele's hand through the crook of his arm and Angrim frowned, apparently unhappy about being escorted by the skald rather than her lover. Cele pulled away, not wanting to be a source of trouble between the couple.

Jorund turned to Angrim and lifted her chin with one well-manicured finger. "Lady Celia is our guest and is helping us. There's no need to pout, my dove." His rich, caressing voice drew a smile and a blush from Angrim. Jorund let his hand trail down her shoulder to her elbow. Then he signaled the group forward. "Proceed." He drew Cele's hand through his arm again, and after a nod from Angrim, this time Cele didn't resist.

Two warriors carrying lanterns went first, then Jorund and Cele. Eirik and Angrim followed, and the other eight men brought up the rear, packing the blankets and food. All carried swords, and none of the men looked very appealing; they reminded Cele too much of Harve. Fortunately, he wasn't coming along, and she didn't have to interact with the others. Jorund kept her close by his side, following the first two men. He wore his own cloak now, and Angrim wore a shorter garment that didn't threaten to trip her.

Jorund turned the force of his attention to Cele. "I haven't thanked you yet, for agreeing to help me." His deep voice rumbled softly. "The people of Nuvinland will owe you a great debt for the return of their Talents, and their freedom."

Cele squirmed inwardly, uncomfortable with her part in this. Returning the Talents to the people seemed like a good thing. So why did she feel so uneasy? "I didn't do that much," she murmured.

"You underestimate your gifts, my lady." Jorund smiled down at her. "And you have other contributions to make."

Her skin tingled as it had when Eirik spoke, only this time with an edge of pain. Cele's unease grew. "What do you expect me to do?"

"Nothing as yet, my lady. Merely allow me to enjoy your company while we go to where the Talents are hidden." Jorund put his ungloved hand on hers, where it rested on his arm. "Then, I hope, you will Find the ones I need."

Cele shivered. *He's trying too hard.* But Jorund's hand felt warm on her own and he sounded so sincere. She wondered what his Talent was. Presence? Persuasion? But Thora had said her amulet would protect her from those Talents. And hadn't he said his Talent had been taken when he was Outcast?

"And then what?" Cele asked.

"We'll return the Talents to our people."

"Will you get your Talent back?" Cele hoped it wasn't rude to ask.

Jorund smiled unctuously. "So I hope."

"How will you get me get home?"

"It's quite complex, my lady. You needn't concern yourself with the details."

Cele stiffened at his, *Don't worry your pretty little head,* answer. "I'd like to know."

Jorund shrugged. "A nimbus of power will be freed when the Talents are released. I'll use the Staff to focus it, say the words I spent years searching for, and invoke the magic hidden by the priests. Then the Bright Road between the Nine Worlds will open, sending you home."

Cele grimaced. It sounded like mumbo-jumbo, but how would she know? She'd never even heard of Talents two weeks ago, let alone magic that worked.

Jorund looked faintly amused. "As I said, complicated."

They walked for a long time. On their occasional rest breaks, Eirik entertained them with stories and songs, creating a surreal, picnic atmosphere, but Jorund never allowed them to pause for long. They stopped when they reached the end of the tunnel. It was a dead end, except for the natural fissure in the face of the far wall. Rubble scattered at the base of the walls made it apparent that until recently, the fissure had been blocked, walled off. A single man stood guard there.

"Knut!" Cele rocked back on her heels.

Knut flicked a nervous glance at Jorund. "Yes, my lady. I am glad to find you well."

Cele stepped forward. The two guards ahead of her and Jorund moved aside. "You killed Lindy!"

Knut took a step back, bumping into the rough wall. "I defended myself!"

"You—"

"He brought me word of your arrival, my dear," Jorund interrupted, taking her arm again and patting her hand. "I cannot hope to prevail over Neven's corruption without the help of good men like Knut. He understood immediately how important you are."

"But he cut Lindy's throat!"

"Sadly, such acts are sometimes necessary to achieve the greater good. Let it go now." Jorund patted her hand then turned to the others. "We'll stop here for the night. Tomorrow we'll finish the last leg of our quest."

Cele glared at Knut but remained silent. She supposed freedom fighters did a lot of things she wouldn't like if she saw them up close. *That's what Jorund's men are, aren't they? Freedom fighters?* But she remembered how Dahleven had grieved over Lindy.

Angrim eyed the dark gaping fissure nervously.

"Here, Jorund? Couldn't we go back a bit? Further from...that?" She gestured tentatively toward the end of the tunnel, not looking directly at the natural opening.

Jorund chuckled. "I'm here, and Eirik, and these other strong men. Do you think a few hundred yards can protect you better than we can?"

Angrim looked at the ground and shook her head.

"Are we going in there tomorrow?" Cele asked. Dahleven's warnings about creatures in the dark natural caverns made her shiver.

"You aren't fearful as well, Lady Celia? Not the woman who so bravely fought her attackers?" Eirik teased.

Cele's skin tingled, and she remembered something else Dahleven said. "Fear is a normal response to danger. That doesn't mean I'm going to let it stop me from doing what I have to. Nor am I going to let it goad me into taking foolish chances." She turned back to Jorund. "Do we have to go into the caverns?"

Jorund's eyes narrowed as he frowned at Eirik. "Yes, my lady, it's the only path to where we must go. Don't give too much credence to the old tales of the Dark Ones. The worst we're likely to encounter are a few blind spiders. You can be assured that I, and my men, will keep you safe."

Dahleven paused before a rough, narrow opening in the side of the tunnel and concentrated on his need for the quickest way to the crystal room of his vision. The pull of his Talent remained constant, urging him into the natural fissure.

Seven of the eight men with him shifted uneasily or stood cautious and stiff; Fender lounged against the wall assuming an air of nonchalance. Two of the other men, seeing him, relaxed and drank from their waterskins. After his vision, Dahleven had been reluctant to include Fendrikanin, but excluding him would have given insult. The younger man had the right to seek glory and honor in battle, after all, and Dahleven refused to believe the future was fixed. The Norns might set the warp of a man's fate, but it was up to each man to weave the design. He was glad to have Fender along to steady the others.

They were all good men, and they'd followed him without question and with little rest, confident that his Talent led them true. Now they waited for Dahleven to confirm what they must suspect: that their path led into the natural passageways they'd been warned away from since childhood. The warnings were more than tales told to frighten children into obedience. Every generation a maid or a child disappeared, and even strong men had been lost without a trace after venturing into the Darkling passageways. The Dark Elves stayed away from the places of men, but they didn't suffer trespassers cheerfully. A man might return whole of body but wander endlessly in his mind, if he were caught by Elven magic.

It didn't matter. If Celia truly was being pressured or deceived into Finding the Hidden Talents, any risk was worth taking. The already contentious Jarls would erupt into open warfare with the power of the Great Talents suddenly at their command. The destruction that Fanlon had sacrificed so much to prevent would come at last—*if* Celia Found the Talents. If she failed, Dahleven wouldn't bet on the length of her life.

It was that risk that drove him on.

Dahleven gestured into the fissure and spoke more confidently than he felt. "This is our path." He settled his plain metal helm firmly on his head, then stepped into the rough opening.

The uneven ground was strewn with tumbled and

fallen rocks. It narrowed to cracks where the walls came together sharply, then suddenly opened deep pits beneath their feet. Some they could jump, others they had to belay across. Dahleven forced himself to ignore the sensation of being watched; he needed all his wits to navigate the cavern safely. To free his hands, Dahleven hooked the lantern to his belt; a thick leather guard shielded his leg from its heat. At times he bent nearly double to avoid a suddenly low ceiling, and he was glad more than once for his helm. The going was slow, but he trusted his Talent; this was the quickest, most direct way to the crystal room.

After a candlemark or more of scrabbling forward, the floor grew smoother—just before a blind end. Dahleven stared, disbelieving. He held the lantern high.

A pile of tumbled rock and rubble barred their way, yet his Talent still pulled him forward.

Fender stood beside him and stared at the wall of boulders, hands on hips. "It will take an army of miners to move this, my lord, or a Stoneshaper Talent. Do we go back?"

Dahleven ignored the men muttering and bunching together behind him. There was no path here, yet the pull of his Talent was strong. He closed his eyes and concentrated. The Crystal Hall was close. "No. The Path is here, Fender. We must go forward." He reached out to lay a palm on the barrier.

"My lord!"

Dahleven opened his eyes and turned at Fender's exclamation, reaching for the hilt of his sword. Fear widened the younger man's eyes.

"Your hand," Fender whispered, "went through the stone."

Dahleven gazed at his hand, turning it over and back again, flexing his fingers. He took off his glove. His flesh looked as it should. Then he reached out again. The rock felt solid. He looked back at Fender. The low brow and nosepiece of his helmet didn't do much to conceal Fender's distress. Dahleven turned to examine the surrounding boulders more carefully. They were all hard and immovable, yet their texture seemed indistinct. He closed his eyes again and stretched out his arm cautiously, concentrating on the pull of his Talent so he wouldn't think about jamming his fingers on the stones. He encountered nothing but a cool mist and he stepped forward into it.

Suddenly he was jerked backward.

Fender's grasp on his wrist was rigid. White showed around his eyes. "You were in the wall almost entirely. The light from the lantern was fading."

"Darkling magic," one of the men muttered.

"Elven witchery," another grumbled.

Dahleven turned to his men and Fender loosed his hold. Some still gaped in horror, a couple looked sick. "This is my path. The barrier is naught but illusion and cannot harm us. Nevertheless, I will not order you into it. I must go forward. If you will come with me, hold on to the warrior in front of you and close your eyes. I will lead you through."

Their faces grim, to a man they linked, fingers tucked in the belt of the man before, leaving their sword hands free. Dahleven nodded. "Your courage brings you honor." Then he chose a brace of men. "Torvald, Seig, I must ask you to remain behind. I am sorry to deny you this chance at glory, but I would have you bear word back to Quartzholm, should the rest of us dine tonight in Valhalla."

The two men nodded, and Dahleven took Fender's wrist, hooding the lantern before stepping forward. He didn't want the lantern to draw attention as they emerged. Nor did he want to imagine what might happen if one of them saw himself inside the illusory wall.

Could one be entombed in the false stone? Better to avoid that ill chance by moving in the dark, even though that held its own risks. "Stay together," he told his men, just before the mist enveloped him.

The floor of the fissure dropped down, and Jorund held Cele's arm to steady her descent. Four of the men carried lanterns to light their way, but the hair on the back of Cele's neck prickled as she stepped into the raw passageway. A vague feeling of being watched had plagued her all night, or what she thought of as night—it was impossible to tell underground. Now the sensation grew stronger. So did an awareness that she wasn't welcome.

"Watch your head," Jorund warned.

Cele ducked, feeling the uneven rock ceiling graze her hair. *I wish I had a hard hat.* She stubbed her foot and lurched forward. Jorund steadied her. Somehow it didn't seem as reassuring as when Dahleven had done the same. *Correction: I wish I were somewhere else.*

"This section is the worst, Lady Celia. A little farther on, the way becomes easier," Jorund promised.

Cele held on to that encouraging thought while she scrambled and climbed between the rough rocks. She clung to it when she leapt across a crevasse in the floor that breathed a warm draft of air up from its depths. It kept her moving forward when she had to crawl awkwardly up a sloping chimney on hands and knees, trying not to trip on her cloak and skirts.

As she climbed out of the confined passage, Jorund lifted her to her feet. He'd kept his promise. She wouldn't be bumping her head on the ceiling here; the rough, natural walls soared to a dim crack over forty feet above, twice the width of the chamber, the length of which twisted out of sight. The floor was as smooth as the halls of Quartzholm.

"We're here, Lady Celia." Jorund drew her away from the chimney's opening with an arm around her shoulders. "Safe and whole. We were given safe passage, just as I said."

"Given by whom?"

Jorund ignored the question and bent close, sweeping his other arm out to encompass the long cavernous tunnel. "Have you ever seen such wealth in one place?"

Hundreds of geodes ranging in size from six inches to over four feet in diameter protruded from the walls or lay scattered on the floor like fossilized eggs. Sparkling inclusions glittered in the lantern light, making the cavern look like the treasure room of a fairy castle. "It's beautiful," Cele breathed.

"This room is a mile long and branches twice," Jorund said, drawing Cele along with him. "It took two years for me to find it, even with the help of my friends. I feared it might take another two years of trial and error to find the Talents I need, until you came along. And thanks to you, I can now open their hiding places safely."

"What do you mean?"

"You Found the Staff. It was the missing piece. Without it, releasing a Great Talent is...dangerous." He lifted his gloved hand.

Cele looked at Jorund's mask, remembered the sagging flesh it concealed. *Is that what really happened to his face?* "How did you get it out of Wirmund's rooms? It was well guarded. I couldn't get any closer than the floor below."

Jorund smiled with half his face. "The Darkling Lords have servants with many skills."

Darkling Lords?

"And I am grateful for you, as well. You're a gift from

the gods, Celia. A Finder of great Talent, and beautiful as well. We shall do well together," he murmured softly, bending close.

Cele's skin stung as if he were lashing her with nettles. The assumption in Jorund's words disturbed her.

"Until you send her home," Angrim said, frowning.

Jorund inclined his head toward Cele. "Of course. Until I send you home."

Cele shivered as Jorund's warm breath caressed her ear. Again, she wondered why he was trying so hard. Why did he feel he had to use Persuasion on her?

Jorund straightened. "Your presence has allowed me to push my plans forward more quickly. Very shortly now, the parley will come under attack, and Neven's power will be broken."

The news hit her like a cold rinse after a warm bath. "But Ragni's there!" Cele blurted.

Jorund looked surprised. "What did you expect, my lady? I've made it no secret that I hope to destroy the Kon's tyranny. Did you think his sons would be untouched by that?"

She hadn't thought about it at all, not really. A chill realization stole her breath. *He's going to kill Dahleven, too.*

Jorund's voice took on a soft, soothing tone. "If they see reason, I'll spare Neven's family. They're not to blame for his excesses, after all."

His voice was as rich as honey, but no longer convincing. *Dahleven will never surrender.* Cele's heart pounded as Jorund's intention became clear to her. *Jorund planned to kill him all along. And what will he do to Kaidlin and Aenid and Ingirid? Give them to men like Harve?*

Cele felt sick. *How could I not have seen this?*

Various things had nagged at her. Things she'd avoided looking at too closely so she could focus on her one goal: going home. Jorund had dangled that carrot in front of her with great skill, distracting her from everything else. Each taken alone could be explained away, but together they were too much to ignore. Eirik's lies. The poison meant for Neven. Knut. Harve's protest that he'd followed orders. *Did Jorund really save me*? Or was it all a set-up? His explanation had shifted the blame smoothly onto Neven, and she'd believed him. She hadn't had the amulet to protect her then. *Was all a lie*?

Jorund took Cele by the shoulders and looked her in the eye. The amulet's warning made her skin burn like biting ants. "Now you must help me again, my lady. As you see, there are thousands of geodes here, but only one holds the Talent that can heal me. As you can see, I have no time to waste. I don't have time to search them all. I need you to Find the correct stone. Then, when I am restored, we shall release the other Talents, and I'll send you home."

Home. Longing flooded Cele's heart. She hungered for all the familiar little things she'd taken for granted. She wanted to watch old movies with Elaine again, eat junk food, and listen to mariachi music. But the cost was too high. Hope shriveled in her breast like a flower in an icy blast. She couldn't cooperate now that she understood the threat to her friends. Not even for a chance to go home.

She made her decision, and prayed it wasn't too late. *Freyr, Baldur, if you exist, please help me. Help Dahleven and Ragni.*

She looked at Jorund's escort of warriors, at Jorund. He would never let her back out now. This first Talent he wanted was for healing. It sounded harmless enough, but once she Found one, he'd know she could Find the others. *Maybe, if I pretend to fail, he'll let me go and move on to plan B.*

Cele returned his eager gaze. "Okay. Let's do this."

Jorund told everyone to be quiet, to let her work. Cele closed her eyes and pretended to concentrate. After several moments, she opened them. "I can't Find it."

Jorund frowned. "Try again. It might have other Talents hidden with it. Fanlon gathered them randomly, and hid them in the dark together."

Hidden in the dark. Cele looked around the cavern. Crystals sparkled in the flickering lamp light, punctuating the black shadows. Shadows that...moved?

She blinked. The shadows were still. *It must be a trick of the light.*

"Try again," Jorund repeated. His words stung, and he didn't quite keep the edge out of his silky voice.

Cele shut her eyes again. Furrowed her brow. Minutes later, she slumped in what she hoped was a convincing manner and declared, "I can't do it."

This time Jorund didn't even try to be smooth. His hand rested on the pommel of his sword and his voice was cold and hard as ice. "You're not having second thoughts, are you, my lady? I know the extent of your gift. You did what no one else could do. You Found the Staff despite the layers of powerful magic concealing it. This should be quite simple by comparison."

A chill zigged down her spine as he tapped his fingers on his blade's hilt. The threat was clear. If she didn't Find the Talent, he'd kill her. No one would ever know what happened to her. She'd just disappear. Dahleven would believe she'd returned to Midgard, as she'd written in her note.

She glanced at Jorund's escort. Most of them looked bored. Maybe she could Find the Healing Talent, and while Jorund was distracted with it, she could get away before he made her Find all the others. It was a long shot, but it was something.

Cele closed her eyes again. Her awareness of Jorund

and the others faded as she imagined a Healing Talent reaching out to ease pain and harm. A dozen barbed hooks pierced her, shredding her flesh in every direction, ripping her apart. One Talent healed catastrophic burns, another restored sight, one regenerated lost limbs, another cured disease. All powerful. All tearing at her. Cele screamed, dropped the image like she'd held a hot pan and doubled over, gasping for breath as the agony slowly receded. *"Quite simple." Right.*

Jorund was talking. "Lady Celia? Where is it? Where is the Talent?"

She didn't have to fake the strain in her voice. "I don't know! The pain—"

Jorund grabbed her shoulders and pulled her upright, his fingers bruising her flesh. His sharp gaze bored into her. "Find it! It's here somewhere. You've Found other things you've never seen. Try again!" He gave her a shake.

Cele trembled with lingering pain and fear. She couldn't face that agony again. Her breath came in short gasps as she stared back into eyes as frigid as the Arctic sea. She looked away. "I can't!"

A sharp slap rocked her head to the side. Her eyes flew wide, and Jorund grasped her chin tightly, forcing her head up. "You can, and you will." He spat the words into her face. She was barely able to nod. He released her. What could she do? He wouldn't accept failure, real or pretended.

"Don't try to deceive me again!"

She tried to shift the image of her search, as she had for Ari. She focused on nothing in particular, not sure what she should be thinking of, looking for, needing. Fear squeezed her stomach painfully.

Cele took several deep breaths to steady herself, then opened her mind. The tortuous ripping began again as she sifted through the many Healing Talents threatening to shred her in a thousand pieces. It felt like her flesh was being torn from her bones. Her Talent drew her in one direction, then shifted again. She started to pick one, then another clawed for her attention. She was barely aware of her hands clenching till her nails pierced her palms, or her guttural screams.

She doubled over, hands on knees, trying to breathe. Black spots danced in her vision, her ears buzzed. Cele gasped shallowly, hungry for air. She knew what a dying animal felt, attacked by vultures overeager for their meal.

A shout and the sharp clang of metal on metal startled her. Cele's eyes flew wide, and someone jerked her roughly aside. They were under attack.

Jorund's attention was riveted on the men charging his position. *He's distracted. I could take him out.* She tried to lift her arm, but echoes of pain made her muscles twitch uselessly. Cele sagged to her knees, unable to move.

chapter twenty-five

DAHLEVEN CHARGED OUT OF the shadows, shouting as the chaos of conflict erupted around him. With one double-handed blow, his sword swept a man's head from his shoulders with a crunch of bone and a spray of blood, letting his momentum carry him past. Across the chamber, Celia screamed as if tortured in Fenris's jaws, and fear for her froze his blood. Jorund Firestarter jerked her back before drawing his own sword.

Dahleven's anger sharpened like lethal ice and he altered his course for Jorund, slipping between men battling for their lives. He wasn't surprised Jorund was behind this. The conniving bastard was just the sort to use sneaking raids and the threat of war to get what he wanted.

Another adversary interposed himself, his blade slanting for Dahleven's shoulder. *Knut!* He should have expected him to be allied with the likes of Jorund. Dispatching him would be a pleasure. Dahleven blocked Knut's sword with his own, then swept his blade down and around at Knut's arm. "You are Outcast, Loki-spawn," he shouted as Knut parried and retreated a step. "Your life is forfeit." Dahleven stepped in, closing the gap and thrusting upward. Knut deflected his blow, their blades clanging. Instead of piercing his chest, Dahleven's sword sliced deep into Knut's thigh. Knut wavered, then brought up his sword again, but too late. Dahleven's steel took him in the throat.

Dahleven had no time to enjoy dispensing justice to Lindy's killer. Another man attacked and Dahleven parried just in time. Their swords met with a joint-jarring screech of metal.

He managed to turn his opponent's blade aside, but the man countered, renewing his attack. He was good, very good, and Dahleven had to retreat a step, then a second, and a third, to keep his skin whole. Around him, the clangor of battle raged. He was only dimly aware that several of his men were down—his focus was his immediate survival. His first adversary had fallen easily, but Knut had tired him, and this man pressed him hard, putting him on the defensive.

Dahleven met a powerful overhand attack with a sharp ringing of their blades. The stroke sent a numbing shock through his hands and wrists. Metal sang against metal as they disengaged. The man grinned, lips pulled back from huge yellow teeth, as Dahleven retreated yet another step.

Yellowteeth's skill no more than equaled his own, but the bastard's strength was overwhelming. He moved too quickly for such power, attacking with the speed and ferocity of a wasp with a sledgehammer. Dahleven had practiced a few times against an opponent with a Talent for Strength; he'd never bested him. But this was no practice match, and Yellowteeth would do more than sting him.

Dahleven thrust under the other man's guard, slicing the inside of his thigh, and ducked a returning swing that would have taken Dahleven's head if he'd been slower. He took another step back and came up hard against the wall. His opponent thrust and Dahleven dodged, hoping the man's Talent would break his sword on the rock wall behind him. His enemy's skill was too great; his sword's tip barely kissed the stone before being swept down and across.

Dahleven dove and rolled. The man was quick. Too quick. He engaged again before Dahleven was quite out of his tuck, knocking the sword out of Dahleven's grasp and sending it scraping across the floor. As though time had slowed, Dahleven saw Yellowteeth grin as his blade sliced toward him in a clean arc, about to sever blood and bone.

"Hold!" Jorund shouted.

The final blow didn't fall.

Yellowteeth rested the tip of his sword against Dahleven's throat, preventing him from rising from his awkward half crouch. The cavern was silent except for a few groans; his fight had been the last. All of his men were down. Fender slumped against one wall, blood masking half his face, just as it had in the vision. It was no comfort to see that of their foes, only Yellowteeth and Jorund still stood. Eirik also was on his feet, but was of no consequence.

Dahleven fisted his hands, wishing they were crushing Jorund's throat, but the sword under his chin forced him to be still. Two years before, the Loki-spawn had been Outcast and stripped of his Talent. Jorund had made a great show of remorse at his trial, but Ragni had known his true heart, and Neven had persuaded the others to Outcast the Jarl permanently. Dahleven ground his teeth, sorry to see the scum hadn't died in the drylands.

"Lord Dahleven, how pleasant to be able to entertain you, though I'd hoped to do so a bit later." The Fire-starter came to stand in front of him.

"I'm glad to disappoint you," Dahleven said. The

sword at his neck wavered, nicking Dahleven's neck. Yellowteeth's trouser leg was drenched in blood below the cut Dahleven had delivered.

"No matter. It's better, I think, that you witness this." Jorund turned and drew Celia to her feet. She looked nearly as weak as she had after Finding Ari. A red handprint marred her cheek. Dahleven felt a surge of anger, and added Celia's injury to the long list of reasons he wanted to beat Jorund bloody. Angrim came with her and tried to cling to Jorund's arm. He shook free of her with less attention than most would give a buzzing fly. She stood with arms wrapped tightly around herself, eyes glazed with hurt.

Dahleven looked at her coldly, thinking of the men she'd poisoned with *soven*. They very nearly hadn't survived.

Celia shivered under Jorund's touch. The shadow of pain stained her too-pale face and Dahleven remembered her agonized screams.

"I'm sorry," she whispered in a strained voice. Tears tracked her cheeks and she wavered on her feet. Jorund's hand lay possessively on her shoulder. Dahleven's muscles twitched with the desire to shove the bastard away from her and smash his fist into the Outcast's face.

"Lady Celia has seen through Neven's deception," Jorund said. "She's chosen to help me by Finding the Staff of *Befaling*. In return, I'll send her safely home."

"*I* was the one who told you where it was!" Angrim protested. "If we'd waited for her to do it you *still* wouldn't have it."

Dahleven ignored Angrim, as Jorund did. *What lies has he told Celia?* Lies made believable by Neven's actions. Dahleven sought Celia's gaze and spoke to her as though they were alone in the room. "Father treated you badly, but he's never lied to you, nor made false promises." Dahleven looked into her reddened eyes, willing her to believe. "Nor have I."

"What about the glowing tales of Fanlon's theft I'm forced to tell each Feast?" Eirik demanded. "Those Talents were never Fanlon's to take, but you and Neven have me paint him a hero."

There was something wrong with that, but Dahleven could think of nothing to say against it. In fact, Eirik's words made sense. Why hadn't he seen it before? Dahleven nodded.

Celia's eyes widened and she glanced quickly at Eirik, rubbing her arms as though they itched.

Dahleven found another argument. "Nevertheless, there's danger in releasing the Talents. The Jarls are too fractious to use such power safely, let alone an Outcast. Look at our history before Fanlon stole the Talents."

"History is written by the victor," Jorund answered.

"Life was better before Fanlon's perfidy," Eirik added.

Eirik's argument was convincing. Dahleven started to nod again.

"No! Stop that!" Celia exclaimed and looked angrily from Eirik to Jorund and back. "If what you're saying was true, you wouldn't need to use Persuasion. The truth should stand on its own."

"An excellent point," Dahleven said.

"We haven't time for this debate," Jorund said abruptly. "Eirik, bind and gag him. I want him to witness the end of his father's rule."

Cele pushed down her nausea and tried to bring her adrenaline-charged body under control. She knew she was verging on shock and pulled the sable cloak tighter around her. The odors of blood and feces mingled with sweat and urine. Cele breathed through her mouth. The smell of death was becoming too familiar.

One thought held hope. Though bound and gagged, Dahleven was still alive.

With Dahleven tied up, the man who'd held him at sword's point sheathed his bloody weapon on the third try, then half fell to a sitting position. "Help me, my lord! That bastard near cut my leg off!" He pressed his hands to the bloody wound in his thigh.

"Tie it off," Jorund said off-handedly, his attention on Cele. "Eirik, take care of it."

The skald moved from Dahleven to the wounded man.

Dahleven sat with his hands tied behind his back, legs laced together at the ankles. A gag pulled the corners of his mouth back, distorting his face. He looked furious.

Cele swallowed hard. She deserved his anger. He wouldn't be in this mess if not for her.

"How is it you are impervious to Eirik's Talent, my lady?" Jorund leaned close, speaking in rich, silky tones. "Do you possess an amulet?"

"A what?" Cele tried to look blank and confused as she kicked herself for tipping her hand. But she couldn't have remained silent. Seeing Dahleven nodding along like a puppet made her sick.

"A protective talisman, my lady. You seemed unimpressed by Eirik's argument." Jorund's eyes never left hers.

Cele forced herself to return his gaze calmly. "Eirik has never impressed me much." She cast a dismissive look at the skald. "Should he?" She hoped Jorund would believe she was naturally impervious.

Jorund raised an eyebrow thoughtfully and surveyed the skinny skald before returning his gaze to Cele. He chuckled. "No. Of course not. But how then do you know he used Persuasion?"

"That *is* his Talent, isn't it?" she asked, as though unsure. "Why else would Lord Dahleven agree with him?"

"Because it's the truth?" Jorund asked.

"I doubt Dahleven would think so."

"Perhaps not. But his opinion isn't important, at present. You know he'll say anything to protect Neven's power and his own inheritance. His goals are entirely self-serving."

Cele managed not to snort. *Says the pot of the kettle.*

Jorund put his arm around her, turning so she couldn't see Dahleven. "No matter. It's time and past time for you to Find the Talents, Celia," he crooned. "I'm sorry I lost my temper with you, but you should not have tried my patience, my dear. Let's put that behind us. I'm willing to overlook your past failures. You're new to this world, after all, and your Talent is young. But it's strong. You Found the Staff. And you want to go home, don't you? All you need do is Find the Healing Talent, and then, after I am restored, you can give me the power to send you back to Midgard."

Again, his rich smooth voice was accompanied by painful stinging. "And Neven's family," she said, playing along. "You won't hurt them?"

"Of course not. My only wish is to return freedom to Nuvinland."

She heard a muffled protest from Dahleven, but Jorund's hand on her shoulder kept her from looking around at him.

She couldn't stand his touch another instant. Dahleven was dead no matter what she did or didn't do. It was just a matter of when and how. Cele stepped abruptly away, brushing Jorund's hand from her shoulder. His silky cajolery made her want a bath. He'd used and deceived her from the start, wooing her with sweet lies just like Jeff had. How could she have been so stupid? Well, no more. Anger and self-disgust overrode her plans for deception.

"No."

"No?" Jorund frowned, but didn't look surprised. "You fail to understand, Lady Celia. *No* is not an option." He drew his dagger. A foot of polished steel gleamed in the lantern light.

Cele stepped back.

"You needn't fear, my lady. I have no intention of harming you. You're far too precious and useful." Jorund took two steps and knelt next to Dahleven. "But Lord Dahleven has plenty of blood to spill."

Fear spiked and she put out her hands. "Don't kill him," she pleaded, before the words even formed in her mind.

"I have no intention of it, my dear. He's too valuable as a hostage." Jorund teased his knife over Dahleven's gloved hands. "Will a finger persuade you? Or must I begin with a hand?" Jorund's half-smile jarred with his flat, practical tone.

The man with the leg wound slumped over, unconscious. Eirik's bandage hadn't stopped the bleeding. Jorund barely flicked him a glance. "I can see you require persuasion, and since Eirik can't provide it, I shall have to." With sudden, surprising speed, Jorund seized Dahleven's bound wrists, flattened one of his hands against the floor, and set the knife against a finger joint.

"No!" Cele screamed. "I'll do it!" Her stomach tightened painfully as her bravado failed her. She knew Jorund meant to kill Dahleven, but she couldn't bear to watch him tortured. She had no doubt he would cheerfully dismember Dahleven until she did as he wanted.

Dahleven shook his head and frowned, drawing his brows down over his stormy gray eyes, protesting inarticulately around his gag.

Jorund looked disappointed and released Dahleven's wrist. "Excellent. Proceed."

Cele looked away, trying to hide her thoughts. With Jorund's last warrior down, she had a chance. He wouldn't expect her to attack. Quickly, Cele considered her opponents. She didn't think Eirik and Angrim would be much of a threat, but they didn't have to be to foul things up.

Jorund's dagger was still against Dahleven's hand. Cele willed Jorund to stand or move the dagger away from him so she could sweep kick it away, but he remained kneeling by Dahleven's side, poking the point of his knife into Dahleven's glove. Small spots of blood bloomed on the leather. *I'll have to chance it.*

"Don't even think it," Jorund said as she started to move. He shifted the knife to Dahleven's armpit. Cele abruptly aborted her assault. One upward thrust would cut the nerves to Dahleven's arm, sever the artery. "I know about your unusual skills in combat, my lady. Though even after you killed Pung I didn't expect such an effective response to Mord's and Orlyg's efforts."

They weren't Neven's men, after all. "You *told* them to rape me?"

"I would have stopped them in the nick of time. Probably. I wanted you grateful to me, and I'm quite aware of Lord Ragnar's Talent, you see. That's why I had Harve chase you home. You had to believe your own story of escape and feel enough fear to cloud the rest."

"You told them to do it," she murmured, "and you killed them anyway. Flogged Harve." She could hardly think past her horror and disgust. How could she have ever believed this man?

Jorund shifted his weight, but his knife didn't waver from Dahleven's flesh. "Enough of this. Find the Talent. And don't try me again, Lady Celia."

Cele bit her lips and tried to ignore the fear that

trembled through her muscles. The thought of embracing that pain again made her sick, but she believed Jorund's threat; he'd start slicing away at Dahleven if she failed again. "I tried! There's too many of them. They're pulling me apart."

Jorund pursed his lips. "Perhaps I wasn't specific. I want the Troll's Talent. It regenerates all injury."

Cele stared. "*All* injury?"

The half of Jorund's mouth she could see twisted in a wry smile. "Releasing a Great Talent without the aid of the Staff was a mistake I won't make again. Thanks to you. Only a Talent so powerful can heal the magical damage I suffered."

So it wasn't Wirmund who'd destroyed his face. He lied about that, too.

Now he could release all the Talents he wanted without harm—now that he had the Staff. And she'd given it to him.

He wouldn't share the Talents; he'd take them all himself. He'd become a dictator, one with the ability to regenerate. No one would be able to stop him.

She couldn't do it. But if she didn't, Jorund would slice Dahleven to bits.

chapter twenty-six

cele swallowed hard. She tried to ignore the shadows that seemed to press ever closer. She looked at the floor, avoiding the sight of Dahleven's anxious face and the men who lay dead and dying all around her. Shoving aside fear and self-recrimination, Cele closed her eyes and tried to imagine a troll. She'd never seen one, though here in Alfheim, that might be only a matter of time. She wrapped the idea of a troll with the power of regeneration and restoration, confined in dark stone. She pushed her worry for Dahleven out of her mind. Steeled herself against the agony she feared. She wanted that Talent, needed it.

Clear and easy, the Talent pulled her. A mere twenty feet away, a small geode called to her. She started toward it, but movement nearby made her startle and turn.

A stunningly attractive man stepped out of nowhere and bowed to her. Black hair fell just past his shoulders and his beardless chin was in perfect balance with his wide brow and high cheekbones. A velvet cloak the color of the summer forest covered a tunic embroidered with autumn leaves.

Where did he come from? He wasn't part of Jorund's group or one of Dahleven's men.Cele glanced at the Outcast. Neither he nor Dahleven, nor Angrim or Eirik seemed aware of the man. Or of anything else.

Four others, two tall, handsome men and two beautiful women moved away, into the shadows, pushing them back.

"You are not looking for that which you desire." The first man drew her attention back to himself with a voice as rich as melting chocolate. Unlike Jorund's words, this man's didn't bring her pain.

He stepped closer, moving with feral grace. Dark lashes framed the man's pale, water-colored eyes, eyes that drew Cele in with the promise of understanding some deeply hidden secret she hadn't known she longed for. She could have stared into his face for hours, but then he blinked and all her questions came tumbling out. "What do you mean? Who are you? Why don't they see you?"

The man smiled slightly. "You cast your light in the wrong corners. That is why you cannot Find what you seek."

But I Found the Troll Talent.

"It is not what you truly desire."

Cele looked closely at the man through narrowed eyes. His sun-bronzed skin was smooth and perfect. Too perfect. He wasn't very good at answering questions, either. She opened her mouth to point that out, but he put a silencing finger on her lips, and this time his smile reached his eyes.

"I am Galendir of the *Lios Alfar*, a Light Elf in your tongue. They do not see or hear me because I do not wish them to."

An Elf. No wonder his skin is perfect.

Then his smile faded, and his expression became serious. "If you wish to Find a way free, you must look for it."

Great. As if Jorund's threats weren't enough pressure, this Elf was speaking in riddles. She started to say, "It's not that simple," but he again held a finger against her lips. She had the feeling he heard her anyway.

The Elf's pale eyes met hers for a long moment. She felt as if his gaze penetrated her soul, as if he saw all her fears and shortcomings. She squirmed inwardly, but didn't look away. She wasn't going to let him intimidate her. "So what do I look for, then?"

A hint of a smile touched Galendir's lips. "What is it you most need?"

A way to save Dahleven. No, more than that. I need to stop Jorund.

"Just so." Galendir nodded. "But you are not seeking it."

"I know! What I need is a bomb! But what do I look for? If I don't know, the Talents will pull me apart!"

Galendir placed two fingers on the side of her forehead. The touch was cool, delicate, riveting. Cele froze as a vision of great power coalesced in her mind, writhing and twining like bolts of lightning, screaming all at once like many voices in the dark and cold. They wanted to be free. To be used. Their strength rocked her like a thunderclap.

"You want me to give him that? Are you crazy? That's just what he wants! After the Troll Talent, anyway."

"It is what he craves, but not what he expects."

She hesitated. *What if this guy is on Jorund's side? For all I know he's trying to trick me into giving him the power to kill everyone that I care about. Ragni said Elves don't interact much with humans. Why does he care about any of this?* Cele opened her mouth to demand answers, but Galendir answered her before she could speak.

"Balance. The Dark Ones revealed this place to their

tool," he gestured gracefully at Jorund, who still seemed oblivious to their conversation. "They sent their minion to retrieve the Staff for him. They weighted the Great Wheel. They would turn it to their advantage, but Light must balance Dark. We sensed their meddling, but couldn't find the way—until your Talent called us. You shine brighter than these others. Now it's our turn. I will guide you, but it must be you who acts."

Cele's heart thrashed painfully in her chest, like a bird confined in too small a cage. She needed a weapon, some way to stop Jorund, but she was afraid. She'd made so many mistakes since she'd gotten here. What if trusting this Elf was the worst? She looked at Galendir, who waited for her to decide.

A warrior doesn't fight herself. Dahleven's lecture echoed in her mind. *Don't let fear keep you from moving forward.*

"You know what you must do," Galendir said.

She did. Cele opened herself, opened the cage of fear and doubt her heart was trapped in.

Something inside unfolded, blossoming within her. The voices of all the Talents murmured to her from their long confinement. First one whisper, then another and another. The multitude blended into a chorus that echoed for her alone, shouting: *Here! Here! Here!*

Finding had never felt like this before. Neither gentle tug nor painful rending, the hidden Talents tried to draw her closer, to find release, but they were sucking her into the dark of their prison.

There were too many. Talents of healing, creativity, destruction. All calling to her. All vying for her attention. All trying to draw her close enough to leap free. She couldn't sort through the multitude. How could Jorund imagine he wanted all of this?

A picture of what she needed to Find appeared in her mind. Cele focused on the image Galendir gave her, held it like a shield, let it guide her like a lantern.

The clamor fell away.

Nearby, a large geode called with a clear voice. Several voices. It held more than one of the Great Talents. She listened closer. The trapped Talents promised power, great power. Deadly power.

She'd wanted a weapon, and she'd Found one. But would it stop Jorund, or arm him with a deadly force?

Cele glanced at the Outcast Jarl, still staring, still unaware, thought of how Galendir had seemed to step out of nowhere. The Elves obviously had powers equal to the Great Talents. "Why didn't you just stop him yourself?"

Galendir frowned. "Freyr has enjoined us. We cannot act directly in the affairs of men. But you can. If you choose. The Great Wheel must turn. Light must balance Dark." The Elf nodded at Jorund and stepped back into the shadows. "Give him what wants. It's not what he expects, but it *is*what you need."

Cele shivered uncontrollably as Galendir moved away, his words echoing in her mind. *What he wants isn't what he expects.*

Jorund blinked and regarded her with a sharp expression. "Did you Find it?"

She could still give him the Troll Talent. She and Dahleven might be able to escape while he was distracted. But she'd already made her choice. Galendir had been cryptic, but he hadn't tried to coerce or Persuade her against her will.

Cele swallowed hard and pointed. Her hand wavered as she indicated the larger geode. She was barely able to speak. "There. That's what you want."

Jorund looked at her closely, and was apparently satisfied by what he saw. He sheathed his dagger and stepped close to the geode, roughly shoving Cele back so she stumbled several steps and fell against Dahleven. "Watch them," he barked at Eirik.

Dahleven groaned as Celia pointed at the geode. His one life wasn't worth it. Jorund would never be satisfied. Once he was healed, he'd ransack the Great Talents, becoming the most powerful tyrant Nuvinland had ever seen.

Celia lost her balance as the Firestarter thrust her away. She tried to catch herself with several awkward steps, but her shivering overcame her and she collapsed, slumping against Dahleven. She looked near Exhaustion, but after a moment she glanced at Eirik, who was watching Jorund, then pushed herself half behind him, sliding slowly until she could reach the ropes on his wrists. He felt her pull weakly at the knots, her trembling vibrating into him where they touched. A moment later Eirik jerked her away.

"Oh, no, my lady, we'll have none of that." With two hands under her arms, Eirik lifted Celia nearly off her feet, then tossed her across Dahleven's legs.

Dahleven's temper flared at Eirik's rough treatment. Celia made no attempt to resist the skinny skald; she barely seemed able to sit up and lean against him. Dahleven had never seen anyone shake so after using their Talent. Her trembling reverberated through Dahleven's chest and he shifted to give her better support. He wished his arms were free so he could hold her—after he killed Jorund.

Jorund knelt by the geode, running his hands over the dark, irregular surface as though he caressed a woman. It was huge, the size of a mountain cat. "Angrim, bring me that box!" he ordered abruptly, pointing.

Angrim blinked, jolted out of her cowering trance, and scurried to comply. She hardly seemed like the same woman who had strutted her allure so confidently in the past.

Jorund took the small wooden box from Angrim and turned away from her, oblivious to the pleading look in her eyes. Dahleven had little doubt that the Firestarter would discard her now that her usefulness to him was finished.

In a few moments, Jorund had assembled the contents of the box. He drew fire from a lantern to light the two bowls of incense he'd put on either side of the geode. He grinned at Dahleven, his eyes both bitter and gloating. "That's the last time I'll have to do *that*," he said. "Soon my Talent will be hot again, and it shall not burn alone. What shall I do first? Tumble Quartzholm to its foundations with an earthquake, or burn her? What will Kon Neven be Jarl of then?" He turned away again and drew a small purple bag from under his shirt. From it he took an amethyst crystal.

A priest's talisman! Dahleven looked on in horror. The last of his hope that Jorund would fail in the necessary ritual faded.

Jorund held the crystal in one hand and the Staff in the other, raising both over his head. He began to chant in the priests' tongue. His words echoed in the stone chamber and the amethysts started to glow. Throughout the cavern, the crystals imbedded in the walls answered, returning and amplifying the purple light.

From nowhere, three tall men and two women came forward. Dahleven startled. The men were strong warriors, the women lush and willowy, and all as finely clad as Jarls and their Ladies on Feast Day. *Elvenkind!* Jorund was oblivious to them. Nor were Eirik or Angrim reacting. Dahleven had heard of such things in fearful tales of the Fey-marked. The Elves used their glamour to hide themselves from mortals. *But why do they show themselves to me?*

One of the men came toward him and Celia, while

the others moved into the vanishing shadows. His hair was black as a raven's wing, as were the lashes that framed his pale eyes. Dahleven's heart thundered in his chest. He strained against his bonds, but Eirik had done a good job of binding him. Were these Light Elves, or Dark? Did it matter? No man encountered the Elves and remained whole and unchanged.

"You're back," Celia murmured beneath his chin.

Dahleven wished Celia had removed his gag. Had she seen the Elf before? When?

The Elf knelt with impossible grace and drew a dagger that looked like sunlight on ice. He sliced through Dahleven's bonds as if they were strands of hair. Dahleven pulled the gag from his mouth, and the Elf put a finger to his lips. The touch was gentle, yet firm as a command. And with that touch came the knowledge that these were *Lios Alfar*, Light Elves.

Dahleven clamped down on the questions he wanted to ask. Why would the Elves free him? What were they doing here, in the deep underground of the Dark Elves? But then, why did Elvenkind do anything? A man erred dangerously if he thought he could understand such things.

Eirik's back was turned to him. Jorund seemed unaware of the Elves presence, murmuring the words of the ritual. Dahleven looked around. The closest weapon was a sword clutched in a dead man's hand five feet away. Dahleven thought his odds of killing Jorund pretty good—if the Elves didn't interfere.

The Light Elf shook his head. "This is not for you to do. Your Lady has chosen wisely."

Dahleven frowned, not understanding.

"Light must answer Dark," the Elf explained. "We felt the Dark Ones shift the balance, but the cause was hidden—until we saw your Lady's beacon. You have our thanks. Now leave the Dark Ones' tool to his fate."

It went against his nature to put his trust in Elven-kind, but he had little choice. He wanted to crush Jorund with his own hands, but with their glamour, the Elves could trick a man into killing his best friend if they chose. Defying the Elf's command bore too great a risk. He wrapped his arms around Celia and she leaned against his chest.

The Elf looked at his companions standing at the edge of the shadows. Figures within the shadows surged forward as if they would go to Jorund's aid, then re-treated as the Light Elves pushed them back with upraised hands that glowed golden in the dark.

The light from the crystals grew as Jorund continued his chanting. Tears stung Dahleven's eyes and he winced at the brightness. The Elf turned back to him. "You are too fragile," he said and stretched his fingers toward Ce-lia's eyes.

Celia blinked when he touched her, then her eyes widened. "Oh!"

"What is it? What did he do to you?" Dahleven raised a hand to push the Elf away even though he could barely see.

"Be at peace. No harm has come to your lady."

Dahleven hesitated, and the Elf placed his palm on her head. She breathed deeply. Her trembling stopped. She straightened as though suddenly stronger. Then the Elf reached for Dahleven's eyes. He pulled back, but the Elf's touch was lighter than a breath of air.

He could see again, without the light hurting his eyes. Startled, Dahleven sucked in a sharp breath.

The Elf had changed. No longer was his appearance that of a human warrior. The raven hair remained, but now it flowed like midnight down the Elf's back to his waist, and his eyes slanted sharply over high cheek-bones. Lithe and strong, his body moved with a strange cat-like grace. He was beautiful—and completely *other*.

The Elf withdrew his long slender hand and nodded, meeting Dahleven's stare with a calm steady gaze. Then he turned to join his companions.

The violet light continued to grow, reflected and multiplied a thousand times by the crystals embedded in the walls. It obliterated everything but the silhouettes of the Elves, but now Dahleven could look at it without wincing.

A sharp, loud *Crack!* made both Dahleven and Celia jump. The light flared and Dahleven's arms tightened around her.

Then Jorund shouted triumphantly, his wild laugh echoing through the chamber.

chapter twenty-seven

Dahleven's throat closed, choked by despair. Now that Jorund Firestarter had the Troll's Talent, no one would be able to stand against him. His capricious will would rule Alfheim. *Why didn't Fanlon destroy the Staff when he had the chance?*

Jorund screamed.

Raw agony tore from the Firestarter's throat. Dahleven shuddered as the horrific shrieks echoed throughout the chamber. He couldn't see what was happening to Jorund. He didn't want to. The excruciating wails clawed and cut. Dahleven winced and ground his teeth, hunching his shoulders against the sound of torment. He pulled Celia close, pressing her head against his chest, trying to muffle the sound of more pain than a man or woman should ever imagine. Celia moaned and clenched her fists on his byrnie.

The screaming stopped abruptly. The light faded. The Elvenkind were gone.

Angrim shrieked, "My eyes! I can't see! I can't see!" Eirik merely stared about him with blank horror.

Jorund lay on his back by the split geode, eyes wide and unseeing, mouth twisted in a rictus of pain. His arms bent tightly to his chest, fingers claw-like. Blood trickled sluggishly from his ears and nose. He was unmistakably dead.

Cele let Dahleven pull her to her feet. She stared at Jorund's body, his tortuous screams echoing in her mind. In all her time on the phones, she'd never heard suffering so horrible. And she'd caused it by pointing to a particular rock. A rock that Jorund had asked for, demanded, as the price of Dahleven's blood and body. Now the Outcast was dead, along with the chance he'd offered her of returning home.

Cele shook her head, ashamed of her gullibility. She still grieved for that lost hope, though not for Jorund. He'd manipulated her from the start. He'd never intended to send her back, but she'd wanted it so badly she'd let herself be deceived.

Dahleven turned her away from Jorund. She became aware again of the fallen men and the wails of Angrim and Eirik. Here was something she could do, something more useful than dwelling on the betrayal and anger Dahleven must feel toward her. "We have to see to the injured," Cele said, pulling out of Dahleven's arms.

With an arm around each of them, she guided Angrim and Eirik to sit against the wall, knowing they'd feel more secure with something solid at their backs.

Angrim's sobbing subsided to whimpers. She looked older and duller, diminished. Eirik was babbling and staring wide-eyed at nothing in particular. There was nothing Cele could do but speak soothingly. They clutched at her desperately, and she had to pry their fingers free to move on to the other injured. Cele felt Dahleven watching her and tried to ignore it, forcing herself to focus on the task at hand.

Dahleven watched Celia for a moment, her face devoid of emotion. *She's holding her heart at arm's length.* He'd seen men react that way after a battle. She moved deliberately, efficiently checking for life in the nearest of the fallen warriors. He didn't like the shadow in her eyes, or the way she avoided looking at him. She'd seen too much death—and he'd failed to protect her from it.

Dahleven knelt by Jorund's twisted body. He regretted not having the chance to kill the Outcast himself, but this was a fitting end to his perfidy. His lip curled in distaste as he pried the stolen priest's talisman from Jorund's convulsed fingers. It was blackened like the geode. The Staff of *Befaling* was another matter. Its crystal was still clear, though a deep crack ran from base to tip. Dahleven gathered them up. *Ragni will want these. They should be returned to the priesthood.*

A groan from Fender drew Dahleven to his side in an instant. The gash to his scalp had left his friend's face bloody, but the flow of blood had slowed, leaving a sticky mess.

Fender dragged himself to sit against the wall, and gently probed his cut scalp. "Having one's head laid open leads to strange dreams, my lord."

"Then keep your helmet on next time," Dahleven jibed, relieved that his friend still had his wits—and his head.

Fender looked around and frowned at the bodies of their friends and foes. "Lady Celia?"

"Alive," Dahleven answered, shifting so she could be seen.

"And that whoreson?"

"Dead."

Fender nodded and winced. "I dreamed Elves were at hand."

A cold grue slithered down Dahleven's spine. "It was no dream." Dahleven's gaze locked with Fender's for a moment in silent understanding. They both knew the world didn't turn as it usually did when the Elvenkind were involved.

Celia appeared at his side then, and held her hand in front of Fendrikanin's face. "How many fingers am I holding up?"

"Three," Fender answered accurately.

"Any dizziness? Nausea?"

"I'm glad to see you well too, my lady." Fender grinned. "But I'm sure there are others more in need of your attention."

"A head wound is nothing to laugh at," Celia said, her voice tightly controlled.

"Even for someone as thick-headed as me?"

Celia didn't smile at Fender's teasing.

Dahleven looked at her closely. "The others?"

Celia's face was a stiff mask. She didn't meet his eyes. "All dead. Two of Jorund's men are still alive...but not for long."

Dahleven closed his eyes. Five more of his men dead. Five more to sing to Valhalla. Five more families grieving.

"There's nothing I can do for them," Celia said softly. "I'm sorry. I'm so sorry. None of you would be here if it weren't for me." She covered her face with hands blood-stained from checking the dead and injured.

Dahleven looked at Celia, startled out of his own pain. *Is that what she's been thinking?* "That's right. If not for you, Jorund might have found some other way to release the Talents, and we would not have known until he destroyed us. He might have taken more time, learned a better magic, and succeeded. Because of you, Jorund got careless. Because of *you*, the Light Elves are grateful to us." He could hardly believe he was saying those last words. *Light Elves grateful to us.*

Celia dropped her hands. Her green eyes glistened with tears. "Your men are dead because of me! Because I believed that son of a bitch!"

"My men chose the warrior's path and understood its dangers. They died honorable deaths, and they will feast in Valhalla tonight. The tale of this battle will be sung for generations."

"If not for me, they'd be singing their own songs! I wanted to go home so badly I didn't think about what I was doing or what it would mean to you. I Found the damn Staff for him! I should have known better, even if he did use Persuasion on me. I just didn't want to see what was in front of my face all along, and *people are dead because of it*! Because of my stupid, selfish, gullibility."

A slow cold anger moved in Dahleven. Neven had dangled Celia in front of Jorund's nose and left her vulnerable to him, pushing her into the Firestarter's web of lies. Neven's plan had borne its fruit, their Outcast enemy was revealed and destroyed, and widespread ruin averted. But all Celia could see were the bodies of his men and her part in their deaths. Neven had brought her to this, but Celia was bearing the weight of it.

He grabbed Celia by the shoulders. "Listen to me! You didn't make those mistakes alone. Jorund was an accomplished liar. He fooled us all for years before he got arrogant and burned Koll's crofts. Even then he almost talked his way out of his punishment. Your *mistakes* saved thousands of lives. Don't you understand? If not for you, everyone in Quartzholm might have been killed by that Oathbreaker!"

Celia clenched her jaw and looked away.

"I heard what Angrim said. It was she who told the Outcast where to look for the Staff. When it came down to it, you couldn't do it, could you?"

Celia remained silent.

"Nor did you know when you Found the Staff that Angrim was Jorund's agent, did you?" Dahleven lifted her chin so she had to look at him. "Did you?"

"No."

"If we were all condemned for what we might have done, we'd all be exiled," Fender contributed. Celia cast a knife sharp glance at him. He raised his hands as if in surrender. "Remember, I'm a wounded man."

"If not for you, the Light Elves wouldn't have been here to counter what the Dark set in motion," Dahleven continued. "It was your 'beacon' that drew them here. I think they sensed you using your Talent."

Cele slumped, as if in surrender. "Then the agony was worth it. When I first tried to Find the Talent he wanted, the damn things nearly ripped me apart."

Celia's words sobered him. He remembered her screams. "And now? How do you feel?" So much had happened, he'd forgotten that Celia was still in Emergence. She'd been weak as a babe before the Elf's touch had strengthened her. He cursed himself for not bringing any *sterkkidrikk*.

"I'm fine."

Fender chuckled. "I think Lady Celia's in better shape than we are."

Dahleven looked at Fendrikanin's bloody face and felt the ache in his own muscles growing. Fender was probably right.

Cele cleaned and bandaged the cut in Fender's scalp,

then helped Dahleven arrange the bodies of their fallen companions, laying them side-by-side with hands crossed on their swords' hilts. Then Dahleven and Fender sang the funerary song. Some magic of the caverns amplified their two voices until they sounded like a choir, sending shivers of longing and loss and hopeful joy racing through Cele's heart.

Afterward, Cele and Fender went on ahead while Dahleven remained behind, executing the law on Jorund's dying men. As Outcasts, the law turned every man's hand against them, and it was more merciful than leaving them to die slowly. Cele thought she should be appalled at the summary justice, but all she could think of was how difficult and unpleasant it must be for Dahleven.

"Are you sure you feel well enough to manage Angrim and Eirik alone?" Cele asked Fender. She and Dahleven were going on to bring news of Jorund's defeat to the parley. Fender would take the same news, and Angrim and Eirik, back to Quartzholm. "You took quite a blow to the head." They walked side-by-side down the spur of tunnel to where Dahleven and his men had entered the caverns only hours before.

"Never fear, my lady. It's the sturdiest part of me—but one." He winked.

Cele made a face and rolled her eyes, but she was glad Fender still felt like joking.

"Besides, Torvald and Sieg are waiting just beyond. I won't be alone long. And I doubt Lord Dahleven will allow you out of his sight for some time yet." Fender's eyes twinkled, and Cele felt herself blushing.

Suddenly Fender flung his arm in front of Cele. "Look out!"

"What is it?"

Fender looked at her strangely. "You almost ran into the wall...Don't you see it?"

Cele looked. There was no wall in front of them, just those to either side. She shook her head and lifted her lantern to peer closely into Fender's face. Was the blow he took making him hallucinate? "Are you sure you're all right?"

Dahleven came around a bend in the passage leading Angrim and Eirik, his face grim. He stopped abruptly. "Where's the wall?"

"*What* wall?" Cele demanded.

"You don't see it either?" Fender asked. He stepped forward and patted his splayed fingers in the air like a mime. "You saw it before. I see and feel it quite clearly."

Dahleven walked forward, hands in front of him, until he was slightly beyond Fender, then stepped back, shaking his head. His gaze locked with Fender's and they shared a grim expression.

"What is it? What are you not saying?" Cele demanded.

"No one has congress with Elvenkind and remains unaffected," Fender said in a voice like bad news.

"Ragni said something like that once," Cele said. "What does it mean?"

"It means," Dahleven said slowly, "that we're Fey-marked. I don't know why he saved us from blindness, but the Elf's touch had greater consequence than our protection. There's a wall of Glamour here, Celia. The illusion doesn't trick our eyes. We can't see it, while Fender can."

Cele stared, blinking at where Fender said the wall stood, then turned back to Dahleven. "Because the Elves touched us, and not him? Then why isn't he blind like Eirik and Angrim?"

"I don't know. Perhaps because they were closer to the magic, or because he was unconscious at the time. He's lucky to have escaped our fate."

"But it sounds like a gift."

Dahleven shook his head. "Few will see it that way. You must tell *no one* about this. People aren't—comfortable—with the Fey-marked."

"*Comfortable*. You mean we'll be ostracized, don't you?" Cele stared, worried for him. "Could you be disinherited?"

"You can rest easily, Lord Dahleven," Eirik said. "I'll say nothing of your affliction—unless it comes up at my trial." He cocked his head at an odd angle staring with wide eyes. "And you, Lady Angrim, can you keep the secret as well?"

The threat was obvious. All of Cele's anger, frustration, and anguish coalesced into a sharp glittering point. She stepped forward and grabbed the front of Eirik's tunic. He flinched when she spoke an inch from his nose, her voice cutting like a razor. "And just how do you intend to get back to Quartzholm, you lying little weasel? Will you lead, or will you leave that to Angrim?"

She let Eirik go with a little shove and he stumbled, awkwardly keeping his balance.

"You wouldn't leave us."

All the anger it was too late to express to Jorund found its mark in Eirik. "Don't try me," Cele grated. "Then again, maybe we *will* take you back. What do you think Neven will do when he finds out you've been in Jorund's pocket all this time? What will your Guild do when it learns you've lied about what the runes revealed?"

Dahleven raised his eyebrows at Cele but didn't interfere.

Eirik blinked rapidly. "I won't say anything. I have nothing to say. I didn't *see* anything."

"Do you have enough honor left to swear to that?" Fender asked. "As Lord Dahleven's sworn man, it would be up to him, not Neven or even your Guild, to choose appropriate punishment, or care for you in your blindness. And what of you, Lady Angrim? Will you swear fealty?"

"Don't be angry with me! Jorund misled me. I'll do *whatever* you want." Angrim cocked her head coquettishly. The gesture seemed like a parody of her former self, now that she no longer sparkled with allure. Something more than her sight was missing. Had her beauty and sex appeal been an illusion, too?

"I'll take your oaths, then." Dahleven stood impassively as Eirik and Angrim got down on their knees and swore fealty to him. Cele wondered if they could really be trusted, but this was obviously more solemn and significant than a casual promise. Cele remembered Sorn's reaction to what Jeff had done, how he'd called Jeff an Oathbreaker. Obviously, a promise wasn't given, or broken, lightly here.

Dahleven accepted their oaths of loyalty; in return, he promised to provide for their needs as long as they stood true. All three of them seemed more relaxed when it was over, as though something essential had changed between them. Dahleven swore them to secrecy, then led them and Fender safely through the wall she couldn't see.

She knew they were through the wall of glamour when Dahleven's waiting men shouted their joy at seeing him and Fender. Their expressions of backthumping relief swung quickly to grim sorrow at the loss of their comrades.

Fender took charge of the small party, giving Eirik and Angrim into the care of Torvald and Seig. Cele and Dahleven watched until the little group disappeared around a curve and the light from their lanterns faded.

"We must go, as well," Dahleven said. "Neven must be told about Jorund as soon as possible."

"Oh, no!" Anguish washed over Cele, and she grabbed Dahleven's arm. "Jorund said the parley was going to be attacked."

Dahleven stiffened. *Father and Ragni are walking into an ambush.*

Even in death, the Firestarter might still begin a conflagration. "That could end all hope of peace. If only one side or the other is attacked, they'll believe the truce has been violated."

Celia released his arm. "Can't we warn them?"

"When did he say the attack would occur?"

"He didn't. He just said soon."

Dahleven cursed. With Jorund, "soon" probably meant the attack had already begun, and they were at least two days away from the parley site. Whatever Jorund had set in motion would be over by the time they got there.

Celia reached out, but didn't quite touch him. "Can we get there in time?"

The words almost choked him. "No. We're too far away." He'd sent men ahead to secure the site. If they did their job—and were lucky—they'd discover the ambush. That might at least save Neven and the Nuvinlanders. But the Tewakwe would still be vulnerable, and if Jorund's Outcasts attacked them, they'd believe the Nuvinlanders false. He didn't see how a tangle of misunderstanding and bloodshed could be avoided.

He still had to try. He had to tell Neven and the Tewakwe about Jorund's treachery and death as soon as possible. That knowledge just might prevent the situation from escalating to war.

Dahleven looked at Celia. She was overtired from two days of captivity, and Finding the Talents, and had seen too much death. She watched him with anxious, red-rimmed eyes. It was madness to take her into the aftermath of battle. Depending on the outcome, continuing skirmishes could harry the Nuvinlanders all the way back to the border, putting all in the area at risk. He should call Fender and his men back, send Celia on to Quartzholm with them.

She must have read his mind. "Don't even think about it." Her face was stern, her voice flat. It was the same tone his mother had used when he was a child, contemplating mischief. "I'm going with you. I won't be kept safe in a box."

Dahleven looked at Celia standing with hands on hips and knew that Fender would have to tie her up to get her back to Quartzholm. Something like relief, or maybe joy, washed through him as he realized he'd have to keep her with him.

A little of the tension drained from Cele's body when she realized Dahleven wasn't going to send her back to Quartzholm. She'd made such a mess of things. She needed to redeem herself, in some small way, and she couldn't do that stuck at the castle. And she didn't want to leave Dahleven.

Dahleven returned to the chamber briefly to gather extra oil and food and waterskins. He bundled blankets and one of Jorund's sleeping pads as well. "It will be warmer than sleeping directly on the cold stone, as we did before," he explained.

Cele agreed as she shouldered the pack and skins he handed her. Heat swept over her as she noted that he brought only one of the narrow pads. The memory of Dahleven's kisses, the feel of his body against hers, made her even warmer.

She dismissed the thought. He'd said she wasn't to blame for what had happened, but she couldn't so easily forgive herself. And no matter what he said, she didn't believe Dahleven could, either.

Cele followed him through the smooth-floored tunnel. Ordinary crystals sparkled to life in the walls as the lantern light struck them, twinkling in the normal way, not glowing as they had before Jorund died.

They had no energy to spare for conversation, leaving Cele too much time to think. The searing light and Jorund's screams, the torn bodies of the dead and dying, the smell of blood and death, all weighed on her mind. Despite Dahleven's words to the contrary, Cele knew she'd put his men in harm's way. Shards of anger and grief cut her heart. She was glad Jorund and his deceptions were dead. She'd kill him again if she could for threatening Dahleven, for luring her to betray the friendship he had offered.

Cele swallowed on a sour stomach. How could she have let herself be taken in by his smooth talk? Hadn't she learned anything from Jeff? Only this time she wasn't the only one hurt. Men had died because of her naiveté. She tore at herself over and over with that thought.

Dahleven led them onward. Shadows and soft lantern light rippled over his body, his form lumpy with various burdens. His movement was sure and strong, but he adjusted his stride to fit hers. Though he had little to say, he glanced at her often. Cele gritted her teeth, expecting to see disgust and condemnation in his face. She wouldn't blame him. She deserved that, and more. But his expression only held concern. Eventually, he called a halt, much earlier than she anticipated.

"Don't stop on my account," she said, despite her fatigue.

Dahleven shook his head, slipping his burdens to the floor. "We traveled hard and fast to reach you, without much rest."

And finished with a battle that killed most of his men.

Cele took the thin featherbed as Dahleven shrugged out of its strap, and unrolled it. "I'm sorry—"

"No more of that." Dahleven cut her off.

Cele swallowed her unspoken sorrow and grief. He was right. What could she say that would make up for what she'd done?

Dahleven shed the rest of his burdens, laying them out with the same orderliness she'd observed that first night by the spring. It seemed so long ago. Then he sat down on the thin mattress with a soft groan.

"Would you like something to eat?" Cele started to rummage in the pack she'd carried, trying to be useful. She handed him a small loaf of bread and a wedge of cheese. Jorund had been well provisioned.

He actually smiled as she sliced and shared out the food between them. "At least Jorund had better taste than to pack journeybread." One of the skins he'd scavenged held a light wine, which they passed wordlessly between them.

When they'd eaten their fill, Dahleven removed his heavy leather byrnie and turned the wick of the lantern low. "Come here." His voice was warm, and he spread his hand to indicate the space next to him on the pad.

As Cele settled next to Dahleven, her heart beat faster, as nervous as she'd been the first night she'd slept between him and Sorn. More so, because now she wanted to be in Dahleven's arms more than any place on earth, and there was no future in it.

Dahleven lay down with a sigh, pulling her against his chest with her head on his shoulder.

"You did well today. You kept your head." Dahleven

spoke slowly. "I don't have the words to tell you..."

His words warmed Cele even more than his body.

"If you were one of my men I'd know how to reward your courage...I've never known such a woman..."

Could he mean it? Did he really hold her blameless for what had happened? He'd said as much before, but it was hard to believe. Cele waited for Dahleven to continue but he said nothing more. His breathing altered. He'd fallen asleep.

Dahleven's earlier words returned to her. Jorund had been a skilled liar, practiced at deceit. Even those who knew him best had been taken in by him. He'd known exactly which of her buttons to push, she finally conceded to herself. Angrim had probably told him what best to tempt her with. He'd dangled the lure of home in front of her with consummate skill.

Maybe, she could forgive herself. A little.

Dahleven came awake instantly, as he usually did, and blinked three times before yesterday's events reasserted themselves in his mind. He focused on what was most important: *Celia is safe.*

Cool relief washed over him. The danger could so easily have been missed. But it hadn't been, thanks be to Baldur, in large part due to the Daughters of Freya. That truth chafed like a new boot, but he would have to wear it.

Dahleven stared into the shadows above them. Celia lay with her back to him, her warm rump pressed against his hip. His body urged him to roll her beneath him. Memories of the soft weight of her breasts in his hands and her moans of pleasure teased him, but her breathing told him she was still deeply asleep. Another of Nature's summons became more urgent. Reluctantly, Dahleven slipped from beneath the blankets, turned up their lamp, and went to answer a different need.

A ruffle of cool air pulled Cele from sleep as Dahleven slipped back beneath the blankets. He curled himself around her, snugging his legs behind hers as close as two spoons in a drawer. Cele drowsily nestled backward into his warmth and sighed, as his arm came around her waist, pulling her closer. Then she came fully awake as he trailed little kisses up her neck.

"You're awake," he murmured warmly, and traced the curl of her ear with his tongue.

A shiver raced down Cele's spine and her heart beat faster. She hadn't expected this—but she wanted it. Craved it. She arched her neck to receive more of Dahleven's kisses.

This is sheer stupidity. She shouldn't let this begin, no matter how insistent her body's demands.

Dahleven's hand stroked down her thigh and back up, slowing Cele's thoughts.

This will only complicate both our lives. She should roll away and get up.

His hand moved up under her tunic to cup her breast. Her nipple was already standing high and he teased it delicately through the thin fabric of her dress, sending a shock of pleasure cascading through her body.

She groaned and rolled to face Dahleven, sliding her hands under his shirt and up his back, savoring his warmth and the feel of his muscles as her finger slid over his skin. He leaned over her on one elbow and his gaze searched her face before his head came down. His lips met hers gently, then pressed their case more urgently. Any doubt she had fled. Cele returned his kisses openly, their tongues twining and caressing.

The world narrowed to sensation and pleasure. She wanted him. Needed him. There was no future to worry about, only now. Cele barely noticed Dahleven's hand at her shoulder as he unfastened the brooch that held her tunic until he jerked and swore, then stuck his thumb in his mouth.

She couldn't help laughing. "I'd hoped I was the one you were going to impale."

Dahleven's eyes widened, and for an instant Cele wondered if her humor put him off. Then he snorted. "Your turn will come," he growled, rolling to his knees and pulling her up to kneel in front of him. He tugged her dress over her head.

Cele felt no awkwardness at her sudden nudity. The chill air tightened her skin, making her even more glad of Dahleven's warm hands as they glided over her. Her need rose as his appreciative gaze swept down her body, stopping at her hips.

"Ah, *there* it is," he said.

Cele paused for a moment in surprised confusion. Then Dahleven touched the amulet bag tied to her thigh. Ragni had said to keep it secret. Did it offend him?

"We have much to thank Thora for, when we return," Dahleven said thoughtfully.

"You knew?"

"Ragni told me." Then he flung her dress aside and kissed her, dispersing her fears.

"You'll never make it as a lady's maid," Cele said, treating his shirt with the same disrespect. Then she moaned softly as Dahleven's mouth surrounded her taut nipple. She almost collapsed with the sweet shock of pleasure. Dahleven held her in place, sucking, nibbling, tugging. She ached with wanting him, but he kept her there, moving only to give equal attention to her other breast. He caressed the first with his hand, forcing Cele to grasp his shoulders as she trembled with pleasure. When he straightened for a kiss, Cele shuddered and reached for his pants.

Dahleven chuckled. "Are you so anxious to be transfixed?"

"You have the advantage on me. I'm anxious to rectify that." She wanted to see and feel all of him. She settled back on her heels and tugged futilely at the laces. "How do these work?"

Dahleven looked down and half-groaned, half-laughed. "It's Loki's work. You've knotted them." A long minute later, they were free and so was Dahleven. Cele sucked in a breath. He was stunning, from the breadth of his lightly furred chest, to his narrow waist, down to his muscular thighs and calves. She splayed her fingers through the springy hair on his thighs, enjoying the feel of the muscle beneath. The shadows cast by the lantern accentuated the hard planes of his body. He was as beautiful as if he'd been sculpted, yet he was no cold statue, but hot flesh.

An instant later, Dahleven pushed her back on the sleeping mat and they pressed together, sharing the delicious heat of their bodies.

"You are beautiful," he murmured, "and strong, and brave."

"Do I need to be brave to make love with you?" She laughed. "Or perhaps I need courage to do this?" She slid her hand between them and ran a finger delicately up the length of his erection. She loved the hard silkiness of him, the way it jumped under her touch.

Dahleven sucked his breath in sharply, delightfully, so she did it again.

"Have a care, my Valkyrie," he groaned and retaliated by stroking her at the juncture of her thighs. Cele gasped as a bolt of sensual delight shot through her and she grasped his shoulders. Dahleven's growl of satisfaction made her blood run even hotter as he bent his head to her breast and the pleasure sharpened. An intoxicating wave caught her up, and her breath came short and fast.

Cele ran her hands over the taut muscles of his arms and back, rejoicing in the feel of him as he trailed sizzling kisses from one breast to the other. His lips closed over one swollen nipple, sending another cascade of pleasure to build the simmering heat within her. He tugged gently with his teeth and another bolt of delight shot straight to her core. She moaned, cupping his buttocks with restless hands, pulling him closer, guiding him between her legs.

He held still for a moment, poised at her entrance, teasing her with tiny movements, building her hunger until she couldn't stand it anymore. She grabbed his perfect glutes and pulled him in, rocking her hips upward to receive him. Heat flashed through her, and every nerve sparked, burning wild and sweet as they moved together. He became part of her, filling her, satisfying a soul-deep hunger.

Cele tightened around him and Dahleven gasped his pleasure. He moved slowly at first, then faster as Cele caught his rhythm and rose to meet him. Her skin burned and tingled as each movement's pleasure brought her higher. Then with a few swift strokes, he pushed her off the pinnacle to soar in ecstasy. Sensation buffeted her, overwhelming her senses. Dahleven shuddered and arched his back, plunging deeply, holding her as if he'd never let her go. Cele flew for endless moments, suspended in joy and delight, only slowly returning to hover somewhere still a little above the earth.

chapter twenty-eight

Dahleven held celia's HAND as they moved through the tunnel. She'd sought his touch often since the morning's lovemaking, and Dahleven was slightly surprised to find he was just as hungry as she was for the contact. The feel of her hand in his somehow made his worry easier to bear.

What would he find when they finally reached the parley site? Jorund had promised an attack. Would the Tewakwe take it as a breach of the truce? Neven could find himself fighting two foes at once. *I don't want to be Jarl just yet.* And what of Ragni? His brother was competent with sword and bow, but he'd been a priest for eight years. All his combat experience was on the practice field; he'd never faced an enemy intent on his death.

The tunnel ended at a fissure that opened onto the hill. Dim light filtered in from outside. This was the closest exit from the tunnels to the parley site, but they were still over a day's walk away from where the Tewakwe and Nuvinlanders were supposed to meet.

"Stay here. I'll scout the area," he said to Celia. He didn't want to lead her out into a running battle or an Outcast encampment.

She nodded and squeezed his hand. "Be careful."

Dahleven shrugged out of his pack and drew his sword. He handed the lantern to Celia. "Count slowly to two thousand. If I don't return, retrace your steps to Quartzholm as best you can. Don't try to Find your way any more than you must. Don't Exhaust yourself."

She stretched on tiptoe to press her lips to his and Dahleven clasped her to him, savoring the feel of her body against his. His cock sprang to life and clamored for attention, not caring that he had other things to attend to. Reluctantly, he released her. She slid down his front and leaned her head against his chest for a moment before stepping away. He gave her shoulder a quick squeeze, then turned and eased through the fissure, lifting an overgrowth of foliage aside with his sword.

One, two, three...

Cele hated this, worrying about someone she cared for, waiting to find out whether he would come back to her in one piece. She noted the irony of the situation. Only four days ago she'd complained to Dahleven about this very thing, yet here she was, obediently waiting for her man to return from...from what? What was he facing out there? She wouldn't know until he returned. If he returned.

Her man. *Is that what he is?* Or was it wishful thinking? Their lovemaking had pushed aside her guilt and doubt. Cele hadn't wanted it to end, hadn't wanted reality to come rushing back with all its questions. What was their reality?

She cared for him, more than she wanted to acknowledge. *Hell, I might as well admit it. I love him.*

Even more, she trusted him. He wasn't Jeff. Wasn't her father. Warmth welled up within her at the memory of Dahleven's touch and his teasing laughter. Fear rose too, with the knowledge that she could be about to lose the happiness and delight she'd only just discovered.

She considered following him for a moment. *I could help him. Watch his back.* Then she thought of Sorn. She could get him killed if she distracted him at the wrong moment.

So she waited, and tried not to let her mind run wild with fearful possibilities.

One thousand seven, one thousand eight...

Dahleven had said they'd be too late to warn Neven and Ragni of the attack, yet he hoped to bear the good tidings of Jorund's demise to them and to the Tewakwe, as evidence of the Nuvinlanders' good faith. It would be a horrible twist of fate if Ragni and Neven had died just as their enemy was defeated. Cele knew that thought weighed heavily on Dahleven, and she ached because there was nothing she could say that would help.

One thousand four hundred thirty-two, one thousand four hundred thirty-three...

What would she do if he didn't return? He'd come back for her if he was able. But if he wasn't? If there was something so bad out there that Dahleven couldn't handle it, she probably couldn't either. It didn't matter. She wouldn't just leave him, maybe injured and bleeding, regardless of what he said. She couldn't.

One thousand eight hundred fifty-eight—

A sound at the entrance interrupted her count and she took a defensive posture, ready to fight if she had to.

Dahleven sidled through the opening. "It's all clear."

Trembling with the release of the fear she'd been suppressing, Cele leapt into Dahleven's arms. Anger rebounded from relief. She pushed an arm's length away to see his face. "Don't you ever do that again! I'm going with you next time. I'd rather die fighting beside you than wait and wonder!"

Dahleven smiled, but it was humorless. "You will *not*." His voice was flat and implacable, leaving no room for negotiation.

"But—"

"No."

Cele pressed her lips together, undeterred. *We'll discuss this again—later.*

It was late afternoon when they emerged from the mountain. Dahleven went first, Pathfinding the quickest way to the parley site. There was no trail, and the rugged terrain made the going difficult. They didn't have the breath to talk, and the need to keep a sharp eye out for Renegades and Outcasts preoccupied his thoughts when he wasn't worrying about the outcome of the parley. As the sun dropped below the western ridge, he chose a small, level space shielded on two sides by tall conifers to set up their fireless camp.

Celia remained quiet even while they ate their cold supper. She'd grown even quieter, if that was possible, as he honored the memory of his fallen men and recounted their exploits. When he finished, they settled together on the sleeping pallet. They were still fairly high on the mountainside, and even at full summer, the nights here were chilly. He pulled the blanket up over the two of them. Celia lay tense and quiet beside him. Something troubled her, but she wasn't sharing it with him.

"Warm enough?" he asked.

Celia nodded, her head pillowed on his shoulder. He should have enjoyed holding her close like this, the feel of her body molded along the length of him. But her spirit was missing, her heart closed, her mind far away.

"What troubles you?"

"Nothing."

He felt her tremble, and her sniff betrayed silent tears. "Celia, what is it?"

"Your men. They were so brave and loyal and good. If I hadn't been so selfish and stupid, they'd still be alive."

Dahleven winced. He'd told the stories of his men to celebrate their lives. He hadn't thought that Celia would take the tales and twist them into a noose to hang herself with.

"You are not responsible for their deaths," he said flatly. "They followed *me*, obeyed *my* orders."

"But you were only there because of me. If I hadn't been so self-centered, so focused on going home, I might have seen through Jorund's lies sooner."

And been abducted and coerced into Finding the Staff anyway. What could he say to her? Celia was kind and selfless enough to sing to a dying man, comfort a grieving father, and rescue a drowning boy. But she wouldn't hear any of that now.

"I didn't realize you held such a low opinion of me," Dahleven said, adopting an aggrieved tone.

"What?" Celia sounded startled. "What are you talking about?"

"You obviously think my character rather poor, not to mention my intelligence."

"Of course not! You're honorable and caring and smart."

It delighted him to hear her say so, but he couldn't dwell on it. "Then it's my judgment you doubt."

Celia sat up and looked down at him. "Why would you say that?"

"Because only a man of poor judgment or low intellect or bad character could possibly care for the woman you've been describing."

Celia's eyes flashed. Her mouth opened then snapped shut again. She glared at him.

"Fortunately, I don't know that woman."

"You're twisting things," she complained sharply.

Dahleven grinned. "I'm in good company then."

Celia looked away, staring off through the trees. Starlight filtered through the branches, playing on the drying tear tracks on her face. Finally, she closed her eyes and bent her head.

Dahleven squeezed her arm. "Truly, their deaths do not lie at your door. You owe no *wereguild*."

She was silent for several long moments, then she sighed and looked back at him. "I know. I thought I'd learned this lesson long ago. At the Dispatch Center we teach the newbies that they're only responsible for what they can actually do. We can't save everyone. But that doesn't stop us from wanting to."

He pulled her down to lie close to him, pleased when she didn't resist. "That desire gives us the strength to strive. But it should be a goal, not a scourge. We mustn't flay ourselves with it."

"Then it's not your fault, either," she said.

"They were my men. I led them."

"What's sauce for the goose..."

"What does that mean?"

"What's sauce for the goose is sauce for the gander," she elaborated. "You did your best. You took the same risks they did."

She'd turned his own words back on him. It wasn't a comfortable experience.

"You don't fight fair," he said.

"Haven't you heard? 'All's fair in love and war.'" She kissed his nose.

Dahleven's heart skipped a beat. Should he hope she'd given him her heart as well as her body? "Is this love, then, or war?"

Celia paused a moment, then softly said, "It's not war."

He captured her mouth, kissing her slowly, deeply, as his heart expanded with delight. "Thank you," he said when he finally pulled away.

"You're welcome." She smiled gently then returned his kiss. He delighted in the warmth of her lips, the soft stroke of her tongue. Then she nibbled her way up to his ear. "You know," she whispered, "I think you have too many clothes on."

"Do you, now?"

"Yes, I think you should take them off."

"But it's cold," he said with mock innocence.

Celia snuggled closer, making his pulse jump. "I think we could heat things up a bit."

The next afternoon, Dahleven carefully picked his way downslope, despite his desire to hurry. He'd started seeing signs of recent battle, scored earth and bloodstains, half a league back. Alone, he might have surrendered to the desire to rush downhill to the parley site, but Celia's presence reminded him of the need for prudence. Dahleven grimaced. In love and war, his desires seemed always at odds with his responsibilities.

The rough terrain of the hillside prevented them from touching as much as they had in the smooth-floored tunnels, but they'd made up for it last night. The image of Celia sitting astride him rose in his mind. Starlight had silvered her silken skin and cast half-moon shadows beneath her full breasts. Cool air and his attentions had peaked her nipples. His cock swelled as he recalled how she'd licked and nibbled her way up his body, teasing his shaft with her tongue before taking him into her. Her uninhibited joy in their lovemaking had multiplied his pleasure.

But what he felt for her preoccupied him even more than the vivid memory of their physical love. He'd meant everything he'd said to her. He respected her bravery and generosity. He admired the way she took responsibility for her actions, though she was too inclined to punish herself. He loved the way she challenged him, heedless of his rank. He loved...her.

The knowledge came to him easily, with none of the dread of entrapment he would have expected to accompany it. He loved her.

He was sorry for her sake that the priests had no magic to send her back to Midgard—but not too sorry. He wanted her here with him.

With him. Making love every night. Waking up together every morning. Laughing over meals. Sharing joy in their children.

Odin's eye. He was expected to make a political alliance. He was heir to Quartzholm and the eldest son of the Kon. He'd been reminded of his responsibility to his family and the Jarldom ever since his Talent Emerged. Lords and Jarls had tendered their daughters to him at every feast day for the last ten years.

He could ask her to be his *elskerinne*. It was an honor to be the chosen one of a Jarl's heir. But Celia wouldn't see it that way. Her ways were too different.

A shout jerked Dahleven out of his tangled thoughts. *"Halt!"*

chapcer cwency-nine

DAHLEVEN'S ATTENTIN SNAPPED BACK to his surroundings. He cursed and extended a hand to halt Celia's progress behind him.

"Who approaches?" a man's voice demanded.

"Lord Dahleven Nevenson, heir to the Jarldom of Quartzholm, and Lady Celia Montrose, under my protection."

Two Tewakwe warriors emerged from the forest shadows. One held a bow with an arrow nocked, the other a bladed club. Nothing about them revealed whether they were Renegades or loyal Tewakwe. Either way, they might be hostile.

The Tewa with the club took in their disheveled and bloodstained appearance. "You look more like *Bahana* Outcasts, escaping battle."

Dahleven's fingers twitched. He hated facing an armed man empty-handed, but he kept his hand away from his sword's hilt. "We have won our battle with the enemy that attacked both our peoples. We bring news of this victory to the Kon and the Kikmongwi." He hesitated, then asked, "Do they yet live?"

"No thanks to you, Outcast."

"We aren't Outcasts!" Cele stepped from behind him, and the archer drew his bow in response to the sudden movement.

"Celia!" Dahleven tried to pull her back, but she moved forward, where she was an easy target.

"Would an Outcast walk openly toward the parley site? Would he have a woman with him? Dressed like this?" She held out her arms. Even dirty and smeared with blood, she was clearly a lady.

After a moment, the archer relaxed his bowstring, and Dahleven's pounding heart settled back into his chest.

The Tewa with the club regarded Celia with narrowed eyes, then said, "You will surrender your sword and dagger, *Bahana*. Then we will find those who will either vouch for you—or kill you."

It went against every warrior's instinct Dahleven had to give up his weapons, but he did it anyway. He could fight these two, but not without risking Celia. At least they were only calling him *Bahana* now, not Outcast.

They continued downslope, with the club-carrying warrior in front and the archer following. Dahleven kept Celia close, helping her when needed over rough ground. She didn't complain, but she'd started to limp. She wore only the thin slippers meant for indoor use.

"Will you tell us what happened?" she asked, pitching her voice so the Tewakwe could hear her.

"The Kikmongwi is victorious," the archer answered. "We have crushed the Outcasts!"

"How did the Nuvinlanders fare?" Dahleven asked.

The warrior in front shrugged. "Many still live."

"Is my brother, Lord Ragnar, among them?"

The Tewa glanced back. "You will know soon enough."

Security was good. They picked up two additional Tewa warriors as an escort and were accosted by sentries twice more before they reached the parley site. As they neared the assembly, several Nuvinlanders grumbled at seeing him under Tewa control while others called out greetings to him.

Dahleven raised his hand in acknowledgement. "All is well," he reassured them, hoping it was true.

The Tewas escorting them exchanged glances and gripped their weapons tighter.

The Tewakwe forces stood rigid and separate from the Nuvinlanders. Apparently, the Kikmongwi had come prepared for any possibility, just as Neven had. Both Nuvinlanders and Tewakwe looked ready to attack at the first sign of betrayal.

At the center of an open area between the two groups of warriors stood a canvas pavilion. The sides were hooked up to admit the afternoon breeze, and a woven mat covered the ground. A dozen Nuvinland and Tewakwe guards alternated around the perimeter. Neven and Loloma, the Kikmongwi of the Tewakwe Confederation, sat on cushions facing one another, in the manner of the Tewakwe. Ragni and a Tewakwe man each sat to the right of their respective leaders. The second Tewa was not Loloma's usual Truth-Sayer, Dahleven noted. Had his regular man been killed in the battle? This could get chancy if the Kikmongwi didn't have the assurance of knowing the Nuvinlanders were dealing honestly with him.

Neven and Loloma glanced up as Dahleven and Celia approached. The only sign of his father's surprise was a slightly lifted brow. He gestured them forward. "Loloma Kikmongwi, you know my eldest son, Lord Dahleven."

Dahleven bowed deeply, honoring Loloma as he would someone of his father's rank. "I am pleased to meet with you again, Kikmongwi." Loloma's dark skin was more deeply seamed with wrinkles than the last time Dahleven had seen the Tewakwe leader, but his black, shoulder length hair was still barely touched with white. He wore a sleeveless doeskin shirt dyed a soft green and intricately beaded across the shoulders. His exposed arms were still strong with muscle.

"And this is Lady Celia Montrose." Neven gestured Celia forward.

Cele curtsied to the Kikmongwi and Neven, hoping her nervousness didn't show. She knew lives were riding on this meeting—she didn't want to do or say something that would screw things up.

The Tewakwe's coloring and features reminded her of the Native Americans of her own Southwest. The Anasazi had disappeared from Arizona about eight hundred years ago. Could these be their descendants? *But how did they wind up here, with Vikings?*

"So this is the newborn," the Kikmongwi said.

Cele looked at him, confused. Neven, Ragni, and Dahleven all looked surprised too.

"You are newly born to the Fifth World, are you not?" The Kikmongwi explained. "Your coming was foretold."

Cele nodded because it seemed expected, though she wasn't sure what he meant.

Loloma regarded her for a long moment, then turned back to Neven, resuming the conversation their arrival had interrupted. "You say it was not you who attacked us. Yet ten of my warriors lie dead or gravely wounded on a field of truce and parley."

Dahleven stepped forward. The Tewakwe warriors shifted closer to him. Dahleven held his hands open at his sides. "I have news you both should know on that matter, if you would hear it."

Both Kon Neven and Loloma Kikmongwi nodded.

"The Outcast Jarl, Jorund Firestarter, kidnapped Lady Celia. He meant to force her to Find his lost Talent. She learned that it was he who organized the Renegades and Outcasts raiding both our peoples. We came to tell you of his part in the raids and the attack on this parley. I congratulate you both on your quick defeat of his men."

Loloma glanced at his Tewakwe companion, and the man cocked his head to the side.

"How did you escape this Jorund, Lady Celia?" Loloma asked.

She had to be careful. Dahleven had warned her that Loloma would have a Truth-Sayer Talent at his side and would know if she lied, and any lie would be considered a sign of betrayal. Like Dahleven, she had to tell the truth, but not too much of it. She couldn't let anyone know they were Fey-marked, nor could she let slip the hiding place of the Great Talents. "I didn't do it alone. Dahleven and his men rescued me. They fought Jorund's escort. Most of them were killed." Cele blinked back the tears that threatened to rise. "Then Jorund performed some kind of magic, and it killed him."

Again Loloma looked at his man, and again the man cocked his head to the side. It must not have been the response the Kikmongwi wanted, because he frowned and turned to Neven. "This Outcast of yours, this former Jarl, has caused great harm to the Tewakwe Confederation. Perhaps he hoped to curry favor with you by attacking us. There are some among your people who would rather take than trade."

Dahleven stiffened. "Kon Neven is not among them," he said in a level tone. "We honor our trade agreements with the Tewakwe. Do you suggest Kon Neven would break that oath?"

Cele held her breath. She might not know much about this world, but she knew that calling the Kon an

Oathbreaker was not a good thing. Her gaze skipped from one man to the next. Tension sparked between them. Even Ragni's face was tight. All the warriors standing at the edges of the pavilion seemed poised for battle.

"He would not have to break it if another provoked a war he welcomed," Loloma answered.

"I saw the Outcasts and Renegade Tewakwe encamped together well within your lands, Kikmongwi," Dahleven said.

"And what were you doing in our lands, without permission? If your purpose there was honorable, why did you not present yourself?"

"I was tracking the men who attacked our borders. I couldn't be sure it wasn't you who gave them refuge, Kikmongwi."

Loloma's expression grew dark. "The Tewakwe do not make war upon themselves. Yet our children cry at night for the loss of their fathers and uncles. Men killed by you *Bahana*, who do not suffer the losses we have."

"My daughter's child is without his father," Neven shot back. "And many more Nuvinlanders have suffered as well."

"What's the matter with all of you?" Cele burst out.

"Celia—" Dahleven touched her shoulder, but she shrugged him off. Everyone else stared in silent surprise, Neven with both brows arced high.

"This is exactly what Jorund wanted! It was Jorund who did this to you. To *both* of you." She turned to the Kikmongwi. "I don't know what Jorund told the other Outcasts to do to your people, sir, but I do know that Kon Neven's family has suffered personally from the Renegade attacks. Lady Kaidlin's husband was killed, and Sorn, Dahleven's sworn brother, was murdered in front of me. Jorund could hardly wait to destroy Quartzholm. He wanted to set you at each other's throats. Don't give him the victory now that he's dead."

Loloma stared at her, then his lips curved in a half smile. He was silent for a moment, then nodded. "It would seem the newborn is wiser than either of us, Kon Neven. Our peoples have suffered equally. I will ask no man-worth to be paid."

"Nor I." Neven leaned forward to clasp the Kikmongwi's forearm. "May we always face our common enemies side by side."

Loloma returned Neven's clasp. "May we continue together in trust."

There was a slight rustle as everyone present relaxed from their hyper-alert state of readiness.

Loloma gestured for his Truth-Sayer to move aside, then turned his attention again to Cele. "Come newborn, and sit beside me." When she and Dahleven were seated, he continued. "Now tell us, how did you come to travel through the door the Late Comers used?"

Cele shook her head. "I don't know what you mean."

"Those who came after us. As in the days of song, the people of Tu'waqachi, the Fourth World, forgot Taiowa was their Father and turned their hearts from virtuous things." Loloma's voice took on a story telling rhythm.

"The sorcerous *Powakas* had turned the hearts of the people. The rains stayed away and the rivers dried. Some of the People remembered however; their *ko'pavi* remained open to the Creator. So Taiowa sent Spider Grandmother to bring his true sons and daughters out of evil to the Fifth World. She told them to dance and call the rain.

"Soon the winds cooled and the sky darkened, all except for a *sipapuni* high above. The clouds released their rain, but it didn't fall to quench the thirsty earth. It spread on the wind and a rainbow ladder appeared; and so the people began to climb."

Cele sucked in a sharp breath. *A rainbow!*

"People who remembered their father Taiowa came from all over, but the Late Comers dallied along the way. 'This land is not so bad,' they said. 'Let's rest here awhile.' They tarried too long. Taiowa pulled up his rainbow ladder and closed the *sipapuni*.

"Many years passed before they saw their error. The evil of the *Powaka* sorcerers grew strong and the land lay sere and parched like a bone in the drylands. The children of Taiowa were dying and cried out for help. Spider Grandmother heard and pitied them. She drew the sign of the rainbow ladder on the bones of the Mother and opened a way for the Late Comers."

Cele remembered the drawing of the arch, the footholds, and the climbing men. *Is that what I saw carved on the rocks?*

"The People rejoiced and climbed into the Fifth World. When they arrived, they hung their heads in shame because they hadn't answered the first call. They didn't join the Tewakwe or the *Bahana*, the white men who had heeded the summons. Instead, the Late Comers traveled far to the south. They live there still."

Loloma's speech returned to a conversational tone. "Spider Grandmother must have shown you her drawing of the ladder, Lady Celia. You are the latest to come, but you are welcome."

"Thank you." Cele hesitated, then asked, "There's no way back, then?" Anticipation pulled her tight as a bowstring. The Tewakwe were her last hope of home.

Loloma shook his head. "We have no magic to send you back. A babe cannot return to the womb, nor can you return to Tu'waqachi. Spider Grandmother brought you here because your *ko'pavi* is open to Taiowa. This is your place. Sing the Creator's praises and listen for his whisper; he has work here for you to do, as we have seen today."

Loloma's words ripped the last of her hope away. All

the things of home, big and small were lost to her now. Her job. Her friends. Her life.

Yet something in her felt lighter. Loloma's words held hope; she had a place here. She glanced at Dahleven, then back at the Tewakwe leader. Maybe she could let the past go. She could move forward.

Loloma spoke again. "But if it is Taiowa's will that you return, perhaps the Katsinas can show you the way."

Distress tightened a fist on Dahleven's heart. Celia still wanted to leave. He shouldn't be surprised, he knew, but he'd hoped he'd given her some hope of happiness here, enough to want to stay.

"You would, perhaps, like to rest now, Lord Dahleven, Lady Celia," Neven said. "Father Ragnar, would you make arrangements for them?"

Ragni stood and bowed first to Neven and then to the Kikmongwi. Loloma gestured to his man, who also rose. It was a courtesy for the Kikmongwi to forego the assistance of his Truth Sayer in the absence of Ragni, and it boded well for the trust the two leaders needed to have in one another.

"I will have my daughter send a dress to you," the Kikmongwi said to Celia. "Kon Neven has no women with him." His tone implied that he thought the fact strange.

"My thanks, Loloma," Neven said.

Celia smiled and curtsied deeply before following Ragni out of the pavilion.

Several paces from Neven's pavilion Ragni asked with feigned innocence, "Shall I secure two tents for you, or will one do?"

The thought of sleeping with Dahleven again quickened Cele's pulse even while she felt anxious about what others would think. She felt herself blushing and was surprised to see Dahleven coloring, too.

"One then," Ragni said, chuckling.

Dahleven's face grew stormy.

"Actually," Ragni hastened to add, "we haven't many tents with us, Lady Celia. I shall give you mine and Dahleven and I can share Father's, if that will suit?"

"Thank you, Ragni," Cele said. "I'm surprised you have tents set up at all. Everyone looked so ready to fight when we got here."

"There was good chance of it, as you saw. But luckily you were here to set us straight." Ragni grinned, but Cele could tell he meant it more sincerely than his words implied. "We defeated the Renegades' ambush yesterday afternoon and established a temporary truce with the Tewakwe. There was no reason not to make ourselves comfortable, especially if we might be fighting again today."

"The Kikmongwi mentioned the Katsinas might know how to send me home. Who are they?" The word probably didn't mean the same thing it did back home.

"That's what the Tewakwe call the Elves." Ragni frowned. "I wouldn't hold out much hope of that, Celia. The Elves don't have much to do with us, and that's a good thing."

Celia couldn't help flicking a glance at Dahleven.

Ragni's brows rose as he looked between them. "There's a tale there, I'm thinking."

"Later," Dahleven growled.

"What can you do about bathing arrangements?" she asked as they paused in front of his tent.

"Not much, I'm afraid. A basin of water is the best I can offer."

The details were worked out. Ragni and Dahleven cleared his belongings from a pavilion that was tall enough to stand in, and nearly five paces across. The water had just been delivered when two Tewakwe women arrived. One introduced herself as Na'i, Loloma's daughter. The other carried a folded bundle and a soft basket slung from her shoulder.

Na'i wore tall suede boots and a calf length dress of brown, finely woven cloth. Though cut differently, it was just as carefully tailored as what Nuvinland women wore. Graduated strands of polished amber hung around her neck, and multiple earrings pierced her ears. Her straight black hair was caught back in a braid. "Please accept this gift," Na'i said. "Momo'a will assist you since you have no women of your own."

The girl with Na'i stepped forward and bowed her head.

Even folded, Cele could see that the blue, doeskin dress Momo'a carried was beautifully decorated with polished lapis and sparkled with beads of blue crystal.

"You're very generous," Cele said. "Thank you."

"You honor me," Na'i said, and left.

Cele stripped and Momo'a began sponging off several days of grime. As she bathed, the Kikmongwi's words sank in and took root. The door home was closed, the matter finished—unless the Elves knew a way. She could try to find them. If she really wanted to go. Did she? Maybe Loloma was right. Perhaps she was meant to be here. She knew Dahleven would say she'd already made a difference. But what about the future?

Momo'a used a wooden paddle to scrape the beaded water from her back. Cele's attention turned to the quiet girl helping her. "When did your people come to the Fifth World, Momo'a?"

"Over five hundred summers ago. But it has been only two hundred summers since we found the *Bahana*, our light-skinned brothers."

"I didn't see any of your people in Nuvinland. Do you ever visit there?"

Momo'a hesitated, then said, "We trade, but the passes are closed by snow most of the year. Travel between us is difficult. We don't visit the *Bahana* often. Some of them have forgotten that we are all Taiowa's children."

Cele winced inwardly. That sounded too familiar. "Are there very many Tewakwe?"

Momo'a patted her dry with a cloth. "The Confederation has settlements all up and down the northern face of the range. We have prospered since Taiowa brought us here. Loloma is Kikmongwi for all."

Momo'a rubbed a spicy scented oil into her skin, and Cele's muscles softened under the girl's skillful hands. She hadn't thought she'd need help dressing, but when the dress was unfolded, she realized she'd never have managed the lacing alone. Momo'a pulled the ribbons tight in back so that the soft doeskin molded to Cele's curves. The hemline was slightly higher than on Nuvinlander dresses, just above her ankles. Matching beaded ankle boots completed the outfit, replacing the slippers she'd worn to shreds scrambling through the forest and over rocks.

Momo'a finished by braiding blue ribbons in Cele's hair.

She was just wishing for a mirror when there was a scratching outside at the tent flap. "I forgot a sheaf of paper," Ragni called. "Could you slip it out to me?"

Cele found the roll of paper and stepped out into the afternoon sunlight.

Ragni's reaction was better than a glass. He grinned and his eyes glowed with not so subtle lust. "Had my brother not already come to his senses and claimed you, I wouldn't allow him another chance. I regret not pressing my opportunity with you."

Cele blushed but smiled at the praise. "How did you know? Did he kiss and tell?"

"Dahleven?" Ragni huffed a soft laugh. "No. My Talent is Empathy, my lady. To my eyes, you and Dahleven are glowing with affection—and other feelings. It's not difficult to guess the reason."

Cele hardly knew what to say. "Oh."

Momo'a emerged, with the basin of used water supported on one hip.

"Thank you for your help, Momo'a, and convey my gratitude to Na'i again, please. I wish I could repay her generosity, but I have nothing to give in return."

Ragni leaned close and whispered, "Your ear jewelry, perhaps?"

Cele touched her ears. She'd worn the diamond studs for so long, she'd forgotten she had them on. They were the only things Jeff had given her that she'd kept. "Of course!" Cele removed her earrings. "Please give these to Na'i for me, along with my friendship." She lay them in Momo'a's palm without a twinge of regret or loss.

Momo'a's eyebrows lifted as the sunlight flashed brilliantly in the gems. "I believe she will be pleased to accept both, Lady Celia."

Dahleven arrived moments later. His muscles strained against a borrowed russet leather tunic and ivory shirt. Parts of her started to tingle as she admired the way his too-tight leather leggings showed off his thighs and rear. She also liked the heated look in his eyes as his gaze swept over her.

Ragni cleared his throat and muttered, "Have pity on me."

"What?" Dahleven asked, as he continued to look appreciatively at her.

Ragni held the paper low and discretely adjusted himself. "Never mind. I've got to go." He strode quickly away.

Dahleven didn't give his brother a second look. "Will you walk with me?" There was an oddly diffident note in his voice.

"Of course."

They climbed up the hill, hand in hand. The sun slanted through the tall trees, tipping the needles with gold, and birds chirped in the branches overhead. An unseen raven cawed. They found a wide, flat rock to sit on, sheltered by a brake of young trees. Cele knew there must be sentries not far away, but couldn't see them.

Dahleven sat close to her, not quite touching. She wanted him to take her in his arms, but instead he leaned forward, hands knotted tightly together, elbows resting on his knees. Something was definitely bothering him.

A feeling of dread stole over her, but she laid a hand on his shoulder. "Just tell me."

"A Jarl shouldn't act impulsively, or only to please himself. He has his people to think of," he stated flatly, not looking at her.

Gudrun's warning surfaced in her mind and Cele's throat tightened. What had she been thinking? That they had a future together? She hadn't even realized she'd drifted into considering long-term possibilities. Here was her wake-up call. Dahleven knew his duty to Quartzholm and Nuvinland. He might want to sleep with her, but his honor would force him to make sure she knew what the rules were.

"Don't," Cele said, pulling her hand away. "I understand. I'm a wildcard in this world. All of your choices have political consequences, including who you sleep with."

Dahleven nodded. "Nevertheless, I want you by my

side, Celia."

Cele's breath caught in her throat. *By his side. As his* elskerinne?

She loved him. She wanted to be with him. An official mistress was, according to Gudrun, a respected person among the Nuvinlanders. They could be together—if she didn't mind sharing him with a wife.

I can't.

Maybe half a loaf was better than none, but she couldn't settle. It wasn't enough. She wanted it all. Marriage. Love. Commitment. "No." Her chest felt so tight she could barely breathe, but somehow she got the words out. "I won't be your mistress."

Dahleven straightened, his eyes wide, mouth agape.

Is he really that surprised at being refused? Abruptly, she stood and walked away from him, stopping beside a massive pine, blinking back tears. She couldn't stay here and watch him marry someone else. She'd Find the Elves. They might be able to send her home. The image of Galendir's pale gracefulness and lithe strength rose in her mind. At the thought, her Talent pulled at her, tugging her attention up-slope. He wasn't far. She could go to them now.

She imagined Elaine's welcoming hug at finding her alive. All the big and little things like movie nights and microwave popcorn, the convenience of cell phones and cars, tampons and modern medicine would be hers again. She'd sleep in her own bed and have meaningful work to do. And if she somehow kept her Talent for Finding, she'd volunteer with Search and Rescue. She'd have a full life.

Why didn't that seem like enough?

"Celia." Dahleven caressed her upper arms, sending an intimate shiver through her body. "Being an *elskerinne* is an honorable thing—"

She opened her mouth to retort, but he didn't give

her the chance.

"—but I do not ask it of you."

Confused, Cele turned to look at him as he took her hands in both of his.

"I will sacrifice and serve the people of Quartzholm in all things but this. I will choose my wife for the sake of my heart, not my position. I love you. Will you wed with me?"

Cele's heart exploded with surprise, hope, and joy, but her mind couldn't quite take it in. "What?"

Dahleven laughed. "I love you. Will you be my wife?"

She searched his face and saw only warmth and— nervousness?

She wanted to accept, but how could she marry someone after knowing him for two and a half weeks? *I knew Jeff for two years, and look what happened.* But Dahleven wasn't Jeff—or her father.

As if he read her mind, Dahleven said, "I'm no Oath-breaker, Celia. I won't leave you alone with my babe in your belly."

Cele's heart fell. "Is that what's behind this? You think I might be pregnant?" Was he just trying to do the right thing? "Don't worry—Thora gave me some of that tea to brew. Besides, you haven't made me any promises. Your honor is safe."

Dahleven looked taken aback. "A babe wouldn't force our marriage, though I would stand by the child in any case. My offer is to *you*, and it *is* a promise."

Hope threatened to choke her. She pushed it down ruthlessly. "Your mother won't like it."

Dahleven smiled. "How could she not welcome the woman who helped save Quartzholm from earthquake and fire? That's what Jorund had planned, after all."

"She'll welcome me, all right." Cele couldn't keep all of the bitterness out of her voice. "As your mistress."

"What?"

"She doesn't think I'll make a good wife for you. She thinks I should be your *elskerinne* since I don't know all the ins and outs of your politics."

"And what decision did the two of you come to about my future?" he asked acidly.

"I told her that since you hadn't asked me to be either one I couldn't agree or disagree...She didn't like that answer."

A smile tugged at his lips. "I expect not."

"Then I told her I was going home, so I would be neither."

Dahleven's smile faded. "If that is your wish, I will help you seek out the Light Elves. Loloma is likely right. The old tales say the Fey once passed freely between Alfheim and Midgard. Though we have no magic to send you back, the Elves must know a way."

Cele sucked in a sharp breath. There it was. She could go home. He would help her. She looked up the mountainside, into the forest, where her Talent told her the Elves lingered not far away.

Then she realized the enormity of what he offered.

"You would do that? For me? But if you took me to the Elves, everyone would know you're Fey-marked!"

Dahleven spoke in a voice tight with emotion. "I can do no less. You saved my family and my home from death and destruction. I will do whatever it takes to see you happy—even if it means losing you."

Cele stared. He would risk his rank and privilege, would risk *everything* to make her happy? On the mere chance the Elves could send her home—if that was what she wanted.

Did she?

Dahleven swallowed. "I know this world is strange to you, but I would have you stay here with me. I love you, Celia. Is it unfair of me to ask you to choose a new life so soon?"

The world expanded with joyful possibilities.

Then reality contracted painfully again. She shouldn't let her judgment be overwhelmed by one that one little word. *Love.* It didn't guarantee happiness. Jeff had used it often enough. "You hardly know me."

"I know your character. I know you're brave and compassionate and honest. The rest is detail. Detail I'd like to spend my life discovering."

Cele was silent, overwhelmed by Dahleven's unreserved declaration. "You'll be Jarl one day," she protested weakly. "I'll want you to change things. Give women greater freedom and opportunity. Can you accept that? And Gudrun has a point. I don't know how things work here. I won't bring the strength of a political alliance with me."

"Father is already working to improve the position of women, and—"

"Neven?" Cele asked, astounded.

Dahleven nodded and grinned. "Yes, and I agree with him, though I'd rather not discuss gender politics just now." He grew more earnest. "The protocol you can learn. And your lack of connection with any of the other Jarldoms is as much an asset as a liability. Alliances can place awkward and difficult demands. Your unusual background will keep the Lords and Jarls and their ladies from easily taking your measure. And Mother already respects your strength and honesty."

"She does?"

"So she said. Don't let her worry you. Not many have the backbone to stand up to her. She rather liked that. She'll accept you as my wife."

Doubt lingered. "Your father will never allow it."

"He already gave his blessing."

Cele gaped. Neven had approved of her marrying his heir? Neven, who had bullied her unmercifully?

Again Dahleven seemed to read her mind. "He didn't

know who was working to topple Nuvinland and bring us to war with the Tewakwe. He hoped you would attract attention, and he needed you to be vulnerable to his enemy's lure."

"He used me as *bait*?" Cele exclaimed, pulling her hands free of his. "And you let him?"

"He didn't ask my advice on the matter," Dahleven growled.

"He could have told me what he had in mind, asked me to help, instead of...using me."

"He didn't tell *me* his plan until I forced the issue. And you couldn't know Neven's plan, or Jorund might have sniffed the lie with a Truth Sayer. That would have put you in even greater danger."

"Even so, why set his dog on me? Gris practically accused me of murder!" Outrage sharpened her voice.

"I know. Sometimes I think the Chamberlain enjoys his work a little too much." Dahleven clasped her fist between his palms. "But if Neven had been kind and helpful to you, would you have listened to Jorund?"

Cele growled. She'd never been so angry in her life, except at Jeff. That Dahleven was right didn't make her any happier. "No," she finally grated out. "I probably wouldn't have, once I was away from his Persuasion."

Dahleven waited silently, stroking with his callused hand until hers relaxed. Gradually, Cele's anger faded. He loved her. How could she stay mad? He traced one thumb over her palm. *How could such a small gesture be so stimulating?* She pulled him closer for a kiss. She'd meant it to be quick, but the moment their lips met, she wanted more. Apparently, so did he.

Dahleven cupped her head and slipped his tongue into her mouth, teasing and caressing. His kiss was better than New York cheesecake drizzled with chocolate. All she wanted to do was nibble him up and swallow him down. His hand found her breast. Had anything ever felt so good? Her nipple rose and she pressed into his palm. He started to pull up her skirt. Cele wriggled against his arousal and Dahleven moaned. Then he froze.

"We can't." He dropped the hem of her dress. "Not here."

Cele blinked, trying to think over the clamoring of her body. "Why not?"

"Sentries."

She groaned. "Damn. I forgot." She rested her head against his chest while she caught her breath. *Maybe we could sneak back to my tent.*

Dahleven interrupted her lustful thoughts. "There's something else. Something you must agree to before we can marry."

A ripple of dread ran down Cele's back. *Now what?*

Dahleven took a deep breath. "Sorn was my sworn brother, and he died without children. Sevond has no one now. I—I've promised him my second son." He tried to keep the hope and despair out of his face. A woman who married for position and power wouldn't balk at his promise. Celia had no such ambitions. His oath could cost him his happiness, but there was no going back.

Celia frowned. "What does that mean?"

"Our son would take Sevondsson as his *paternavn* and at his fifth summer he would go to live with Sevond as his own blood. He wouldn't inherit the Jarldom even if our other sons were lost to us, may Freyr forbid."

Sevond lived in Quartzholm. The child wouldn't be lost to her. He'd be closer than if he were fostered with another Jarl. Dahleven searched Celia's expression. Her customs were different than his. Could she give up a child, even if she could see him every day?

He saw the anguish in her face and knew what she would say before she spoke. He could barely hear her words over the knife thrust of anticipated pain.

"I can't do it. I'm sorry. Family is everything to me. My mother kept me and loved me even when her folks pressured her to give me up for adoption. I don't think I could give up our child."

Dahleven clenched his jaw, making the muscles jump. He nodded once. He could find no fault with her. "It's not uncommon for us to foster our children away from home. I never thought before how it must rend a mother's heart. Or a father's." Giving a child they'd made together into the care of another, even Sevond, now seemed more than he could do. But his word was given. He looked up, directly into her eyes. The love and understanding in her gaze stole his breath.

"You did it out of compassion." Her tone was gentle.

She might forgive him, but there was no getting around this. He looked down at their clasped hands, dreading the answer to his next question. "Will you return to Midgard, then?"

She was silent for a long time. When she spoke, she sidestepped the question.

"I think Sevond may release you from your promise."

Dahleven's heart skipped a beat and he looked up sharply.

"Will you keep a secret?"

"As long as doing so is within my honor, yes."

A grin stole over Celia's face. "Aenid is pregnant with Sorn's child."

Delight burst in him, filling his chest. "Truly?"

She nodded and recounted the tale of Aenid and Sorn's love for each other.

My sworn brother knew more than sisterly love before he died. Dahleven laughed and hugged her and didn't bother to wipe away the joyful tears that tracked his face. When he could speak, he said, "Sevond will be elated by this news. I believe you may be right. Knowing Sorn lives on through this child will likely give him sufficient reason to forgive my vow."

He drew her close, and Celia nestled under his arm. It felt so right, as though she belonged there. Nevertheless, the tension still in her shoulders told Dahleven that her mind was unsettled. She had not yet given him an answer.

"What if Aenid's child is a girl? Will that make a difference?"

He didn't flinch from the truth. "Boy or girl, my promise stands. It's Sevond's choice alone whether to release me from it." Dahleven fell silent, waiting for her decision.

Cele thought of the time she'd spent with Sevond, remembered the stories he'd told about his family. He was a good man, and he'd obviously been a loving father. Sorn had spoken of him with great affection. *But to give up our child, even to him...*

She ought to be angry with Dahleven for making such a rash promise, for forcing her to make this choice, but she didn't have it in her. She understood why he'd done it. She took a shuddering breath and blinked at the tears that stung her eyes.

Stay or go, she would face heartbreak.

She couldn't give up a child, but she couldn't give up Dahleven, either.

Don't let fear stop you.

"If I stay, you have to promise you'll never again make a decision that affects us both without me."

Dahleven lifted a brow. "And you as well."

"Fair enough." Cele nodded and sealed the promise with a kiss. She barely noticed the single sharp caw of a raven.

"I want a long engagement," she added, when they broke apart. "And don't even think about taking an *elskerinne*."

epilogue

Cele smiled as Father Wirmund held Aenid's child above his head with two hands. The little girl was small and pink, with a thick thatch of dark hair that was Sorn's gift to his daughter.

"Let Freyr bless thee, and Freya guard thee, and may Baldur be your guide. From this day forth, all shall know thee as Kaleth Sornsdatter." Wirmund intoned the concluding phrases, then handed the little girl back to her mother.

The assembly hall was filled to capacity. Quartzholm was crowded with those who had arrived early for the Midwinter Feast, and all had been invited to the Naming Day Ceremony. A spontaneous cheer erupted and continued until Neven stepped forward. The baby, who had cooed happily throughout the ceremony, now let loose with a sharp cry. A ripple of laughter ran around the room, then all were silent again.

"Let us all now honor the gods and my new-named great-granddaughter by feasting in their honor!"

The crowd cheered again and began to disperse to

the banquet hall. The family would make an entrance the near the dais, but not until the guests were seated. On this occasion, Sevond would join them at the head of the room.

Dahleven's arm stole around Cele's waist while they waited.

"Kaleth is a pretty name," she said, leaning back against his chest.

Dahleven put his other arm around her. "What names do you like, for our daughters?"

"Kathryn, I think. And Amanda, for my mother."

"Only two?" he teased.

Before she could answer, Sevond approached, holding Kaleth. "My lord Dahleven?"

Dahleven straightened, leaving one arm around Cele's shoulders. She tensed, trying not to hope too much. Sevond had not yet rescinded Dahleven's promise, and though neither of them had spoken of it, they were growing anxious that he might still want their son to replace the one he'd lost.

Sevond looked down at his granddaughter with glowing eyes. "She is perfect. And she'll never go to fight and die in the drylands." He looked back up at Dahleven. "I release you from your oath, my lord. It was generous, and it helped me through a dark time. But this little one is enough for an old man like me. It is enough to know my Sorn continues through her."

At last! Cele wanted to laugh and clap her hands, but she merely grinned.

"Only, there is one thing I would ask as a condition, my lord."

Cele's heart stopped. A condition. What price would he ask?

"I would have you name your second boy after my Sorn."

Dahleven shook his head. "I can't do that."

"What?" Cele cried. *Has he lost his mind?* "Of course we—"

"Because I plan use that name for my firstborn son."

Tears brimmed in Sevond's eyes. "You do my boy great honor. Thank you!" Sevond looked down at the little girl in his arms. "Did you hear that, Kaleth? A Jarl will one day bear your father's name." Sevond bowed and went to tell Aenid.

"Don't ever scare me like that again," Cele said softly, punching his shoulder. Then she hugged him. They were free. The last shadow on their happiness was gone.

"That was well done, Dahl," Gudrun said, approaching from behind.

"Thank you, Mother."

Gudrun looked at Cele with her usual piercing gaze. "And you, my daughter-to-be. Can we set a date now, for your final vows?"

Cele smiled back into Gudrun's eyes. "Whenever you like, Mother."

thank you!

Thanks for reading *DANGEROUS TALENTS* and allowing me to entertain you for a few hours. If you enjoyed this book please tell your friends, and take a few minutes to leave a review on the site where you purchased it. It doesn't have to be long, just a few thoughts about what you liked will help other readers know why they might like it, too.

Authors depend on word of mouth and reviews from their fans, but very few readers leave reviews. Your opinion can make a real difference.

Make sure you sign up for your free story, too! My newsletter subscribers will be the first to know about sales and special offers.

ABOUT THE AUTHOR

Frankie Robertson writes fantasy and romantic fiction with an otherworldly twist. She also writes the sensual *Victorian Secret Romance* series inspired by mythology, fairy-tales, and cryptozoology as Francesca Rose.

Frankie has lived all over the country, but now lives in the Sonoran desert with her husband in southern Arizona. Her backyard is often visited by hawks, coyotes, javelinas, and bobcats, which don't get along well with the bunnies, quail, and lizards. She brings a varied background to her writing, including experience as an investigator with the Western Society for Paranormal Research.

BOOKS BY FRANKIE ROBERTSON:

The Vinlanders' Saga
DANGEROUS TALENTS
FORBIDDEN TALENTS
DEBTS
DARK WINTER'S NIGHT

The Celestial Affairs Series
LIGHTBRINGER
GUARDIAN
APOSTATE

Celestial Affairs: The Trust
BETRAYED BY TRUST

Stand-alone Titles
VEILED MIRROR
NIGHT MOVES: A Short Story Sampler

TITLES WRITTEN AS FRANCESCA ROSE:

The Victorian Secret Romance Series
WITH HEART TO HEAR
YETI IN THE MIST
YETI YULETIDE

Made in the USA
Las Vegas, NV
01 July 2022